Passion . . .

Brent pressed his mouth down on her cool, chaste lips. His hands roamed over her taut virginal breasts and he was overcome with a powerful desire for the alluring sixteen-year-old.

"Now," Morella said, molding her young body to his. "I want you to do it."

Once more he crushed her to him. What if he was a lot older than she? It was not uncommon. He was not yet forty and he had so much to give her. He could make Delamain Castle her own. Lady Delamain. And somehow it seemed so right that the baby he had saved so long ago should become his wife. She would no longer be a foundling, but a lady of status with her own home and servants.

He put a hand under her skirt and began to caress her thighs, gently lowering her to the ground. Shortly he would see her beautiful nubile body that he had so often imagined in his dreams. She was panting and moaning now and held up her arms for him as he lay down beside her, beginning to unfasten his breeches.

Just as he bent to kiss her, a movement made him look up and there was Analee standing before him, her eyes severe, her full red mouth twisted in scorn. Suddenly he held not Morella in his arms but Analee, and they were again in that moonlit glade making love on the forest floor as he was about to do here.

"Do not do it," Analee said, speaking clearly. "If you touch her you will regret it all your life," she said, and held up a hand in admonition.

Brent sat up and, rubbing his eyes, looked at her again; but where she had stood was only the blackened half-trunk of a blasted tree. Analee had gone.

Also by Katherine Yorke:

FALCON GOLD

Falcon Fury

Katherine Yorke

PINNACLE BOOKS   NEW YORK

This is a work of fiction. Although some of the characters in this book were real people, and the historical events mentioned did take place, most of the main characters and events portrayed herein are fictional, and any resemblance to real people or incidents is purely coincidental.

FALCON FURY

A Pinnacle Book. First published in Great Britain in 1981 by Macdonald Futura Publishers

First printing, August 1982

ISBN: 0-523-41746-2

Cover illustration by Aleta Jenks

Printed in the United States of America

PINNACLE BOOKS, INC.
1430 Broadway
New York, New York 10018

Author's Note

As far as I can ascertain them, all the historical references in this book are true. For many years after the failure of the Rebellion in 1745 Prince Charles Edward Stuart wandered as an exile until 1766 when he went to Rome on the death of his father, the Old Pretender.

His obscure life during his years of exile has been pieced together by many authors and I have consulted all the sources available. He did form a liaison with Clementina Walkinshaw who had met him during the Rebellion, and she did join him in France and bore him a daughter, Charlotte. She left him in 1760 and never saw him again though Charlotte joined her father in Rome in his old age and was created Duchess of Albany by him. Her story alone is a fascinating one.

Clementine Walkinshaw's sister Catherine did serve the Princess of Wales and at one time the court of the Prince and Princess of Wales was known to be a hotbed of Jacobite intrigue. So it is surely not idle to speculate that Catherine's own feelings about the Prince, whom her family had served for so long, may have been equivocal. It is however pretty certain that, with the rest of her family, she disapproved of her sister's relationship with the Prince. There were those however who still maintained that she was a Jacobite spy, though the evidence seems to suggest very strongly that she was not.

In writing the present volume, the third in the series, I am especially indebted to the following:

Berry, C. Leo. The Young Pretender's Mistress. Charles Skilton, Edinburgh and London, 1977

Corbett, Julian S. England in the Seven Years' War. Longmans, Green & Co, London, 1907

Savory, Sir Reginald. His Britannic Majesty's Army in Germany During the Seven Years' War. Oxford, 1966

Sherrard, O.A. Lord Chatham: Pitt and the Seven Years' War. The Bodley Head, 1955

Williams, Basil. The Whig Supremacy 1714–1760. Oxford, 1962

Williams, Basil. The Life of William Pitt, Earl of Chatham. Longarms, Green & Co., 1913

K.Y.

FALCON FURY

Chapter One

Watching the children play by the side of the lake on the small safe beach that Nat Hardcastle and his men had constructed especially for them, Analee smiled. The contentment in her heart was, she knew, secure and lasting. Her husband had loved her for over five years now; he was never far from her and when he went to London or abroad on the King's business he wrote to her every day. The proof of their love was two more babies, little Charlotte, now four, and three-year-old Beyrick who romped on the pebbly shore with young Robert, Nelly's child, a year older than Charlotte. Clare and Duncan, more grown-up, were sailing homemade boats from a tiny wooden jetty and around them nurses and servants fussed while Analee gazed contentedly at her brood, feeling that she had at last achieved some satisfaction in a life full of turbulence and heartache.

To compare Beyrick and Duncan was to realize how truly her husband's child Beyrick was—even at three he was a small edition to that fearsome giant with his great hooked nose and massive frame. Such was his size that his birth had been difficult even for a woman as strong as Analee. He seemed to enter the world fighting so that even at the commencement of his life he resembled his father, the great warrior known to friends and enemies as the Falcon, the bird of prey.

"See how different they are," Analee murmured to Nelly who sat beside her in the shade because she was expecting her second child. Analee liked the sun and sat with her head back to receive the full benefit of its rays on her healthy olive skin. She closed her eyes and her body was suffused with warmth as from a lover's

1

embrace; she thought with longing of the tender administrations of her husband—away in Hanover to be with his ailing monarch George II, who in his dotage spent more time in his beloved native land.

"Beyrick is the very image of his lordship," Nelly concurred, twisting awkwardly in her chair as though unable to find a comfortable position. Analee opened her eyes and glances at her with sympathy, knowing well that cumbersome feeling as the baby, nearing its time, shifted about in the restricting confines of the belly. "There is no doubt that *he* is his son." Nelly glanced slyly at Analee who, with a smile on her face, shut her eyes again and once more succumbed to the rays of the sun.

"You are the only one to know the truth, Nell."

"It is sealed in my heart forever, your ladyship."

Suddenly there were sounds of scuffling on the tiny beach, childish voices raised in anger and Duncan, Lord Blair, heir to the great Falconer estates, administered a blow to his sister Lady Clare and sent her reeling into the water. Her ladyship fell on her bottom, her legs rising high in the air, her curly locks resting on the lake's still surface. For a moment Lord Blair glared at her and then, glancing at his mother, made off for the shelter of the wood as fast as his long legs could carry him. The three younger children stopped their games, gazing at their elders with concern.

Analee jumped up and made swiftly for the water's edge, but Nat Hardcastle was there before her and scooped Lady Clare, crying more from humiliation than actual bodily harm, into his arms. Eight-year-old Clare kicked her legs furiously, showing the many flounces of her petticoats, now soaking wet, and demanded to be put down, vowing all the things she would do to her brother when she caught him.

Analee took her in her arms, gratefully accepting her from Nat, and set her down gently on the ground, kneeling so that she was scarcely taller than the child

2

and gazing into the dark eyes resembling her own. "Clare," she said chidingly, taking her daughter's hands in hers, "I foresaw this. You must not goad Duncan. He is by inclination good, but you tease him so that all he can do is to hit out, because otherwise he is the mildest and most polite of boys."

Indeed Duncan's manners were impeccable, his disposition regal, invariably gentle and courteous. Everyone remarked on the dissimilarity between him and his father, at a loss to account for the difference that was one of temperament and mien rather than looks.

"He has no need to cast *me* into the water, Mama," Clare said, looking threateningly in the direction of the wood where Duncan was being pursued by two of the menservants. "For he is stronger than I am."

"But his nature is milder. If you call him a coward he will react like a strong man, like Papa. You would never call your Papa a coward, would you?"

Clare's expression softened; a look of hero-worship came into her eyes. "Oh, Papa is no coward, Mama. I wagered Duncan that he could not swim the lake, that he dared not. Papa would have dived immediately into the water . . ."

"But Papa is a grown man!" Despite herself Analee laughed and took the child in her arms, kissing her. "Of course Duncan cannot swim the lake and doubtless even your Papa, the mighty Falcon, would not care to venture into its icy water. For despite the temperate nature of the day, the streams that feed the lake are cold, my darling, even in the most benign weather. They come from high up in the mountains, from the hidden recesses of the rocks, and maintain their crystal quality even when they are absorbed by the vastness of the lake."

Clare, wide-eyed, stared at her mother as though she was expounding mysteries that, although beyond her childish comprehension, she knew to be exciting. Already Clare was tall, with a sturdy, pliant body. Unlike

3

her mother, her skin was fair, but her eyes were dark and surrounded by exquisite long lashes which she fluttered unashamedly when wishing to make a conquest of the opposite sex. She flirted outrageously with her father who sat her on his knees and laughingly called her a minx, saying that she was just like her mother.

Clare was a child of love, conceived before Analee and the Falcon were married, before there had been any break in their relationship, any rift in their love. The rift had long since been mended but it remained delicate tissue, not as hardy as the rest of the body and more vulnerable to any undue strain. It was like the scar over a boxer's eye which his opponent makes for to try and reopen the wound and bring about his downfall.

Beyrick and Charlotte came after the wound had been made and healed—they had tried to cement the love of Analee and the Falcon. And Duncan? Duncan was a very special child, the heir to the estates of the great Lord Falconer but, unknown to him, not his child at all.

Analee watched anxiously as she heard the servants crashing about in the wood and then sighed with relief when she heard Duncan squeal and knew that he was safely captured. She smiled at Nelly. "They have got him. I must punish him for hitting his sister; but not too hard. It was not altogether his fault."

"It was not his fault at all!" Nelly snorted. "She is a virago, that one. She is too like her father and . . ."

"Her mother?" Analee raised an eyebrow, the gentle rocking continuing, a smile on her lips. "Aye, she is our child, the fruit of our loins. Do you recall those days, Nell, when I was a servant at Falcon's Keep? Do you remember Mrs. Ardoine and her birch? It was all so long ago." Analee sank lower in her chair and stretched her feet out before her, wriggling her toes and gazing at them. Analee had never got out of her gypsy's habit of easing off her shoes whenever she got

4

the chance; she scarcely ever wore them in the house and was not averse to walking barefoot through the woods, the soles of her feet hardened from years of trudging over the land.

"I remember," Nelly said quietly. "I am not likely to forget and am thankful those days are past."

"I too am thankful they are gone," Analee said, raising her hand to shade her eyes from the bright glare of the sun which was almost directly overhead, reflecting up from Derwentwater with the fierce unrelenting brightness of a shining mirror. "But sometimes I wonder . . . you remember the freedom, Nell, of our way of life? Waking in the morning with the sun as it rose from behind the mountains, the fresh dew on our faces . . ."

"Aye, and an ache in our backs," Nelly said practically. "Our bellies empty and not likely to be filled. No thank ye, Analee, I much prefer being the maid of a fine lady, my husband the manservant of a great lord!"

"A *maid*, Nell?" Analee looked incredulously at her beloved companion. "Nay, a friend. The only true friend I have or am ever likely to have. No servants you and McNeath, but friends, true friends, of my lord and myself."

Nelly looked at her mistress, her eyes brimming with tears of emotion. "You are no gypsy, as you know, Analee, but a great lady, the daughter of a lord. Now that we know the truth of your birth, a truth which I always guessed, you honor me more than ever in saying that. When I think of my own humble birth, the shame of my brutal father and compare . . ."

Analee stretched out a hand and grasped Nelly's. "Do not speak so, my dear friend. Put all those sad memories behind you, as Reyora once bade you. Do not think back on the past."

But Analee knew that Nelly had once been got with child by her father and such bestiality was hard to forget and forgive, even though among the gypsy people it

5

was not uncommon. Brewster Driver had been a rough, harsh man and his family went in constant fear of him.

"Perhaps he has been hanged long ago as a horse thief," Analee went on thoughtfully, remembering those far-off days when she had briefly stolen horses for him. "It would be no more than he deserved."

"My father a horse thief and yours a lord," Nelly sighed, nursing her swollen belly. "There is such a gulf between us, Analee."

"That is stupid talk, and let us have no more of it. Ah, here is young Lord Blair, safely captured I see."

The Master of Blair, squealing pitifully, his legs hanging against his capturer, Nat Hardcastle, was brought over to his mother and deposited gently on the ground by the side of little Clare who, her tears dry, was gazing at him with the contempt of the first-born. When she saw Duncan set down beside her she kneaded her fists in her eyes and looked as though she were about to start bawling all over again. Analee held up a warning finger.

"Now hush, Clare. If there are any more tears you will be sent inside. Do not taunt Duncan and he will not harm you or if he does I shall soon put a stop to it, and if your father hears of it . . ."

Duncan's face clouded with fear. He seemed to go in mortal dread of his father, who indeed with him was a stern parent, whereas to the rest he was tender and indulgent. He told Analee it was because Duncan was his heir and he must grow up accustomed to fear and respect his father; but Analee often wondered if there was another reason—if, in some intuitive way, Angus knew Duncan was not his child but the offspring of a man he despised and hated, Prince Charles Edward Stuart, the Young Pretender, now an exile wandering on the Continent. This hostility between father and son saddened Analee, who thought of the relationship between the King of England and his eldest son, traditionally one of mutual dislike. But how sad old King

6

George had been when his heir Frederick, poor Fred, had suddenly died four years before. Angus said that he had been a broken man ever since.

"There is no need to fear your father, Duncan," Analee said gently. "Do not look so anxious. As long as you do as you are bid he will always be just; but he would not like to hear of you knocking your sister into the water."

"Oh pray do not tell him, Mama," Duncan pleaded.

"I will say nothing," Analee patted his shoulder, "as long as there is no repetition."

"There will not be, Mama."

Duncan glared at Clare and toddled away as swiftly as his six-year-old legs would carry him.

Despite the quarrels of her children the scene was one of such domestic bliss that Analee's good humor remained undisturbed. It was good to be a mother, a beloved wife eagerly looking forward to the homecoming of her husband. Yes, despite what she said, it was even good to be a marchioness, the natural daughter of an earl, a woman of society with a high place in the hierarchy of the country. Had she not met the Kings of England and France, been on good terms with the Pompadour, and also with the Princess of Wales who had even invited her to be a member of her suite? But, more than this, had she not lain with the man who fascinated so many women, the last of the Stuarts, regarded by many as the heir of England's rightful king? Had not his seed grown within her and produced a fine sturdy child? Her eyes followed young Duncan to the shoreline and, briefly, her eyes misted with tears at the thought of the hapless fate of his father, a penniless exile and now, according to reports, a feckless rake and drunkard.

In many ways little Duncan seemed to emulate his real father. He was a beautiful-looking child with enormous charm. Yet he was moody and capricious, alternately sulking and giving vent to moods of wild elation.

7

He was unfailingly courteous and polite and yet he could be very wild and savage as when he had thrown Clare in the water, not caring whether she sank or swam—or was it that he knew that in his small protected world there would always be servants to guard his behavior, to prevent him or those he upset coming to any real harm?

Analee was almost asleep in the sun when she was aroused by one of the servants, who, dressed in the full Falconer livery, correctly attired even despite the informality and the heat of the day in scarlet coat and breeches and snow-white cravat, was entering the quiet glade by the lakeside, a few hundred yards from the house. Analee sat up as the servant bowed low, his eyes lingering for a moment on the bare brown feet of his mistress.

"Madame, Miss Delamain begs that you will receive her."

"Miss Delamain? Emma is here?" Analee looked at Nelly and quickly rose from her chair. "Did you hear that, Nell? I have not seen Emma since I went over to Cockermouth, oh let me see, it was shortly before his lordship's terrible illness . . ."

"It was five years ago, your ladyship. I remember it as though 'twas yesterday. It was the year 1750 and I was expecting Robert." Nelly glanced at her son, who had resumed his romping with little Charlotte and Beyrick.

"Aye, and our paths have never crossed since. I had the feeling Emma was avoiding me. She never accompanied the Riggs when they came over here and was never there when I visited them. I must go and see her at once. Nelly, I leave the children in your care and do not hesitate to administer rebuffs and rebukes when you think it necessary. I will try to persuade Emma to join us for luncheon by the lake."

"It is almost ready, my lady," Tom the manservant

bowed. "I know cook is well advanced in her preparations for it."

"Let us make haste then."

Analee smiled at Tom and, gathering up her skirts, bade him precede her along the path through the wood that led to the house.

Inside, Emma was standing by the long, low window that overlooked the lake. She was still thin though not as haggard as Analee remembered her; certainly not the beauty that she had once been before she journeyed to America in her fruitless quest to recapture her love, Stewart Allonby. Momentarily Analee felt a pang on account of Emma's resemblance to her brother, Brent. It was something in her expression rather than facial similarity or coloring; also her gestures and the way she turned aside from the window and regarded Analee as she came into the room.

"Emma!"

"Your ladyship."

Emma dropped a slight curtsey.

"Oh, Emma," Analee grasped her hands. "Do not 'your ladyship' me. I am Analee, your old friend. Am I not?"

Emma's hands were limp in hers. The expression in her eyes when she met Analee's gaze was hostile and suspicious. She ignored the question. Analee let her hands fall, gesturing towards a chair.

"Pray sit down, Emma. I am delighted to see you."

"Your ladyship is very kind. I came on a whim as I was journeying between Cockermouth and Delamain castle where I am once more living with my mother."

"You are living there permanently again? I did not know." Analee gazed for a moment over the lake, seeing in her mind's eye a small laughing creature darting across the lawn. Morella. It was impossible ever to put Morella completely out of her mind; not a day passed but she spent some part of it thinking about

9

her. It was as though she had lost her first-born, even though she lived only a few miles away.

"Mama is very frail now. She needs me."

"I am sure she does."

"It really was because of Mama that I came."

"Oh?" Analee's eyebrows were raised interrogatively.

"Mama is pining for news of Brent. The worry about him makes her ill. She thought . . . you . . ."

Emma gazed searchingly into Analee's eyes.

"I have heard no word of Brent since he departed from here some years back. He is no longer part of my life, Emma. All that is finished."

"We thought you might know something."

"Nothing." Analee shook her head firmly, feeling a little band of steel encircle her head. She had, she *must,* put Brent Delamain, Morella's father, firmly out of her mind. He had only ever brought trouble, alienated her from the Falcon. It was on his account that the Falcon had nearly once killed her; it was really because of Brent that that great fissure had occurred in their lives. Yet he had said he would love her forever. In her heart she knew it was true. She sighed. "I am sorry, Emma; sorry to know that in her old age your mother still grieves for her son."

"Of *course* she grieves for her son," Emma snapped. " 'Twould be unnatural not to. I am sorry I disturbed your ladyship." She pursed her lips and Analee could see her jaw working as she gritted her teeth. Emma would be about twenty-seven. Already she had the markings of an embittered old maid.

"Will you not take off your cloak, Emma, and stay with us awhile?"

Far from removing her cloak, Analee perceived that Emma was actually fastening it and drawing her gloves over her ringless fingers.

"I thank your ladyship, but I wish to proceed with my journey. I must apologize for disturbing you."

10

Emma turned towards the door but Analee ran in front of her and barred her way.

"I cannot let you go like this! You know that I regard your family as my own; that I venerate your mother and love your cousins the Allonbys, aye, and your brother Brent. Too much has passed between us over the years, Emma, for you to regard me with such scorn."

"I do not *scorn* you, Lady Falconer." Emma's lips began to tremble and Analee realized that she had been keeping herself strongly under control. "I *fear* you! I fear the impact of the woman known as the Enchantress on all whom I love."

"But that is absurd . . ."

"It is not absurd! Did I not know of the passion my brother Brent had for you, so much so that it destroyed the very foundations of his marriage? And did I not know of the impression you made on Hugo Fitzgerald so that he put his own life in danger . . ."

"Hugo Fitzgerald!" Analee looked sharply at Emma. "You spoke of my impact on all whom you love. Is Hugo Fitzgerald among them then?"

Emma's pale face was suffused with color, her eyes bright. She lowered her head.

"I did not mean to say his name."

"Ah, but you did. You also said I endangered his life. I did *not*, Emma. He was that perfidious type of person who is known as a double spy. He pretended to be loyal to Hanover and at the same time to favor the Stuart cause. To this day I swear I know not where his true allegiances lie."

"Brent nearly killed him. For *you*. Because of that he would not look at me again when he returned wounded from here. He moved to Whitehaven and never again set foot in the Riggs' home at Cockermouth, at any rate as long as I was there. Yes, I found him personable and attractive. I also thought he looked with favor on me; but no, it was the Enchantress . . ."

"Oh, Emma, this is nonsense." Analee stamped her foot with anger and went to the window, her arms akimbo. The sun was now directly above the house. She hoped the children were being given their lunch as it was long past noon. "I a married woman, the mother of several children. I am happy and contented and in love, aye," Analee turned to Emma, her fine eyes blazing, "in love with my *husband*. There is no other. Now he is in Hanover but he returns soon and I will go to London with him for the rest of the year. He allows me a few weeks in Lakeland at the best time of the year, the late spring and early summer. There is no room in my heart for any but Lord Falconer."

"You told me that before, but it was not true. Every man who sees you is enraptured by you."

"Oh that is absurd! I assure you I am as chaste as a nun while my lord is away. I look at no other men and if they look at me I cannot help it, I am sure. I have not seen Hugo Fitzgerald or Brent Delamain for years and know not what has become of either of them."

"You once gave Stewart a spell," Emma whispered urgently, the color of her cheeks growing higher. "Will you not do the same for me?"

Analee vividly recalled the day that she had given Stewart Allonby a spell here at this very house, and he had cast it on the lake to flow in the direction of Emma's home. She had fallen in love with him, returning his passion for her; yet it had not lasted. Away in America he had found someone else and spurned Emma when she ventured after him. Analee suddenly looked at Emma and held out her hand.

"I will do anything for you, Emma, but I have not cast a spell for years. I have forgotten my gypsy ways. Besides, my spells do not always work; they did not work for Mary, for Brent did not fall in love with her again and she remained estranged as his wife. I have not seen Hugo Fitzgerald for years and we parted on such bad terms I doubt if he even thinks of me."

12

"Then why does he not look at *me?* What have I done to him?"

"Because your brother wounded him maybe?" Analee said gently. "His pride was hurt?"

"Or because I am too plain," Emma said bitterly. "I am not sufficiently attractive for him."

"That you can do something about," Analee said. "You do not need a spell to enhance your looks; but I have a suggestion to make. If you will stay with me for a day or two I shall send for Reyora, my old friend the *cohani.* She is full of magical spells that will surely be sufficient to ensnare Hugo Fitzgerald, if you are sure you want him." Analee lowered her voice and gazed at the floor.

"Why should I not be sure? He is a very personable man."

"Oh, there is no question as to his looks. It is his disposition and nature that worry me."

"All that has changed. He is a solid businessman working for Ambrose Rigg. He has no truck at all with politics now. I know that, Analee. Times are very different, the Hanoverians securely on the throne. No one any longer believes the Stuarts have a hope. Hugo has become the very model of respectability; a pillar of society." She clasped her hands together, her eyes alight.

"I do not think you need any spells," Analee said gently. "If he could see you as I see you now, flushed with love and alive with hope, he would desire no other. The ability to entrance him is there, in you *yourself,* Emma."

"But he will not even see me, Analee. If he hears I am with the Riggs he will not come near. I beg you to help me. I beg you."

Emma watched as the blood from the rabbit dripped slowly into the pot containing her own menstrual blood. Fascination at the process warred with horror and repugnance. She had gathered herbs under Analee's direction from the surrounding hills and ditches and ground them into fine powder with a pestle and mortar, mixing them with her spittle and urine. When Reyora had come and discovered that her woman's flow was due, she said that this was the most suitable, most propitious time for a spell of such power that it would enslave any man—for the rabbit's blood represented his, and her own menstrual blood was a sacred fluid, a symbol of potent fecundity.

The blackbird wriggled in the secure clasp of Analee's hands as Reyora spread the mud-colored liquid over its back, murmuring soft words of incantation.

"How will it work?" Emma said breathlessly.

"The bird will alight on his head or shoulder and he will be immediately transformed and will think only of you. This is a most powerful spell; I myself have to spend some time preparing for it in order to be strong enough to send the power. Analee and I once sent a bird as far as Germany where it cured the Falcon stricken with a mortal illness. But this is a softer spell, a love spell, and the bird does not need to die as the other did."

"Why did it need to die?"

"To give life, of course. This on the contrary must not die. It is a female ready for mating. By the time she finds your beloved she will have mated and by settling on him will impart some of her own fecundity, filling him with lustful thoughts."

Emma blushed as Reyora looked gravely at her.

"We are dealing with elemental things, my dear—you must not be afraid of love."

"But why will his thoughts turn to me and not another?"

"That is part of my spell. It is because your essences are mingled in my magic potion. As the need in his loins grows urgent, a picture of you will appear in his mind, as an object of desire. He will find he cannot rid himself of it and will seek you out. When his eyes

14

alight on you he will realize that it is *you* he wants and he will fall deeply and irrevocably in love with you. You must be sure that you want him, for the spell is binding."

"Do you really want him, Emma?"

The bird wriggled again in Analee's hands and for a moment looked as though it would fly off, but her hold on it tightened.

"Yes, I do."

"Plighting your troth over this bird is more important than the wedding vow. Now you must place your hand on the bird's head and repeat some words after me. Are you ready?"

Reyora took Emma's right hand and dipped it in the murky liquid. A powerful stench assailed Emma's nostrils and she felt a spasm of nausea.

"Now you must stroke the head of the bird and say these words after me. Are you ready?"

"Yes." Emma felt herself begin to tremble as Reyora took her stained fingers and placed them on the head of the bird.

"I, Emma Delamain."

"I, Emma Delamain."

"Do swear."

"Do swear."

"That I wish to be bound to Hugo Fitzgerald."

"That I wish to be bound . . ." Emma's voice trailed away and she swallowed hard. She glanced at Analee, who gave her a reassuring smile. Emma's voice strengthened. ". . . to Hugo Fitzgerald."

"That I wish to lie with him and give myself to him."

"That I wish to lie with him . . . and give myself to him."

"In the marriage bond forever."

"In the marriage bond forever."

"I swear by the gypsy lore."

"I swear by the gypsy lore."

15

"There, it is done."

Analee suddenly released the bird and it flew upwards, scattering drops of the liquid onto Emma's head. It appeared to hover momentarily over her as though seeking direction and then it turned its beak westwards towards the coast, flying low over the lake towards the Borrowdale valley before it disappeared from sight.

Emma, gazing at her hands stained with the muddy, nauseating liquid, was overcome by a feeling of total revulsion; her forehead, too, was stained with the drops left by the bird and she felt unclean, putrid like the liquid.

But Reyora gazed at her with satisfaction, cleansing her own hands with grass she had pulled from the side of the neatly cut lawn. "The spell had gone well," she said. "The drops of liquid shed by the bird are an excellent sign. Now tip the remaining liquid in this bowl in the lake, in the direction the bird has flown, and then go up to rest resisting the impulse I know you have to cleanse yourself. As you sleep you will dream of your beloved. Before morning breaks the bird will have mated and before evening will rest upon him."

"I know not what to say," Emma said falteringly, looking from one to the other. Then she knelt and emptied the bowl into the lake.

"Say nothing," Analee reassured her. "But go upstairs as you are bid and lie down. Nelly will rouse you later and help you to wash and change your things; but now obey Reyora and all will be well."

The two gypsies stood watching Emma go slowly towards the house, keeping her dirty hands well away from her dress like someone fearful of being caught in a foul deed.

"Well, you cannot blame her." Reyora said, taking up the bowl that Emma had left by the side of the lake and cleansing it with grass. "I hope she is not mistaken in this man. It is a very strong spell I have woven."

16

"I know it, dear Reyora. You have lost none of your *cohani* powers."

"Indeed they are more potent than ever. I recently killed a man from two hundred miles away. He had defiled one of our young girls, scarcely thirteen years of age; taken her in a ditch and left her almost dead. We knew not who he was nor where he had gone. Some weeks later he was found in a field in Kent, pierced through the heart by a stake. Everyone said it was a witch. Indeed it was. It was I."

"But how did you come to know this?"

"He carried in his pocket a bracelet he had stolen from the young girl; his first motive was theft before his gross passions overtook him. He was a member of another tribe, the Louth gypsies from Cornwall. They had passed this way. One of the women of our tribe was married to a Louth gypsy. She knew the story and returned the bracelet knowing it was he. The tribe have done all they could to make recompense for the deed of one of their number. I relieved the poor child of the result of this carnal encounter."

"She was with child?"

"Unfortunately. But I took it very near the time so she felt very little pain. I healed her mind, too, and she has forgotten everything."

"Dear Reyora, clever Reyora," Analee said fondly, remembering Reyora's successes with her in the past. "How glad I am to have you for a friend."

Reyora put an arm about her as they strolled towards the house. "Now, Analee, tell me how it is with you? I told you, did I not, that things would be better. And have they been?"

"Oh, yes!" Analee stopped and looked at her friend, her eyes shining. "I have two more beautiful children and the undying love of my lord. I . . ." her smile faded and she came nearer to Reyora. "Why do you look like that, old friend? Is aught amiss?"

"I told you, Analee, that for you life would be sor-

17

row mingled with joy, joy with sorrow. You have just had great happiness as I said you would. Now you must be prepared for a little change. But do not despair. Things will right themselves again, after a time."

"It is to do with the Falcon?" Analee whispered anxiously, and took hold of Reyora's arm as the sage nodded her head.

"Oh, Reyora, do not let him be faithless to me yet again. I cannot bear it. Oh surely it is not another illness? Do not say . . ."

"I say nothing, my dear," Reyora said calmly, fastening the large carpetbag she carried after depositing in it her phials of potions and spells. "I cannot deflect the course of events. I can only prepare you for them and assure you that evil will not triumph forever. It cannot. Now show me your children once again, dearest friend, and I will give them my blessing before I go. I love them all as though they were my own and anything I can do to protect them from life's ravages, I shall. You can depend on Reyora."

Chapter Two

Hugo Fitzgerald stood on the jetty at Whitehaven watching the hatches being battened down on the fishing wherries that would go out with the evening tide. The cargo of French brandy which the boat had carried was safely out of sight in the warehouse, hidden under bales of legally imported cotton and tobacco. Hiding the contraband was merely a formality because all the customs men in Whitehaven were in the pay of Ambrose Rigg, whose smuggling activities formed the basis of his considerable fortune.

He himself was growing richer every day, Hugo

18

thought with satisfaction, because his share in it was increasing, too. It was a fine prosperous business in which nine-tenths went to Mr. Rigg and a tenth to the revenue. There had to be some token payments to the Exchequer because the scale of Rigg's activities was so vast. He was one of the most important men, if not *the* most important man, in Whitehaven.

Rigg had always been lucky in the men he employed. Brent Delamain had served him faithfully until circumstances had obliged him to leave, and Hugo had taken his place. Hugo was even better than Brent because Brent was essentially a man of action, whereas Hugo had a keen business brain. Hugo liked figures and his acumen had enhanced the business which Rigg had built up so assiduously over the years, and which he was now content to leave to run itself because his own interests were in his large and growing family and his fine estate on the outskirts of Cockermouth.

Hugo looked at his watch and then up at the pink sky. It was a fine evening. He was due to dine with the Riggs and give his report to Ambrose, who came into Whitehaven far less often than he used to. Hugo hailed the master of the wherry and, putting his hat on his head, turned towards the quay when an object seemed to drop out of the sky and land on his shoulder. Startled, Hugo swiftly moved his hand: there was a flutter of wings and a bird flew off, ascending swiftly towards the sky. Hugo brushed his shoulders with his hand and swore, examining his fingers.

"Curses! Damned bird!" he exclaimed and, getting out his handkerchief, wiped the bird's dropping off his shoulder, irritated that a good coat should be soiled. Once in the warehouse he climbed the stairs to his room and removed his coat, rubbing the shoulder with clean water until the stain had gone.

That it was a curious incident never occurred to him. He combed his hair and whiskers, changed his cravat and, putting his hat on his head, went round to the back of the warehouse where his horse was saddled and ready for him.

A great white napkin was spread over the vast circumference of Ambrose Rigg's belly. Above it, his face was red and his greying hair frizzy but sparse. His nose was full of large pores, resembling a pincushion, and threaded with tiny red and purple veins. The hands which frequently raised his glass to his lips were soft and podgy, and a large diamond glittered on his middle finger. Ambrose liked the sound of his own voice. He wanted everyone to know about his success however often they had already heard the tales of his inauspicious start, his childhood of respectable poverty. Although he was only in his early fifties, his experiences seemed to have stretched a lifetime. He remembered Queen Anne and the accession of George I, the 1715 Rebellion and the discontent at home.

"They were very uneasy days," Ambrose said, trapping a large belch in his napkin and looking guiltily at his wife. "Pardon, my dear, but that was an uncommonly good dinner. Mutton and caper sauce is, in my opinion, an unbeatable combination."

Sarah Rigg smiled her frosty smile. Her husband's manners were certainly better than when she had married him, but they would never be those of a gentleman. She fanned herself with her own napkin and pushed back her chair. "It is very hot," she said. "Too hot for mutton, I think."

"It is never too hot for mutton. What, Hugo?"

Hugo had been looking at Mrs. Rigg, noting the sour expression on her face, the downward turn of her mouth. There was little doubt she was carrying a child again. He marveled that such a corpulent man and such a disagreeable woman could ever contrive to couple at all. The thought of it quite stretched the imagination.

20

"No, sir. I enjoy mutton at any time. But if Mrs. Rigg . . ."

"Aye, she is with child again. I saw your glance. She breeds every two years. Is it not so, my dear?"

"Alas, yes," Sarah said, tetchily fanning her hot face. "So it seems."

"It is the will of God, my dear," Ambrose said complacently. "The will of God and my own not inexpert endeavors . . ."

"Please, Ambrose!" Sarah said sharply, looking at Hugo. "I do not care for this kind of conversation."

"I'm sorry, my dear." Ambrose winked at Hugo and then looked at the door as a servant entered bearing another dish. "Good, plum pudding I hope. Boiled mutton and plum pudding . . ." He slavered with greed, rubbing his podgy hands.

Hugo felt a spasm of nausea and closed his eyes at the sight.

"Are you quite well, Mr. Fitzgerald?" Sarah was looking at him curiously. "Does the food not agree with you?"

"On the contrary, Mrs. Rigg. It is so good I . . . I am bereft of words."

"Then you will have some plum pudding?"

"If I may." He leaned over and took the plate from Sarah's hand, observing a look of grim satisfaction in her eyes. She was a woman he did not understand. He knew she did not like him but he did not know why. He was polite, hard-working and dependable. Yet she never tried to increase their intimacy or call him by his Christian name. He felt she merely tolerated him. She was, of course, Brent Delamain's first cousin. Maybe that had something to do with it, yet she was said to disapprove of him too. Even when he thought of Brent he felt his stomach curdle. If ever there was a person he detested . . .

Ambrose had two helpings of pudding before he spoke again. Sarah, Hugo noticed, enjoyed her food, too. He thought of her breeding again and the idea seemed quite incredible. How did such a formidable, severe woman even bring herself to the requisite degree of tenderness, and submission? He felt a stirring in his loins and was shocked. Surely thoughts of Sarah could not . . . ? He did not desire her in the very least.

"It is time you were breeding, too," Ambrose said, as if reading his mind. "You must be thirty."

"Thirty-two, sir."

"Aye, I thought so. Well, I did not marry until I was turned forty. But if I knew then what I know now I would have started sooner. One cannot enjoy one's children if one is older, as younger folk do. They romp on the floor with them and all kinds of things. And now a new baby. I will be in my seventies when he is grown up."

Hugo saw Sarah look at Rigg. He could tell the words on her tongue although they were left unsaid. She wondered why he didn't stop and leave her alone. Hugo wondered the same thing. He knew Ambrose always patronized the best brothel in Whitehaven when he was in town. Maybe there was some satisfaction in bedding the severe Mrs. Rigg, getting her with child; or maybe he deemed a very large family an essential tribute to the memory of one who had started with nothing?

"I have a mind to marry, sir," Hugo surprised himself by saying. "But who?"

"Who?" Ambrose roared. "There are any number of pleasant damsels in Whitehaven and Cockermouth."

"But I do not know any, sir."

"Then that is your fault. You work too hard."

"Does female company not attract you, Mr. Fitzgerald?" Sarah Rigg's tone was rather taunting, Hugo thought.

"Indeed it does, ma'am. Maybe it is true that I do work too hard."

"I would have thought you would be most sought after."

Sarah Rigg gazed at him and Hugo felt himself blushing. It was as though she had divined the lascivious course his thoughts had taken. He actually saw her smile, a rare expression. In fact the smile transformed and softened her features and made her seem younger than he thought she was, although he had heard that she was a good bit younger than Rigg. Maybe not much older than himself.

"I am not in the circle of balls and parties, ma'am. I do not have the time."

It was true he had no time. He worked as hard at Ambrose's business as though it had been his own. And indeed it was his hope that Ambrose would make him a partner. He worked hard with this object in view. "Rigg and Fitzgerald," why not?

Hugo Fitzgerald slept badly. He tossed and turned in his bed and seemed to wake every few minutes. Yet he only heard the cry of a night bird, the whinny of a horse in the stables. Towards morning there were the sounds of the servants stirring early in the house, of water being drawn in the yard and the cattle being fed. He got up and looked out on the pleasant rural scene that lay before him, the mountainous range that led to Ennerdale and Wastwater or, over in the west, towards Derwentwater. The early morning mist obscured the most distant hills and the pungent smell of wood smoke assailed his nostrils. He saw a young girl busy in the yard below, hauling a bucket of water from the well. She was tall and well-built and as she turned, bent over by the weight of the pail, she seemed to look up at him and his heart turned over.

Emma. It was Emma Delamain. He leaned over the window sill but the young girl passed nonchalantly beneath. Of course it was not Emma at all. Emma. He went over to his bed and lay down, his hands cradling his head.

He had not thought of Emma Delamain for years. Why should he think of her now? He had scarcely known her, a subdued, ill-looking girl who had been jilted in America and had crept home to lick her wounds. He now recalled her height—she was tall for a woman—and the beautiful rich quality of her chestnut hair. Her face was pale and too thin, but her eyes were deep in their sockets and her lids rather opaque. Her nose was long and straight, her mouth firm. It was said she had once been a beauty. He wanted to kiss the mouth, to encircle that slim waist with his arms. He suddenly felt an overwhelming desire for her and he leapt out of bed and stripped off his nightshirt, dowsing his throbbing body with cold water.

At breakfast he was like a man in a trance.

"Did you not sleep, Hugo?"

Ambrose was tucking into a dish of ham, lamb chops and coddled eggs. He lifted a tankard of ale to his mouth and took a large draught. His attitude was that of a man in the last stages of starvation.

"Not very well, sir."

"Ah! You need a woman."

"I think I do, sir."

Ambrose looked at him with surprise as though not expecting his remark to be taken seriously. "I meant it in jest. Doubtless the mattress was too soft or the pillow too hard."

"No, I think I do need a woman, sir. A wife."

"Ah, it was my remark about breeding that troubled you." Ambrose wiped his mouth on the sleeve of his coat, ignoring the napkin fastened to his waistcoat, and smirked. "Yet your wages should buy you enough in the way of carnal satisfaction, eh? They have some very good wenches at Mrs. Earnshaw's."

"I was not thinking of prostitutes, sir, but of a wife. As you said, I should be wed. I am of age."

24

"Ah, you are certainly that!" Ambrose chuckled and, pushing back his chair with difficulty, waddled to the sideboard where he helped himself to deviled kidneys, fried potatoes and a piece of liver. "Is there someone you have a mind to wed? You are in love? Is that it, eh? Come, my boy, you can tell me." Ambrose sat heavily in his chair, then leaned conspiratorially over to Hugo, putting a hand on his arm. "My good lady suffers from sickness in the morning and will not join us."

Hugo leaned back, pushing his plate away from him.

"You have lost your appetite, too! Who is it? Who is the fortunate wench?"

Hugo put his hands in his pockets and gazed at the ceiling. "What think you of Emma Delamain, sir?"

Henrietta Delamain clasped Analee's hand and held it briefly to her bosom. "Dear, dear Analee, how lovely to see you again! But such a brief visit? Can you not stay longer?"

"Now now, Henrietta," Analee said, following her hostess into the long drawing-room of Delamain Castle. "I have only come to enquire after your health and then I must go to Falcon's Keep to await my husband."

"So your holiday in Lakeland is over?" Henrietta pointed to a chair and also sat, facing her guest.

"For the time being. We had some beautiful weeks there. But I miss my husband."

"Of course." Henrietta searched the face of her guest, about whom there were always so many rumors—that she had been a gypsy, that she was the daughter of a nobleman, that she possessed magical powers. None or all of them could be true for all Henrietta knew. Cooped up in this grim castle in the middle of the country, seldom visiting London, she often felt cut off from life. "And how are your children, Analee?"

"Oh, they are very well. The younger ones are adorable; Clare full of character and spirit; and Duncan . . . well, very much his own person."

Analee glanced out of the window as though willing herself to see that curly blond head bobbing about on the lawn.

"Oh, you are so fortunate in your children." Henrietta passed a hand across her brow. "To have sons, what would I not have given . . ." Henrietta wrung her hands and looked at the ceiling. "But still, thanks to you and good Reyora, the matter seems no longer to trouble my husband. He has become reconciled to my barrenness and accordingly more tender towards me. The question of an heir to this great place continues to trouble him. Brent, of course, could not inherit because he is an outlaw. Unfortunately the title would pass to a distant cousin, but our eldest daughter, Mildred, could possibly inherit some land and part of the estate. George has lawyers seeing to the matter."

"But surely he is in good health and not likely to die?"

"Oh yes, he is in excellent health; but you know there are always unforeseen circumstances and my husband is a very cautious man. He so longed for an heir."

"Maybe you will have one in the course of time."

"I doubt it, dear Analee. I doubt it very much."

"And what news of Mrs. Delamain and Emma?"

"They are well. Emma lives again with us, you know, or rather with her mother. She seldom visits us at the castle, being content to brood on her thoughts. Alas, I fear she will never marry, but be an old maid, an embittered spinster dwelling on past memories. I never saw a girl so changed. She was such a beauty. Charles Edward Stuart has a lot to answer for; the ruin of some of our family and many a broken heart, to say nothing of broken lives. Happily George took care to make prominent display of his loyalty during the Rebellion. He commanded the local militia and has at least saved the honor of this branch of the Delamain family."

Henrietta looked searchingly at Analee who, it had been rumored, had also shared a double loyalty during the Rebellion—to her husband, a Hanoverian commander, and to the renegades. But Analee was still looking out of the window, filled with an understandable sense of agitation. For she had not come to see Lady Delamain or even Emma, but her own daughter Morella who lived with her grandmother in the dower house of the castle.

Morella was Analee's first-born, a love child, the fruit of her brief affair with Brent Delamain. During the Rebellion they had become separated and fate had intervened so that Morella, then a baby, had been given shelter by Brent's mother who was unaware of the relationship. Or did Brent's mother suspect? Analee remembered how she had looked at her when she had visited the castle to take Emma away prior to her unsuccessful voyage to America.

"Sir George's loyalty indeed does him credit," Analee murmured. "Could we walk in the garden do you think, Henrietta? It is such a lovely day."

"But you need not journey on today, surely? At least stay the night. It is past noon."

Analee had risen early, the journey across the lake and from Keswick to Delamain Castle had taken most of the morning. It was true she was tired. The Falcon was not due until the following day. Moreover if she wanted to see Morella . . .

"I will stay," she said. "But I must leave first thing tomorrow. Pray be good enough to send one of your servants to bring my bag from the carriage."

"Of course." Joyfully Henrietta got up and went to pull the bell rope. "Nelly is not with you?"

"Nelly is about to have a child. Oh, how I dislike being parted from her at this time. I am hoping my lord, who comes with her husband, will allow us to re-

27

turn to Furness for the birth. But she is well looked after; the midwife who assisted me is waiting to attend her."

"And Reyora?"

"Reyora is only called if there are difficulties. We do not expect them with strong Nelly."

"That woman is a treasure. I am sure it is she who has brought about this change of heart in my husband."

"It is possible," Analee said, fastening her cloak loosely about her. "It is quite possible."

"She comes over to see Morella and always pays me a visit. She is strangely drawn to that child."

Analee felt her heart skip a beat. Reyora had saved Morella from certain death after the gypsy camp in which she was born had been destroyed by the vanquished remnants of the rebellious army.

"Morella must be what, ten or so now?" Analee was sure her voice would give her away, but Henrietta prattled on without appearing to notice anything.

"She was born in the year of the Rebellion, 1745. Yes, she is ten. She is a tall, strong child, a curious girl. I never understand her myself."

"Oh, why?"

"She is so grown-up. One would think her a lot older, and she is so wise! I find myself listening to her with great respect."

"Oh, you do see her then?" Analee murmured. "I recall you once said that you did not have her in the castle for fear she would contaminate your own children on account of the mystery of her birth, the obscurity of her origins."

A blush of embarrassment spread over Henrietta's homely features and she avoided Analee's eyes. "Did I really say that? What an odious person I was. You see it is since, through you, I came to know Reyora that I think I have discovered the true meaning of goodness,

28

and anything connected with Reyora could not be bad."

"I am glad to hear you say it," Analee said, following her hostess along the stone corridors of the castle, down the broad staircase and out of the great double doors.

It was a beautiful day, warm but balmy, and the trees stirred in the wind. Only in the north country did one find such a profusion of greenery, Analee thought, due to the heavy rain, the dark richness of the soil. She thought of the hot streets of London, of the bustle and confusion of the Court and her heart ached to remain here; but it was not to be.

"Would you like to see Emma?" Henrietta said when they had taken a measure by the side of the rose garden, admiring the profusion of blooms, inhaling their heavenly scent. "She returned much refreshed after seeing you. I believe she stopped a few days longer than she intended."

"Yes, she did. We got on well, I am glad to say."

"Poor girl. She will never wed. She will remain a spinster to look after her mother. Another heart broken by Charles Edward Stuart!"

"Has her mother forgiven me for helping her to go to America? I often think how different Emma's life might have been if I had not assisted in that folly."

"Oh, you meant well. I know Brent was behind it, and Emma is stubborn like all the Delamains. Well, she learned her lesson. No man is to be trusted. Ah look the door opens and there is Emma."

Analee turned as Emma started to run along the path from the dower house to the parterre between the rose gardens, her arms outstretched.

"Analee! They did not tell us you were here."

Analee went towards Emma and caught her hands, kissing her. "I was not sure I would be able to call. I am on my way to Falcon's Keep. But I couldn't resist it."

"*And* she is to stay the night. I insist that you and your mother dine at the castle. Sir George will be delighted. He is due back from Whitehaven this afternoon."

"Whitehaven?" Emma's voice faltered and she looked at Analee.

"Aye. He does a lot of business with Rigg, you know. Uncouth though Rigg may be, he is related to Sir George through Sarah. I would be the first to disclaim the connection but it appears he is on the way to being a very substantial landowner. Money, of course, is no respecter of persons; providing one has the knowledge, anyone can make it."

"I found Mr. Rigg very agreeable," Analee said, looking sharply at Henrietta. "He is a kindly man, his hospitality quite lavish. Like me he was not brought up to be used to the finer things of life and consequently appreciates them the more."

Henrietta's chin trembled at the implied rebuff and Analee thought she was about to burst into tears.

"My brother thinks very highly of Mr. Rigg," Emma said quickly, "and of his business acumen in particular. He . . ."

But Analee was looking at the house where a tall, fair child stood in the doorway gazing at her. Without speaking or looking back, Analee walked slowly towards her and stopped in front of the child whose gaze remained unwavering. Then she dropped a curtsey.

"Do you remember me, Morella?" Analee bent down and lightly clasped her hands. "You have not seen me for some time. What a big girl you have grown into."

"Lady Falconer," Morella said in a high, clear voice. "Aunt Susan saw you from the window."

She turned and behind her was Brent's mother, Susan Delamain, supporting herself on two sticks, a rictus of pain vying with the smile on her face. As Analee gazed over Morella's head at her, she knew that Susan knew everything. She dropped her head in acknowledgement.

"Mrs. Delamain."

"Lady Falconer, what a very pleasant surprise. I wanted to thank you . . ."

"Thank me! I thought you would censure me."

"Oh no." Susan hobbled slowly over to her and Analee could see the painful, swollen joints of her hands that clung to the sticks. "What had to be had to be. Emma would have contrived somehow to get her own way; but since her last visit to you she is a different person. You have given her life and hope—how, I know not."

Still holding Morella's hand, Analee turned to watch Emma walk slowly up the path chatting to Henrietta.

"She is beautiful again."

"Yes, her looks have returned. It is as though the past nine years of bitterness had never been. I think she is reconciled to her lot. They call you the Enchantress, I believe. You have enchanted Emma."

"Oh, not I," Analee said gently. "I think she felt rested and, yes, peaceful by the side of our beautiful lake. Derwentwater never fails to weave its spell on those who seek its balm. Many a time I have journeyed there depressed and ill at ease and within a few days . . . How Morella has grown!"

Analee looked at the child, who was still staring at her, a grave, thoughtful look on her face. How like Brent she was. There was not a trace of her mother about her. She had Brent's blue eyes, Brent's blond hair, the firm Delamain mouth, slightly stubborn like Emma.

How foolish it was that no one knew the truth, Analee thought bitterly. How absurd to pretend . . . but no, what purpose would it serve? If the truth got out it would undo her marriage to the Falcon and cause only unhappiness and resentment among those she loved.

31

Yes, she was sure Mrs. Delamain knew; the look in her eyes still told her so. She knew, or she had guessed.

"I remember you very well, Lady Falconer," Morella said clearly. "I remember the last time you were here, and I remember you driving away with Emma, and Aunt Susan crying afterwards."

"Oh, did you cry?" Analee looked compassionately at the frail woman in front of her. In years she was not old but she looked it; the skin over her face was like parchment and her large luminous eyes bright, as though with incipient fever.

"I knew Emma was going away and I did not know when I should see her again. But I trusted you, Lady Falconer. I have always trusted you."

"Come and see my dolls," Morella said, pulling Analee by the hand. "And the doll's house Uncle George had built for me."

Laughing, Analee allowed herself to be dragged along the corridor and pulled upstairs. When they got to Morella's room she realized they were alone and no one had followed them. It was the first time she had ever been alone with her daughter, her first-born, in many ways her dearest child because the most deprived. Her room was large and airy and overlooked the river that ran alongside the castle, stretching all the way to Penrith. Analee recalled passing by the side of that river when she set off with the Driver family on the journey that was to change her life. She had passed by this castle . . . it seemed like another age.

"What are you looking at, Lady Falconer?"

"The view, my darling. It is so pretty, is it not?"

"Why do you call me your 'darling'?"

Analee felt a lump come into her throat and she leaned against the window sill, willing the tears to go from her eyes.

"I think you are a very sweet little girl. You *are* a darling. Now, show me your dolls."

Beautifully dressed and kept, they sat on Morella's

bed, propped against the wall. There were fair dolls and dark dolls, rag dolls and wooden dolls. And there was a sumptuously dressed doll with long dark hair, the expression on its face familiar . . . Morella picked it up and held it out.

"This is you, Lady Falconer. See how like you it is."

Analee grasped the doll and stared at it. She felt a prickle run down her spine and her heart began to pound with apprehension.

"This is an incredible likeness. See, this dress is even like one I have. How came you by this?"

"Reyora gave it me. She is the gypsy who found me when I was abandoned by my mother. She brought me here and left me with Aunt Susan. I am an orphan, Lady Falconer, and but for Reyora I would have died. She gave me the doll because I admired you when you were here last. I said what a lovely lady you were . . ." Morella sighed and pushed her flaxen hair away from her face. "I said I wished I had someone like you for a mother."

"Oh, Morella!" Analee fell to her knees and clasped her daughter in her arms, pressing her close, feeling the vibrant warmth of her young body. Her eyes were wet with tears which ran down her cheeks and onto the blue basquin bodice of her elegant gown.

"Why are you crying, Lady Falconer?" Morella pulled herself away and stood gazing at Analee.

"Because you have a mother; I'm sure you have one who loves you. One day perhaps you will find her and then be happy ever after, as in the story books." Analee brushed the tears from her eyes and stood up.

"I don't know how you can say that. I have no mother. She abandoned me. Why should she look for me now? I hate my mother for abandoning me, for leaving me to die before Reyora found me. I hate her, I hate her!"

"Oh you must not say that," Analee seized her again

and held her by the shoulders. "What did Reyora tell you of your mother?"

"That she could not look after me. That she had to go away. She *said* she loved me very much. I do not believe it."

"Oh she did love you! I am sure of that," Analee said, her voice breaking. "I feel it in my bones."

"Are you really an enchantress?" Morella said shyly. "Can you see into the future and the past?"

"No, I am not an enchantress, but I have certain powers. I know you have a mother and that she loves you, and that one day you will know who she is and you will be happily reunited." Analee knelt and kissed her face, hugging her close. "I promise you that."

"In the meantime will you pretend to be my mother?"

Analee laughed and got to her feet. "You have very kind people here who look after you. Your Aunt Susan, Emma, Sir George and Lady Delamain. They love you and will look after you . . . until your own mother comes. Now we must go down." She put the doll back on the bed and smoothed its clothes. "There, Lady Falconer," she admonished the doll in a grave voice. "Be sure you look after Morella and see that she behaves."

Downstairs there was the sound of a commotion, doors banging and dogs barking. They hurried to the window to see what was happening and there below, on the lawn in front of the house, they saw a man approach and Emma shyly waiting to greet him, while a groom held the man's horse and dogs yapped at his heels. In the background Sir George Delamain sat on his large roan watching, a smile on his face. Then he turned away and rode up to the castle.

The man quickened his step and, when he was near to Emma, held out his hands. His face was alight with happiness and something else: love. Hugo Fitzgerald.

Analee back away from the window but remained in its shadow, too fascinated not to watch.

"What is it?" Morella said, tugging at her dress.

"Sshh," Analee held a finger to her lips and smiled, her hand reassuringly on her daughter's shoulder. "This is a moment when no other should be present."

"But *who* is he?"

"He is a friend of Emma's. Mr. Fitzgerald."

"Why does he look so happy?"

"Because I think he likes her. See . . ."

"She likes him, too," Morella said firmly, clasping the window sill. "She looks very happy, too."

After their greeting Hugo stood back and pointed the way along the path for Emma. Briefly his hand encircled her waist and lingered a moment. She seemed to merge into him and as they began to walk slowly towards the copse by the side of the river, Analee thought how well suited they were. The spell had worked.

"Come, let us go down and see Aunt Susan." She clasped Morella's hand tightly. "This is very exciting . . ."

"Will they get married?"

Analee laughed, raising her head. "Oh, it is too soon to say. They might."

Downstairs Susan Delamain sat in her accustomed chair by the fireside, though the fire was unlit and a large bowl of flowers stood in the grate. The windows were open and a shaft of sunlight fell on the polished boards of the floor. She smiled at Analee.

"Did you see?"

"Mr. Fitzgerald."

"She likes him very much.".

"Then I'm glad."

"But he never seemed to want to see her. He showed no interest in her. She spoke of him a great deal. I wonder what changed his mind?"

"He would be a very lucky man," Analee said, sitting opposite Mrs. Delamain and holding Morella round the waist. "She is too good for him."

"Who is to say?" Susan clasped her stick with her swollen fingers. "He is better than nobody. I do not like the thought of the empty years which stretch out for Emma unwed. An unmarried woman has no place in our society as I, a widow, know. I know too well the loneliness and I had my children to comfort me." She smiled at Analee and nodded to Morella. "She likes you very much, too."

"I'm glad," Analee said, meeting the gaze of Emma's mother. "I love her. She is very precious to me."

"I know," Susan Delamain said. "I know she is."

Chapter Three

"A toast," Sir George said, getting to his feet and raising his glass. "A toast to Emma and Hugo."

Everyone stood up except the newly betrothed couple.

"To Emma and Hugo."

Analee looked over the rim of her glass towards the happy pair. Emma was transformed by her happiness; even the simple dress she wore seemed to enhance her looks, her gleaming chestnut hair, her face no longer pallid but with a roseate glow as though she spent a lot of time in healthy outdoor pursuits. Hugo could hardly take his eyes off her and then, at that moment, he turned and met Analee's glance. His smile vanished and his face went ashen as though he had had a sudden sharp shock. Analee dropped her gaze, the toast was drunk, and everyone sat down; but when she glanced at him again Hugo was still staring at her and

36

Emma had a puzzled expression on her face and seemed to look at him for reassurance.

"I never thought when I went to Whitehaven that I would return with a fiancé for Emma," Sir George said with satisfaction, turning to Analee who sat on his right. "He is fair smitten with her as you can tell. 'Twas only his modesty that made him decide not to speak before, a feeling of unworthiness. He has had to make his own way in the world."

"I know that," Analee said. "And I hear he is doing it very well."

"Oh very well. Rigg has it in mind to make him a partner and now, with this good marriage, it will make him all the more acceptable. I'm delighted, I must say. The Fitzgeralds are good solid supporters of the King, and Emma is marrying into a family of staunch Hanoverians, not like those Allonbys. In them no good lies." Sir George lowered his voice so that his mother would not hear. "Hugo is far better anyway than that worthless Stewart, although we do hear he is prospering in America. It is not that he doesn't work hard. It is his loyalties which are suspect. Once a rogue always a rogue."

"I hope not," Analee murmured, thinking what a rogue Hugo Fitzgerald had been—flirting with her, pretending to be loyal both to the Hanoverians and the Stuarts. She wondered if she had been right in bringing this marriage about. But Sir George obviously had no doubts about the man who was to be his brother-in-law, and indeed Hugo, with his open good looks, his dark curly hair and blue eyes was an attractive man. There was an air of integrity, of honesty about him that was quite deceptive. He had once declared himself in love with Analee; she hoped that infatuation had passed.

Gradually she saw Hugo's color return and for the rest of the meal he carefully avoided looking at her, all his attention being reserved for his fiancée until the women left the table while the two men concluded the dinner with brandy and cigars.

Analee took Susan Delamain's arm as she made her way painfully along the corridor to the drawing-room. She was as light as a bird but Analee was aware of her weight as she leaned against her for support.

"Thank you," she murmured, looking gratefully up at Analee as she put her into a chair. "It is a great effort for me to move about as I used to. How happy I am to know that Emma is to be wed. It is such a weight off my mind, Lady Falconer. But I have another worry . . ."

She gazed at Analee, who drew up a chair and sat next to her. Henrietta and Emma had gone up to Henrietta's room to freshen themselves.

"Sometimes I feel I do not have long to live. If I die, what will become of Morella?" She looked earnestly at Analee, who once again met the older woman's eyes. "I had thought Emma would always take care of her," Susan Delamain went on, "thinking that she would not marry. But now what will happen?"

"I thought Lady Delamain spoke very fondly of Morella," Analee said slowly. "Very different from the last time I was here. I am certain that in the unfortunate event of your death Morella will be well taken care of."

"Are you *quite* sure about that?" Susan leaned forward, lowering her voice even though there was no one else present.

"Quite sure," Analee said. "I will give you my word."

"I know Morella means a lot to you. There is an affinity between you."

Analee nodded without speaking and pressed the older woman's hands. Some things did not need putting into words.

Analee listened sharply in the dark. Some thing, some noise had awoken her. The windows were wide open because the night was hot and a bough of a tree beat against an open window. But it was not the sound of the tree. Analee was sure of that. She stirred uneasily in her bed and then sat up. Someone was in the room. Her heart slowly began to thud against her ribs.

"Who's there?" she said, wishing she had put the catch on the door. A sudden draft sprang up and she knew the passage of air between the door and the window had been disturbed.

She quickly got out of bed and reached for her robe. Then she stole silently around the bed so as to put it between her and the intruder. "I will scream if you do not speak," she said. "In a trice all the servants will rush in."

"Do not scream," a voice whispered. "I wish you no harm."

"Hugo!" She groped on the bedside table and struck a tinder to light the candle. Her hands trembled and she felt them encompassed by two large ones.

"There is no need for light, my Analee. We can do what we have to just as well in the dark."

"Hugo, are you mad!"

His arms encircled her and brought her down on the bed. His breath came heavily and he began to pluck at her nightgown. She started to struggle and gasped: "I will scream unless you stop at once. Your whole life will be ruined, Hugo, if you rape me."

"It is not rape, my Analee. It is love. I want you to love me, too. I think you once did."

"That is utter nonsense. I never loved you—in fact I despised you. Your cunning and duplicity made you contemptible in my eyes."

"That was a long time ago. I am no longer interested in politics. The Hanoverians are safely entrenched; but I am interested in you. I feel I will love you forever."

"But you have just this very day proposed to another. You had the air of one wildly, nay, passionately in love. Have you taken leave of your senses?"

"I thought I was in love until I saw the quality of your glance. My heart seemed to dissolve. I knew I loved the wrong woman, that I had made a mistake. The Enchantress was enchanting me again. I have a hopeless passion for you, Analee, and I am sure that once you feel the impress of my ardor you will be the same." He pulled again at her robe, his hand groping for one of her luscious, full breasts. Analee felt half stifled with the weight of his body on hers. He put a knee between her legs and tried to prise them apart. She gritted her teeth.

"If you violate me, Hugo Fitzgerald, you will not live to see Whitehaven again. Lord Falconer returns home tomorrow and will hear of this."

"Ah, but will you tell him? Will you *dare* confess? Will not his rage be directed against you, too?"

"You do not care for your life?" Analee struggled as he roughly lifted her nightgown above her waist and began to fumble at her groin.

"I care only to know you. After that I think I have no more desire in the world."

With a swift movement he threw himself upon her, attempting to straddle her, his own nightshirt lifted over his hips. Analee took a deep breath and, making a superhuman effort, bit deeply into his wrist. She felt the blood gush over bared bosom and, with a cry, Hugo lurched off her and fell onto the floor. Quickly she left the bed and ran to the door. But with her hand on the hasp she waited. No sound came from behind her except a stifled sob of pain. She knew she had nearly bared the flesh to the bone.

"Shall I call for help?" she said in a low voice.

"No, I beg you. I pray do not. I am unmanned."

"You are lucky you were not properly unmanned," Analee said, creeping over to the bed and groping once more for the tinder. "Next time I will sink my teeth in

40

a more vital spot and then see if you ever have children."

"I think you would, too," Hugo groaned bitterly. "You are a vixen."

Analee struck the tinder and lit the candle. The scene before her was quite appalling. The bed was covered with blood and Hugo lay on the floor, the flesh hanging from his wrist where Analee's sharp teeth had bitten into it. His nightshirt was still around his waist and the member that had been so eager to force itself into her lay flaccid and puny against his thigh. He looked a pathetic, comical figure and Analee smiled with contempt as she looked about her for something to bind his wound.

"How we shall explain this I do not know," she said. "Luckily the explanation will be up to you because I depart at first light. The maid will think my woman's flow overtook me to soil the bed, though to be sure it looks like a carnage."

She went to her valise and tore some strips from her clean underlinen which she soaked in a jug of cool water. Then she knelt by his side and began to stanch the blood.

"I did not know my own strength," she murmured pitilessly. "You were fortunate I did not sever the hand. I hope this will cool your ardor for good, Mr. Fitzgerald, as least so far as I am concerned. You will never get the best of me. Never." She pressed the loose flesh back into place and swiftly bound the wound. "I hope it does not become infected, for then you might die. I do not think, though, that my spittle is poisonous."

"*You* are poisonous," Hugo snarled. "You are a viper."

"Oh come, may not a woman defend herself?"

"I did not intend rape, you knew that."

"I know that your approach was violent, sir, too violent for my liking. Your gestures were violent and your

41

member was ready to prod me. You would have taken me against my will and, for all I know, impregnated me with your vile essence. Save it for that good woman whom you intend to marry, Mr. Fitzgerald, though I do not envy her having you for a husband. You are a deceitful man, sir, and this deceit follows you through life. You pretended to love both the Hanoverians and the Stuarts and now you pretend to love Emma Delamain, doubtless for base motives of your own."

"It is not true," Hugo gasped, sitting upright and nursing his aching wrist. "I was suddenly overcome by a passionate desire for her. I bethought me that it was time I wed and Emma seemed the most suitable, the most desirable person imaginable. I wanted none other . . . until I saw you gaze at me over your glass this evening, those bewitching eyes haunting me. They will haunt me until I die."

The first rays of dawn were glowing through the trees and Analee decided to pack so that she could be ready to leave when it broke. She had made her farewells the evening before, saying that she would break her fast on the way, for she had no idea when the Falcon would arrive and she wanted to be there to greet him. She threw back the sheets and stared down at Hugo who, crestfallen, still sat on the floor, his nightgown awry, his face a mask of self-pity. Knowing about the spell, Analee suddenly felt sorry for him and also troubled that her own peculiar fascination for men, of which she was not unaware, was stronger than gypsy magic.

She folded her arms and stared down at Hugo, prodding him with a foot. "You must be off now to your bed."

Pathetically, Hugo held out his arm towards her. "What shall I say about this?"

Analee shrugged. "You must say what comes into your mind. You are an expert at deception, so something should occur to you. And then, dear sir, permit me to give you some advice. Contrive to be married *soon* to Emma Delamain and to make her as good a husband as she will make you a wife. Work hard and diligently and put your liking for deception, for intrigue, as far from you as you can. For it will only cause you trouble as it has already. Moreover, forget me and never mention my name again."

Analee gave him a final little shove with her foot and he struggled to his feet, clasping his injured hand. Without a word he tottered over to the door and Analee opened it for him, standing silently to one side as he passed her without glancing at her again. She shut the door and carefully put the catch on it. Then she went over to the basin and, despite the chill of early morning, stripped and washed herself all over with cold water as though to expunge the memory of his attempts to defile her.

Analee lay in her husband's arms, aware of the gentle, satisfied rhythm of his body as he slept deeply after making love. She felt imprisoned in his grasp; a willing prisoner. Lying in their large bed at Furness, the afternoon sunlight glinting on the paneled woodwork of the walls, she was suddenly reminded with amusement and also revulsion of her encounter weeks before with Hugo Fitzgerald. What would the Falcon have said if word of that had ever come to his ears? Would he be lying as contentedly as he was now with a smile on his lips even in sleep, the relaxed fulfilled expression of a man who has had his senses gratified as often and as satisfactorily as he could ever have wished.

The Falcon stirred and the hand that lay loosely over her breast suddenly grasped it. When she looked round his large brown eyes were open, staring at her.

"What time is it?"

"The sun is high, my dearest. It is late afternoon."

The Falcon sank back and stared at the ceiling, his

fingers caressing Analee's breast from time to time, stroking and squeezing the nipple until it was upright.

"What enjoyable weeks we have had, Analee," he said, glancing at her. "Full of tenderness and love; but it is time soon to return to London. I hear the King is already asking after me."

Analee tried to conceal a spasm of dismay.

"So soon, Angus?"

His lordship raised himself up on an elbow and looked at her with amusement.

"*Soon?* My darling, it is almost a whole month that I have been here in the north. Do you not realize that a man with my many commitments and duties has no right to such protracted leisure?"

"And do you want me to come with you?"

He stared down at her, frowning.

"Of course I want you to come with me! Are you not my *wife?* Do you not have duties towards me—duties besides these which you so obviously enjoy fulfilling?" He leant down and ran his tongue lightly over her bosom.

"But I have duties to the children too, Angus. The life for them up here is so good, so fresh and wholesome after London."

"Then leave them here, my dear," the Falcon said testily. "They will be well looked after."

"But I miss them, Angus. Besides they see so little of you . . ."

"My dear Analee," the Falcon swung himself off the bed and sat on the side scratching his chest. "I assure you that I hardly ever saw my father when I was small and, as you know, my mother was dead; but for all that I came to little harm. Is it not so, my dearest?"

Analee avoided his eyes. Much as she adored her husband, she considered him remiss as a father. He was not one to play with his children or to take overt pleasure in their company. At times he hardly seemed aware they were there and was frequently irked by

44

them, especially Duncan. The sight of Duncan invariably drew a frown from the Falcon. Consequently the boy avoided him. Analee sighed and got out of bed on the opposite side.

"I am waiting for an answer, Analee."

She turned to him, her expression unsmiling. But still she said nothing.

"I said, 'but for all that I came to little harm.' Does your silence mean you disagree?"

Analee got up and put on her robe, shivering slightly as she fastened it about her person.

"I wish you cared more for the children, Angus."

"But I *do* care for them!"

He got up angrily and put on his own robe, a heavy velvet affair embroidered with gold thread. "How can you say I do not care?"

"You take so little notice of them. You would leave them here for months at a time."

"And what is wrong with that, pray? My dearest Analee, I know not about children who are brought up in gypsy camps; but those of the aristocracy are taught to be rarely seen and never heard. Above all, and at all times, to be subservient to their parents—an attitude that a good wife should heed *too*." He looked at her severely and stalked through to his dressing room, banging the communicating door sharply behind him.

Analee sighed. Sometimes she felt she could scarcely talk to the Falcon about anything serious at all. Except in bed he regarded her with an air of amused toleration as though to emphasize the degree of difference in their stations in life. In many ways she knew that to him she was indeed a chattel—a beloved precious one, perhaps, and much valued—but nevertheless still a possession.

Duncan stood trembling in front of his father, his chin quivering, his hands behind his back. Yet despite his fear there was, withal, an attitude of defiance and Analee knew this was what so enraged the Falcon: that

45

Duncan was unimpressed by his father's anger. He wore blue trousers, blue stockings and a white shirt, the sleeves rolled up to show his strong young brown arms. Analee could see the fingers latching and unlatching behind his back, the only sign that he was nervous. In front of him stood Lord Falconer, six feet six and a half inches tall, his black brows gathered in a knot in the center of his forehead, his eyes glinting with rage.

"The fact, sir, that you disappeared for over an hour and no one knowing where you were *is* a matter of the gravest concern. You were disobedient and defiant and your behavior deserves a good whipping."

It was only a trifle—he was found almost before he was missed—but Analee knew that the Falcon enjoyed finding fault with Duncan for the least thing while the other children could get away with murder.

"You are not even sorry, are you, sir? I can see the light of defiance in your eyes."

"I did not think it a very grave matter, Father. I wanted to look at the traps Nat had set in the wood. I could see the house the whole time."

"Yet when Nat called you did not come. Being in charge of you, he was beside himself with worry."

"I did not hear him, sir."

"I don't believe you, Master Duncan. You must know that any brigand can make off with you if you are found unattended. They could demand a large ransom to restore you to your family. They could kill or maim you, you the heir to the great estates of Falconer."

The Falcon's voice was bitter. Analee knew that the Falcon never ceased to grieve that Duncan, his least favored son, was his heir. As he unfastened the belt on his waist Duncan visibly began to tremble. It was not the first time his father had administered a thrashing.

"Take down your trousers, sir, and arrange yourself over that chair." The Falcon pointed an imperious finger at a wooden chair near where Analee sat, and flexed the strap in his hands with every sign of enjoyment.

Analee suddenly remembered how he had physically abused her when they were first lovers and how he had once nearly killed her, suspecting her of infidelity. He was a cruel man who enjoyed cruelty for its own sake. He enjoyed inflicting suffering. She put out a hand and got to her feet, but Angus turned to her, snarling.

"Pray be seated, Analee! I want you to witness the chastisement of this young man, the apple of your eye."

"I beg you, sir . . ." tears came into Analee's eyes and she looked at Duncan, whose piteous glances at his mother were more than she could bear.

"Beg nothing, my dear. Now bend over, sir."

Duncan falteringly tugged at the buttons of his breeches but the Falcon, livid with impatience, strode over towards him, reached out a great fist and tore the breeches, exposing his son's backside. Then he pushed him over the chair and raised the thick belt, bringing it crashing down on the small bare rump.

With every stroke Analee felt nausea; the savagery with which her husband applied the lash showed her how he enjoyed it. His lips were drawn back in a rictus of pleasure and his eyes gleamed. Every time the strap came crashing on his buttocks Duncan quivered, but uttered not a sound, his small hands tightly grasping the side of his chair until his knuckles were white.

Three, four, five . . . with every stroke Analee inwardly implored him to stop and then she saw Duncan sag and droop over the chair. Her hands to her mouth, she ran across to her husband and struck him on his broad back.

"Stop, stop . . . you are killing him! Stop!"

The Falcon turned angrily round looking as though he would start to belabor his wife, a fine bead of froth showing at his mouth. He shoved her unceremoniously to one side and turned round to resume his task on the practically senseless boy, but Analee dived in front of him and stood protectively over Duncan.

"My lord, I forbid you to touch this child again. You must thrash me first. You said you aim was to protect him from brigands and kidnappers. Do you protect him from them only to kill him yourself?"

She turned round and clasped Duncan, who remained inert over the chair, tenderly drawing up his torn breeches over his raw buttocks. Then she wrapped her arms around him and gently rocked him in her arms. His head lolled to one side and his eyes flickered. She sat on the chair and drew him close to her, her eyes wet with tears. She stroked his brow and kissed him, hugging him all the time. She didn't look at her husband at all, but was aware of him strapping the belt again round his waist.

"Well 'tis enough," he mumbled, a shade sheepishly, Analee thought.

"'Tis more than enough," Analee said, gazing at him with contempt. "You ought to be ashamed of yourself hitting a young child with such force. Your own son. 'Tis as though you wished him dead."

The Falcon looked at her and she met his gaze. His face was puzzled.

"'Tis true I do not love him and I know not why. My own son, my heir . . ."

"Sshh," Analee cautioned him as Duncan began to move. "It would not do for him to hear you. You had best leave us now and I will see to him."

Lord Falconer gazed once more at the inert boy as though at a stranger then, with a sigh, put on his coat and walked swiftly out of the room.

Analee waited for a while crooning over her child and then, when he was sufficiently recovered to walk, she helped him up to his room and laid him gently on the bed. She bathed his tender backside with cold water, rubbing a sweeting smelling balm into it, and

48

then she dressed him in his nightshirt and put him face downwards on the bed.

"My father hates me," he said, his eyes blinking rapidly with tears. Because she could not lie, she put a hand on his shoulder and stroked him gently, nuzzling him with her cheek.

"*I* love you very much. Your father is a fierce, impatient man."

"I hate him."

"You must not say that, Duncan! You must try and understand him. One day you will be the great Lord Falconer and you will honor his memory."

"I never shall. He loves the others but he hates me. His face changes when he looks at me. I want to love him but I cannot because of the hate I feel coming from him for me."

Analee marveled that such wise words came from such a young head. He was scarcely out of his baby clothes, yet he expressed himself so well. Instead of a child of six he was more like one of eight or nine. His precocity was remarkable and this, too, was resented by the Falcon.

"I hope he goes away soon," Duncan continued, beginning to sob onto the sheet, kneading it with his hands. "I hope he never comes back."

Analee straightened up and looked out of the window. In the distance she could see the snow-capped mountains at the end of Borrowdale. It was a rainy day and there was a chill in the air. Somehow it seemed expressive of the concern she felt about her husband's behavior since they had had their tiff in the bedroom two days before. Since then he had been moody and talked increasingly of returning to London. She deeply regretted now bringing up her concern about the children. Perhaps he didn't like to be reminded that he was an indifferent parent. Perhaps in his heart it made him feel guilty and this violence towards Duncan was a way of releasing his spleen. Better she had not spoken than to have caused this outrage.

Gradually Duncan's breathing grew heavier and he fell into a deep regular sleep. She covered him with a light blanket and tiptoed softly from the room, leaving the door ajar in case he called.

The house was quiet, the smaller children taking a walk with Nelly and her two-week-old baby who had been born while Analee was still at Falcon's Keep. It was another boy, named Dermot after her husband's father. Nelly would stay at Furness to look after the children while she and Angus returned to London alone to take their place at the Court.

There were once again rumors of war. The French were trying to undermine the English in India and America and the continent of Europe was buzzing with rumors. Some said that the French were again paying court to Bonnie Prince Charlie, to offer him support for a rising at home to occupy the English forces. Analee knew that Angus was immersed in politics, growing increasingly uneasy with the Pelham brothers, the Duke of Newcastle and his brother Henry, and plotting with William Pitt, whom he considered more capable of running the country. At one time there was talk of the Falcon going to command the English forces in India; but the King was anxious to keep him at home. He was one of the few men he trusted. Some said he would like the Falcon to succeed the Duke of Newcastle as Prime Minister.

Analee went along the corridor to the bedroom which she shared with her husband at the end of the house. It overlooked the lake and the mountains and, for most of the day, was filled with sunshine when there was any. But this was a grey, dull day and Analee pushed open the door feeling tired and in need of a rest. The sight of her husband using such violence against her small son had shocked her deeply.

The Falcon lay on the bed in the middle of the large

room. He still had on his boots and his jacket, but his eyes were closed. Analee was about to go out quietly again when he opened his eyes.

"I have been waiting for you. I have a need of you."

He smiled at her and lifted a leg as though to have her remove his boots. His eyes were lazy and amorous, a smile played on his lips. The thought that his violent action against her son had aroused his desires sickened her.

"I have things to do in the house," she said and went to the door.

"Come here."

Analee stopped, but did not look back. Then slowly she advanced towards the door again.

"I said, come here—wife."

She put her hand on the door knob and glanced behind her. Her husband still lay on his back, his face turned towards her. The smile had been replaced by a cruel grimace. Analee felt sudden fear striking her heart and closed the door. Reluctantly she stepped back into the room.

"Has your violence aroused your desires, my lord?"

The Falcon leapt off the bed and, seizing her, threw her down on to it. He stood over her, a towering giant, his hands on his hips.

"Now listen here, woman. I'll tolerate no impudence from you, just as I do not care for disobedience from my son. I am the complete master of this house and I want you to know it."

"I have no doubt of that, my lord," Analee said fearfully, remembering only too clearly the occasion when he had violated her in Paris, half killing her. Although he had never been so violent since, she knew what he was capable of. There was some demon lurking at the back of his heart ready to disperse the gentle tender part of his nature, of which she had seen much in the past five years, surrendering to his frequent demands, gladly bearing him two children. She loved An-

51

gus Falconer because she had willed herself to do so, to forget the past; but the past was always there, like a threatening shadow. She knew it and she was afraid of him, love continually warring with apprehension and unease.

Analee looked up at him, her eyes pleading for tenderness. She felt if he despatched her love again it would not easily come back.

"Get undressed," the Falcon said, and started to remove his breeches, turning his back on her. There was no tenderness, no dallying, no love play that made the act such a delight.

Obediently she sat up and began to unfasten her bodice. She took it off and put it neatly on a chair, then her skirt; she only wore simple clothes while at home in Furness. She turned round and saw that Angus was lying on the bed, as naked as she was. But he didn't look at her, his head was cradled on his hands and his eyes rested on the ceiling. She lay down beside him and gently encircled his body with her arms, leaning over to kiss his nipples. She felt him tremble and, without any endearments, he raised himself and straddled her, penetrating her before she had time to realize what was happening. His stiff member tore at her flesh and hurt her; there was no love in her for him, no desire. He took her roughly and discharged himself after a few short thrusts like a stallion. Then he fell off her and, pulling the bedclothes over himself, was immediately asleep. He had not even kissed her, as though she was some harlot, some doxy to be taken and thrust aside. The tears ran down her face and she turned her back on him, weeping silently.

She lay there for an hour, not daring to leave; she heard voices as the children returned from their outing and the smell of food as the dinner was served. Someone knocked on their door, but when there was no answer they went away again. Finally the Falcon woke,

52

yawned and sat up, his head tousled. He looked at her good-humoredly.

"I am very hungry. Send a servant up with some dinner for me."

"Yes, Angus."

Analee got obediently out of bed and quickly dressed. Her husband didn't even look at her, but had turned on his side again, his face resting on his outstretched palm, his eyes closed. She wanted to give the door a good bang to shatter his complacency, but she closed it gently—she would keep the rage locked in her heart because she could not hope to win against the power of the Falcon.

Downstairs there was a bustle of humor and activity. The older children sat at table, Nelly presiding at their head. She glanced up as Analee came into the room and her face clouded.

"Is all not well, my lady? Where is Duncan?"

"He is resting. His father gave him a hiding for getting lost. I have come to get food for his lordship who would dine in his room. He is out of humor today. I will take food up for Duncan, too."

"And yourself, my lady? Will you not eat?" Nelly looked at her anxiously. "You do not look at all well. Let me send food up for you."

"No, I prefer to eat with you, as much as I can for I am not hungry. I will go and see Betty and arrange for his lordship's food to be sent up. I will prepare something nourishing for Duncan myself."

Analee went into the kitchen and busied herself with instructions. Then she took some egg custard and sweetmeats for Duncan, arranged on a tray with a little posy of flowers. Once she would have done it for her lord; but not now. Not ever again maybe. She did not go near his room all day and at night would have had a bed made up for herself in a spare room had she dared.

The Falcon rose at dusk and went to his study. He

said he would dine there alone and he did. Two bottles of wine were sent in and some brandy. Analee dreaded the night and she went to bed early although this was no protection. To her surprise she fell asleep and when she awoke it was dawn and the place by her side was empty. In alarm she got up and, putting on her robe, went downstairs to his study. A candle gleamed under the door. With trepidation she knocked, leaning against it, her heart hammering.

"Come in."

The Falcon was sitting at his desk writing. He looked haggard and his eyes were bloodshot. A glass of brandy, untouched, stood by his side. He didn't look up as Analee came in. She stood behind him and said timidly, "Is all well, my lord?"

"Aye, it is well." He stopped writing and looked up at her. "I am altering my will. I do not believe Duncan is my child. In law he is, so he will inherit my title. That I can do nothing about; but I will leave him as little property and money as I can."

Analee's hand flew to her mouth.

"What are you saying, Angus? Has your rage made you insane?"

He turned in his chair and looked at her gravely.

"Analee, you have not been faithful to me. You know it and I know it. All the men ogle you and you are slave to their desires. McNeath told me you had bedded with Brent Delamain and I wager he is the father of Duncan; he was in Paris at the same time as us. I cannot trust you, Analee, and, because of that, I cannot love you."

The Falcon's face was sad and Analee went up to him trying to take his hand, but he withdrew it from her and put it on the desk, grasping his glass of brandy with the other and taking a large draught.

"Angus, how can you speak thus to me? Your affair with my half-sister, Lady Constance Craven, was the scandal of London. You are known as a womanizer and kindly do not trouble to deny it. How can you talk to *me* of infidelity?"

The Falcon got up from his chair with an oath and seized her roughly by the arm.

"Don't you dare to speak to me like that, Analee. *I* am the master of the house, the master of your body and your soul. You depend on me for everything you have, everything you are. I gave you my name, my love, my children. Without me you would be a gutter gypsy, a wanderer in the fields, a prey to any man. As it is you have flaunted your wealth, *my* wealth, and your looks to ensnare men. Do not think I don't see how they observe you, lust for you. I know you too well, your love of the amorous arts, to think you capable of resisting them."

"My lord," Analee said in a trembling voice, "you do me grave injustice. It is true I am yours in body and soul and love only you. I have been faithful only to you. All your children truly *are* your children, the fruit of your lordship's seed. You should know the power of my love for you, for I have given you proof of it countless times. You enrage yourself unnecessarily with this irrational jealousy. How could I look at another man when I have you for a husband?"

Analee stared boldly at him, her expression submissive but also defiant. If she knew that she lied to the Falcon she had good reason to do so. As long as his suspicions remained suspicions she was safe; but if he knew the truth he would kill her. He would kill her and throw her body in the lake and, being such a powerful lord, no one would put him on trial. They would remember she was a mere gypsy, even though the natural daughter of an earl, and forget all about her. Looking at him she realized that her old fear of him was returning again to displace the love and rapture of the past few weeks. With a man of such uncertain moods how could she ever feel secure? She thought of their loveless lovemaking earlier on—the Falcon had not treated her like that, like a common doxy, since the early days of their relationship when to him she was just a passing fancy, a woman he had picked up in a gypsy camp, never divining how passionately and hopelessly he would shortly fall in love with her. Was he now falling out of love? She remembered Paris and she remembered Lady Constance. It was only too easy to recall these bad bitter memories with someone as volatile and unpredictable as her husband.

The Falcon looked momentarily uncomfortable after Analee's speech and took another draught of brandy, his hand riffling through the papers on his desk. He had a night's growth of beard and looked unkempt.

"Well that's as may be," he murmured. "I have only your word for it. How is it that Duncan is so unlike me, so stubborn, so unruly?"

Analee gave a faint smile.

"If I may say so, my lord, those are two of your very attributes. Are you not a stubborn, passionate man who takes not kindly to discipline? Your son is very like you, in temperament and in looks."

The Falcon stared at her but she did not falter; she met his gaze unflinchingly, staying the panic in her heart.

"I like him not; but I will reconsider disinheriting him. Maybe he will improve as he grows older. He needs a stern tutor to discipline him. I will separate him from his brother and sisters upon whom he is a bad influence and send him to Falcon's Keep with a man of iron discipline and good learning. I will teach the young puppy to conform."

Angus grimaced with satisfaction and rubbed his jowl. He scratched his chin and looked at Analee.

"So, you *do* love me, eh? You had best prove it again. Get you upstairs and be ready to receive me."

Time was when he would have taken her in his arms and tenderly embraced her, gently undressing her with

56

words of endearment. Now he ordered her upstairs like a strumpet to fulfill his desires.

Well if that was what he wanted, a strumpet she would be, not the wife of his bosom, the mother of his children; not a marchioness, but a common whore who prostituted herself for gain. And, in this case, what she wanted to gain was not jewels or finery or title, but her life and the welfare of her children. For these objectives, particularly the latter, she would do anything.

Chapter Four

The Falcon was restless to be gone from Lakeland. Having made his decision about Duncan he lost no time putting it into practice; but sent him back to Falcon's Keep with McNeath who would look after him until a tutor arrived from London. Analee was only allowed a brief, tearful farewell of her eldest son. Fearful of showing her emotions in public, she took her intimate farewell of him in her bedroom where she hugged him and kissed him, promising him that she would always look after him, protect him from his father's ire.

"For Papa is essentially *good*, Duncan. What he is doing is for your welfare. You must always remember that."

Duncan had rubbed his behind, still sore from his thrashing, and looked at her distrustfully.

"Why is he sending me away, Mama?"

"Because he wants you to be taught. We are going to London and he thinks you will be distracted there. It is for your own good. I will write to you every day, my darling, every day . . ." Tears came into Analee's eyes as she knelt and kissed him. She felt his little body stiffen and knew that he distrusted her, too. In his small world there was no one he really trusted.

"Ma'am, his lordship . . ."

McNeath advanced, his face wrinkled with compassion, and held out his blunt strong hand towards Duncan.

Analee brushed away her tears and pushed Duncan gently forward. "There, my darling, go with good McNeath. He will look after you . . ."

Analee turned away and buried her face in her hands. She did not watch them go out, but lay on her bed sobbing, hearing the sound of the coach as it went slowly up the drive towards the road at the foot of Cat Bells.

There was a movement in the room and she drew herself up in the bed, thinking it was her husband. She wanted to show him a brave face, for Duncan's sake. She had begged him not to send their son away, but he had refused to listen to her. Once his mind was made up on anything, nothing deflected him from it.

Analee tried to keep up a show of good spirits for the sake of the children and the household; but her heart was heavy especially because, since his whipping of Duncan, an estrangement had grown up between her and her husband that affected the tenderness of their marriage bed. Every time he took her in his arms she recalled a man to whom violence was no stranger, one who had once beaten the daylights out of her and left her near death. One who would thrash the tender flesh of a young boy until it bled. When he reached for her she trembled involuntarily, only hoping that he would think it was desire.

Now she trembled as a hand was laid on her shoulder. But the gesture was tender and womanly and she grasped the slight, familiar hand. "Nell."

"Oh, Analee, what has become of his lordship? His behavior is so strange of late. Even McNeath comments on it."

Analee struggled up, smiling bravely at her old friend. "His lordship is restless, Nell, anxious to be back in London. I think I have detained him too long. You know he is much older than I and does not get the same pleasure from young children. They irritate him. He is a man used to action and the bustle of cities and I fear the country bores him. He will soon recover his old form when we are back in London. Of that I am sure."

Analee turned her head away so that Nelly would not observe her expression. But she realized she could not withhold the truth from someone who knew her so well.

"There *is* something wrong, Analee, isn't there?" Nelly spoke softly and sat on the bed beside her mistress with the familiarity of one accustomed to taking such liberties. Analee suddenly leaned over to Nelly and buried her face in her matronly bosom, for Nelly had gained weight since, as young women, they had scrambled over the fells together.

"Oh Nell, I as so unhappy. You know it, you have sensed it. His lordship and I had words one day last week and nothing has been the same since. I accused him of not being fond of his children and he resents it bitterly. Of *course* he is fond of them, Nell . . ."

"Not so as you'd notice," Nelly sniffed and patted Analee's back. "Sometimes he hardly seems to know they are there. He never seeks them out and they all go in fear of him, especially Duncan. My goodness how he blanches when his father passes. Runs and hides he does . . ."

"But Nell, my husband is an important man. An *older* man; a lord, a Marquess. We do not really understand such folk, you and I. His lordship says that the aristocracy are bred to ignore their children. He was. For all I know, he may be right."

"Well," Nelly said firmly, "it is not *my* way and it is not *your* way, whatever his lordship may say. I consider it very strange behavior. His lordship is a moody man, that we know. But things are alright . . . between you, Analee?" Nelly searched her face anxiously.

"They are not as good as they were; but I am sure they will be alright again. It is a temporary phase. That is all." Analee wiped her eyes and, straightening up, blew her nose vigorously, leaving it shiny and pink. "We have enjoyed such rapture in each other's arms that I cannot believe we will not again. At times I fear him remembering what he can be, what he can do. Seeing him hit Duncan . . . affected me. I tremble a little now when he embraces me; but it will pass. When we return to London all will be well. The only thing that really grieves me is his attitude to Duncan, the fact that he cannot abide him. Did one of the others offend him as much he would not feel the same."

"But it is singular that he dislikes Duncan, for his young lordship resembles him so."

"That is exactly what I say, Nell! It is very strange, as if he divines the truth. Of course I strenuously deny it."

"Oh, of course! You *must*. If he knew the father was his arch enemy the . . ."

Analee put a hand to her lips and looked anxiously at the door. "Do not say it, Nell. Do not say the name. If he were to hear he would kill us both. There, kind, good Nell; go down and bring me some broth to restore my spirits. I must keep myself strong for the sake of my children. I must conceal my feelings."

Nelly reached into her pocket and produced a large white envelope. "I bring you this. It came by special messenger."

Analee took the envelope and, examining the writing, saw the small crest on the pocket. "Mr. Rigg has a crest?" she smiled. "He, too, will be ennobled next."

"It is from him?"

"It is from Sarah. I know the writing." Analee tore it open and quickly perused the contents. "They want

60

us to visit for the wedding of Emma and Hugo. Oh, I think we should not go."

"But why not?"

"In case, on seeing me, Mr. Fitzgerald declines to go to the altar! I dare not. The sight of him makes my lord so jealous. I tell you what, Nell, I will invite the Riggs before we go. They can come with their children for the day and we will contrive a happy family party." Analee glanced at her slyly, her accustomed good spirits returning. " 'Twill be a change, will it not, to see my good lord in his unaccustomed role of a family man?"

The Rigg family, not to be outshone by the might of the Falcon, traveled to his home in Lakeland in style with three carriages, four outriders, numerous servants and a nursemaid for each of the youngest of their six children. When Analee saw the long procession wend its way along the road and through the gate she stared at it at first in amazement and then with laughter, muffling her giggles as Nelly put the finishing touches to her simple toilet.

"Perhaps they have come to stay for a week."

"They are only here for a few hours, Analee."

"*En route* to Delamain Castle perhaps, but still a formidable retinue."

Analee decided to put rings on her fingers after all or the Riggs might feel insulted. Then she glanced at her face in the mirror and patted her thick luxuriant hair before going quickly downstairs to join the Falcon who was already standing at the main door, his mouth agape. He turned as he heard Analee.

"You did not tell me they were stopping."

"They are not, Angus. It is only a visit. I think it is done to impress."

"The carriages cannot all fit into the drive." Angus gestured to an equally dumbfounded servant and told him to go and stop the third carriage from trying to approach the door.

"They will have to walk," Angus said bad-temperedly. "What a carry-on." He put his hands behind his back, thrust out his jaw and stared aggressively at the interlopers as though at an invading army.

And, indeed, the scene had aspects of an invasion as the grooms reined the horses, postillions hurried down from their perches, carriage doors were flung open and a variety of people, old and young, descended to the ground. The number of servants from the Rigg household outnumbered those from the Marquess of Falconer by about three to one, and they scuttled about all attired in a gorgeous livery of emerald green and yellow that Mr. Rigg had had designed by a tailor in Carlisle who also worked for Lord Lowther.

But almost all, male and female, were outshone by the corpulent figure of Ambrose Rigg himself as he carefully descended the small ladder let down from the carriage, clutching the hands of two stalwart servants who stood on either side.

Mr. Rigg had chosen to be clad in purple from head to foot, or rather from the neck where his coat began to his knees where his breeches ended. It was not a gentle nostalgic purple of the kind favored by old ladies, but a hectic thrusting purple such as adorns the persons of bishops, judges and others prominent in society's hierarchy. It was the color of rich gentian accentuated by the high gloss of the rich silk imported from the Indies. His waistcoat was of a pinkish purple, more the tones of a foxglove, and heavily adorned with purple braid woven in the silk mills of Macclesfield. His high starched cravat, of pure Brussels lace, frothed at his throat, and his stockings were of the sheerest white silk fashioned in Leicestershire. His black shoes were adorned with gleaming brass buckles and from the sleeve of his frilly shirt flopped a large white handkerchief stained with snuff. His full bottomed whig was slightly awry, due to the bumpiness of the journey over the hills from Cockermouth. His red face was puffy

62

with lack of sleep, such had been his excitement at the prospect of a meeting at last, as an equal, with the great Lord Falconer towards whom he now advanced trying unsuccessfully to bend his solid body deferentially at the waist.

The Falcon regarded this apparition with all the amazement of a general on the field surprised by an unanticipated attack. His mouth hung open and he slowly descended the steps towards the paved courtyard.

" 'Tis Mr. Rigg, my lord," Analee whispered, scarcely able to suppress a smile, but doing so quickly as she saw the neat, though ample, figure of Mrs. Rigg encased in sensible brown buckram follow a few paces behind her spouse. She in turn had a trail of small Riggs behind her though Henry, who was thirteen, was taller than his parents. Elia, eleven, and no beauty, had something of the imperious look of her Allonby ancestors. Norman, nine, and Caspar, seven, were both smaller editions of their father. Augusta, who had looks unlike any of the other Riggs, was four and Joanna Rigg, whose looks it was difficult as yet to ascribe, was the baby.

As Ambrose seized the hand of the Falcon, his expression of delight akin to apoplexy, his wife came to his side and the junior Riggs formed a straight and respectful line behind their parents as though waiting to be presented.

"My lord!" gushed Ambrose Rigg, wringing the noble hand. "You have no idea what an honor it is for my humble family to be received by your lordship."

Ambrose Rigg bent so low over the hand that Analee thought at any moment he would kiss it. She hastily came forward smiling, while the Falcon remained dumbfounded, content to let his hand be wrung until it pained him.

"How very pleasant to see you again, Mr. Rigg, Mrs. Rigg," Analee turned to Sarah and embraced her on the cheek. "And all your children—my goodness! How you've grown, Henry, and Norman, I hardly recognized you. But, my dear little Elia, you are bound to be a beauty . . ." Analee leaned and kissed her cheeks, pinching them with her fingers while the children all registered their various degrees of pleasure at having their names remembered by their distinguished hostess who had not seen them for three years.

"May I present my wife Mrs. Rigg, sir?" As Ambrose pompously brought Sarah forward the Falcon recovered his composure and thankfully took the hand of Mrs. Rigg, perfunctorily bending his head to kiss it.

"Ma'am, I congratulate you on your progeny."

"Oh, thank you, Lord Falconer." Sarah Rigg, whose home Furness Grange had once been, found her tongue and smiled gratefully at his lordship. The past was still too full of sad memories for Sarah to have looked forward to the visit with any sense of pleasurable anticipation. Even though she knew that Analee had vowed to restore the estate to any of the Allonbys who lawfully returned from exile, it pained her to think that the ancestral Allonby home was in the hands of strangers.

His lordship righted himself and was about to escort Mrs. Rigg into the house when his eye was caught by a movement from the second carriage and a young woman stepped from the door to the ground, daintily picking up her skirts as she came down the small set of steps placed for her. Rigg hurried over as fast as his fat legs could carry him and took the elbow of the young woman, leading her back to the reception party. Analee raised her eyes and looked enquiringly at Sarah; but, before she could reply, Ambrose said:

"May I present to your lordship and your ladyship Miss Anna Cameron, my sister-in-law, who has lately come from America?"

The Falcon opened his eyes wide in admiration, his demeanor immediately and subtly changed by the appearance of this young woman. Analee observed how he squared his shoulders so that he appeared to advance his height an inch or two and brushed some imaginary specks of dust from the front of his coat. Analee having seen many times the effect of female beauty, not the least her own, on his lordship, knew that the Falcon was impressed, as indeed she was herself.

For Anna Cameron was no raw-boned red-faced American from the backwoods, but a beauty with red-gold hair and large turquoise eyes which gleamed with youth and excitement and, maybe, a suspicion of belladonna which Italian ladies used to make their eyes shine. She was small in stature but exquisitely proportioned, like a miniature figurine of Meissen porcelain with a narrow waist, a high full bosom and the whitest sloping shoulders which were only partly covered by her dress of white gingham dotted with small red and blue spots. Her bonnet of the same material partly framed her face into an attractive oval and her red mouth was elegantly formed yet relaxed and friendly as her brother-in-law, clearly relishing his role, led her over to their hosts. Miss Cameron dropped a low curtsey and the Falcon, still preening himself, bowed and bent low to take her hand and help raise her up.

"Charmed to meet you, Miss Cameron." The Falcon's hooded eyes gazed into hers and lingered for a long moment.

"I am so honored to make your acquaintance, Lord Falconer," Miss Cameron said, blushing only slightly as she turned and dropped a similar curtsey to Analee, "and your ladyship."

"How do you do, Miss Cameron. You are the sister of Stewart Allonby's wife?"

"Yes, Elizabeth is my sister! 'Twas she who kindly arranged that I should come to this country and stay with Mr. and Mrs. Rigg before proceeding to London."

"Ah, you are going to London?" The Falcon said with undisguised interest in his voice.

"Yes, sir. I am staying with friends of my father, Mr. and Mrs. Peto of Cavendish Square."

"Peto? Peto?" His lordship screwed up his nose, gazing at the sky as though for enlightenment. "I know them not, I fear. Peto, Peto. Let me see. Know you anyone by the name of Peto, my dear?"

"I assure you, sir, they are not in the least well known or distinguished." Miss Cameron said with another faint blush. "They are wealthy merchants who came recently to this country from America where they were near neighbors of ours. Mrs. Peto very much missed her family."

"Ah, merchants . . ." the Falcon said as though dismissing the idea from his mind. "No, we would not know such people."

Analee saw Sarah turn red at the remark and the pleasant smile vanished abruptly from the face of Miss Cameron, a young lady whose own family fortune was founded on trade.

Rigg, however, appeared unperturbed and gestured towards the house with his small, plump hand. "This was the Allonby estate, my dear; in your brother-in-law's family for generations."

"Aye and like to be restored someday," Analee said, the expression of rage at her husband's disparaging remarks being quickly dispersed by her anxiety to make their guests feel at ease.

"Stuff," the Falcon said uncompromisingly. "I have no intention of restoring it. The Allonbys are traitorous folk who betrayed this country, saving yourself; ma'am, always saving yourself." The Falcon made an exaggerated gesture towards Sarah, who however did not appear altogether mollified by it. Her lips were drawn together in a straight, disapproving line expressive of irritation and unease.

"They were not traitors, my lord, but had their own points of view," Analee said firmly. "Had the Stuarts been successful, it is your lordship who would now be

66

languishing in exile with your estates maybe in the hands of the Allonby family. It was a matter of loyalties. The Stuarts, after all, were once the legal kings of England."

"Mistaken loyalties if I may say, ma'am," the Falcon said with a display of good humor as unaccustomed and it was unexpected, winking broadly at Miss Cameron who appeared discomforted by the exchange. "You see, my wife *will* argue with me, Miss Cameron. I hope they bring up women to be more respectful of their spouses where you come from."

Miss Cameron laughed with relief, showing dainty even teeth. "Oh no, I assure you, Lord Falconer, quite the contrary. The women of the new world are very spirited in their attitudes towards their menfolk. Not *all* of them of course."

"Not *you*, I hope," Angus said flirtatiously, drawing nearer to her.

"I am not wed, Lord Falconer. I cannot say what I will do." Miss Cameron smiled at him archly and Analee felt a tremor of irritation which she was careful not to show. She knew that, but for the presence of this nubile young woman, Lord Falconer would have pounced on her spirited remark with his customary bullying attitude.

"The women in America are certainly different from us," Sarah Rigg said, taking the hand of her youngest son. "They have a much harder life. They have to become accustomed to being as strong as the men. Some of the tales Anna has told us you would not believe, Lady Falconer. Women besieged by marauding Indians, having to endure deprivation and starvation for weeks on end."

"Indeed it is not only the Indians who behave like savages," Angus said gruffly. "You should have seen what some of the fleeing Stuart troops did. Why, I recall the slaughter in the camp of gypsies . . ." The

67

Falcon paused and looked at Analee, who blanched and put her hands to her face.

"Oh do not, Angus. Even to recall that scene to this day . . ."

"Ah, you see!" His lordship said with satisfaction. "So much for the Stuarts."

"I assure you my brother-in-law is not like that," Anna Cameron said defensively. "He is a perfect gentleman, the very model of what we always imagined a well brought-up Englishman to be. He is kind, considerate, just to the slaves, beloved by everyone, adored by his wife and children . . ."

"Ah, there are children?" Analee said eagerly.

"Oh yes, Lady Falconer, three already."

"My goodness, such a large family!"

" 'Tis our tradition, ma'am," Ambrose said pompously, looking smugly at his brood. "The Allonbys breed well."

"Come and take some refreshment," Analee began ushering them into the house before Sarah could protest at her husband's vulgarity. "Our children await the arrival of yours with great anticipation though they are mostly younger, I fear. Your elder children might perhaps like to take a boat on the lake after they have eaten?"

"Oh, capital!" Norman said. "May we, Father?"

"Of course, my boy," Ambrose purred, rubbing his hands together, delighting in such intimacy with the aristocracy. "Her ladyship is too kind. Too kind."

In many ways it was a successful day even if not quite the scene of family conviviality that Analee had anticipated, for the Falcon made no attempt to conceal his admiration for Miss Cameron. He insisted on personally showing her the house, especially the older parts that had come from the ancient Abbey of Furness when the house was part of the monastery lands, and the gardens that had been so lovingly laid out by John

68

and Stewart Allonby before their defeat in the Rebellion.

He paid such court to Miss Cameron that from time to time Analee perceived Sarah or Ambrose Rigg steal a quick glance to see how she was taking it; but she pretended indifference, or ignorance, and kept a relaxed smile upon her face which was not easy for her to maintain. Sarah had informed her that Anna was just twenty-two—the age the Falcon liked, though older than her half-sister who he had seduced five years before. Doubtless Miss Cameron was also a virgin, and doubtless much taken by the attentions of the powerful Falcon. Doubtless too she would be unable to resist his charms, if forced upon her.

"Miss Cameron must visit us in London," the Falcon declared as the sun began to sink over the hills and the time for departure drew near. "Must she not, my dear? You could introduce her at Court."

"I would be delighted, Angus," Analee said sweetly. "Nothing would give me more pleasure."

"I am sure the Princess of Wales would be much taken by her—well-bred young women from the new world are a rarity at court."

"Her Royal Highness is a widow," Analee said to Anna. "But she has recovered remarkably from her bereavement and brings up her young son, George, to succeed his grandfather. She is a woman of much spirit."

"Oh, what you say is so exciting!" Anna clasped her hands together and gazed starry-eyed at Analee. "I cannot believe my good fortune. Ambrose, Sarah, do you hear—I might be presented to Her Royal Highness the Princess of Wales?"

"Aye, and to His Majesty himself, why not?" the Falcon said idly, taking snuff and passing the box to Ambrose who groveled once again—he had done little else all day—with gratitude and took too large a pinch, making himself sneeze. His wife gazed at him with her usual disapproval, and averted her eyes from the spectacle of his bulbous red nose, brown with snuff, being encased in his already stained handkerchief. The Falcon, of course, would never be caught in any such gaffe, delicately taking just the right amount between his finger and thumb and positioning it at just the right angle in his nostril. "I am well in with the Court," he continued, dusting his nose with his spotless handkerchief and ignoring the antics of Ambrose. "His Majesty would, I am sure, be delighted to receive Miss Cameron. He is old, of course, and feeble, but still the King of England. And Lady Yarmouth too, Queen in everything but name . . ."

Analee glanced at her husband, whom she knew rumor said had received the formidable countess's favors. Lady Yarmouth was known to have a weakness for him and to be able to refuse him nothing—not even her bed. The thought of her husband copulating with the King's mistress was beyond Analee's comprehension; but at least it was only for gain, to be privy to the inner secrets of the Court and Cabinet. There could not be a spark of physical attraction. She much preferred that to his sharing a bed with such as Anna Cameron who was far more likely to ensnare his passions and cause untold mischief to her and her family.

"When shall you be in London?" the Falcon said with deliberate vagueness. "Soon?"

"She will not stop for the wedding." Ambrose quickly took his fourth glass of port. "It would not do for Emma to find her with us."

"Ah," his lordship nodded wisely. "Emma of course having been rejected by Stewart?"

"Exactly," Ambrose agreed sagaciously and put the delicate glass to his thick lips.

"So when is the wedding?"

"Next month. Young Hugo is very uxorious, eager to be wed. He is building a fine house on some land I gave him outside Whitehaven. It will not be ready, of

70

course, so they will lodge with us for a time. But if your lordship and your ladyship would be good enough to take young Anna here under your protection in London I know she will be in the seventh heaven."

Analee had no doubt at all that she would. She was glad to see them go, but sorry to think that, all too soon, she would see Anna Cameron again. She thought of Reyora and her warning, and somehow Anna Cameron seemed like the harbinger of misfortune.

Chapter Five

Prince Charles Edward Stuart put down his tumbler full of whisky and stretched his legs in front of him. Brent observed how his hand shook as he placed the glass carefully on the table by his side. The Prince's appearance shocked Brent even though he had heard how much he had deteriorated since his long, fruitless ten years of exile began. Yet there was still a kingly quality about him, the air of a man used to command. Brent remembered how much he had revered and loved him. He looked at him sadly and shook his head.

"But I assure you, Delamain, there *will* be war in Europe. The French are eager to use me for their own ends and I them for mine. I have not waited all this time in vain."

Charles picked up his glass and, downing its contents, held it out imperiously towards Brent. "Pray fill my glass. This is the best whisky from Scotland. I still have my contacts, my loyal followers, whatever you may have heard."

Brent assumed an expression of innocence, but the Prince wagged a finger at him. "I can see you do not think so. You have heard rumors of me, false malicious rumors. I assure you I have many loyal followers. What

71

kind of life do you think I lead here, hounded from pillar to post? Even now my residence in Basle is under perpetual surveillance. I come here to Paris—to the house of my friend and banker Waters—skulking through the night. But, Delamain, I promise you this time we shall triumph. We shall . . ."

Brent shook his head again. "I beg your Royal Highness not to deceive yourself. The Hanoverians are too well established in England. The King is secure on the throne . . ."

The Prince's face, once so lean and handsome, now heavy and dissipated, glowered. "Do not call that imposter 'King' in my presence, Delamain! You should know better. They call my father the Pretender! It is *he*, Prince George of Hanover, who pretends. Kindly hand me my glass."

Brent hastily refilled the glass and handed it to Charles, who sipped the contents eagerly. All that Brent had heard about his heavy drinking, his dissipation was true. The Prince had aged in the last few years and his once splendid figure had thickened. "I beg your pardon, your Royal Highness, I am asking you to face reality . . ."

"Do not talk to *me* of reality, Delamain!" The Prince thumped his knee and some of the liquid spilled from the glass on to his crumpled, faded suit. There was even a patch on the pocket. Brent recalled how immaculate his old leader had once looked even in war, how brilliant his court in Edinburgh before the tide turned against him. Bonnie Prince Charlie, how the ladies loved him. Even his wig looked as though it was never combed and fitted him badly. "I know all about reality. I live in it constantly. It is you who are in dreamland. Know you that King Louis of France has in mind to marry me to his daughter, Madame Adelaide? That he is full of plans to restore my father to his throne, and that I am to lead a fresh invasion of

England? Know you that, Delamain? I see you still look disbelieving."

"It is hard to credit, sir, with our own forces so dispersed."

"I assure you it is true," Charles said petulantly. "Louis will do all he can to provoke cousin George. I have sent for you to offer you a place at my side, as my right-hand man. You will come to live at Basle so as to receive my orders daily. I want you to carry messages between Switzerland and France, and France and England. The Princess of Wales is at the heart of the English efforts to have me restored. I want you to go to London and make the acquaintance of Mrs. Catherine Walkinshaw who is housekeeper to the Princess."

"I cannot go to London, sir, I fear for my life. I cannot set foot in England. Lord Falconer in particular desires to hound me . . ."

"Ah, Lord Falconer," the Prince said thoughtfully, emptying his glass yet again and handing it once more to Brent. "You know that Lady Falconer to whom you once introduced me is sympathetic to our cause? May she not be of help?"

Brent's heart leapt. To see Analee again he would risk his neck. "I believe Lady Falconer is an intimate of the Princess of Wales. I might contrive . . . Mistress Walkinshaw, you say?"

"Aye, she is the sister of . . . well I suppose you know all about Clementina Walkinshaw, my common-law wife?"

Brent gazed at the ground. "I did hear rumors, sir. . ."

"Oh come, man, all the world knows it and that we have a child. Mistress Catherine is the sister of my good lady and would do all in her power to help our cause. Yes, you get Lady Falconer, the Enchantress, to come to your help once again. And give her my respects should you see her." The Prince smiled, as though at a pleasant memory, his face transformed.

Sister Mary Gertrude sat in the convent parlor, her hands tucked in the sleeves of her habit. The black nun's veil had finally obscured any traces of beauty and her face had the pallor of those who enclose themselves for a long time indoors. Her luminous eyes gazed at Brent and she thought over his words. Then she shook her head. "I would have naught to do with him, Brent. So many good people have deserted him. Why, last year even the devoted Goring left him to go into service with the Prussians."

"I know, that was a blow to the cause. The Prince treated Goring so badly. It is because he is so short of real friends that I feel I cannot fail him, Mary."

Brent looked at his former wife and found it impossible to recall the days when he had loved her, been under the spell of her golden beauty many years ago in Lakeland. The nun's black habit had come between them forever. But it had made her a friend, a confidante he badly needed. He had come for her counsel.

"But, Brent," she said in her soft convent voice, cultivated after years of speaking in whispers, "I thought you had left the service of the Prince? Did you not go to America to seek your fortune there?"

"I found the country too rough," Brent replied, beginning to pace restlessly up and down the convent parlor. He stopped in front of a statue of St. Scholastica, the sister of St. Benedict, founder of the order to which Mary now belonged. The gentle ageless plaster face, illuminated by the soft glow of candles gazed down at him. "I liked not the life. I prefer the ways I know in Europe. The new Americans are crude, thrusting people. They think of nothing but money. The work I didn't mind; but the way of life . . . no. They cannot rest without news of the mother country. They ape France and English fashions in ridiculous ways. They have houses modeled on our styles and their servants wear liveries and wear white gloves. But their use of slavery is quite abhorrent to me. Scarcely a laborer in the fields is a free man. Many of those who are not black slaves, imported in vile conditions from Africa, are indentured men, like Stewart was, sent over there for crimes committed in England. The way they treat their servants and slaves is appalling. They do not think of them as human beings."

"You are too kind, Brent," Mary said gently, remembering how passionately and for how long she had loved him, a love that had now been sublimated in that higher duty that she owed towards God. "You have too gentle a nature. I would to God that it could be used to some higher purpose."

"Of what kind?" Brent turned from perusing the countenance of the statue, clothed, like Mary, in its black Benedictine robes, and looked at her.

"Did you ever think of offering yourself to God, too? I have found such happiness within these walls, Brent."

"As a priest?" Brent looked at her incredulously.

"Why not? Or a monk. It is a tradition in both our families, the Allonbys and the Delamains. Don't forget your brother Tom who as a priest also died for the Stuart cause in the Rebellion."

"I am not like to forget," Brent said grimly. "But I have no calling, no vocation. I am not attracted to the life, Mary."

"Are you sure?"

"Quite sure."

Brent thought of Analee and his conviction that one day, one precious day, she would be his. As long as she was alive, married to the detested Falcon or not, he would remain in the world.

"Is it still Lady Falconer for whom you pine, Brent?" Mary spoke quietly, but the tone of her voice was sad. But for Analee she and Brent would still be married, maybe the parents of the children Mary had always longed for. Analee the Enchantress had intervened and crushed their love.

75

"Of course I pine not for Lady Falconer," Brent said gruffly. "I have not seen her for years. I hear she has borne more children to that, that . . ."

Mary held up a soft white hand. "I can see that you *are* still enamored. You can hardly bring yourself to say his name—the Falcon."

"Ah, say not that wretched name," Brent snarled. "How I hate the man."

"Then it *is* Analee . . ."

"You know I can never forget her."

Mary got to her feet and went over to him in the gliding, unhurried steps of the nun. She seemed to have diminished in size since she had taken the habit and she gazed up at him, placing a hand on his arm, even though convent rules forbade any contact with a man. "That is why I suggested you should become a priest. Your closeness to God will help to put her out of your mind. She has enchanted you, Brent, and only God can undo so powerful a spell."

"You believe she has enchanted me? You believe in magic?" He gazed down at her in amazement. "You, a woman of prayer, believe all that?"

"Of course. There is good magic and bad magic. Good magic comes from God—that is the spiritual side of our nature. Prayer is magical, its power and the transformation it can bring to our lives, I know." Mary permitted herself a brief, bitter smile. "Who knows better than I the power of prayer? The balm that it can bring to the soul in trouble?"

As Brent's expression changed to compassion—for he knew that she referred to her love for him—she let go of his arm and turned away, a bent, rather aged figure though she was scarcely thirty years old. Although her convent life had given her the repose she so earnestly sought, it had both aged her and made her ageless. She was no longer a young woman but she would never be a very old one. The regularity of the life, the healthiness of the routine, would give her that white unlined

76

skin that also deprived her of her femininity, her sex. Her shorn hair was hidden forever under the veil, her unlined brow obscured by the white wimple which almost hid her eyebrows. She had been such a beauty; blue eyes, golden hair, a fresh, healthy complexion . . . only the blue eyes remained and their rich color, almost sapphire, was fading because of so many hours spent in the dark, eyelids tightly closed in prayer.

"Aye, I *am* still enamored of Analee," Brent said quietly. "I'll confess it. I no longer think of her as much, but when I do it gives me pain, physical pain here in my heart." Brent touched his chest. "I wandered throughout America trying to forget her, but to come back to France . . . Ah!" Brent took a deep breath and looked at the ceiling. "It means that only the Channel lies between us."

"The Channel *and* Lord Falconer!"

"Aye," Brent lowered his eyes dejectedly as though the vision he had just witnessed had faded. "Aye, Lord Falconer. Child of Satan if ever there was one."

"Only prayer can defeat a son of Satan," Mary said, sitting down again and placidly crossing her hands. She momentarily closed her eyes as if in prayer.

"Then you must pray, Mary," Brent said urgently. "You must pray that he may be overcome."

"I will pray that the will of God will be done," Mary said, opening her eyes and gazing at him. "What it may be I know not, but that it will be done."

"Amen," Brent said. "In the meantime what am I to do, Mary? You who are nearest to me of all women, nearer even than my sister Emma. What shall I do with my life since I do not feel the call of God to be a priest?"

"I do not think you should ally yourself with the Prince," Mary said firmly. "Even in the convent away from the world we hear all kinds of things about him."

"That he has a mistress?"

"Not only that, but that he treats her badly. He

77

abuses her and fights with her in public, oh yes, even in the streets of Paris. He is always drunk and abusive to his friends, who desert him in droves. He will not visit that pathetic old man, his father, who languishes for sight of him in Rome, or reply to the letters of his brother, Cardinal York. He is dissolute, intemperate, vicious, trusted by no one, deserted by his friends."

"Yet I remember him as he was. Ten years ago what a different tale we had to tell. Full of hope."

"Aye, but a decade has passed and one must be reasonable."

"Charles II, the Prince's illustrious ancestor, was restored to the throne after a longer period wandering in the wilderness."

"Yes, but England did not have a lawful popular king on the throne. Cromwell was dead. We have had over forty years of the Hanoverians. They are here to stay, Brent. The Stuarts will never be restored and I speak as a faithful servant of His Majesty King James III in Rome. Were his son more like that saintly man than I would have more hope for the Cause. As it is I have none."

"I will do one last thing for him," Brent said. "Not be his henchman in Basle, but I will do as he asks and go to England."

"Where you may be apprehended and hanged. Remember it is not so long since poor old Archibald Cameron met his end."

"I do not think they will hang any more. They are granting pardons, restitutions of estates. As you say, they are very secure. But, Mary, there is a storm brewing not only in Europe but in India and America between the French and English. It was very evident when I was in America, the hostility between the English and French who are building a line of forts from St. Lawrence to Mississippi in an effort to divide the country. The Prince says that King Louis has offered him assistance to conquer England. He is very buoyant, very optimistic. And there still are traitors at Court. The Princess of Wales perpetuates the hostility traditional between the heir to the throne and the monarch and is said to nurture known Jacobites among her suite. One of them is no less than the sister of the Prince's mistress, Catherine Walkinshaw."

"Oh, but she has been there for years, maybe twenty or more."

"Aye, but she is still a spy. She regularly sends messages to the Prince. Her family were all staunch supporters of the Stuarts. The Prince would have me approach her and find out how lies the land, and to approach her I must first approach the Princess, and to get near her I must seek the help of the only woman who can bring it about . . ."

"Analee," Mary said sadly, looking at him. "The Marchioness of Falconer. That is the real reason you wish to go to England. I knew that sooner or later she would have a part to play."

"Mary, can you not arrange it for me?" Brent said urgently, going over to her and lowering his voice. "Arrange a meeting with Lady Falconer in one of your convents, say somewhere in the country, not too far from Dover."

"You know we have no convents there, Brent. The nuns were sent packing after the revolution of 1688. But stay, I do have a thought. One of our nuns is from an aristocratic family in Kent who were deeply divided over the Rebellion. Half of them joined the Prince but the other half strongly supported King George."

"Rather like our own family."

"Aye. Well, the equivalent of Sir George Delamain is Lord Goodacre who lives not far from Folkestone. His wife is a loyal supporter of our cause—all the women favored the Prince and the men the Hanoverians. Her sister came to France to become a nun. I am sure Lady Goodacre will gladly receive the Marchioness of Falconer, if she is willing, and will make arrangements to disguise you. There, it is all I can do."

Brent bent down to embrace her, such was his gratitude, but Mary abruptly turned her face away, her eyes closed, her lips silently working in prayer to keep her from temptation.

Although acquainted with the name Goodacre, Analee could not think why she had received a letter from her ladyship urging her to visit Kent. The missive had been delivered with a good deal of secrecy, the bearer of the letter begging to be allowed to give it personally into her ladyship's hands and then waiting downstairs for a reply.

"*I am acting for someone,*" the letter stated cryptically. "*If your ladyship will be so good as to make the journey an Important Person will be forever in your debt.*"

The Prince! The Important Person could only be he. Analee got up from her desk and paced the floor in agitation. The Prince had sent for her again. She knew about the rumors of war—all London was full of them and the wealthy were sending their riches to the country. She had sworn to abjure him and love only her husband; but her husband had betrayed that love yet again. She rang the bell and the servant who had brought her the message appeared. "Is the messenger from Lady Goodacre here?"

"Yes, my lady."

"Ask him to come up. Is his lordship at home?"

"No, my lady."

Analee nodded with satisfaction and stood at the window looking into the formal garden of Falconer House, until there was a timid knock at the door and a young man stood awkwardly on the threshold, his hat in his hands.

"It is so good of Lady Goodacre to invite me," she

said. "Tell her that I will accept. It is today week is it not?"

"Her ladyship begs you will stay a night or two."

"I am not quite sure, because I know not my husband's movements. He may make it impossible for me to accept."

"I understand, my lady," the servant bowed.

"But tell Lady Goodacre I will contrive it somehow. See, I will pen her a short note." Analee sat at her escritoire and began to write rapidly, dipping her quill several times in the ink. Then she sanded the paper, sealed it in a crested envelope and gave it to the servant, together with a sovereign. "All being well I shall see Lady Goodacre today week and stop a day or two."

The servant bowed and withdrew, putting the sovereign safely in a deep pocket.

"Goodacre," the Falcon said, looking suspiciously at Analee. "How came you to know Lady Goodacre?"

"I met her at Court, Angus."

"But why should she want us to stay for no reason?"

Analee recoiled at the word "us." "I think she is being hospitable. We liked each other."

Angus yawned. "Lord Goodacre is a profound bore. He can talk of nothing but his gun dogs. Well, you may go if you like, but I shan't." Angus looked shrewdly at Analee, calculating that his chances of making a conquest of Miss Cameron in her absence were good. She had so far shown not the least inclination to respond to his amorous advances and seemed determined to remain in the good books of Lady Falconer, who she appeared to admire. Well, he would see. Few women could resist his charms if he was determined.

"No, Angus, I feel my place is by your side," Analee said without a hint of sarcasm.

Since her arrival in London the previous month, Analee had befriended Anna Cameron and to her surprise found that her company was invigorating and refreshing. Not only was she eager to learn, but her stories of life in Maryland were a source of endless interest to one who enjoyed travel and new experiences as Analee did. Although Miss Cameron could not have remained ignorant of the Falcon's interest in her she did nothing to respond to him by the slightest alteration in her behavior. Analee supposed her indifferent to his advances, indeed shocked by them, as any well brought-up girl should be.

For her part however, she wished that Miss Cameron would soon return home so as to retain the purity of her state. "Why no, I insist that you visit your friend Lady Goodacre," Angus said ingratiatingly. " 'Twill do you good to visit the country again."

"Oh, I am touched that you should think of me," Analee said unemotionally. "I would not have thought that my comfort was your lordship's paramount concern of recent weeks."

Angus looked sharply at her and raised a threatening finger, shaking it in front of her face. "Now listen here, my dear Analee. I am a patient man, I trust, but I will not continue to endure these snide remarks on your part. How mean you that I have not had *your* comfort in mind?"

Analee gazed steadfastly at him, as she played with the emblem made of Falcon gold which hung round her neck.

"I fear your lordship has grown indifferent towards me. Your embraces are not as tender as they used to be or, alas, as frequent. Do I displease you, my lord? Your absences are both many and prolonged. If I have aught to say you do not appear to listen. Have you grown tired of me, sir? Is there perhaps another fortunate lady vying with me for your affections?"

The Falcon reddened and turned sharply on his heels as though wishing to avoid the omniscient, penetrating light in those fiery dark eyes.

"What you say is tosh, my good woman. Of course you do not displease me! But you must remember I am not as young as I was. Perhaps my vigor has diminished—though I hope not. I am a busy man with frequent demands made on my time from all quarters. This fact alone should be enough to explain my frequent absences from home. Alas, I cannot always take you with me because these are occasions of concern only to men, those of us who by our station in life are entrusted with the governance of the nation . . ."

"What you say is doubtless all very true, my lord," Analee said evenly. "However I cannot help hearing gossip—people delight in tittle-tittle you know—that would have you gracing *as a single man* the tables of many illustrious hostesses in London. Why is it that these ladies are privy to such august counsels and I am not?"

The Falcon stared moodily out of the window, still avoiding her gaze, his hands thrust behind his back in his customary attitude of defiance.

"Some things are hard to explain, my dear. There are certain women in London who are both well-born *and* well-educated. You alas, through no fault of your own, are neither. These matters we discuss would be quite beyond you."

The flush on Analee's face grew deeper, suffusing her neck and the swell of her bosom. She clenched one of her hands and angrily kneaded it into the palm of the other.

"The rumors that get around my lord, do not concern weighty matters discussed at the dinner table; but what happens *afterwards* . . . Besides *I* am the daughter of a lord, as well-born as your lordship, almost."

The Falcon threw his head back and laughed cruelly. "Nay, conceived in a haystack and born in a gutter, the daughter of a common gypsy. It was just St. March's fanciful idea that you were his daughter.

Maybe he wanted to get nearer to you for base ideas of his own. Eh? Has he tried to fondle you while pretending to have sired you? Eh? Eh?" The Falcon turned towards Analee, his handsome countenance spoiled by an ugly leer.

Analee was suddenly seized with such contempt for her husband that for all the world she would have picked up the iron poker that lay in the grate and hit it about his head. She felt the sweat spring to her brow and clenched and unclenched her fists. "How can you talk so evilly, Lord Falconer? Surely the Devil himself is with you. You have made the land so fallow that he had embedded himself deep inside you. To entertain such a notion when you so welcomed the news, told me you had always known I was well-born . . ."

"Ah, that was different," the Falcon said, continuing to smirk. "I would say anything in those days, besotted with love of you, anything to please you. I thought it most unlikely the whole time, I must say. What proof does he have?"

"My mother's name was Morella. The circumstances were just as he said . . ."

"But *you* did not know that."

"But I did. I knew one part of the story and he the rest."

"You put the words in his mouth."

"I did not."

"The idea in his head."

" 'Tis not true!" Analee's breathing quickened.

"Ah, yes. No doubt he had it in mind to lie with you. One day he would . . ."

"Stop, my lord! How can you be so base? You think I would lie with my own father?"

"I think you would do anything, Analee," his lordship said loftily, taking his snuff box from the pocket of his vest. "At heart you are a whore; the profligate way you have behaved with me has been disgusting. You flaunt and display yourself in a way one would not ex-

84

pect from a well-born woman. She would not have the
instincts you have. That is how I know you are the
daughter of a common gypsy folk—aye, mother *and*
father—and not a lord."

"Because I enjoy the arts of love, sir, you wish to
make me feel ashamed?" There were tears in Analee's
eyes, but tears of rage, not regret.

"You have no modesty, Analee. No real lady would
enjoy the carnal act so much. That is the prerogative
of men, whose playthings women are. However roughly
I launch myself upon you you are always ready to ac-
commodate me, as though you enjoyed it."

"So that I will not be hurt, sir! If I refused you, you
would tear me apart as you once did. I have never forgotten that you nearly killed me."

"You enjoyed even that, you slut. Rape in the gutter
is really what you desire . . ."

The sting of Analee's hand across his face took the
Falcon by surprise. He staggered momentarily and then
put his hand to his cheek, staring at her. "How *dare*
you!" He raised his free hand as though to hit her.

"I will do it again though you tear me limb from
limb. I am your wife, Lord Falconer, a peeress of the
realm. Yes, you have given me your name and raised
me to the peerage of England. As such I am known to
the King, to the Princess of Wales, who has given me
the privilege of treating me as a familiar. I am the
mother of your children, lords and ladies all. Nothing
can undo that even though you divorce me and put me
in a convent, or confine me in a dungeon. Maybe you
have one in Falcon's Keep in mind for me? Nothing
can undo what you have done. I am your wife and as
such I will not submit to your insults and abuse."

"You have no rights . . ." The Falcon's hand still
lay against his painful cheek, but he seemed to change
his mind about striking her.

"Oh yes, I have."

"You are subject to me, body and soul."

"The law would not allow you to kill me; but I am not your concubine. I pity you, Lord Falconer, that you hold womenkind in such small regard. Maybe had your mother lived, had you known the gentleness of her love, you would not treat me, or women, thus. It is because I know how capable of tenderness and affection you are that I grieve to see you behave like an animal. Now you would make my son, Duncan, grow up like you, deprived of a mother's love. Send me away by all means, Angus; but let me be with Duncan. Let me give to him all the love that you will not permit me to give you."

Angus took his hand away from his cheek and slumped in a chair, his long legs spread out before him. His head hung on his breast and he gave a deep sigh. "You talk so well, Analee, that sometimes I feel you must be of noble birth. Yes, you have the temperament of a lady, but the morals of a whore."

"I have never been ashamed of liking the amorous arts, sir, of knowing how to please your lordship in bed. As a woman I have had my full satisfaction, and the privilege of breeding your lordship's children. I know not why you have turned against me, or what I have done. Whatever happens in my life, Angus, I will always treasure the memory of these past five years and the good times that preceded them, when we were first lovers, first wed, had our first child.

"You are a powerful man, easily bored. You seek perpetually for fresh entertainment, new things to do. It seems to me that you need another war, my lord, and no doubt you have taken your share of other women although I would that you would not seduce young Anna, much as you may wish to. She is a gently reared girl and 'twould ruin her for life; moreover she does not appear brazen, from what I have observed, as that hussy my half-sister, Lady Constance Craven, did."

A sparkle came into the Falcon's tired eyes. "What

you say about Anna Cameron is rubbish, but about Lady Constance you are right. Yes, she had your dispositions all right, your whorish inclinations. Maybe St. March sired you after all. Constance certainly delighted in being bedded by me. I hope she gives her husband such pleasure."

"And I hope he approves if she does," Analee said with asperity, "seeing he is a grandee of Spain and you consider it unladylike to enjoy the pleasures of the bed."

"Lucky man," Angus sighed. "Lady Constance Craven now a Spanish duchess. I think she will be stifled by the Court of Spain. Maybe a little of the formality of it would suit you. Do you care to visit her?"

"No, thank you, I do not care to see Lady Constance again. I am of a jealous disposition, my lord, even of someone who no longer cares for me and affects to despise me. She caused me such suffering and heartache. I would not be a woman if I were not jealous."

The Falcon laughed and rubbed his knee. "There are things I still like about you, Analee. You have spirit. You . . ."

From the look in his eyes Analee knew that the conversation had bred lewd thoughts in his mind. In a moment he would order her upstairs to perform the marital duty that he affected to despise her for. She felt such rebellion in her heart that she decided to refuse, whatever that would precipitate, when the door opened and a servant, bowing very low, said: "Miss Anna Cameron begs your ladyship to receive her. She is waiting downstairs."

"Oh, I had forgotten that she was coming," Analee said with relief. "The Princess of Wales has graciously asked us to take tea with her."

"Ah, Leicester House again, eh?" the Falcon said,

eyeing her suspiciously. "You are still hobnobbing with that old Jacobite crowd?"

"We never discuss politics, sir. Her Royal Highness is much more interested in the arts and related matters, as well as the welfare of her children and her hopes for the marital happiness of the Prince of Wales. Pray show in Miss Cameron," Analee concluded, turning to the footman who had announced her. As she said this she noticed the Falcon get up and start to preen himself with sly glances in the mirror, his hands on his cravat, straightening his wig. Then he turned with an eager expression to stare at the door.

Analee held out her hands to Anna in greeting as she came through the door, noting the freshness of her looks, the eager smile on her face. She wore an enchanting gown of patterned orange silk, with a round décolletage and a broad collar of chiffon edged with lace. On her head she had a close fitting cap of white muslin under a natural straw "bergère" hat with a turned-up back. She responded to Analee's embrace with her usual warm affection and then curtsied without a trace of flirtatiousness to the Falcon.

"My lord."

Angus took her hand and kissed it, bowing low. He held it in his for a second longer than necessary, gazing into her eyes. "My dear Miss Cameron, you look exceptionally ravishing today. You are sure to find a beau in London who will throw all he has at your feet. I wager you have one already. Eh?"

"Lord Falconer, you are too kind," Anna said unaffectedly, smiling at Analee. "Indeed it was not my intention to find a husband over here, but to enjoy myself and that I am doing thanks to you and her ladyship."

"But why not?" the Falcon said, reluctantly letting her hand fall. "There are many young noblemen who would feel honored to give you their name. Indeed

88

were I younger and, of course, free, I would not hesitate."

Miss Cameron's smile vanished and she looked at Analee with embarrassment. "Your lordship is so kind; but the charms and accomplishments of Lady Falconer are the talk of London. I hear nothing but praise wherever I go."

"Ah, but you have an advantage over Lady Falconer, my dear, and one she would not deny," the Falcon said waggishly. "You are educated. She never had any learning and you I understand are familiar with the classics. Nor could she play a note, while I have heard you perform, to my considerable delight, on the pianoforte. Your voice also is divine. Whatever else Lady Falconer was when I married her she would not deny that she was singularly ill-accomplished. She could neither read nor write."

A silence fell in the room and the color of Analee's face heightened. "It is true, my lord," she acknowledged with a slight smile, "that I was a common gypsy, as your lordship has not infrequently pointed out; when you did me the honor of giving me your name; but I believe that you were not displeased then, and that since that time I have done much to make up for my lack of education. It is true that I do not read Latin and Greek or speak French like your lordship, but I can now read and write. I have mastered the household accounts, I am a good breeder of children and, I believe, not clumsy on the dance floor. I have made the best uses I could of what little nature has given me."

"Oh, Lady Falconer, you have!" Miss Cameron said admiringly, turning away from the Falcon as if to indicate her displeasure. "What would *I* not give for your beauty and accomplishments. *You* are the talk of London."

"We must go," Analee said, glancing at the clock on the mantelpiece. "It would not do to keep the Princess of Wales waiting. She is yearning to hear about your adventures in America and I believe the young princesses will be at her tea today."

Miss Cameron clasped her hands with excitement and stared at Analee with delight. "Oh, I can hardly believe it! What will my parents say when they hear this?"

"Ah, but what would they say if you were presented to the King?" Angus said, circling her and, like a stag scenting a doe, endeavoring to catch her eyes again.

"The King, my lord? Would Lady Falconer arrange it?"

"I can get someone *far* more important to arrange it," the Falcon said dismissively. "Lady Yarmouth *herself* is prepared to present you to the King."

Analee looked sharply at Anna and then at her husband, her eyes smoldering. "But I could present Miss Cameron, Angus, as I myself have been presented at Court."

"Oh, my dear, do not bother yourself. Besides I know you mean to go away for a few days. Take a week, as much as you like with Lady Goodacre," the Falcon waved a hand at her, as though desiring to spirit her away, while edging nearer to Anna, breathing lustfully. "Take two. I assure you it will give Lady Yarmouth much pleasure to act in your absence. Much pleasure—almost as much as it will me."

The expression of excitement in Miss Cameron's eyes turned to apprehension but, as she tried to look for help to Analee, the huge frame of the Falcon came between her and his wife and all she perceived was the look of naked desire on his face.

Chapter Six

The journey to Folkestone was accomplished at a leisurely pace in one of the Falcon's comfortable carriages with two postillions and an outrider. They took the Dover road, which was considered safer because it was busier and there was less chance of apprehension by highwaymen. Analee was familiar with the route until Dover because she had traveled on it so much when she and the Falcon went to France at the end of the previous war. It was, on the whole, a happy time and she sat back in her seat thinking on those days, surely never to be recaptured? She sighed and glanced at her maid, but she was asleep. How Analee missed the companionship of Nelly, who was at Furness looking after the children. She wished she could join them.

At Dover the carriage took the coast road through Folkestone to the ancient Cinque Port of Hythe, and then climbed a steep hill to the imposing castle that stood on its brow with a magnificent view of the Romney marshes. Indeed on a clear day the coast of France could easily be seen.

They had stopped at an inn near Canterbury over night, but still Analee was tired and glad of the glass of Madeira that her hostess offered her as soon as she had greeted her in the courtyard and taken her into the long drawing-room.

"It is so kind of your ladyship to come," Lady Goodacre said, fussing around Analee. "As you can imagine it is an important mission."

"I am intrigued, I must say," Analee said, loosening her traveling cloak and sipping the wine. "You took a risk, did you not?"

Lady Goodacre looked at her proudly. "I would do

anything for the cause, Lady Falconer. I am of Scottish descent; Annabel McCleod was my maiden name, and our branch of the McCleod family has always been loyal to the Stuarts. Alas, the Goodacres have been the other way and during the Rebellion my husband and I were at loggerheads. Our immediate family are split, too, but of course time has done much to heal that. We have little doubt that the Hanoverians will remain on the throne—alas!" Annabel Goodacre wrung her hands, pacing up and down.

"You would still like the Stuarts to be restored?" Analee looked at her over the rim of her glass.

"Of course, Lady Falconer! They are the Lord's anointed, appointed by God, upholders of our Holy Catholic Faith. Of course I would like them to be restored. I pray for it daily. Do you not?"

Analee looked into the fire that had been lit against the September chill. "I would like it above all things but, like you, I do not think it will happen."

"And like mine, too, Lady Falconer, your husband is not only a committed Hanoverian but a general in the army of the King!"

"Aye, it is a difference that has often come between us," Analee said sadly, gazing at her hostess. She was a pretty woman about ten years older than Analee, but her face seemed prematurely lined as though from the tension and suffering she had undergone, and her black hair was flecked with grey. "We have not met before, Lady Goodacre, have we?"

"No, Lady Falconer. My husband, though a good man in many ways, does not allow me to go to London, where he is sure I will scheme and plot with those that gather round the Princess of Wales at Leicester House. Of course I would not. I am so unimportant no one would listen to me. But my Stuart loyalty is unquestioned, and when my sister, who is a nun in France, made this request I was delighted and honored to be of service."

92

"Is he here?" Analee said breathlessly.

"Yes," Lady Goodacre lowered her voice to a whisper. "He is asleep. He came into Rye by the night tide and only went to sleep this morning. He is weary from his journey."

"Oh, how I long to see him," Analee looked yearningly out of the window. "To think he is in this very house. No wonder you feel honored."

Lady Goodacre looked at Analee with a slight frown but continued, "It is always an honor to serve the cause, Lady Falconer. Alas, how many of the Prince's previously loyal followers are defecting. Even Lady Primrose, an erstwhile friend of mine, talks against the Prince whom she formerly so admired. I often feel that he is like Our Lord, betrayed by those who once loved him the most."

"And does he plan to see others here?"

"*He?*" Lady Goodacre looked at her with surprise, when the door slowly swung open and in its shadow stood a tall man gazing at Analee. She got to her feet and sank to her knees in a deep curtsey.

"Sire," she said and held up her head as the figure by the door came into the room.

"Analee."

Analee stared up at him, and a feeling of such faintness overcame her that even on her knees she swayed and would have fallen to the ground if Brent had not quickly knelt beside her and supported her under the arms.

"My Analee." He rested his head against hers and clasped her gently to him. Analee heard the door shut and realized they were alone.

"Brent." She could hardly utter his name. All her love for him came sweeping over her, flooding her heart and banishing the memories of past unhappiness. She leaned against him and her eyes misted with tears. She could feel the swift thud of his heart and knew that

93

he felt the same. His lips brushed her face, his body against hers trembling.

"Analee, my Analee. Always my Analee whatever happens, whatever you say."

He held her away from him and looked at her, smoothing her hair back from her brow. Then he kissed her wet eyelids, her cheeks and when his lips met hers he found them ready for him, merging with his, her passion as demanding as his own. As she clung to him he encircled her completely with his arm and then, reaching beneath her bodice, he cupped one of her breasts and felt the exquisite luster of her skin, the nipple already hard and erect with desire.

Finally they broke apart and, still panting, he sat beside her on the floor and took her hands between his, looking into her eyes. "I hardly dared hope you would still feel the same. It has been five years."

"I feel I love you more," she said simply. "We are never parted in spirit, Brent."

"Never a day passes but I think of you, wherever I am, whatever I am doing—on the seas or in America or France, and last thing at night I always call your name to waft me on the tide of sleep."

"I thought you were the Prince."

"I realized that when I saw you curtsey."

"Lady Goodacre said it was an Important Personage."

"Am I not an Important Personage?"

"Oh you are, you are." She touched his chest, her hand lingering over his heart. "I hope we have not shocked her ladyship. She left the room right quickly I see."

"I am sure she will be discreet. She is a good person."

"I hope not too good to disapprove of us. Have you not noticed sometimes that the closer people are to God, the more distant and the more critical of their fellows they became?"

94

Brent laughed and, helping her up, led her to a sofa which looked on to the fine view of the marshes and the sea. A terrace ran along the front of the house and the door leading on to it was open so that they could see the golden-pink band of sun as it settled beneath the western horizon.

"How long are you here for, Brent?" She took his hand again. "And what is your mission?"

"The Prince has asked me to be his right-hand man."

Analee stared at him, not knowing whether to be sorry or glad. "And will you?"

"No." Brent shook his head. "No. It is ten years since the Rebellion and I am weary of wandering, of being an outlaw. His cause is lost and everyone knows it but he. But because of the love I once had for him I agreed to come to England to try and see Mistress Walkinshaw, the sister of the Prince's mistress. But it is too dangerous for me to go to London. Even here I imperil Lady Goodacre by my presence. So I thought of you. You must see Mistress Walkinshaw for me."

"Then it is true that Clementina is his mistress?"

"He lives with her. They have a daughter, Charlotte. They travel around like fugitives from justice and the Prince is reputed to treat her badly. Even by not marrying her he dishonors her. No one respects him for it, but he still hopes to wed a Daughter of France."

"Poor woman," Analee said sadly. "Of course I know Catherine Walkinshaw. She has been in a household of Princess Augusta for many years. She is now her housekeeper."

"You know her well then?"

"Yes, we are acquainted. I am one of the few the Princess allows into her private apartments."

"And is she still a Jacobite?"

"We never talk of politics. We never have. The Princess is too aware of my relationship to the Falcon. She was very kind to me the other day when I introduced a young American friend to her, the sister-in-law of Stewart."

"Anna Cameron!" Brent said with amazement.

"You know her?"

"Of course. I stayed with Stewart in Maryland and the Camerons gave a ball for me. Anna is a beautiful young girl."

"It is a wonder you did not fall in love with her." Analee looked at him slyly and his grasp on her hand tightened.

"Do not mock me. With your face etched in my mind how can I ever look at another? I will never marry unless it be to you."

Analee lowered her head and brushed yet another tear from her eye. "You know it can never be. Though the Falcon's feelings towards me have cooled yet again I still do not think he wishes to divorce me. Even if only to goad me he will keep me. He has already sent my eldest son Duncan away from me because I love him so much."

"That swine has made you terribly unhappy," Brent said angrily. "He treats you like a plaything. How you tolerate it I do not know."

Analee looked at him, her eyes clear and untroubled. "I loved him. I never hid that from you. He spoke to me with a strange magic . . ."

"Loved. You said *loved*!" Brent rose to his feet with an exclamation. "Is it possible that you could be finally out of love with him?"

Analee gazed somberly at his excited face.

"I cannot be certain, Brent. He arouses such a conflict of emotions within me. When I am away from him I see him in a different light from when we are together. Yet recently I nearly came to hate him as he taunted me in London about my birth and lack of education and indirectly accused my father of desiring carnal relations with me."

"The man is a monster!"

"He is also jealous of me, as I am of him. He is much talked about in London for the attention he pays to women. Yet he denies this to me and says his powers are waning on account of his age. He is no longer as . . . attentive to me as he was."

"Good! Would he could withdraw his cursed attentions altogether."

"Maybe he will, but even then I cannot leave him. My children are too important to me, Brent. And I cannot forget that for many years I have lived with the Falcon in the greatest harmony and bliss. For that at least I am grateful."

"Do not speak to me of bliss," Brent said ferociously. "Even to imagine you in his arms makes me want to throw myself over that cliff."

"You must accept it, Brent," Analee said quietly. "You know that I always loved the Falcon. I fell in love with him when I never thought to see you again, and his love I was ready to remain until I died had he not mistreated me so. I told you I loved him but I also told you he was a hard man, a difficult man to know."

"How *could* you after he nearly killed you in Paris, raping you and half strangling you? How *could* you?"

"Because I was nothing," Analee said simply. "Women have no rights in this world, as you know, Brent. I was his wife, his possession. I had nothing of my own, nowhere to go. And I loved my children though wealth meant nothing to me. It never has, of that I can assure you."

"I believe you," Brent said grudgingly, sitting by her side again. "You are too honest and noble a woman to desire a person's wealth."

Analee gazed at him and took his hand.

"You are my great love Brent, because you are steadfast, honorable and true. But the Falcon is my passion. I can only ask your understanding and forgiveness, even if I do not deserve it."

"You do deserve it, Analee." Brent gazed tenderly

97

into her eyes. "Yet I do not believe that we did not have passion. We *did*, and we could so again. I would do anything to have you, Analee. Anything."

Analee looked into the eyes of the man who had loved her with such devotion for so long. How happy they would have been; of that she had no doubt. He would not have given her the fame and fortune of the Falcon, but of what use was that from a man whose passion so quickly turned to scorn? They would have lived abroad perhaps, in exile, but their love would never have wavered. How much had she sacrificed to become Marchioness of Falconer?

"Well, maybe my lord will one day put me aside in favor of a younger and more educated woman to preside at his table. He certainly has an eye for young Miss Cameron. He was *most* anxious to encourage my visit here. To get me out of the way, I suspect."

"Oh, she turns many a head," Brent said. "She was much sought after when I was in Chesapeake, but not by me I assure you. Besides, I fancy she too would have an eye for a fortune but, even more, a title because her family has wealth. Titles are very popular with Americans who have foresworn them to live in their new country."

"I like her," Analee said firmly. "She is an unaffected girl, spirited. The Princess of Wales was much taken with her and I believe she is to be presented to His Majesty while I am here."

"*You* will not present her to the King?"

"His lordship, my husband, thought the Countess of Yarmouth more suitable. I even understand there is to be a little supper given by her ladyship, with the King and my husband as the only male guests."

"That dreadful old whore," Brent said with disgust. "That disgusting crab . . ."

"Tush, Brent," Analee said with pretended indignation. "You are talking of the mistress of the King."

"Frau Wallmoden. That's what she was when he

98

brought her here just to be his whore. Countess of Yarmouth indeed! What an ordeal for Anna, three old drones driveling over her beauty."

"You do not talk of my husband, I trust, as an 'old drone'?" Analee looked at him wickedly.

"He is certainly twice her age, is he not?"

"He is," Analee nodded. "But he is a well-preserved man, certainly not an 'old drone.' Had he desired my love he would have retained it."

"And has he lost it, Analee? I must know." Brent sat beside her again, looking earnestly into her eyes. "I *have* to know. Has he lost it forever?"

For a long while Analee looked out at the scene before them, then she got up and went to the door. A mist was rising from the marshes and the sun on the horizon had changed into a red ball of fire which would suddenly disappear, causing night to fall. She thought of Brent's dangerous journey over the marshes and shivered.

"I cannot be sure, Brent, that it has gone forever. He has certainly tired of me as men do tire of women, whether temporarily or for good I know not. It is well known. He has had what he would of me, enjoyed my best years and perhaps he now would take another wife. He is not content with injuring my pride by parading his mistresses although in London he takes care not to do it in front of me. Knowing my temper he doubtless fears I would tear out their eyes, and he would not be wrong. I think he would marry someone more worthy of bearing his illustrious name—maybe a German princess or a member of the high English nobility. I doubt whether even Miss Anna Cameron, beauty as she is, would do, as he has no need of her money, and her family, besides being Jacobite, is not noble. No, he will toy with her and try and seduce her; but he will not wed her."

"You think he really will divorce you?"

As Brent continued to look at her incredulously, Analee considered her reply.

"I am *not* sure about divorce. I have given him no grounds. I am a faithful wife, a good mother. Besides I too have my friends at court and my father, you know, is the Earl of St. March, even though he lives most of the year in Spain. I am not a complete nobody as his lordship likes to pretend. He will have to take care. Very great care. Besides," Analee turned her enchanting smile on him, "I have my spells. I have not forgotten my old gypsy magic entirely."

"I would wed you, Analee."

"Alas," Analee turned to him sadly, drawing him to her so that they both stood in the doorway of the terrace, arms around each other. "It is not to be. You cannot return to England and I cannot leave my children. I would die if I were parted from them and his lordship knows that full well. I would never sacrifice my children to my love, even to you, Brent. Even to you. Now you must tell me what it is I must do, for our hostess will think us rude if we do not go and see her."

"I want you to talk to Mistress Walkinshaw and report to me. Ask her what is the extent of Jacobite support in London, who would rally to the Prince and so on. She will know everything. She will have all the facts at her fingertips."

"And then?"

"You will send a letter through Lady Goodacre to her sister in the convent. Mary will give it me."

"Ah, Mary," Analee's eyes clouded. "You see her?"

"I visit her in the convent."

"And is she happy, Brent? Has she any regrets?"

Brent swallowed and grasped Analee's hands. "She has accepted the Will of God. She thinks He wanted her to be a nun and she has found peace. She says you were His instrument in this because her love for me was very powerful. God works in mysterious ways. She is like a sister to me, a close friend."

"I am glad. And the Allonbys—John and his wife? Are they happy?"

"I think so. He pines for England and no longer believes in the cause. His wife is a Frenchwoman, Thérèse. She is a good Catholic and a good wife to John and mother to his children. They have three babies."

"I'm glad. I have always said I will restore Furness to him if he is pardoned."

"He says he will never seek a pardon. He will never live under the Hanoverians. He is content to spend the rest of his life in France, and Stewart is now an American. Furness is yours forever, Analee."

"Unless the Falcon takes it away," Analee said. "Who knows where his wrath will lead him?"

Brent turned to her and enfolded his arms about her again. She remembered the moonlit night when they had first loved each other. How long ago it was. She felt the impress of his maleness against her and knew he desired her. She longed to melt in his arms, to spend a night of love with him. Her loins ached for him. She looked up into his eyes. He was still her *gadjo*, more beloved now than before. He had lines now on his face that made him look older but also stronger, and his once gold-blond hair was ashen-colored. But his deep blue eyes were still vivid and as she looked at them all she could see mirrored was herself, his eyes blazing with love for her.

"When must you go?" she whispered.

"Tonight."

"Tonight? Oh, Brent, *not* tonight!"

"I came in on the tide and I'm going out on the tide. We can trust no one and I dare not linger here. Lord Goodacre's servants are loyal to him and might betray me. I wanted to take this risk just to see you once again."

"Then we must kiss and part," Analee said, her heart heavy with grief. "Until we meet again. When will that be?"

"We are never parted," Brent said, pressing her to him. "But one day we will be together forever. It is only a matter of time. Your gypsy promised me. She promised."

"I did not know I was assisting at a lover's tryst, Lady Falconer," Annabel Goodacre said the next morning as Analee, heavy-eyed because of lack of sleep, sat facing her at breakfast. She had watched Brent by the light of the moon as his horse, escorted by one other, made its lonely way down the path from the castle and struck out across the misty marsh lands. She felt that with him went the only man who had ever really loved her not only for her body, as others did, but for herself. He would not toss her aside as the Falcon had done because he sought new pastures in which to take his pleasure. He would love her when she was old and no longer the object of women's envy and men's desire.

"You misunderstand, Lady Goodacre," Analee said with dignity. "It was no tryst. You must know I was expecting the Prince."

"But when you saw Mr. Delamain, you almost fell into a swoon." Lady Goodacre sat upright in her chair as though she were reprimanding a recalcitrant child.

"Mr. Delamain is a *very* old friend. All his family sacrificed themselves for the cause. One brother was killed. He himself was sentenced to death and his cousin, Stewart, deported to America. The whole family was dispersed. Of course I swooned when I saw Mr. Delamain. I thought he, too, was dead."

"Oh." Lady Goodacre primly wiped her mouth with a starched napkin and broke a piece of freshly baked bread. "I am sorry if I misunderstood."

"Indeed you did misunderstand," Analee said with

asperity. "Though you can be forgiven in the circumstances. I did not come here to deceive my husband."

Lady Goodacre, who had heard all the rumors about the amorous exploits of the Falcon, would not have been all that surprised if she had; but as a good Catholic she could not tolerate infidelity, however justified. Her face broke into a smile. "Let us be friends, Lady Falconer. I assure you I have need of them, exiled as I am in this remote part of Kent. My husband and I have never really become reconciled because of our differences in the war. Of course I have been an obedient and docile wife and borne him children, but even they divide us. The girls are still all very partisan for Bonnie Prince Charlie, even little Amelia who is only seven."

"Oh, I would *love* to see your children," Analee said. "I have heard them running about, but in this great house I could not find them. My own children are at our house on Derwentwater. I miss them every day."

"You should bring them to visit," Annabel Goodacre said. "We should like nothing better." She leaned over and said earnestly, "I hope you will forgive what I said earlier, Lady Falconer. I am, you know, a pious woman, and I misunderstood what I saw. I believe a woman should be true to her husband whatever justification she may have to be otherwise. The marriage bond is for life, is it not? I know that Sister Mary Gertrude, my sister's companion in the religious life, and Mr. Delamain were once wed; but even then he is not free to marry again, not in my eyes. God has joined them together and only God can put them asunder."

Analee gave a delicate cough and finished her coffee, pushing the cup from her. "I believe they were never joined in the physical sense, Lady Goodacre. The marriage was not consummated."

"Oh!" Lady Goodacre looked embarrassed and found something very interesting to stare at on the floor. "I am sorry. I did not know."

103

"I feel we should not judge other people when we do not know their circumstances. Is it not so?" Analee gazed at her hostess, who looked past her to hide her confusion.

"I do agree, Lady Falconer. I seem to be doing everything wrong this morning. Oh I do hope you will stay a few days. I can't tell you how much having a friend here will cheer me up. Will you stay? Can you? *Please*."

Analee thought of the misery of her life at their house in Piccadilly, her jealousy as the Falcon went about making amorous conquests. She was tired and felt rather ill. The bracing sea air would do her good. Besides, the Falcon did not want her back. He had told her.

"I would love to stop a few days, Lady Goodacre. But you must promise to call me Analee. Then we can really be friends."

King George II was an old and feeble man and his passion for routine was as meticulous as ever. He liked to do everything at the same time every day whether he was at his palace in St. James's, or his beloved home Herrenhausen in Hanover. The Falcon found Court life stifling and the men around the King were as old and stuffy as His Majesty.

But it was obligatory to be seen a lot at the Court. Especially now with the political uncertainty at home and the threat of trouble abroad. The Falcon was an intimate of William Pitt who had been in the government since 1754 and was known to be anxious to hold the reins of command tightly in his own hands. The Falcon could sense a greatness in Pitt that he had never seen in the Pelham brothers, but he feared that he was too unstable to govern the nation. He was excessively preoccupied with his health and was thought to have periods of madness when he did not move from his home.

The Falcon was restless. Part of what Analee had said was true. War and battles suited him. He was always at his happiest when chasing the enemies of the King. He was fond of feminine company to soothe him after hours of political discussions in the corridors of power at St. James's or Hampton Court, and there were several beds in London where he was welcome so long as the husbands of the women in question were not in them too. It was a world of subterfuge and deception that he enjoyed—providing he was not cuckolded in turn, which was why he guarded Analee so jealously.

The supper given by Lady Yarmouth, ostensibly for him but really to present his new attachment Miss Cameron to the King, had been an outstanding success. She had looked ravishing in a gown of turquoise blue that matched the radiant color of her eyes, and her flame gold hair was twisted around a velvet bandeau of the same color, while she wore turquoises at her throat and on her wrists. The King was palpably charmed and seemed to recover some of his former zest for life.

The Falcon had collected Anna himself in his carriage, but had not deigned to enter the home of the Peto family in Cavendish Square in case they saw it as a sign of approval. He did not mix with trade. It was all he could do to stomach the dreadful family of Rigg, and that was only because there were family connections that he could not ignore, much as he deplored them. After the supper the Falcon also took her back; but he did not touch her or do other than kiss her hand before his servant saw her into the house where the candles were still ablaze and the doors open in welcome. The Peto family had even put on a large supper in the hope that the Falcon would honor their home; but he did not. He knew how to play his cards, and women found men irresistible who did not pursue them too obviously—at first anyway.

The Falcon felt a commotion in his breast regarding

Anna Cameron that he could not recall experiencing for many years. Maybe Lady Constance Craven had been the last one to move him thus, but she was only seventeen and he knew that, whatever her hopes, it could only ever be an affair. He wanted to bed her, but not to take her as his wife. Besides, then, he was still in love with Analee. They called her the Enchantress and for long she had enchanted him. He never thought he would tire of her, but he had. He was of an age when he needed something big and important in his life. He was not of that mold of men who are made for a lifetime of selfless, mature love. He had not married until he was in his late thirties, and now he was only a few years off fifty. Who knew how many years were left to him to have one last passionate fling, especially with rumors of a new war in the offing?

The day after the King's supper he sent Miss Cameron roses and the day after that a brooch made of gold filigree surmounted by exquisite diamonds and rare pearls. The day after that he sent a note to ask her to another small supper given by a friend of his at his house in Mayfair. The friend, a major in the Falcon's regiment, and his wife had been well instructed, and withdrew after supper was served to the amazement of Miss Cameron, who had found them good company.

"But we are alone!" she exclaimed, looking at the Falcon in surprise. The Falcon put a large hand over hers and pressed it.

" 'Twas what I intended."

"You *planned* this, Lord Falconer?"

"Aye." The Falcon gazed into her eyes and withdrew his hand. He knew exactly how to deal with women, even reluctant ones. He could never recall not making a conquest.

Miss Cameron looked flustered but reassured by his apparent calm. She had not known how to deal with the brooch, thinking it too rude to send it back. She was not altogether accustomed to the ways of the En-

106

glish aristocracy. So she hid it beneath her underlinen, away from the prying eyes of Mrs. Peto.

"Have some lobster," Lord Falconer said. "I hear it is excellent." He poured a glass of fine white Burgundy wine, and gazed into her eyes again as he toasted her. "To us," he said.

She blushed and sipped at her glass. Then she raised her eyes and stared at him in her frank American way, placing the glass by her side. "I think I misunderstand you, Lord Falconer. I am *very* friendly with your wife."

"Exactly," Angus said with equanimity, gnawing at the claw of a lobster. "I am looking after you while she is away. She asked me to."

"Oh! Oh, pardon." Miss Cameron smiled and relaxed visibly with relief. His lordship also smiled, but inwardly. She would be hard to get, but he would get her.

The next night he took her to the theatre, again in a crowd of friends so as to avoid scandal at being seen with her in public, and the night after he contrived for a handsome unattached equerry of his to escort her to a ball at Court. Once there, the equerry pleaded the call of unexpected duty and hurried away and the Falcon, conveniently at hand, stepped into the breech. He took care not to dance every dance with her, but again he took her home.

"When will your wife be back, Lord Falconer?"

"Very soon," he said, kissing her hand as she was helped down from the carriage. "She will be so grateful to me for looking after you."

The Falcon felt he was head over heels in love. The titillation had worked as much on him as he hoped it had on her. He passionately desired her; he yearned to get between her loins and make her his. She obsessed his thoughts and he dreamt of her at night, seeing those deliciously sparkling eyes, that minx-like mouth, the surprisingly direct air, that taut virginal bosom so prominent and white in her low-cut evening gowns.

Analee wrote that she was enjoying herself and he sent a personal messenger to say he was immersed in affairs of state and she should stay as long as she liked. Not a day passed but he did not arrange to see Miss Cameron, and as yet he had not even kissed her lips. He was an ardent but patient wooer. He had arranged for her to be escorted to a ball given for the young Prince of Wales who would succeed his grandfather in the event of his death—which some thought would not be too long delayed. The ball was at Hampton Court and the Falcon, though restraining his impatience to bring her there, looked forward to the long drive back to the city when it was over. He would contrive to stop in order for her to admire some part of the river and there . . . His lordship shivered with expectation as he eagerly surveyed the couples who came in through the huge doors.

She was late. He cursed and looked at his watch, aware of the many flattering female glances that alighted on him. In his general's uniform, scarlet coat, buff breeches and black boots, he knew he looked particularly fine. Really he could have any woman he chose. He held himself up and squared his shoulders. Why, then, should he choose this snippet, this daughter of tradespeople from the new country? In every way she was unsuitable, but she enticed him. He was in love.

"Ah, Falconer," an unfamiliar head bowed, and he glanced curiously at the newcomer. "Edward Goodacre, Lord Falconer. We have met before."

Angus surveyed him through his quizzing glass and smiled. "Why, Lord Goodacre. What an unexpected pleasure to see you. I would have expected you to be in Kent entertaining my wife."

"Alas," Lord Goodacre said, accepting a glass of champagne from a passing servant, "I have not had

108

that pleasure. I seldom go to the country and my wife never comes to town." He glanced at the Falcon as though expecting that, as a man of the world himself, he would understand this state of affairs.

"Your wife never comes to London?" The Falcon exclaimed with surprise.

"Never." His lordship shook his head vigorously. "Confidentially, Lord Falconer—I know I *can* tell you this in confidence—I never trusted my wife."

"Ah?" The Falcon smiled understandingly. He felt he should take a look at Lady Goodacre if she was a person of the kind her husband seemed to be suggesting.

"Oh, not in the way you imply, Lord Falconer," Lord Goodacre said hurriedly, frowning with displeasure. "The virtue of my wife is unquestioned. She is a devout member of the Roman Catholic Church, alas. Also, I am sorry to say, she is a convinced Jacobite. That is why I never allow her to come to London. I do not want her to fall into any intrigues that may be still afoot—not that I think many are. God bless his Royal Majesty." Lord Goodacre raised his glass and turned towards that part of the room where the old King was making his arthritic way among a group of courtiers with Lady Yarmouth on one side and George, Prince of Wales, on the other.

The Falcon meanwhile gazed, thunderstruck, at Lord Goodacre. "Your wife is a *Jacobite*?"

"Aye, I am sorry to say, Lord Falconer. I can assure you that my own sympathies never . . ."

"Oh, I know that, I know that," the Falcon said impatiently, with a dismissive flourish of his hand. "I know quite well you are a loyal subject, etcetera, Goodacre. Alas, in quite a few families, my own as well I regret to say, there are these divisions of loyalty. However, what intrigues me is, if your lady never comes to London—*never* you say . . . ?"

"Oh never, never, Lord Falconer. I have not allowed

109

it since the Rebellion. She has come no further north than Maidstone and only visited *there* once."

"Then," said Lord Falconer, lowering his voice menacingly, "how comes she to be so well acquainted with Lady Falconer?"

"Ah!" Lord Goodacre put down his glass and scratched the side of his wig. "That's a point."

"My wife mentioned she was particularly friendly with Lady Goodacre."

"Yes, my wife told me the same."

"Then how did they meet? Lady Falconer has never traveled in Kent that I know except to go to France, and always with me. I have never met your lady wife, to my regret," the Falcon added insincerely.

"That is very strange, Lord Falconer. Your wife is not Scots by any chance? Mine comes of a branch of the McCleods."

"She is certainly not Scots," Lord Falconer said with exasperation, his opinion of Lord Goodacre's acumen sinking fast.

"I did not think she was. Then it cannot be that, that they knew each other as girls, for instance." Lord Goodacre trailed off helplessly.

"*I* think they have never met," Angus said, his suspicions growing to enormous proportions. "I am beginning to suspect some dreadful plot is being hatched in the quiet countryside of Kent."

"Oh, my goodness gracious!" Lord Goodacre exclaimed nervously. "My wife would never land herself . . ."

"It is what *my* wife would do that worries me," Angus said. "You do not know Lady Falconer."

Chapter Seven

Although she trembled inwardly, Analee gazed at her husband with composure, her head proudly raised, her hands neatly folded and relaxed in her lap. She had never once avoided the Falcon's eyes all during their long and painful interview, for she knew that would be her undoing. She still wore her traveling dress, having been summarily sent for from Kent and escorted by a lieutenant of the Falcon's troop. She felt like a prisoner being led to her doom.

The Falcon had started politely enough, the cat teasing the mouse, enquiring as to how she had enjoyed herself, the state of the weather in Kent and so on. At first she thought he knew about Brent's visit, that somehow his spies had discovered even that fact; but then she realized it was her relationship with Lady Goodacre which interested him. How came she to know her? The reason for the sudden visit? Analee thought very rapidly, as she had all during the long journey to London, what explanations she could give, trying to anticipate his questions. In some things she had been right; but in how she came to know Lady Goodacre, seeing that worthy woman was known not to be allowed to visit London . . . . She wrestled inside herself for an explanation, seeking desperately for a solution.

"You had never been to that part of Kent, Analee, had you?"

"No, my lord."

"Not even when you were a wandering gypsy?"

"That was in the West Country, sir, before we came north."

"Then my question remains to be answered, Analee.

111

How *came* you to know Lady Goodacre, that she could address you in terms of such intimacy?"

Analee met his gaze unflinchingly, those hard black impenetrable eyes that burned in his face like nuggets of coal.

"I am acquainted with Lady Goodacre through the Allonbys, sir. She is a friend of that family of many years standing. Despite my devotion to the Hanoverian cause, and loyalty to his Majesty King George, sir, I do retain friendship for those who were so good to me; you know that. They once saved me from cold and starvation and, indirectly, led to my reacquaintance with your lordship—though whether the memory of that pleases you now or not I am not bold enough to say."

Analee lowered her head but her eyes were glinting in a manner very far from humility. She still did not know what this was leading to—whether he knew about Brent. If he did she might as well go to her room and take poison; he would never forgive her. She rather felt though that if he knew about Brent he would have been more violent; this was more in the manner of an interrogator bent on discovering the truth. He might well come to the use of the rack, but not yet.

"Ah, the Allonbys," the Falcon said, straightening himself and leaning an elegant elbow against the mantelpiece. "There *is* a Jacobite connection. I thought so. Lord Goodacre hinted as much when he told me the reason he refused to let his wife visit London. I have *unmasked* you, Analee!"

"Not at all, my lord." Analee raised her head again, meeting his gaze. "Your lordship is wrong to insinuate a political motive in this meeting of two poor women. After all what power have such as we, Lady Goodacre and myself, compared to the might of men? Lady Goodacre has never had any political dealings, being a loyal wife and devoted mother. Her family, it is true,

112

supported the Stuarts, but how many others did the same? Is loyalty a sin, sir?"

"Yes it is, in some cases," the Falcon snapped.

"Well I beg to differ, I think you would value it highly, my lord, if you were on the defeated side. Supposing the Stuarts had won—would you have deserted the cause of Hanover? No, my lord, I know you too well. You would not." Analee took a deep breath and crossed her fingers before she went on. " 'Twas Miss Cameron who brought me news of Lady Goodacre, through Stewart Allonby. His sister Mary was her friend and I wished for news of Mary."

"Ah, I see. It was Miss Cameron, was it? Is *she* come among us as a Jacobite spy?" The Falcon's pulse quickened. Had that vixen . . . but no, if she had wanted to spy on him she would have been nicer to him, she would have responded to his overtures. After all, she was not a young girl, but a woman of twenty-two years. He had had a very hard time with her in the carriage after the ball at Hampton Court. She had threatened to leave the coach and find her own way home if he did not order his driver to recommence the journey. She had looked as though she meant it. He had felt very disgruntled and full of chagrin. But it only whetted his desire. He wanted her more than ever. What a chance, now, to see her again.

"Of course not, Angus," Analee said impatiently. "She has no connection at all with the Jacobites."

"And why should *you* want to know about Mary Allonby? To find out where the scallywag of a husband is, is that it? Eh? Eh?"

"Why should I wish to know where he is, sir?" Analee said trying to keep the relief out of her voice. So the Falcon did not know. Inwardly she thanked God. "I am married to you, a faithful wife, the mother of your . . ."

"Oh yes, yes I know the mother of my children, all

113

that sort of twaddle," the Falcon interrupted her rudely, waving his hand. "I have heard it all before."

"It is true. I have not seen Brent Delamain for years. It is said he is in America, so Lady Goodacre thought." Analee decided that it might be judicious to put two thousand miles between herself and Brent and then she regretted it. Anna Cameron! The Falcon would question her! She began to be afraid of the web that, subtly, was being woven round her—a web of lies and deceit, partly fabricated by herself. The Falcon, like a great spider, sat in the middle.

"I think I will question Mistress Cameron," the Falcon said in silky tones. "I will summon her here before you have time to see her privately and fill her with your lies. *I* will observe her reaction for myself. I think she is still in London."

"Do you not *know*, my lord?" Analee said with heavy sarcasm. "Surely she has been under your protection?"

"I have scarcely seen the girl," the Falcon said tersely, "except at Court of course. She seems well enough taken care of by the younger generation. I said I would introduce her at Court and I have done my duty. 'Tis all."

He turned away abruptly, whether to disguise his confusion or not Analee was unable to tell, and pulled the bellrope. He ordered a servant to go directly and fetch Miss Cameron from Cavendish Square and take no excuses, and then he abruptly left the room.

There was nothing she could do. Analee went upstairs to her bedroom and slowly changed from her traveling clothes; then she lay on her bed for a few minutes feeling utterly dejected. They had traveled all the way from the castle without stopping and she was exhausted; she was also frightened and unsure of herself. For once she was in the wrong; her husband was right to be suspicious, he had every cause. She only felt really secure when she knew she was not to blame.

Now she was not only lying but endangering those she would give her life to protect. Well, if necessary she must give her life; it would be worth little, anyway, if he found out. Then she thought of her children, and her eyes brimmed with tears.

It seemed a very short time before a servant knocked on her door and announced the arrival of Miss Cameron.

As a change from the previous encounter with her husband, now he was all smiles. He, too, had changed into a royal blue *justaucorps*, a coat that hung loosely from the chest, the long skirts stiffened with buckram. Under this he wore a long sleeveless waistcoat of oyster-colored silk with matching breeches fastened at the knee and round-toed black leather shoes fitted with metal buckles. Around his stock he wore the solitaire, a black ribbon tied into a bow under the chin, which was considered extremely smart. His wig was short, its queue tied with a black ribbon. He seemed to have made every effort to look like a young blade without appearing ridiculous; and he had succeeded. She thought he must have spent all the time since they parted grooming himself for the occasion. In a way it amused her as she stood by his side ready to receive Anna Cameron.

Miss Cameron, when announced, sped into Analee's arms and kissed her. "Oh, Lady Falconer, I have missed you so much! Did you enjoy your visit?"

Analee returned her embrace and then kept her hands on her shoulders while she studied her face. She had to be careful not to try to convey any message either with her eyes or by pressure from her hands. The Falcon would be observing her closely. She merely *willed* Anna to be receptive to her gypsy vibrations, those mysterious messages she was able to send by almost magical means.

"I have missed you, too. I hope his lordship took care of you?"

115

"His lordship was very kind," Anna said guardedly and Analee was aware of the shifty, guilty look she gave the Falcon. Her heart sank.

"We scarcely met at all," the Falcon said airily. "I told you I was busy with affairs of state. But I saw to it that Miss Cameron was well looked after."

Anna glanced at him again and Analee saw a faint blush steal up her cheeks. If the Falcon had offended her maidenly susceptibilities there was hope. She doubted if this well-controlled miss from the new world would be as ready to yield the priceless jewel of her virtue as her wanton sister Constance had years before.

"And what is the reason for you sending for me?" Anna said disarmingly, accepting the chair the Falcon held out for her. She gave Analee that frank open smile that seemed incapable of deception.

"I wish to bring you Lady Goodacre's greetings," Analee said, willing in her heart for Anna to understand. Miss Cameron however gazed at her with some surprise.

"I understand you are acquainted with Lady Goodacre," the Falcon said, the tone of his voice changing so as to sound slightly menacing.

For an instant Anna looked from him to Analee and then, her own expression unchanged, she said brightly, "Why yes, but only indirectly."

Analee felt that, for a girl of twenty-two, she was of a marvelously perceptive and diplomatic disposition. Her gypsy spells had undoubtedly helped. Anna was saying things without really knowing why. Analee knew she had her in her power. She intervened quickly.

"I was saying to his lordship that I sought news of Mary and John Allonby, and that, through Stewart, you directed me to Lady Goodacre whose sister is a nun in the same convent as Mary."

The Falcon looked annoyed and tried to interrupt, but Miss Cameron said with great naturalness and ease, "Yes. Stewart was very anxious to have news of his brother and sister. He wants me to visit them when I go to France. I shall hope to stay with Lady Goodacre on the way." She smiled with the greatest naturalness at Analee who thought that she would never know what she had done. Or perhaps she did. There was nothing the Falcon could do now.

"I like not my wife having truck with Jacobites," the Falcon said sulkily, like a bad loser who has lost at cards. "You would do well to steer clear of them, too."

"But, Lord Falconer, is not His Majesty, gracious King George, securely on the throne of England?" Anna raised her well-shaped eyebrows in some surprise. "Does he not have an heir and numerous progeny to secure the throne? I believe the only heir to the Pretender James in Rome is his son who is unmarried and childless. What danger is there to the well-established and much beloved English monarch we have today?"

"Unmarried but *not* childless," the Falcon said viciously. "He has a natural daughter and drags her around like the millstone she undoubtedly is."

"But she is surely no threat to the throne?"

"Oh none at all," the Falcon said, roaring with laughter. "A bastard *and* a girl. What chance has she?"

"Oh I don't know," Analee said, her eyes glinting dangerously. "Was not I *myself* a bastard *and* a girl. What is more I was also a common gypsy. Who would ever have thought I would become Marchioness of Falconer—bastard, a girl *and* a gypsy? Would *you* have thought it, my lord?" She stared haughtily at her husband whose complexion grew mottled with rage.

"This is where your raw, humble origins show, Analee. No real lady would talk like that in front of one of such refinement as Miss Cameron."

"Oh, I assure you I am not offended." Anna Cameron nervously clapped her hands together. "I heard Lady Falconer was a gypsy, but I never . . ."

"Thought to hear such a tale?" Analee looked at her. "Quite. So you see the daughter of Prince Charles may find herself one day on the throne of England, or maybe his son if he had one . . . ?" She gazed innocently at the Falcon who looked as though he was about to have an apoplectic attack.

"I could have you in prison for treason the way you are talking! Let me hear no more of it." The Falcon looked angrily at the fob watch at his waistband and clicked his fingers. "I have an appointment with Mr. Pitt and Lord Ligonier. Both are convinced we shall have war before a twelvemonth is out; although all this frenzy about the threat of a French invasion is ridiculous. 'Tis started by the French—and fanned by the Jacobites, the few there are. May I escort you home, Miss Cameron?"

Every time he talked to her his voice became softer and his expression gentle, even amorous, Analee thought. Yet she liked the girl; her open good nature was appealing.

"Do stay and take tea with me," Analee said. "I am sure we have a lot to say to each other. I can tell you all about Lady Goodacre!"

Analee looked brightly at the Falcon whose face was now purple with irritation. He plucked at the braid on his handsome new coat and seemed about to crush the delicate face of his timepiece in his hands. Through trying to be too clever he had got himself into a thoroughly awkward situation. But, looking at them both, he knew there was nothing he could do. He must rely on Anna's discretion. If Analee heard about the scene in the carriage he would never hear the end of it. But it was not a thing that Miss Cameron should want noised abroad either. How he had managed to raise her skirts and fondle her thighs—alas, only too briefly—before she slapped him hard. He glowered at Analee, smiled at Miss Cameron, kissing her hand and then glanced at

118

himself in the mirror, straightening the black band at his throat.

"Do not keep Mr. Pitt waiting, my lord," Analee said pointedly. "He may keep you out of the government if he ever forms one."

Neither woman spoke as they heard Angus's heavy footsteps run down the stairs. Then Analee sighed and rose to pull the bellrope. They went to the window and looked out on the bleak landscape. The October weather was cold, a freezing wind blowing endlessly from the east. Analee shivered.

"Thank you," she said, turning to her guest.

"I know not what I did. The whole thing bewildered me."

"I could see that. Yet your replies helped me enormously. Thank you again."

"I hope I have not been guilty of assisting in a deception, Lady Falconer?"

"No. Perhaps of saving my life."

"It is as grave as that?"

"It is very grave."

"It *is* to do with the Jacobite cause?"

Analee stared at the young girl, wondering if she had got herself into a worse situation than before. "It is in a way."

"Oh, how thrilling!" Anna clapped her hands together and came over to Analee. "I am devoted to Bonnie Prince Charlie, Lady Falconer! What tales Stewart has told of him, and Brent Delamain his cousin who visited him last year. His landing at Eriskay, his swift victories, his charm and ease in command. My family of course have always supported the Stuarts."

"But from afar, 'tis not the same thing. So you met Mr. Delamain?"

"Yes. He was there for about six months. He was very restless."

"Did you . . . like him?" Analee tried to control the jealousy in her voice.

119

"Oh, very much."

"He is a very personable young man, is he not?"

"Oh he is not *young*, Lady Falconer! He is well over thirty! But he was personable enough. Quite a few of the unattached women set their caps at him. But Stewart told me he was in the grip of a strange enchantment—a permanent love for a woman who was now married with children; but he had vowed never to marry anyone else. Knew you this tale?"

"I heard something of it," Analee said lightly, her heart leaping with joy. "It happened before the Rebellion."

"I never saw him so much as glance with interest at another woman. Yet he was always very polite and a good dancer. It was rather romantic, this tale of his faithful love."

"And have *you* ever had an attachment?"

"Oh, one or two flirtations, nothing more. I am not of a mind to marry until I have travelled and seen something of the world. You have no idea how tedious life in Chesapeake can be."

"But *will* you settle in Chesapeake?"

Anna looked at her in surprise. "Why, I suppose so, Lady Falconer. I never thought any different. My two sisters have."

"Would you not like to stay in England maybe? Marry a man of title and wealth here?"

Anna Cameron appeared never seriously to have considered the matter. She looked at Analee with wide-eyed surprise that made Analee wonder whether a girl of her age could really be quite *so* innocent.

"I had not given thought to the matter, Lady Falconer. It is true there are one or two men kind enough to pay me attention."

"One or two! I heard that you were quite a sensation at Court."

"Oh, how kind!"

"And the Princess of Wales took to you most kindly. You are a great success."

"Her Royal Highness was most gracious. What a tragic loss her husband must have been. Now she will never be Queen."

So Miss Cameron *was* ambitious, Analee thought—the main thing in her mind being that Princess Augusta would never be Queen, not that she had lost a husband. She wondered just how open and simple her new young friend was.

A footman entered and Analee gave the order for tea then, when he had left, she moved her chair nearer that of Anna Cameron.

"To return to Lady Goodacre."

"Yes, Lady Falconer?" Miss Cameron opened those dazzling turquoise eyes very wide. Her prominent lids were almost opaque and her face had a sculptured, classical quality.

"I did want to see her in connection with the Allonbys. That was quite true."

"I see."

"The trouble is we had never met and Lord Falconer thought we had."

"Oh." Miss Cameron appeared to think this a very grave matter.

"I knew he was very suspicious of the Allonbys because he has always suspected me of harboring Jacobite sympathies on account of my friendship for them."

"And have you, Lady Falconer?"

"Shall we say I am . . . sympathetic." Analee hesitated in choosing the correct word. "But I am not a traitor. My husband, as a senior general in the army of the King, always has my first loyalty, my undying devotion."

"Oh, quite." Miss Cameron's thoughts flew to the Falcon's behavior during his wife's absence, the scene in the carriage by the river. She had had to fight him off, fearing for her virtue. She suddenly felt sorry for

121

Analee who was such a beautiful woman; who did not deserve to be made cuckold in this matter. But the Marquess was a very attractive man. Miss Cameron was flattered by his attentions even though she disapproved of him and never expected to respond to someone who was at least as old as her father, if not older. She found her thoughts straying to him more and more and she would look every day at the little jewel under her linen in her drawer. He must think very highly of her to have selected such an expensive present. She would put it on her bosom and imagine being seen in company with him, smothered with jewels, all eyes turned to admire her . . . as they did now; but there were, she knew, also whispers. The Falcon had a reputation. It made her slightly ashamed of being seen in his company for fear of what people would say, the tongues that would wag, sullying her good name.

But she thought of him a great deal; he aroused feelings in her that no man had before. To be a Marchioness . . . she looked at Analee and suddenly reddened. She felt so disloyal and faithless to this good friend. Her guilt was why she had helped her by lying. Anyone could see that husband and wife didn't get on. He obviously wanted some excuse to get rid of her and she, Anna Cameron, would not sully her conscience, disrupt her peace with God by assisting in such a foul deed.

But she had put Analee on her side. Now they both liked her . . . very much.

"You are very thoughtful, Anna," Analee said, gazing at her with some consternation. Her guest had fallen into a brown study and the leaping flames in the grate were reflected in her large translucent eyes. What a color they were, like the sun on some dappled lagoon the like of which Analee had only ever heard about from people who returned from the West Indies.

"I was just thinking," Anna said guiltily, "how un-

122

fortunate it is that families had to be divided by this sad affair."

"You mean Stuarts versus Hanoverians?" Analee enquired, not altogether convinced by Miss Cameron's explanation and then, as she nodded, "It has been the same for generations. It has gone on since James II, the father of the present exile in Rome and grandfather of Prince Charles, was expelled in 1688 from England. It was right that he was the true King and his son, the heir of his body, his successor. But people tried to pretend he was not his real son. The Hanoverians were only very distantly related to the English royal family, through a daughter of James I, the Queen of Bohemia. It was such a tenuous connection that few thought it would ever be realized; but then religion came into it and religion is a very strong emotion. The Whigs were determined to keep the Catholic Jacobites out. They succeeded. 'Twas from Mary Allonby I learned all this, and I have studied more since. I remember the day she told me—oh, before the war in far-off Lakeland and I a gypsy to whom she had given refuge. She was the mistress of the house . . ." Analee shook her head. " 'Tis a sad, sad tale."

"I know you have been very good to the Allonbys," Anna said gently. "Stewart is very grateful for it."

"Is he happy?"

"Oh yes. Very. He and Elizabeth are well-matched, although she is very strong-willed. But she loves him so much because he is so handsome that he can do what he likes with her. They have three lovely babies, two boys and a girl."

"Will he ever come home, do you think?"

"Never. He says his place is in America. And, because he is pro-Stuart, he is against the English government and thinks it should not have so big a say in the colonies' affairs. Many Americans think the colonies should rule themselves and are pressing for the right of

123

self-determination, to have their own houses of assembly and make their own laws."

"Really?" Analee looked rather shocked. "You mean there is rebellion?"

"Oh not yet. The French are the problem at the moment. They want to try and drive the English colonists into the sea; but once we have got rid of the French then we shall set about ruling ourselves. It is only a matter of time and Stewart is prominent among those who think this way. He would love to get even with the English government for dispossessing him of his lands and birthright."

"Take care not to let the Falcon hear you talk like that," Analee said, moving to one side as the footman, followed by a succession of lesser menials and maids, brought in the tea things. "Or he will have you shipped back to America . . or even clapped in irons."

Miss Cameron's face grew round with pretended apprehension and Analee, liking her more than ever, burst out laughing and impulsively kissed her cheeks, relief in her heart once more.

Mistress Catherine Walkinshaw, Housekeeper to Her Royal Highness the Princess of Wales, looked severely at Lady Falconer, her sensible mouth pursed in a disapproving rosebud. She was a stout woman, not remotely good-looking. It intrigued Analee to wonder what her younger sister looked like to have captured the heart of the man who, at one time, most women in England or Scotland would have given their lives for to say nothing of their virtue. Although she had lived for many years in England, Mistress Walkinshaw retained her strong Scots accent and her hair was plainly dressed and sensible, like the rest of her.

"Your ladyship is greatly mistaken if you think I have any truck with the Jacobites," Miss Walkinshaw continued, scarcely opening that prim mouth. "Whatever my family thought or may think, *I* am a loyal supporter of His gracious Majesty King George. And, moreover, since my unfortunate sister dishonored our family, many more of us have gone over to the other side, so shocked were we all by the way she openly disported herself."

Miss Walkinshaw clamped her mouth shut and produced a gold snuff box from the pocket of her capacious gown. "Do you take snuff, Lady Falconer?"

"No thank you, Miss Walkinshaw." Analee looked with interest as Miss Walkinshaw expertly put a pinch in each nostril and gave a large sniff, her eyes suddenly watering.

"Do you not think it is the Prince who has behaved dishonorably in not marrying your sister? She must love him very much and has borne him a child." She saw Miss Walkinshaw wince and hurried on. "I think that is very praiseworthy, very noble and loving. Do you not think so?"

"I do not indeed," Miss Walkinshaw said, her mouth rounder than ever, "and I am surprised that you do. She is living in sin and her child is a child of sin. We acknowledge her as no relation of ours. My family has suffered severe hardships for the Jacobite cause, as you may know, Lady Falconer; my parents went into exile and endured great poverty. But for my sister to have behaved the way she has, has brought shame on our family name. My mother has sworn that she will never speak to her again and means to keep to this. I know."

"I am sorry to hear you speak thus," Analee said quietly. "I know not your sister, but when a woman gives her heart to a man as she has done I think she is to be admired, not scorned."

"You can think what you like, Lady Falconer," Miss Walkinshaw said firmly, agitatedly tapping her snuff box. Clearly she was suffering from emotion and the strong pungent powder helped to calm her. "Your opinions are your own affair; but I do not wish to hear my sister's name mentioned again. It is no concern of

125

mine. I would never scheme or plot against this beloved monarch. Believe me."

"I do," Analee said with conviction. "I do not know how I came to be so misinformed. Please forget we have ever spoken."

"I would like to know how you did come to be so informed," Catherine Walkinshaw said, "as aspersions are obviously cast on my loyalty. I shall speak to the Princess about this."

"Oh pray do not, Miss Walkinshaw," Analee said quickly. "It could lead to too much trouble. I was simply told that you . . . kept in touch, that is all."

"Well, you were misinformed and I am not in touch. I am surprised at you, Lady Falconer, with your husband having the high position he has, the ear to the King at all times."

"I assure you I am no traitor," Analee spoke softly. "But, like you, I have been well acquainted with those who, for reasons of their own, were loyal to the Stuarts. I am simply assisting them, and him . . . the Prince."

"He has no chance at all, you know," Miss Walkinshaw said, modifying her tone from one of strict disapproval into chattiness. Despite the sobriety of her ways she was known to enjoy a gossip. "Princess Augusta used to talk of him kindly but no more. She is too dependent on the goodwill of the King. Before she was loyal to her husband who was forever plotting against his father, as these Hanoverians do. The present King plotted before that against his father George I. I think the late Prince Frederick thought he might conspire with the Stuarts to topple his own father; but God punished him for his disloyalty and struck him down in his prime." Miss Walkinshaw's eyes glinted with satisfaction at the thought of divine intervention on such a massive scale. "Aye, in his prime. 'Twas the wrath of God. And if you take my advice, your ladyship will

126

keep well away from such treasonable activities in case God should wreak his vengeance against *you*, too."

Miss Walkinshaw clamped her mouth tight shut again like a trap and folded her hands firmly on her lap sitting up straight as a ramrod, bristling with righteous indignation.

And, indeed, Analee felt she had fallen into a trap. By asking her to speak so openly to one as close to the Court as this woman, had her beloved Brent unwittingly betrayed her?

Chapter Eight

The casual gardener was a tall powerful man and Dulcie, one of the parlor maids at the Castle, had her eyes on him from the moment he came to help cut down the dead wood in the park surrounding Goodacre Castle. She would spy at him out of the window and when the gardeners and the woodsmen gathered together for food, she made sure that she was around, too.

In no time at all Dulcie and the gardener were trysting to the outbuildings and it was not long after the first encounters, the first gropings and kissings and squeezings, that he bedded her in the hayloft in the far barn on the estate.

She was a lovely piece of comely flesh and, knowing that as soon as he had what he wanted he would have to go back and report to his master and never see her again, Gwyn Dyffed took his time in finding out what he wanted to know.

"I liked ye since I first set eyes on ye," Dulcie said to him one day after they had completed their lovemaking and were resting comfortably in the warm hay that had only been gathered in that summer. From the slats in the pigeon loft high in the barn, the sun shone on the dried golden grass and the soft cooing of pigeons enhanced the idyllic nature of the late afternoon. "Will you be stopping 'ere long?"

Gwyn looked at her slyly. The work in the woods was hard but, as a trooper in the Falcon's regiment, he was used to hard work and Dulcie was different from the usual run of soldier's doxies. She was clean and well spoken, a local girl, and the hunger with which she returned his embraces made him hopeful that she was choosy about whom she lay with.

"I can't stop long," Gwyn said, kissing her pink, rounded breast only partly covered by the hay. "But I'll be back. I like it in these parts—especially your parts," he said, drawing back the hay to inspect her thighs, rounded and ample with a dark hairy turf at the center.

"Do you wander about, then?"

"Aye, seeking work, casual."

"And do you always have a good time like this?" She winked at him and stuck out her saucy pink tongue.

"I *try*, but I don't always succeed. Do you get many strangers in these parts? Many visitors?"

"What do you mean?" Dulcie partially sat up and stared at him. "What are you after?"

"Nothing. I just wondered."

He put his mouth firmly down on hers so as to replace the suspicious gleam he saw in her eyes with the lights of love. He was a big man and she squealed as he positioned himself upon her again and recommenced the timeless ritual of mating.

"You aren't half strong," she said after it was over. "I never knew anyone do it as many times as you."

"It's practice," he said, laughing.

"Oh, you're *that* practiced then, are you?"

"You wouldn't like a man that wasn't, would you now?" He looked down at her pink flushed face and kissed her pert nose.

128

"I'd like a man vigorous like you, but faithful. Would you think of settling here?"

"I might, and I might not. You must be nice to me."

"Like what? Aren't I nice enough?" She wriggled her hips and he slid out of her, his essence spilling onto the straw and changing its color from canary gold to dark yellow. He covered her with his arms and gazed into her eyes.

"I'm looking for someone, a man who owes me money. He didn't pay me and I want to find him. Until I do I shan't settle."

"Oh, *that's* why you ask them questions," Dulcie said, smiling. "Everyone says you asks a lot of questions. I can see you mean to 'ave him."

"I do," Gwyn said. "He cheated me."

"What was his name?"

"I can't tell ye; but he was a landowner, a nob. He employed me for three months without pay. I thought he might have been here, visiting."

"Visiting here? No one ever visits here."

"No one?"

Dulcie screwed up her fetching amber eyes and Gwyn's heart began to beat more quickly. The Falcon had promised a large reward as well as promotion if he got the information he was after.

"Nay. Lord and Lady Goodacre don't get on. He stops in London and she is alone here with the children. There are only two in the schoolroom now, the rest grown up."

"And she never sees *no* one?" The dismay showed on Gwyn's face and he leaned back in the hay resting his head on his hands.

"I only recall one visitor in the past month—a beautiful lady from London, ever so elegant—she stayed about a week and they spent all their time walking and riding, playing with the younger children. She was the wife of some very big nob in London, gentry."

"And she was here all by herself?"

129

"Oh aye, except for her maid, and the servants who had ridden with her. One of them was not bad-looking, but not like you." Dulcie looked at him archly. "I never saw such big muscles, or a big . . . you know," she stared at him, dimpling and blushing.

"And how many of *them* have you seen, you saucy wench?" Gwyn tried to sound roguish, but he felt disappointed and defeated. He would have to go back only to report that Lady Falconer had been here alone. He felt privileged to have enjoyed the confidence of his commander, to be given such an important mission; but there was nothing to tell.

"I'm *very* choosy," Dulcie said. "The last man I had was a sailor from France . . . Oh, that reminds me," she put a hand to her mouth and sat up. "There *was* somebody else here, but I never saw him, only in the distance."

"Yes?" Gwyn was seized by a feeling of excitement.

"He came with the sailor but only stopped twenty-four hours, then he left."

"When did he come?"

"The day that grand lady came from London. I recall it because the sailor was a lusty man like you and made eyes at me in the servants' hall over dinner. We tumbled in the woodshed at night. He had to leave soon after that."

"Those Frenchmen carry the pox, they say," Gwyn said, feeling a little less enthusiastic about his paramour. He would carefully examine his member when he got to his room. Little bawd, going with Frenchmen, not as selective as he thought.

"This one didn't," Dulcie said indignantly. "He wasn't just an ordinary sailor."

"I thought you were more choosy?"

"I am." Dulcie looked at him indignantly. "You're jealous."

"Who did he come over with?"

"Someone to see Lady Goodacre. I know no more. I
130

didn't wait on that day so I never saw him. It was all very secret; none of us were allowed near him. In fact very few knew he was there; I heard him speak though, and he had an English voice; he wasn't a foreigner."

"You couldn't say at all what he looked like?"

"No. But he couldn't have been your man."

"Why not?"

"Because he came from overseas with the Frenchie."

"He came from France?"

"Oh yes. You're sure you're not a government spy or something like that?"

"'Course I'm not," Gwyn said, closing his eyes at the thought of the reward he would get. "Do I look like one?"

"Yes and no. You look like a soldier to me."

"I was in the war but I left it because the pay was awful. We must go, Dulcie. We shall be missed."

"I'm cold, too," she said, shivering. "I wish I had your body to warm me every night."

"Maybe you will," he said, kissing her lightly. "Go on back to your duties at the house; and take care you tell no one about our talk."

"Who could I tell?" she said.

She ran back to the house while he set off towards the wood. She felt almost in love with him and made plans as to how she would try and ensnare him to stay. Maybe Lady Goodacre would give him a permanent job on the estate, if only he could find the man who owed him money.

But the next day, when she slipped away to keep their tryst, no welcoming lover rose up from the straw. The barn was empty, and the day after that the same, and the day after that. The temporary gardener had gone.

The Falcon had never really known torment like this; it was as though he had a sickness. Every other woman

131

he had been sure of, even Analee, but not this one. She pretended she didn't care, and did it very convincingly. He would do anything just for a glimpse of her because, now that Analee was around, he had to be even more circumspect than before. What was more, Anna and his wife got on so well. They went for drives together, rode in Richmond Park or attended little tea parties given by various ladies of title. Anna even called the Marchioness by her Christian name; their friendship was very galling to the husband of one and the would-be suitor of the other.

She was very, very reserved with him—he'd hardly spoken to her since the encounter in the carriage on the way back from Hampton Court. His only hope was that she didn't return the jewel. Surely she knew the meaning of a present like that? As long as she kept the jewel he felt some hope.

Then Gwyn Dyffed returned with his report and the Falcon's whole outlook on life changed. His unerring instinct for trouble had proved correct.

Analee was sewing in her sitting-room when he burst in, flinging back the door and shouting at the top of his voice. He had felt such pleasure that it was difficult to contrive to appear angry; but he managed it. His veins bulged at his neck and his eyes were like forks of lightning. She put down her sewing and gazed at him.

"What is it now?" she said calmly. Knowing how much she irritated him she had been prepared for some outburst; he would contrive something, she knew.

"You outrageous slut," he said. "You *did* go to a rendezvous at Castle Goodacre."

"I know not what you mean," she said, her hands suddenly starting to tremble.

"You did, you did, you *did*! I have had a spy there and he reported to me today. He did his work well. You received a man who came from France. Who was it?"

"I must deny all knowledge," Analee said with a calm she did not feel. "I received no one."

"Someone came there when you were there, accompanied by a French sailor."

"What makes you think he came to see me?"

"Then he did *not* come to see you?"

"I saw no one." Analee looked into his face, knowing well how to lie to save others as well as herself. She should have known that her husband would be thorough. Oh, would she had never gone! But it was no use now.

"Was it the Prince?"

"What an absurd thing to say! Why should the Prince—I assume you mean Prince Charles, knowing how your mind works—come to see me?"

"No, it would not be him. Besides, I know where he is. We have him constantly under surveillance. You know I shall have Lady Goodacre on the rack for this, don't you?"

Now the panic she felt almost overwhelmed her. She could stand torture, but Lady Goodacre . . . and what for? Maybe he was bluffing. She tried conciliation. She got up and smoothed her skirt, put a hand to her hair, composed her features. "Angus, my lord, if you would send me away, send me; but do not contrive artificial circumstances, do not involve good and innocent people. Will you never cease your Jacobite witch hunt, cease your suspicions? Because your nature *is* suspicious, Angus Falconer. You thrive on intrigue and suspicion as some need light and air. The Rebellion is past these ten years, the Prince is undone, he has lost all his support, his followers have dispersed. The second Hanoverian King is a feeble man and the third, a strapping young Prince, prepared to succeed him—who knows when, any day now.

"If you wish to put me away, put me away—I find this life intolerable, existing with a man I loved but

133

who no longer loves me, who is vexed by my very presence. Let us separate, Angus. I will go . . ."

"You will go where *I* put you," Angus said, seizing her arm and snarling into her face. "I'll have you sent to the Tower for high treason."

"Everyone would laugh at you. Known Jacobites are having their estates restored. I believe one or two are even at the Court. They would mock you. You are making plots where none exist. You are becoming a foolish man, in your dotage . . ."

The wrath on Angus's face increased and he twisted Analee's arm behind her, his face an inch away from hers. "You are a traitor, you are consorting with traitors, you try only to injure me, sully my name. You think I am easily misled but I am not . . ."

"*I* think that, Angus? Oh, fie!" Analee said, her face beginning to pale with pain. "Leave off my arm, I beg you . . ."

"You're a whore, you cuckold me; you're a Jacobite, you deceive me; you're a necromancer, a . . ." With every word Angus twisted her arm a little more behind her back and the tears started down Analee's cheeks.

"Angus, if you do not let me go you will . . ."

The Falcon brought Analee's arm right up behind her back to her neck and, as her face contorted with agony, he gave it a savage twist and there was a loud snap. She closed her eyes and swayed and, surprised by his own strength, Angus stepped back and gazed at her with consternation as she fell senseless to the floor, her arm at an awkward angle beneath her body.

He stood and looked at her and wished he had killed her. He hated her so much and she would always be a thorn in his flesh, a hindrance to his ambitions.

He pulled the bellrope and went to the door shouting to the servant who ran quickly up the stairs.

"Fetch a doctor! Lady Falconer has fallen and broken her arm. Hurry up, man, or I'll have you whipped."

Analee knew it was the end; but she felt no remorse. Not even the broken arm was as painful as the bruise to her heart. The last time he had injured her he had been full of anguish, but not this time. He didn't even come and see her as she lay in bed, but sent instructions that as soon as she was fit she was to travel north. Then he went on maneuvers to Somerset with his regiment without saying goodbye.

She made no farewells except to send a note to the Princess of Wales saying she was leaving to visit her children. She sent the same note to Anna Cameron, who had tried to see her; but Analee wanted to see no one. Now that her marriage to a man, once so beloved, was finished, she felt empty and hopeless inside— much, much sadder than she had imagined.

She was also frightened. Having gone so far, she wondered how much further the Falcon would go. She felt he would go to the bitter end to find out the truth and she feared for her innocent friend, Lady Goodacre.

Usually when she traveled north, Analee broke her journey at Delamain Castle, but this time she felt no such desire. She wanted to recover, to regain her strength; to mend both her broken arm and her broken heart. She went straight to her beloved home on Derwentwater, the refuge she always sought when in pain. As she came over the water and the familiar outlines of the house appeared through the mist on the lake, she began to weep and when she saw Nelly and her children lined up to receive her on the jetty, she broke down completely and had to be helped from the boat. By night she had a fever and the following day she was delirious.

"Is her ladyship dying?" Nelly said to the doctor who had been hastily summoned from Keswick.

The doctor shrugged. "She should not have traveled with that arm. How came she to break it? She must have been in great pain. 'Tis swollen to such a size."

135

"I know not, sir. I have scarcely got two sensible words out of her since she arrived."

"The pain caused by the jogging of the carriage over five days must have been considerable. I am shocked his lordship let her travel thus."

"I believe he is away, sir."

"Ah, that explains it. It will be her ladyship's impulsiveness because I know his lordship to be a kind and compassionate man."

Nelly grimaced behind the doctor's back; then saw him out of the house.

"We shall have to send for his lordship if she gets any worse," he said, getting onto his horse and looking down at Nelly. "I fear those poor children will soon be motherless."

Nelly ran upstairs weeping, and flung herself across Analee's hot and restless body as she lay on the large bed she had once shared in such love with the Falcon.

As Nelly wept she felt a hand on her back and looked in surprise to see that Analee's eyes, though bright with fever, were open.

"You must fetch Reyora, Nell. Fetch her quick." Then she lost consciousness again and her breathing became harsh and more rapid.

Nelly rushed down the stairs and sent two servants, each to take different routes, to fetch Reyora and bring her back at once. They were not to stop for a single moment on their way there or on their way back, whoever brought her.

All that day Analee's hot body twisted in the bed and Nelly tenderly bathed her, frequently changing her chemise and sheets. Analee would call out and clutch Nelly, but did not appear to recognize her. Then at about five in the afternoon she grew calmer and a steady rattle began in her throat. She opened her eyes but she did not see. She was dying.

Nelly dried her eyes and went downstairs to fetch the children. Even though she could not recognize them they must take farewell of their mother. Clare led the others into the room, clasping Beyrick by the hand, and bade them all kneel by their mother's bed. The awful rattle continued and Nelly knew it was just a matter of time.

"You must kiss your mama," she said brokenly. "She is very ill."

"Is she dying?" Clare said in her grown-up voice.

Nelly couldn't reply. Her heart was too full and she knelt down and lifted little Charlotte onto the bed.

"I will kiss Mama and make her well," Charlotte said and put her little rosebud mouth against Analee's hot cheek. Then Beyrick followed and finally Clare took her mother's hand and held it against her heart. Then she burst into tears and Nelly bade the servant, who was with them in the room, take the children out again.

"I cannot leave Mama. I will not!" Clare sobbed and tried to get on to the bed with her mother. "Oh Mama, Mama. Do not leave us."

"Your mama will not leave you," Reyora said, still breathing hard from the journey and putting her firm hand on Clare's shoulder. "I promise you that, little one. It is not her time. Now go, and good old Reyora will make her better." Reyora smiled at the child, already glancing anxiously but with practiced skill at Analee and reaching into her bag for her lotions and unguents. "Take them out, Nelly, and then come back to assist me."

Nelly did as she was bid and when she came back Reyora had taken the bedclothes off Analee and was running her capable hands carefully over her body, lingering on her arm.

"It is this where the poison comes from. I suppose *he* did it . . ."

"I know nothing," Nelly said, still too distressed to speak logically. "I only heard Analee was coming home; when she arrived she already had the fever."

137

"He did it. I know. He is a violent man and she is in the most terrible danger from him. Would that we had not saved him when he lay so near death in Germany. I thought then that it was a mistake, but what could I do? She loved him and as long as love is left one is powerless against evil. When her love for him is dead it will no longer be necessary to save him."

"And is it dead?" Nelly asked, marveling at the way Reyora's skilled hands were tending the wounded arm, rubbing soft unguents into it and binding it with leaves impregnated with creams and herbs until a gorgeous fragrance filled the room replacing the smell of sweat and the fear of death.

"I hope so," Reyora said, looking at her patient. "I think so. I knew she was ill, you know. The messenger was no surprise. I felt uneasy and kept on seeing her in my mind, except that I did not know where she was. I thought that perhaps she was in London."

"Would she have died without you?"

Reyora shook her head. "I think not. It is not her time. We all have a time you know, Nelly, though one can postpone it as I did with the Falcon in Germany. Next time I will make sure it is not postponed."

"She loved him so much . . . and he her."

"But he is not a good man. He was momentarily redeemed by her love; but he is bad. The badness will come out as it has now. She is surrounded by his evil desire to do her harm." Reyora's hands wove an imaginary aura around Analee, describing a large arc. "There." She patted Analee's arm gently and laid it by her side. "It will heal and the poison will slowly ebb from her body. You go and rest now, Nell, and I will stay with her. Tell the children that next time they come to see their mama she will greet them with a loving smile."

Nelly burst into tears and, kneeling, kissed Reyora's hand. "Oh, Reyora, without you . . ."

"Without me neither of you would be here," Reyora

138

said, smiling, and patted her shoulder. "Go now and I will tell you when Analee is ready for some warm broth."

Reyora sat with Analee through the night, watching the fever ebb and the swelling in the arm go down. Occasionally she replaced the herbs that bound it and at dawn she went into the garden and gathered fresh ones and fresh leaves from the coniferous trees and laurel bushes. She bathed her face in the icy waters of the lake and watched the sun break over the hills. She was very tired, but happy. When she returned to Analee's room the first beams of the sun bathed the room in a rosy radiance and Analee lay quiet and breathing normally, her eyes clear and free from fever, wide open.

"Reyora," she said simply. "How did you know?"

"You sent for me. Even when near death you murmured my name. But I knew," Reyora said, sitting by her side and taking her hand. "I knew you were unwell because you were distressed."

"It is as though I waited to be home to be ill," Analee said, still speaking in a feeble voice, "so that you could be with me. Home, my Lakeland, my only home—not Falconer House, not Falcon's Keep, but here, Furness Grange. I would he would leave me here all my life."

"Perhaps he will."

Analee shook her head. "He hates me, Reyora. He has such a hatred for me that breaking my arm was only a symbol of breaking me. He wants to do me great harm."

"I will not let him," Reyora said. "I will stop him."

Analee shook her head wearily and the sweat broke again on her forehead. Reyora wiped it with her hand and stroked Analee's brow.

"There, there, you must remain calm."

"I have done so many foolish things," Analee said. "So very foolish, endangering others."

"You have lain with another man?"

139

"Oh no!" Analee managed a weak laugh. "But I saw Brent again briefly, and took a message from him to a servant of the Princess of Wales. I have endangered myself and other good people, and for what? The Rebellion is dead."

"I will never forget what they did to our people," Reyora said bitterly. "I recall the destruction of the Buckland gypsies by the Prince's men. Now he has his punishment. I am glad."

"But it was not he! He was not there! They were savages, disappointed with defeat and gone amuck."

"But the Hanoverians slew no one when they came to power. They have given this country peace."

Analee looked at Reyora and weakly returned the pressure of her hand. "My dear Reyora, much of what you say is true. Were the Falcon not such a cruel man and on the Hanoverian side, I would love them more. But the Prince once held me in his arms, he gave me a child. He comes from a long line of kings. I honor his memory. For Duncan's sake I do all I can for his father."

"Ah," Reyora said. "Now I understand. You do it for love, not power."

"You once said Duncan was the child of a great man. It was he."

"I understand," Reyora said gently. "You are always governed by your passions, Analee."

"The Falcon knows I saw someone at a house in Kent. If he finds it is Brent Delamain, God knows what he will do. He will divorce me, but he will not let me stay here. I shall be universally disgraced. He will order me to some barren place away from my children, my friends. He will leave me there for life like I heard tell the father of King George II left his mother. For thirty years she languished in prison for love."

"I will not let it happen to you, Analee. The days of the Falcon are numbered."

"Oh no!" Analee looked at her in alarm. "You *must*

not harm him. My children, what will they do . . ."

"I do not say *when*," Reyora replied calmly. "The days of all of us are numbered, after all. *I* certainly will do nothing to harm him . . . but nothing to save him either. He is already on borrowed time."

"I wish you had not told me that," Analee said brokenly. "I have some lingering love for him."

"Then you are foolish," Reyora replied, stroking her hand. "You must try and put him from your heart— you must, you must or he will only cause you more unhappiness than you are able to bear. I have not supernatural powers, Analee. I cannot alter the future, only influence the way things happen. Believe me you are in great danger—not physically, but for your own peace of mind. Great events are going to happen that will affect us all, but you in particular. Did I not promise you bad and good, bad and good for several years?"

Analee nodded, blinking through fresh tears. "If I had known I would have preferred death. To lose the Falcon's love . . ."

"For a time it will continue, but one day you will find a greater love. I also promised you lasting happiness. And that will come to pass too . . . sooner than you think. Now send for your children, my dear friend, so that they can be reassured their mother is not dead."

And as the children were brought in and ran to her bedside crying with joy, Reyora stood in the shadows at the back of the room looking at the happy scene, her eyes hooded with the wisdom of one who can see not only the past, but the future too.

Chapter Nine

All London was beginning to talk—or rather, not *all*; but that small, fashionable, select portion of the population that mattered: those who had both wealth and breeding and who frequented the Courts and the upper echelons of high society. In short this small, but very powerful section of society was talking about Miss Anna Cameron and her relationship with the Marquess of Falconer.

By the spring the gossip was such that Mrs. Peto, in whose house Lord Falconer had still not put one foot, was thinking of writing to Anna's mother appraising her of this very distressing situation regarding her daughter and a man not only married, but a premier Marquess of England. Mrs. Peto was both titillated and shocked by it; but one thing was certain, she could not get a word out of Anna, not one single word other than an exclamation accompanied by a look of shocked surprise equal to Mrs. Peto's own.

"Lord Falconer is like a guardian to me, Mrs. Peto!"

"But Mr. Peto is your guardian," Mrs. Peto averred, flustered.

Anna gave her that look of disdain which now came easily to one who, though of democratic upbringing, knew that she was desired by a famous nobleman.

"Alas, Mr. Peto is not, I believe, accustomed to those reaches of society to which Lord and Lady Falconer have access. Is he?"

No. He was not. Mrs. Peto looked at her feet; they had never even been inside the Court, never mind seen the King or the Princess of Wales.

"I still think it is wrong, Anna. People are talking. I know. I may not move in the very highest reaches of society, but we are well enough placed to know what people are saying."

"And what *are* they saying?" Miss Cameron said, shaking her pretty head, the well-dressed curls bobbing up and down.

"Well, that you and Lord Falconer . . ."

"Yes?" She raised her head, showing the delicious dimple in her determined chin.

"That you and he . . ."

"Come to the point, Mrs. Peto."

Mrs. Peto hung her head. "I know not how to put it delicately."

"We are not lovers, Mrs. Peto. I am not his lordship's mistress, if that is what you are suggesting."

Mrs. Peto went crimson and raised her hands to try and hide her face. "Oh, my dear, never was such a thing even *remotely* suggested."

"Then what *is* being suggested?"

Those clear turquoise eyes began to sparkle with interest. How the Falcon would have enjoyed this exchange, Anna thought. How he would have loved crushing Mrs. Peto and her absurd, middle-class insinuations.

"I think the suggestion is, that is to say people *think*, the relationship is too close. Lady Falconer after all is . . . his lawful wife." Mrs. Peto finished lamely and felt her hot cheeks. This little miss was making a fool of her. Mrs. Peto had seldom known a girl change as much as Anna Cameron had in the six months since she came to London. Not only physically but in every way. She was more beautiful, more poised, more elegant, more sure of herself, and . . . Mrs. Peto, with her natural modesty, would not have known exactly how to put into words the next thought that came to her mind. There was a quality about young Anna Cameron that a woman had when she felt fulfilled *as* a woman, when she was beloved and loved in return. Mrs. Peto knew quite well that the only person who could have brought

143

that about was Lord Falconer because, to her certain knowledge, Anna had eyes for no other more eligible and younger men.

Not that there were not a lot of them about. They were mostly dashing young officers acquainted with Lord Falconer and ambitious for promotion and preferment with all the talk about war. They escorted Anna everywhere, picked her up, brought her home, danced with her . . . but when the Marquess appeared, and invariably he did, they melted away like ripples on a pool, only to converge when their presence was required again and his lordship exited discreetly from the scene.

"Lady Falconer knows full well what his lordship is about," Anna said, studying the toe of her delicately shaped silk slipper. "She is detained in Lakeland through ill health. Besides, his lordship is often abroad at the court of King Frederick. When he is here he is kind enough to keep a *paternal* eye on me. I'll thank you not to listen to gossip, Mrs. Peto."

And Anna flounced upstairs and sat on her bed wondering how she could get away from this place. She was nearly twenty-three. She knew she was at her peak. She was beautiful, accomplished and desirable. How much longer would she remain like this? How long would the Falcon's infatuation last, when his own wife was considered such a beauty, a woman who, though just thirty, had never lost her looks. Indeed, some said she was more lovely than when he had married her. Anna was aware, as well as gratified, that the Falcon had sent his wife away because of her. She admired Analee, she was a little afraid of her; but now that she felt her position more secure she no longer liked her so much, because how could you continue to like the woman whose place you eventually hoped to take?

Anna knew that the lecherous Falcon really only wanted her youthful body, and would be content to

144

make her his mistress; but as soon as she took that step she was finished. Having possessed her, his ardor would cool. She knew enough about his reputation in particular, and men in general, to be sure of this. She didn't want merely to be his mistress—to be taken up and discarded when he was replete, like so many before her. She wanted to be his wife.

There was no doubt, as the year 1756 got into its stride, that there was going to be a war. In Europe the continental powers were openly preparing for it—France, Austria and Russia against Prussia and England—and in India and America the first salvos had already been fired. The fear of the invasion of England died down, but troops from Hanover and Hesse still remained to protect the kingdom. They had been hastily summoned by George II because of the poor state of the English army.

The Falcon was excited at the prospect of war. He trained his men unmercifully and plotted to get rid of the hopeless Newcastle (his brother Henry Pelham was dead) and put William Pitt in charge of the country. But the King couldn't abide Pitt and many thought that he would have to wait until the old man died. Pitt and Falcon were alike, they were both egomaniacs and thought they could do things that no one else could. Their mutual admiration was equally based on mutual self-interest.

The Falcon thought most about war, but he gave almost an equal amount of time to thinking about Miss Cameron. He arranged their meetings with all the strategic skill of the great commander he was. He took delight in deploying his forces here, withdrawing them there and entering himself to make the assault. He tried to make the encounters casual and always delightful. Sometimes when he was expected he did not turn up at all. He knew that this was still the best way to get a woman. He thought it was the only way to get

Anna Cameron. He had never known such a willful filly in his life; she had the bare bit between her teeth and would not let go. She was altogether fresh and delightful.

He was wildly, madly in love with her.

The Falcon only ever managed really to get her to himself at the intimate little suppers he got his subordinates to organize. Over an exquisite meal in elegant surroundings with a warm fire in the grate and the candles glittering on the table, he felt he was at his best; witty, light-hearted and amorous.

On this particular evening in March he had taken special care with his always meticulous toilette. Though his darling did not know it, the house in which they were going to have supper after the theatre would be available for him all night.

This was the night he was determined to bring to fruition all his plans. The thought of the carefully planned—oh, planned for how long!—seduction being achieved at last filled him with an almost unquenchable burning in his loins. He had been careful not to lie with a woman for a whole week so as to savor the moment of rapture to the full. Once *she* became his mistress he would totally discard all the others and be faithful only to her. He had every hope to taking her to Potsdam in the spring. He remembered the delicious seduction of Lady Constance and was careful to put in his pocket the little sponges that were so necessary a precaution on an occasion like this, besides providing the most delicious opportunity for closer examination of the orifices of the beloved. The veins in his neck swelled with desire and he had recourse to a large glass of water to cool himself down.

The Falcon scarcely knew what the play was about; he certainly never recalled its name or who was there. He didn't even sit next to Miss Cameron, but some distance away with a bevy of young officers and their

146

ladies in between. But he sat in his seat in the box just behind and to one side of her, so that he could observe her profile, the lovely classical lines of her bosom, the sculptural curve of her neck. Not once but a thousand times he imagined her nude and he squeezed the little sponges deep in the recesses of his pocket longing for the time when he would put them into use. In the course of a whole night in her arms, surely several times? He felt like a young man again, a stud, one to whom sleep was only necessary in order to induce further vigor. How he would please her! He would show her what it was to make love with the Marquess of Falconer.

In the light from the stage she half turned to him and, briefly, their eyes met. Then she turned away again, a little smile playing on her mouth. A mist arose in front of the Falcon's eyes and his head swam. He was sick with desire.

The supper was pregnant with emotion. The atmosphere was so right. He had taken Miss Cameron into the house in Half Moon Street and bade goodbye to the guests even before she realized they were to be alone.

When she did she stood at the foot of the staircase and looked at him with a wondering eye. He seized her arm and hurried her upstairs. All the servants were from his household and his regiment; his own picked men. There was even a maid waiting for her in the dressing-room so as to give her a feeling of confidence, that she was not alone in a house full of men.

She smiled at him playfully across the table and he leaned over and took her hand. Oh, the exquisite turn of the lips, the provocative dent at each side of her mouth—how sensual! He had not even kissed her. He almost groaned at the thought and poured some more wine with a hand that shook.

"It has been a lovely evening, my lord, but then every evening with you is." She returned the pressure of his hand with a slight, very slight squeeze. "I know not what I shall do when I return home."

"Home?" the Falcon said, sitting bolt upright. "What do you mean, return home?"

"I have to go back to Maryland, my lord," Miss Cameron said with feigned surprise, batting her long black lashes against her very clear ivory cheeks. "I cannot stay here forever."

"But you can't go now!"

"But why not? Your lordship and her ladyship have been kindness itself. You have *both* given me the sort of life I never dreamed to aspire to. In fact, it will be hard for me to settle down in Chesapeake!"

"You don't need to settle down in Chesapeake," his lordship said thickly. "You can stay here."

"Oh, but my lord, I cannot. You know that. You must know that people are talking, sir."

"Talking?" his lordship barked imperiously.

"About us."

"Ah. Huh." The Falcon got up and strode from the table, his hands behind his back; but he couldn't take his eyes off her. How bewitching she looked tonight in a gown of primrose yellow, the petticoat flounced and furbelowed, the overskirt edged with ribbon and bows and worn over an oval hoop. Her décolletage was edged with ruching and, in the center of her bosom just at the V of her deep cleavage, was a saucy little bow as if to focus the eyes of her admirer on that crucial and important part of the anatomy.

There was a becoming flush on her cheeks and, in his mind's eye, he saw it spread down her neck and over her bosom as when a woman is engaged in the ecstatic emotions of love. He shut his eyes, the vision almost overpowering him. "Ah, they talk about us, eh? What do they talk about?"

"That is just what I said to Mrs. Peto, sir; but she said she would write to my mama."

"Oh, that common trollop!"

148

"Exactly, sir. She is not a trollop, that I do know, but she is certainly excessively common. I regret that I have associated far below the station enjoyed by your lordship in society."

"But 'tis no fault of yours!" The Falcon exclaimed coming to her side and looking down at her. "And believe me, you are far above them in every way, a jewel, an adornment to the social life of London."

"Alas, Lord Falconer, you are too kind." Miss Cameron lowered her eyes modestly. "I know quite well that I must seem very raw and gauche to you, a rude product of the open classless society of America . . ."

"Oh, my dear, do not say that." The Falcon impulsively threw himself on a knee beside her and, taking her hand, pressed it to his mouth. "You are unique, without equal, no one can match you for attainment, beauty, dignity. You are in every way a perfect specimen of womanhood and I yearn only . . ." The Falcon paused, his heart beating wildly, and looked at her.

"Yes?" She scarcely spoke above a whisper, her own heart undergoing some slight commotion, the meal forgotten.

"I yearn only to make you mine." He raised himself and took her with him into his arms as he regained his full height. Then he crushed her to him, kissing her lips, whose firm yet silky texture he had so much imagined in his tormented waking dreams. He could feel the quick swell of her bosom and he tried delicately to reach down inside her décolletage, but suddenly a vise-like hand grasped his wrist and he jerked back his head and looked at her in surprise.

"Stay, my lord! I am not to be fondled like a doxy." She swiftly resumed her seat and put her glass of wine to the lips he had so freshly kissed.

"Oh, my darling Anna," he pleaded, again on his knees. "Do not torment me. If you knew how I desired you. I will be a very tender lover, my sweetest. I will

149

not hurt you when I introduce you to the delights of love. For you are made for love, Anna. Your body proclaims it. Come." His lordship, his confidence apparently recovered, got up again and and took her hand. "Come see what I have for you."

Miss Cameron looked at him in surprise and, since she had no appetite, allowed him to lead her from the room. He took her along a deserted corridor, up another flight of stairs and along another corridor. Then at the end he opened a door and, standing back, propelled her gently inside. "See?"

Anna Cameron gaped at what she saw. An enormous four-poster bed, with sheets turned back, stood in the center of the room. Candles burned on tables at either side and on a dressing table on which also stood a mirror, an assortment of boxes, and brushes and combs. On one side of the bed there was a freshly laundered nightshirt and cap and on the other a long flimsy chemise. A fire roared in the grate and on yet another table there stood wine in a cooler, two long-stemmed glasses and a variety of fruits and sweetmeats. She heard the door close behind her and she stared back in panic. The Falcon leaned against the door, his face simpering with adoration.

Anna took a deep breath and walked into the center of the room before turning to face him. "Lord Falconer, may I ask the meaning of this . . . this outrage!"

"Outrage?" said the Falcon, nearly choking with surprise. He came over to her and quickly took one of her trembling hands. "My darling, this is not outrage. I thought you wanted it, too." He tried to take her again in his arms. "Oh if you knew, my Anna, how I have waited for this moment. How I have longed . . ."

She shook herself free and stationed herself near the door her eye on the key which, she perceived, he had not turned. "Lord Falconer, you greatly misunderstand if you think that, raw and naïve as I am, without the

150

benefit of high birth or a noble family, I would give myself to you as a common whore."

"Oh, not a *whore*, my heart," the Falcon said, once again rushing over to her. "No common whore. Oh, God forbid, my darling, for you to imagine I would ever think of you like that . . ."

He tried to take her hand, but she snatched it away. The expression on her face was furious and her breath came in short sharp gasps as though she was in desperate need of air. In another age, in another place, Miss Anna Cameron would have made a fortune as an actress.

"Do I understand that you are asking *me* to go to bed with you, my lord?" Miss Cameron put another inch on her height as his lordship's seemed to diminish. "That I would allow you to dishonor me, *me*, Anna Cameron, whose father, Hector Cameron of Chesapeake, though not of noble birth, has a family at least as old as that of Falconer? Moreover, my father is one of the wealthiest men in Maryland and I have been brought up as the daughter of a gentleman and a landowner. If you think I would lightly part with my prized virginity to a man who, however distinguished and noble is *twice* my age, *married* and the father of numerous children . . ." Anna Cameron threw back her head and laughed at him mockingly, then turned and swiftly unlatched the door, stalking down the corridor the way they had come.

Lord Falconer whose carefully laid plans had anticipated this possible outcome—after all, had he not tried to dally with her before?—knew she would be met in the hall and escorted home. He lay on the bed and stared at the ceiling. Then he sent for his valet and told him to get a woman with all despatch. Any woman would do. Any woman at all.

The next day, Anna Cameron received another jewel. It was a rope of pearls with small equally matched dia-

151

monds at every fifth place. Inside was a card on which was scrawled in his lordship's bold hand, *"I will not be deterred."*

Anna smiled to herself and put the card to her lips. Then she placed the precious necklace next to the brooch in her bottom drawer after holding it for some time round her neck, admiring her reflection in the glass, liking what she saw.

Mrs. Peto was quite overcome at seeing the Marquess of Falconer step out of his carriage and walk up to the door. She nearly fell over herself as she received him in the hall. He took care not to take her hand, but bowed slightly and she led him into the immaculate parlor apologizing for the state it was in and for the absence of her husband who had gone to Plymouth.

"Plymouth?" boomed his lordship.

"He is looking for passages for us to return to America."

"Return to America?"

"Why yes, sir." Mrs. Peto curtsied. "We are to escort Miss Cameron home."

The Falcon looked at the ceiling and groaned inwardly. "Is she here?" he said.

"I will fetch her to your lordship this instant."

Mrs. Peto curtsied again and went out of the room backwards, as one who is in the presence of royalty.

Anna had seen the Marquess arrive; but kept him waiting a further fifteen minutes despite the pleas of Mrs. Peto. Then, when she was ready, she slowly made her way downstairs, telling Mrs. Peto she should take care not to listen at the door or his lordship would have her deported to the colonies. Mrs. Peto, who had had every intention of doing just this, fled upstairs to her sitting-room. Who had not heard of the awful power of the Falcon?

Anna Cameron curtsied low and the Falcon bowed. Then he kissed her hand and raised it to his lips.

152

"What is it you want?" he said.

She didn't reply but gazed into his eyes. There was enough laughter in her own to give him hope. "You know I cannot be your mistress," she said. "I cannot permit it. Whatever else other women may do, I am not like them."

"Of course not."

"I have heard of Lady Constance Craven and others. I know they were young, too, even younger than I; but they ruined their reputations irretrievably."

"Lady Constance subsequently married a duke," the Falcon said placatingly.

"Yes, but I believe she had advantages that I have not," Anna raised her eyes to him and fluttered her long black lashes. "Powerful connections, important friends, an aristocratic birth. When one has all these things, little peccadilloes are easily forgiven; indeed they are sometimes expected of those of high birth. For a girl like myself, whatever I may say about my father, it would be ruin. When your lordship tired of me I would be sent home in disgrace. Even in America no man would look at me for all would know of my reputation. I might be married to a woodsman and live in a hut; but no one else would touch me. My father might even disinherit me, for I would bring shame on his name. My sisters are married respectably and well. I would share his fortune with them as we have no brothers.

"What is there for me, Lord Falconer, if I do what you wish? And believe me, I am honored that you should desire me so much." She gave a little curtsey which his lordship found enchanting. He felt his heart would snap in two. He bowed his head and then took his seat in a large chair, spreading his long legs before him. She stood by his side and looked at him. He took her hand and gazed up into her eyes.

"You are quite right, Anna. You are absolutely right. If I had not been so besotted with love, so blinded with desire, I would have seen it for myself, a

153

selfish whim that would ruin you; but I would never tire of you, my darling, never have given you up."

"Ah, you say that now, sir."

"It is true. Have I not courted you for months, with what reward? Only one kiss. Have I not been rebuffed by you, my plans set awry? As you are kind enough to say, I am not without attractions and I know it. Women do not seem to experience difficulty in acceding to my demands. I know not why, but there it is. Only you, Anna; only you have refused me for so long. And I believe you mean it. So, what is it you want?"

"I want to go home, sir; because I cannot stand the torment of this life with you."

The Falcon let go her hand and jumped up. "It torments you, too? You desire me as well?"

"I love you, my lord. Surely you know that "

The Falcon groaned openly and fell to his knees clasping both her hands and kissing them. "Oh, why did you not say it before? Why did you leave me in such misery? Why did you make me think you did not want me?"

"Surely you knew I wanted you, my lord, because I did not refuse your advances, your many, many invitations? Surely you knew what I felt?"

"But how could you love a man like me? As you say, I am so old. I did not dare hope."

Anna put a hand on his head and stroked his brow with her thumb. "To be by the Falcon. Is it possible? But to love the Falcon, yes, that *is* very possible. It is not merely that I am flattered, but I am overwhelmed by your attraction. And if you are as old as my father, that was said in pique. You are a very handsome, attractive man, my lord."

"Then what shall we do? What shall we do?" The Falcon closed his eyes and kissed both her hands, pressing them against his heart.

"I know not what to do, sir. It is not in my power." She lingered on her words and the Falcon opened his eyes and looked up at her. Then he rose, dusted his knees and took her to a sofa where he sat beside her, still holding her hands.

"Power?"

"There is nothing *I* can do, my lord. It is something only you can do about . . . your wife." She gazed at him and she could see the thoughts that flashed through his mind by the expression in his eyes.

"Analee?"

"Well yes, sir, she is your wife. But as long as she remains so, we cannot proceed any further."

The Falcon was silent and Anna's heart sank. She had overplayed her hand.

"Analee," the Falcon said quietly to himself over and over again. "Why did I never think of it?"

"Think of what, sir?"

He looked at her, his eyes very grave, his expression solemn. "Getting rid of her. Isn't that what you mean?"

"Getting rid . . ." For a moment she panicked, thinking of his violent reputation.

"Divorcing her, you idiot girl! Divorce! Aye, I'll divorce Analee and . . ." He put an arm round her waist. "Marry you. *That* is what you want, isn't it? Why didn't I realize it?"

Anna Cameron licked her lips and felt a fresh tremor of fear. "I do not want it; but if you want me . . ."

"It is the only way to have you, you little minx— and, by God, I'll get you!" The Falcon laughed and slapped his thigh. "You want to be a marchioness? Then you shall. I will divorce Analee and we shall be wed. Aye, wedded, and *then* I'll bed you, you little . . ." The Falcon's black eyes turned almost red with desire.

"But first the ring," Anna said. "If you think it can be done. Divorce is, I believe, not very easy, my lord."

"No, it is not easy; but it can be done, especially for someone in my position. It requires an act of Parliament." The Falcon stood and went to the window, rubbing his chin. "I could divorce her on the grounds of adultery, but better of treason . . . *if* I could find out whom she saw in Kent before I sent her north. *If* I knew she consorted with Jacobites. *If* I had proof."

"Treason? Not adultery?"

"Aye, maybe that, too; 'tis harder to prove, but I suspect she went to Lady Goodacre to meet an emissary of Prince Charles. Analee was always thick with those Jacobite rascals. Now if I could find out . . ." he slapped his forehead and came back to the sofa, sitting next to her again.

"You know Lady Goodacre, do you not?"

Anna remembered the lie. Oh, how foolish she was; but then she had not thought that one day she would be within an inch of being a marchioness. "Yes, of course, sir."

"Aye, because 'twas through you that my wife went to see her."

"I only knew *of* her, sir."

"Aye, aye. *Of.* It makes no difference. I will *send* you as my emissary. Ingratiate yourself with Lady Goodacre and find out who this person was. And take care you don't dally with any of the servants there as my last spy did!" Angus threw back his head and laughed but Anna Cameron was not amused.

"My lord, if coarseness comes into this I shall think again."

"Oh, my darling, my angel." Angus threw his arms around her and kissed her cheek. "I cannot *wait* for you to be my marchioness, and make a real gentleman out of me. And I am sure you will. Everything will be very correct and aboveboard in our household."

"Was it not before?" Anna smiled, a quiet mysterious smile.

"Well, it certainly will be now."

"And no straying, my lord, *if* I am your wife. I shall

156

keep a careful eye on you." She gave him a warning look and his heart turned to jelly.

"Oh, my darling, as *if* I would ever need to."

If Anna Cameron felt like a traitor she was careful not to let it trouble her. After all, bringing about a divorce—hardly ever heard of—in order to be a marchioness, was playing for high stakes. One had no longer to think about one's orderly upbringing, one's religious training and code of conduct. Marchionesses in this world were few. There were certainly none in Chesapeake, Maryland, or Baltimore for that matter.

She felt she had changed; that she had risen to a different plane. She had not only captured the love of an important man. He was willing to put off a very beautiful and powerful wife for her. Surely she, Anna Cameron, must be something exceptional to accomplish this? Surely she was rather apart from ordinary mortals, in another realm altogether? She no longer thought as she used to. She *was* different.

The thought of this difference, this new apartness, stayed with her during her journey to Kent; the knowledge, too, that she was going to deceive a woman she didn't know and, possibly, bring danger upon the followers of the Prince she admired. Had she not been brought up as a Jacobite? To detest all things Hanoverian? Ah yes, but that was before she had fallen in love with a Hanoverian general—or rather, not so much fallen in love with him (after all he was so much older and it really was difficult to feel passionately about a father-like figure)—as wished to marry him. And the more she thought about it the more she determined to marry him; to be the Marchioness of Falconer. She decided that nothing, family loyalties or political allegiance, would be allowed to stand in her way.

Lady Goodacre adored company, and what else

could she say to a friend of Lady Falconer's other than how glad she was to see her? She hoped she would stay a few days and explore with her this lovely part of Kent. Anna Cameron was not yet a hardened practiced deceiver and even *she* felt ashamed at the extent of Lady Goodacre's hospitality. She was really only passing through, she said; she couldn't stay long.

At least she agreed to stay the night and over dinner she entertained her ladyship with an account of the developments in Maryland, the fears of war and yet the hopes of getting rid of the French. Annabel Goodacre kept on looking carefully at the beautiful girl opposite her, wondering which side she was on, how much she could be trusted.

"Stewart Allonby is the brother of a nun who is in a convent in France," Lady Goodacre said cautiously, after telling the servants to leave them alone. "In religion she is Sister Mary Gertrude. My own sister Felicity is a nun in the same house. That is how I know the Allonby family . . . and the Delamains."

"And that of course is the connection with Lady Falconer," Anna said, her beautiful turquoise orbs seeming to understand for the first time. "Of course I see it now!"

"I understand Lady Falconer is unwell."

"Alas." Anna Cameron's features suitably composed themselves into an expression of distress. "But I understand she is a prey to ill health."

"Oh?" Lady Goodacre said sipping her wine. "She looked extremely healthy to me. Rumor has it that she is of gypsy stock."

"Oh yes, she is. There is no doubt of that."

"Then I would have thought her very strong."

"I believe it is partly a nervous indisposition."

"Really?" Annabel Goodacre looked unconvinced. "A pity. I liked her so much. She was here in the autumn. I hope she will come again."

Anna Cameron was beginning to feel her visit was

158

pointless, for at that moment her ladyship signaled for the servants to re-enter and all personal conversation ceased. She felt she had not really established a rapport with her hostess and the next day she had said she would go.

But because she was lonely and, a good deal of the time, rather sad, Lady Goodacre enjoyed her wine, especially when she had company. She also enjoyed a glass or two of Madeira or port after dinner and on this evening she threw back the doors that led onto the terrace, her face rather flushed. "I really feel I need air," she said. "See, it is such a lovely evening. So mild for this time of the year. Come, let us take a turn on the terrace."

She turned to Anna Cameron, who thought the evening was distinctly chilly and wrapped her shawl closely around her. However she accepted Lady Goodacre's arm and went with her onto the terrace.

"Oh, the view is marvelous!" she said. "Quite breathtaking. Is that the sea?" She pointed to a ribbon of silver gleaming in the distance ahead of them.

"Yes, it is the Channel and when the weather is clear you can see France."

"Really?" Anna caught her breath and was glad she had come outside. She pulled her shawl more tightly round her, aware of Lady Goodacre's arm closely linked in hers. "I long to go to France."

"You must have friends there?"

"Oh, yes."

"I suppose your family support . . ."

"Of course." Anna gave her arm a comforting squeeze. "Cameron, you know."

"No doubt related to poor Archie Cameron who was executed long after the Rebellion?"

"I think there was a connection," Anna said cautiously, knowing there was not.

"Do you think they will ever return?"

Anna felt she had to be careful. Because she was

here on a secret, devious mission she could not be sure that Lady Goodacre was not devious too. "I don't know."

"But you hope so?"

"Of course."

"And Brent Delamain, would you see him in France?"

"I think he is in America. We saw him in Maryland last year."

"Oh no. He is here."

Anna stopped and a little *frisson* passed along her spine. "Here?"

"Well he *was* here; he is not here now."

"You mean he was *here* . . . at Castle Goodacre?"

"Yes."

"Oh, I wish I could have seen him!" Anna felt her heart skip a beat.

"He was here only very briefly; then he went to France. I don't suppose I should tell you this, but I know you are a friend. He came to see Lady Falconer. But of course you must not tell anyone, never breathe a word."

Suddenly Anna wished she hadn't come; she wished she had said "no" and let the Falcon do his own spying. She wished she were not ensnared by him, not so desirous of becoming a marchioness. She remembered her brother-in-law Stewart, that implacable foe of the Hanoverians, her friendship for Brent . . . what could she tell Lord Falconer now?

"I think we should go in," she said, starting to tremble. "It is getting cold."

"Oh, I do *wish* you would stay on," Lady Goodacre said pressing her arm. "I am so glad you came."

Chapter Ten

Analee saw the small troop of soldiers riding swiftly along the road below her as she walked over Manesty Moor, arm in arm with Nelly, on her way back to the Grange. She stopped and, shielding her eyes against the strong spring sunshine, pointed with her finger.

"I think we are being occupied by the militia, Nell! Or maybe we are at war!"

The two women looked at each other in surmise and began to run down the moorland laughing like girls, their hair flying in the wind. Analee felt that nothing could detract from her happiness now, after these months surrounded by the love of her children and servants in her Lakeland home. Except that she knew the Falcon was alive she never heard from him. He made no communication and sent no instructions. But at last she was content and at peace. She no longer sought to identify her life with his.

They reached the house just as a servant was issuing forth towards the way they had come. When he saw Analee he was already breathless and, stopping, bowed. "My lady, there is an officer to see you."

"To see me?" Analee's hand flew to her breast. "Oh, I hope nothing untoward has happened to the Falcon!"

At the back of the house she could see the men who made up the troop watering their horses and quickly she ran inside, along the passage to the front drawing-room. An officer she did not know stood at attention and saluted her. Then he bowed.

"Lady Falconer, Colonel Middleton, madam, of the garrison station at Carlisle. Your obedient servant, Lady Falconer."

"How do you do, Colonel?" Analee was still panting

from her run and her cheeks were flushed. Colonel Middleton had heard of the legendary beauty of her ladyship, but even he was unprepared for what he saw—her black hair tumbled about her face, her black bewitching eyes gleaming with health and vitality, her enticing chin tilted at a provocative angle. "I hope there is nothing wrong with my husband?"

The Colonel swallowed and lowered his gaze reluctantly from the vision of female beauty to a piece of paper he held in his hand. "No, madam. Lady Falconer," he cleared his throat and his fingers tugged at his tight, stiff collar, "Lady Falconer, I regret, ma'am, that I have orders to apprehend you and convey you to Carlisle Castle."

"Apprehend *me*, sir?"

"For treason, ma'am."

The Colonel's face was as scarlet as his uniform and his collar seemed to have become unbearably tight.

"That is what is writ on this paper, ma'am." The Colonel made a pretence of studying it carefully to hide his embarrassment.

"Treason?" Analee threw back her head and laughed heartily, then good-naturedly pointed to a chair. "Pray, Colonel, do sit down and loosen your collar. I will send for refreshment for you. You will find there is some error."

"There is no error, ma'am, alas, though I confess I do not understand it; but these were my instructions given to me by the governor of the castle himself. And it has the stamp of a very high authority in London."

"The King's I hope," Analee said loftily, "for nothing less will do for me."

"I am sure the governor will show you the document, ma'am. I am come to take you there, Lady Falconer."

"To Carlisle Prison?"

"Yes, ma'am. Those are my instructions and I have no alternative but to obey them. I am sure everything

162

will be sorted out there and your ladyship will soon be restored to your freedom and your estates."

"I see." Analee went over to the bellrope and gave it a sharp tug. When a servant entered she asked him to send Nelly to her quickly and then she turned to the Colonel.

"I must bid farewell to my servants and children, sir, for who knows when I may see them again?"

"Oh, very soon, Lady Falconer, I am sure of that. I daresay there is some muddle that will soon be sorted out. I am distressed to bring you this news, my lady. I . . ."

"Do not distress yourself any further, sir, but enjoy your refreshment. I may bring my maid with me, may I not?"

"Of course, ma'am."

Analee went swiftly from the room greeting Nelly as she approached the door and, taking her upstairs, told her what had happened. Nelly clasped her face in her hands and burst into tears.

"Oh, Analee, how could this be?"

"It is his lordship who is behind it, never fear. This is some devious plan of his to get rid of me. Well, I have good and powerful friends, Nell. I do not believe that they will let this happen. I will demand to be sent to London, to the Tower if need be, and then I can set things happening. Now, Nelly, I want you to come with me because I need you; but I want you to send two messengers. One for Reyora who must come and look after the household in our absence and one to Sir George Delamain who, whatever his faults, will I believe be aghast at this news and will do what he can to help me. Run quick, Nell, and organize this and then hasten back to help me pack my things."

The Governor of Carlisle Castle bent low in the presence of his distinguished prisoner and put the piece of paper in her hands almost supplicatingly. "See for

163

yourself, Lady Falconer. It is signed by the Duke of Newcastle."

And indeed it was, with a mightly flourish, too, as though by someone pleased with his work.

"My husband's close friend," Lady Falconer murmured. "I wager His Majesty would not have put his hand to a document like this."

"It says you are arraigned on a charge of high treason, ma'am, and are to be held here until a trial is arranged."

"I desire to be tried in London where all may hear of it, sir, and not skulking up here out of the way where I may be condemned unheard. Is the dungeon ready, sir?"

"Oh, ma'am, no *dungeon*," the governor said, attempting a nervous laugh. "A suite of rooms has been prepared for your ladyship where you shall have all the comfort you can desire, and what food you order shall be put before you. I assure you, ma'am, I am only doing my duty."

"I am quite certain of that, governor," Analee said bestowing on him the smile that would ensure he would forever be her slave. "I am certain you are."

The Falcon looked pale but triumphant. The deed had been done. He had bullied his pusillanimous friend into signing the document that committed Analee for high treason. All he had to do now was to bring this information to the ears of the King. This was the part he least liked; Analee was a favorite with the old monarch.

Anna Cameron looked pale, too, and not so joyful. She felt that the consequences of accusing and arresting his wife would be far more serious than her swain seemed to think. As she stared at the paper that brought news of Analee's arrest her hand trembled.

"Oh, Angus, do you not think you go too far? Would adultery not have been less serious?"

"Aye, and harder to prove. I do not know she has lain with other men, for sure; but I do know she met the perfidious traitor Brent Delamain at Castle Goodacre and if necessary Lady Goodacre will be prepared to swear it."

"You have asked her?" Anna felt herself blushing, knowing that her treachery was responsible for having brought this about.

"I have told Lord Goodacre what transpired. He was horrified. I said if his wife did not testify against Analee I should have her clapped in irons and committed to prison for treachery too."

Anna thought of the timid, gentle person who had given her hospitality and she blushed even more. The Falcon put an arm round her waist and drew her to him pressing his lips against her cheek. Even though they were betrothed she permitted him no liberties, no intimacies other than a chaste peck on the cheek. He yearned for her more than ever, this delicious nubile person who made herself so inaccessible. What a jewel to be prized!

"There, my love, do not worry your pretty little head. Now I have a surprise for you which I hope will please you. I have in mind to purchase a house for you where you will have your own servants and not the surveillance of that remarkably common Mrs. Peto."

"Oh, Angus. Is it possible?" Anna forgot about her treachery and, clasping his hands, looking into his eyes.

"Of course it is possible! You will be chaperoned by an old friend of mine, Lady McKeith, a lady of the greatest respectability. For all anyone knows it will be her house, for I feel we must maintain the greatest discretion until this difficult time is over. I must appear to be grief-stricken that my wife is apprehended for treason. I shall wear a black band."

The Falcon roared with laughter and poured two glasses of Madeira, one for his darling and one for himself. He carried them over and, putting a glass into

165

her hand, raised the other in a toast. "To us, my dearest."

"To us, Angus." Anna Cameron raised her glass, and only the look in his eyes gave her any confidence or strength to face the future. There were certain things that even a young lady of determination and character from Chesapeake found somewhat daunting.

The Falcon put down his glass and stood with his back to the fire rubbing his hands. It was cold even for April. He gazed at his bride-to-be relishing his power over women, even a woman of such spirit as this. To think he had never sampled the delights of her body. No woman had ever resisted him for so long, certainly not that wanton Analee, who had given her body to him even before her husband was cold in his grave. What a disgusting whore she was! He wrinkled his nose with distaste at the memory, forgetting how he had adored her. As soon as he had his divorce he would set about disinheriting all her children on the grounds that they were bastards. He would breed afresh from the delicious body of Anna and oh, how he would relish doing that! What a girl of spirit and daring she was, what a companion. As he gazed at her an idea came to him and his look changed from simpering adoration to thoughtful calculation.

"I have just thought of something, my dear."

"And what is that, my lord?" She came shyly up to him and stood by his side, an arm timidly stealing about his waist. Even her touch on his thick coat made him tremble.

"If we could get that traitor here to stand trial, *too*, then we would despatch the business all the more quickly."

"Which traitor, Angus?"

"Why, Brent Delamain, my darling. He and Analee together in the dock. Oh, how I should like that!" The Falcon gave a fiendish chuckle, going over to fill his glass with more wine.

"Ah, Angus, can you not leave well alone? Is it not sufficient to have her languishing in jail?"

"Languishing!" Angus gave a short. "My dear, you know not what you say. My wife is not one to languish. Oh, no! She will have her jailers all eating from the palms of her traitorous hands; she will be lying with them each in turn at night, strumpet that she is. Oh, compared to your sublime virtue, my darling, your maidenly chastity, you have no idea what a whore Analee is. That I could permit her to bear my children fills me with nausea." The Falcon passed a hand across his head and closed his eyes as though sickened by the vision.

Anna Cameron gave her betrothed a shrewd look. If chastity was the way to retain the respect of the Falcon perhaps she would do well to remain a virgin forever.

"Now to business." Angus opened his eyes and went briskly to his desk. He sat down and began writing. "I am going to use you again, my treasure."

"In what way, sir?"

"I am going to send you to Paris to seek out Delamain."

"Oh, Angus, I cannot do that," Anna cried in alarm. "I have done enough harm."

Angus turned round and looked at her. "Harm? You silly goose, what harm?"

"I have been . . . very disloyal to a friend already. Have I not done enough?"

"You have not been disloyal, my poppet. You have been very *loyal*. Loyal to our Hanoverian King. You have made yourself worthy to be my Marchioness. When His Majesty hears how we have apprehended the traitors together he will undoubtedly make me a duke and then, my angel, you will become a duchess."

A duchess! Anna closed her eyes and swayed slightly. A duchess. However would they react in Chesapeake to *that*? "What must I do?" she said.

167

Sir George Delamain did not look well. His face was always rather pale, as of one who spends a lot of time poring over figures, but his skin now was positively translucent and he had lost weight. He gazed at Analee piteously and she put a hand on his arm.

"Pray sit down, good Sir George, and I will have a glass of wine sent in to us."

"Thank you, my lady." Sir George sat heavily down in the chair indicated by Analee and passed a hand across his brow. "Believe me, Lady Falconer, this has been a severe shock to my family."

"And mine, Sir George," Analee said, sitting in a chair by his side. From the windows of her suite she had views over the flat countryside, but in the distance she could see, on a good day, the hazy peaks of her beloved Lakeland.

Except for the fact that she was not allowed to leave the precincts, she did not feel contained in any way. She could walk in the pleasant grounds, eat and drink what she liked, see whom she pleased and generally behave like the lady of distinction she was, rather than a common prisoner. The governor was never less than extremely deferential and her letters, the many that she wrote, were uncensored and sent to London by special messenger.

And Analee had not been idle. Her quill had flown swiftly over paper and one of the first letters she had sent had been to the friend and patron who had once offered her a position in her suite—the Princess of Wales. She knew that at the moment it was useless petitioning the King; the influence of Lady Yarmouth would not be in her favor. In fact it was doubtful whether a letter would get to him that Lady Yarmouth had not seen first. Even ministers of the crown had to seek an interview of the monarch through his powerful mistress. But she did write to Lord Bute who, besides being a close friend and ally of Prince Augusta, was an influence on the young Prince George, and who knew how soon he would succeed his grandfather?

"Lady Delamain took to her bed for several days when she first heard the news of your apprehension and incarceration."

"How sorry I am to hear that," Analee said, thankful for her own robust good health. "And you look none too well, Sir George."

"Ah, I have found it a hard winter. I have had many fevers and indispositions and am in a weakened state; and now this news . . ." Sir George blew his nose vigorously in his large handkerchief and Analee perceived that his eyes had filled with tears. "There is of course no *doubt* that Brent did come to Kent?"

"None at all, I'm afraid; but he did not come to plot treason. I think he has hopes of a pardon from the King."

"Oh?" Sir George looked at her with consternation. "Without grounds, I trust?"

"You would not like him back, Sir George? After all, is he not your heir?" Analee looked at him sadly thinking of the irrational force of family feuds; but the brothers had never been close.

"No, I would *not* like him back, Lady Falconer." Sir George thumped the floor with his stick. "He was always a ne'er-do-well. The bulk of my estates and fortune will pass to my daughters, the title and castle to a cousin. I have it all arranged. I never want to set my sights on Brent Delamain again and this latest incident . . ." Sir George wiped his eyes. "What will it do but bring fresh dishonor on my family? Have we not had enough? Must we go through it all again? Did I not speak for Stewart at his trial? Must we go on suffering, we of the family who have always been loyal to His Majesty?"

"I think you owe it to your family and yourself to speak for your brother, Sir George," Analee interjected gently. "I know he wants to give up the life of a wan-

169

derer and settle down. If you could say that your brother had made approaches to you through me for a reconciliation, that would put a completely different complexion on things, would it not? There might never even be a trial. Surely you would wish to avoid *that* scandal, Sir George? A trial in London for high treason? I assure you I will make the biggest splash I can. The trial of Catherine of Aragon before King Henry would pale in comparison to mine."

Looking at her Sir George believed her; but suddenly the dark in his mind was illumined by an unlooked-for, a completely unexpected ray of hope. "There would be *no* trial? No scandal?"

"None. You would go direct to a source near the King—I have one in mind—and say that Lord Falconer is quite mistaken in his suspicions. That Brent wants to make amends and return to England. That he met me for this purpose hoping I could influence his lordship; but I knew it was useless. However I have spoken to you about the matter, and Brent has been in touch with you again . . ."

"But it is all lies, Lady Falconer." That honest baronet looked perplexed and the Marchioness got up and walked with stately splendor, as only she knew how, over to the fireplace. She warmed her long fingers on the flames; she closed her eyes and made a wish— she wished as only she could, willed as only she knew how.

She willed him to do her bidding. She willed it with all her heart.

"It is the *only* way, Sir George, to save your family. You wish that, do you not? I am sure the scandal will kill her ladyship and bring the name of Delamain into infinite disrepute—such that you never suffered before. And I assure you Brent will always be grateful, and so shall I."

He looked into her eyes and knew he had to do as he was bid; he had no alternative. "I will do it, my lady." He bowed his head and suddenly he felt a little better. He did not feel so cold and the arthritic pains left his limbs. He looked at her and smiled. She really was an enchantress, there was no doubt of it at all.

"I knew you would, good Sir George. You are very wise. Now we must send an emissary to Brent, someone we can trust. Someone who will say what is afoot."

"But who can we trust to do such a thing?"

"There is a young girl in London who is very close to the Allonby family. Her name is Anna Cameron. Her brother-in-law is Stewart."

"Miss Cameron? I know of her," Sir George said, avoiding Analee's eyes.

"Of course you know of her. She stopped with the Riggs, did she not? Now if you could see her . . . why pray, what is it, Sir George?" Sir George had gone ashen again and avoided her eyes. "Are you not well? Let me send . . ."

"No, Lady Falconer," Sir George held out his hand as she got up to pull the bellrope. "I had hoped to spare you this."

"Spare me what, Sir George? Speak."

"This Anna Cameron, the one you mentioned, the sister-in-law of . . ."

"Yes, yes, pray go on, sir."

"Rumor has only just reached me, my lady, and rumor it is I assure you, that it is on her account that you are in this jail."

Analee sat down abruptly and tried to compose her features. "*My* account? Pray explain, Sir George."

"It distresses me to say it, Lady Falconer."

"But say it nevertheless."

"It is said, my lady, only rumor mark you, that by bringing this trumped-up charge of treason his lordship wishes to divorce you and put Miss Cameron in your place."

Analee felt her head reel and steadied herself on the arms of her chair. Why had she not known it or

171

guessed it? Why had her powers not told her about this? Were they deserting her? Was she too much a lady and less a gypsy? Why had she put Miss Cameron so firmly out of her mind, hoping she had gone back to America? She remembered those turquoise eyes and she thought they would haunt her for the rest of her life.

"Then it must be Emma," she said without emotion—Sir George was afterwards to relate how uncannily calm she was—"for who else can we trust?"

Emma Fitzgerald, scarcely six months married, listened to her brother with amazement. Fortunately her husband was in Whitehaven and not privy to this extraordinary story.

"But you expect *me* to go to France?"

"There is none other."

"What about yourself?"

"They would never receive me. At least you owe Brent some loyalty, for he helped you."

"But what do I owe Lady Falconer? Nothing."

And then she remembered the spell. But had the spell really worked? It had brought Hugo to ask her to marry him; but it had not brought to their marriage the love and rapture she had hoped for, nay expected. Her husband was a cold lover, an indifferent spouse. He spent most of his time at his bachelor quarters in Whitehaven and buried himself more in his work than ever before. She lived with the Riggs, and went every day to supervise the building of her own home. She hoped that when it was ready Hugo would give her the love she desired and, with it, children. For so far she was barren.

"It is not what you owe or do not owe Lady Falconer, my dear—though, poor woman, I feel sorry enough for her; her husband has some plan to put her away and marry another."

"Oh?" Emma looked at him with interest.

172

"Aye, Anna Cameron has caused any amount of mischief in that household."

"Anna Cameron? You do not mean the sister-in-law of Stewart? The one that stopped here?"

"The very same. The Falcon is enamored of her and desires to divorce his wife and make her his marchioness."

"Anna Cameron," Emma said wonderingly. The sister of the woman she had the greatest cause in the world to hate—Elizabeth Cameron, whom Stewart had preferred to her. "Then perhaps I *do* owe something to Lady Falconer?"

"How is that, Emma?"

"I would not like to help Miss Cameron's advancement one jot. I would do all I can to prevent it."

"Well, that is capital," her brother said, wriggling in his seat uncomfortably. "I had no idea you felt so strongly, especially as you are well and happily married. At least, I trust you are happy?" George looked at her doubtfully. "Are you?"

"Of course I am, dear brother. It is true my husband is excessively devoted to his work and I am often on my own; but I see to the building of our house and I help Sarah with the new baby, and . . ." she gestured lamely, "there is plenty for me to do."

"You know that Hugo has no love for our brother, my dear?"

"Of course I know it. His name is never mentioned here."

"Then how shall you explain your journey?"

Emma looked at him thoughtfully. "I shall have to take Sarah and Ambrose into my confidence. They will think of something. They are the only people we can trust."

But Ambrose was doubtful as to the wisdom of the venture. He picked his nose thoughtfully and then surveyed the contents with interest before popping them into his mouth. His wife grimaced with disgust and

173

looked down at her new infant asleep in her arms—the most beautiful of her children yet. She hoped the last. Oh, how she hoped. She was forty and felt past child-bearing. Someone had told her that if she suckled the baby for a long time she could not conceive while she was doing so. In that case, she felt, she was prepared to suckle it forever. Before, she had employed a wet nurse; but not now. The trouble was that as she grew older her milk seemed to get less plentiful. She sometimes felt the baby did not have enough to eat.

"I have small regard for your brother, as you know," Sarah said to Emma, rocking the baby in her arms. "He has always been irresponsible. 'Twas he who sent you on that perilous journey to America, that ended in such unhappiness. Why should you risk your life for him?"

"I am not risking my life!" Emma expostulated, regretting she had decided to tell the Riggs. Ambrose, after all, thought a great deal of Hugo.

"How do you know you are not?" Sarah said quietly. "Getting involved in spying and plotting. It is neither safe nor wise."

"I agree," Ambrose said, beginning to excavate the other nostril. "Oh, I agree." Then he looked at the frown on Sir George's face and remembered the amount of business they did together. It would not do to annoy the baronet. On the other hand he did not wish to anger those who might advance him in the future. With his entry into civic affairs he hoped one day to join the ranks of the gentry himself, at least as a knight. It was difficult to know what to do.

"It is our family name," Sir George said with an air of desperation. "Emma's as well as mine. Lady Falconer prophesies a scandal the like of which will completely undo our family. She swears that as a peeress she can demand trial in the House of Lords and . . ."

"Oh dear," Ambrose shook his head nervously. "Scandal on that scale . . . oh, dear."

"And I can see her doing it," Emma said.

"And I." The baby burped in its sleep and Sarah rubbed its back. "You will have to go to see Mary," Sarah said after a while, nestling the baby in her arms again. "You can tell your husband that you wished to see her on my behalf. We are anxious about her welfare and I cannot go because I am suckling my baby. You can stay in the convent with her, you will be perfectly safe, *and* she remains on good terms with Brent. She will know where he is to be found."

Ambrose sat back with a sigh of satisfaction. The security of his trade with Sir George was assured. That was really all that mattered—trade and the making of money and, he thought, looking at his latest progeny with satisfaction, the siring of children to whom to pass on his fortune. But perhaps they now had enough. Seven lusty children, four boys and three girls. Besides, he didn't want to wear Sarah out so that she could not bring them up. That was her job now, to look after his home and rear his children. His needs were perfectly well satisfied by a beautiful young mistress he had recently set up in Whitehaven in a little house at the back of the town. She was only twenty-two, the widow of a sailor, grateful for his patronage and experienced in the amorous arts. She was absolutely ideal—clean, wholesome and rather naughty. The sailor had taught her some most interesting ways in bed that he himself had learned in foreign parts.

Ambrose Rigg wriggled in his seat in satisfaction, his mind on carnal delights and the satisfaction of knowing that he led an industrious, successful and most rewarding life. Let others do as they liked, he thought, let others do as they liked.

Sister Mary Gertrude was surprised at the unexpected visit of her brother Stewart's sister-in-law. She had had no word of her coming and was in retreat. The Reverend Mother gave her permission to see her and Sister

Mary Gertrude broke her silence with reluctance as the devotions before Easter were important to her. She was surprised by the beauty of Stewart's sister-in-law and wondered if she resembled her sister Elizabeth. If so her brother was a lucky man; but earthly beauty no longer mattered to Mary. The only beauty now for her was the cross of Christ.

"It is dangerous for you in Paris," Sister Mary Gertrude whispered, gazing at the lovely girl opposite her. "France and England are on the verge of war. Did you not know?"

"Oh, I know," Anna Cameron said. "The French and the English have been openly skirmishing in my country for a long time. Two years ago, in 1754, Colonel Washington was routed by the French at Fort Duquesne and is itching to have his revenge. No, I am not afraid of war."

"But why have you come?"

"Because I wished to see the Allonby family, you, your brother and, if possible, Brent Delamain before I return to America. Stewart will wish to have first-hand news of them. I daren't go back without seeing you all. I shall probably never cross the waters again, but settle down as a good housewife in Chesapeake." Anna Cameron lowered her eyes modestly, not even having the grace to blush, despite the perfidy of lying in this holy place.

"I wonder you have not wed already," Mary said. "You have such beauty; but you must not stay here long. Any enemy of France will be in danger here."

"*I* am no enemy of France!"

"Are you not?" Mary looked at her gravely and smiled. "Good. The English are welcome here so long as they do not support the Hanoverian government. You can come and go safely if you are a Jacobite. Are you one?"

"Yes," Anna whispered, but this time she did blush.

"I thought as much. You would hardly be Stewart's

sister-in-law were you not. You can stay in the convent for a few days while I arrange a meeting for you. John and his family live at Plessy just outside Paris."

"And shall I see Brent?" Anna's voice faltered and she coughed as though from an obstruction in the throat.

"Alas, I do not think so. I do not even know where he is. Somewhere on the Prince's business doubtless. He grew very excited a few months ago when there was the prospect of a French invasion of England."

"I know, the English were in a ferment about it."

"Then, as you know, plans miscarried. Some say the Prince was too timorous."

"Then I shall not see Brent?" Anna could scarcely conceal her disappointment.

"Did you particularly wish to see him?" Mary smiled at her, thinking how attractive this lovely girl would find her former husband. But would he look at her, with his obsessive love for Analee? Hardly. Mary wished that Brent would find someone he could love and settle down with. Maybe Anne Cameron *would* do after all; she was certainly very lovely. Then he could go back to America with her and live in harmony away from the Prince's influence and the proximity of Analee Falconer only a few miles across the water. "It will not be easy; but I think I can arrange it. You will have to be patient. But we have our Lenten services all this week in the convent chapel. You are welcome to share our devotions."

"I should like nothing better," Anna Cameron said, clasping her hands piously and raising her eyes to heaven.

The Good Friday devotions seemed endless, the chanting went on interminably and the beautiful singing of the nuns, though pleasing to the ear, did nothing to ease the feeling of hard wood on delicate knees. Anna Cameron rested her bottom on the bench of the pew behind her and listened to the craving of her stomach. It seemed hours since she had eaten. She glanced at her maid but she was asleep, her chin resting on her hands.

A week had passed and Anna was fretting. The streets were judged so unsafe that the Reverend Mother would not let her go out, even with her maid and a convent servant. Troops were roaming the streets at all hours and no young woman was safe in them unless she had the protection of the veil. Not even soldiers molested nuns—French nuns anyway. It was a different story in foreign countries where they raped and pillaged at will.

Entering the convent chapel Emma saw the beautiful girl immediately and wondered who she was. With her black veil and subdued clothing obviously some postulant come to see if she had a vocation.

Emma was a loyal member of the English Protestant Church and all this popery was offensive to her—the Allonbys and the Delamains had been split in religious matters as much as in political ones, although Emma's mother was a Catholic and her eldest brother Tom had been a monk. Like her brother George, Emma had chosen the Protestant faith. Had she married Stewart Allonby she would gladly have embraced Catholicism; but Hugo, too, was a Protestant and so was Sarah Rigg.

The beautiful girl glanced at Emma standing at the back of the chapel and then she turned her head and pretended to be absorbed in her devotions. Emma could not make out any of the nuns in the choir. She had been told that Sister Mary Gertrude would still be many hours in the chapel during this long Good Friday service. Emma decided to leave her bags at the convent and go straight to her cousin John Allonby. It was vital to find Brent and tell him what had happened to Analee. To try and get him to petition the King and return home.

Emma slipped out of the chapel and gave quick instructions to her maid and the sister porteress at the convent door, together with a message for Sister Mary Gertrude. The hired carriage that had brought her here from Boulogne was waiting outside together with the servants she had engaged. She had been warned not to travel without male protection.

She got into the carriage with her maid and gave directions to the driver, then she leaned back and closed her eyes, the steady jogging of the carriage making her sleep again.

John Allonby stared incredulously at Emma as his wife, Thérèse, led her in through the door of his study.

"You do not recognize me?" she said, smiling and letting her hood fall back.

"My dear Emma . . . of course," John went over to her and took her in his arms. "Of course; but you are a woman, no longer a maid."

"Aye, a married woman." Emma stepped back and gazed at him.

"So I heard." The smile left John's face. "So I heard."

"Doubtless from Brent. He and my husband are old enemies."

"I'm sure it is in the past," John said quickly. " 'Twas all a long time ago. I am sure Brent wishes you every happiness."

"Then he can tell me himself for I have come to speak to him. Do you know where he is?"

John went over to his desk and taking up his long clay pipe filled it slowly with rich Virginian tobacco. He indicated a chair to Emma and smiled at his wife. "Would you bring us coffee, my dear?"

Thérèse gave a little bob and nodded her head, smiling at Emma.

"She speaks no English, alas."

"She seems very nice. I long to see your babies."

179

"You must tell me about Sarah—seven now! Somehow I never saw Sarah the mother of seven."

"I think she will be the mother of twenty if she does not take care! Mr. Rigg is very uxorious, very keen on establishing a dynasty."

John wrinkled his nose and put a spill from the fire to his pipe. "I found it very hard to be fond of my brother-in-law."

"His personal habits are disgusting; but his heart is good. He is a kind man; he sent the money for me to return from America, he did not reproach me for my folly as Sarah did. He gets on well with my husband. I like him."

"Good." John nodded, getting his pipe to draw satisfactorily. "After all, that is the most important thing. You have your priorities right, Emma. I am glad. You must tell me all about . . ."

"In time, John, in time. But I want to hear all about Brent. It is very important that I see him. Please tell me how I can find of him."

"That is very simple," John said. "He is upstairs playing with my children. He arrived here only an hour ago; in Paris only yesterday. He is always very mysterious about his movements. He will be so excited when he knows you are here." John beckoned and, her heart beating with excitement, Emma followed him from the room.

Chapter Eleven

Emma scarcely recognized Brent romping on the floor with his nieces and nephew, laughing, his clothes awry, his hair tousled. She had been so used to seeing him serious and grave in the years of the Rebellion and after, in his years as a refugee. As she opened the door

180

he clutched at three-year-old Hélène who fell on top of him giggling with laughter, and then he gazed at her and she saw that his eyes immediately went to the place he had left his sword.

"No, Brent. 'Tis I." She held out her hands and he took them, using them to lever himself up from the floor. He looked as though he did not know whether to be glad or sorry to see her.

"Emma." He clasped her hands and kissed her cheek; but she could feel no warmth emanating from him. He didn't know whether or not to trust her, so much was clear.

"I come as a friend, Brent, your sister."

His expression relaxed. "Of course, what else, Emma?"

"I know you do not like my husband."

"Ah, but I am not married to him," Brent said lightly. "For which I thank God." He put on his sword belt and, turning, introduced the children to her. There was only a year between them all—Hélène, the eldest, three, Eustace, two and the baby, Marie, still in the arms of her nursemaid who sat on a nearby chair. Emma hugged them all and murmured endearments but they looked at her uncomprehendingly. "They know not a word of English," Brent said.

"Of course not. But you speak French very well."

"I have to pass as a native at times," Brent said, waving to the children as he closed the door behind Emma and himself. "Or I will be killed for an English dog. It is not safe here for you, Emma. Were you stopped on the way?"

"No. My coachman and servants are French. I came by boat to Boulogne and Rigg's agent had arranged for me to hire them there."

"You came *all* the way by boat?"

"Yes, from Whitehaven. Ambrose thought it was quicker. I was very sick!"

"The seas around our coast are treacherous. It is what has kept the English safe—so far anyway."

"So far?"

"The Prince is very hopeful of a successful invasion."

"And you, Brent?"

They had reached John's room and he stood up to greet them as they came in, looking anxiously from one to the other.

"Oh, we are speaking, John. Never fear!" Brent said laughing and putting an arm lightly round his sister's shoulders. "Even though she is married to a traitor."

Emma shook herself away and looked at him furiously. "My husband is no traitor, Brent, but a good and honest businessman. He has no truck with politics now."

"I wish I had not either," Brent said, sitting in a chair and accepting a glass of wine from John. He gazed at Emma and nodded his head. "Aye, truly. I wish I were a free man able to live in England."

"You are no longer loyal to the Prince?" Emma looked at him sharply.

"I am as loyal to him as I can be. That is, I would not betray him; but I cannot trust him. The Prince I loved, for whom our brother gave his life, is not the man he was. No one trusts him anymore. He drinks too much, makes too many enemies and takes too many chances. He is always moving around in disguise—and some think him ridiculous. He was recently seen wearing a false nose like Marshal Saxe! He sent me to England on a fool's scheme and nearly had me arrested; but for Analee I would have been."

"Analee? How came she into that?"

"I knew it was folly for me to risk being seen in London so I came only to Kent and asked her to approach the sister of the Prince's mistress. Clementina Walkinshaw, who he said was loyal to the cause. The sister, Catherine, would have no truck with it at all, or conversation with Analee. She said that her family had completely rejected Clementina. Analee endangered herself even by mentioning it and had it been I, I should have been apprehended and sent to the Tower. Even the Prince's mistress is not loyal to him and old friends like Lady Primrose, Goring and others speak against him loudly. He asked me to be his right-hand man, and when I went to see him in Basle to tell him about Analee's visit he castigated me for not going myself and said *she* was a traitor! He was so drunk he almost threw me out of the house and had it not been for the intervention of Clementina I should have had nowhere to stay.

"I am finished with the Prince. I tell you that."

"I am glad to hear it," Emma said and quietly, quickly told him what she had come for.

For a long time after Brent sat with his head bent on his chest and his eyes closed. After a while Emma perceived that tears were stealing down his cheeks and when he opened his eyes they were red and full of suffering. "She is in jail, for me?"

"Accused of high treason—treason against the monarch and punishable by death."

"I must go to her at once!"

"That is folly, Brent," John said, putting his glass to his lips. "Emma has a plan."

"You are to approach the ambassador here and ask for a pardon. You will swear that you will have no more to do with the Prince and that you wish to return to England. The King is granting clemency to many people now because the throne is so safe."

"But what about the invasion scare at the end of last year? I hear there had been nothing like it for years."

"It died down. Pitt did not believe there would be an invasion and people are listening to his views more and more. Some say he will be asked to form a ministry and run the country."

"He is detested by the King," John said.

183

"No matter. That is what we hear, although in Cumbria we are not exactly at the heart of affairs; but Mr. Rigg is keenly interested in politics and one day hopes to be mayor of Whitehaven."

"Indeed?" Brent tried to look grave, but could hardly keep himself from laughing. "Perhaps they will ask *him* to run the country. I can just see old Rigg at the helm."

"Do not mock him, Brent."

"I do not mock him. I *respect* him. If it were not for your husband I should still be working for him. Anyway I have to see the ambassador. Go on."

"George is going to London, maybe he is there already. He is to see Lord Bute who, he thinks, will be sympathetic to you. Lord Bute is a close friend of Princess Augusta who loves Analee. Everyone in London is aghast at what has happened. They think for Analee's sake the King will listen kindly to you and grant a pardon."

"And what about the powerful Falcon?"

"The Falcon is still powerful, but not as much as he thinks. He is very friendly with Mr. Pitt, who is disliked by the King, and people also disapprove of a liaison he has formed with a young woman. They think he wants to put away Analee and take her for his wife."

Brent shot out of his chair and clasped his sister by the shoulder, staring into her eyes. "Say that again? He wants to marry another?"

"So it is said—to Miss Anna Cameron, who is distantly related to us through marriage."

"*Anna Cameron.*" Brent sat down heavily and took a gulp of his wine. "Miss Anna Cameron of Chesapeake?"

"The same. The Falcon has become infatuated with her."

"Well, she *is* very beautiful," Brent said as though dubious about the whole thing. "But compared to Analee, how could any man desire . . ."

184

"Oh, other men *do* find other women desirable, too, you know, Brent," John said lightly.

"Yes, but the fiend has wed her; she loved him! What greater joy can any man wish for? She has borne him children—oh, would she had borne *me* children." Brent gazed at the ceiling, his hands clasped as though in prayer.

"Your chance of wedding Analee may not be as remote as all that if the Falcon divorces her," John said quietly. "All the more reason to try and legalize your right to be in England, to plead for a pardon."

"I will do it. I will do it," Brent said, jumping up. "Oh, the very thought . . . quick, how soon can I see the ambassador?"

He looked eagerly at Emma who smiled quietly.

"It will not be as simple as that; but plans are afoot. We shall go back to Paris together where there should be a message for me at the convent. Mary was at prayer and I did not see her. Come, I will take you to see Mary and try to discover what news, if any, there is from London."

On the way back to Paris from Plessy, on the outskirts, brother and sister talked as they had not had the chance to for a long time. Emma was more reserved, saying little about her marriage; but Brent, in the presence of so close a relation, let all pour forth—his disillusion, the unsatisfactory nature of his wandering life, his pent-up longings for Analee.

"She has ruined your life," Emma said grimly, staring out of the window.

"Oh no. Since I realized the cause was lost, 'tis the only hope I have had for the future. I knew her marriage with that tyrant would not endure. She was bewitched by him, impressed by his position. If the war had not intervened to part us *I* would have married her . . ."

"And been disinherited by *your* family," Emma said

185

tartly. "You never had anything to offer her, Brent. Lord Falconer had everything."

"She did not want riches or title. I know that. With me she would have had happiness. With him she has had nothing but misery, sadness and abuse. Yes, I would like to go back to England, to get work and become respectable again. *Then* I shall be worthy of Analee."

Brent sat back with a deep sigh of satisfaction; but Emma wondered if he really found self-deception so easy. He had no fortune, and what sort of work could he get? He could not work with Rigg now that Hugo had his place; and even if he could get some work like that, would the Marchioness of Falconer, used to great estates and many servants, settle down to such a life? Would she want to?

"Let us go first to my lodgings," Brent said, sitting up as the carriage entered the narrow streets of Paris clustered with buildings. "Mary may have left a message for me there. I doubt whether we can disturb her devotions before Easter Day is out."

"Mary knew you were here?"

"Yes, I sent a message round yesterday. I am stopping in the house of friends just near the convent. I told her I was going to see John first because I knew she would be at her devotions."

"Mary at least will be glad to see the end of your life as a wanderer."

"Aye. She will have peace at last."

"It is what she wants?" Emma looked at him in the gloom of the carriage.

"Yes. She said she never doubted now that she had a vocation. It was the will of God that our marriage should founder."

"I see." Emma pursed her lips and thought not of the will of God, but of the almost frightening power of the Enchantress. Did she not make Hugo fall in love with her? He told her that he had had a sudden vision

186

of her, Emma, after not thinking of her for years. Then why, *why* was their marriage less than satisfactory, his devotion less than total? She yearned to have a home and a child. Yet although they lay together often enough, when he was home, his lovemaking lacked passion. She always had a feeling of dissatisfaction, of disappointment afterwards. Was this why she did not conceive? She thought again of Analee; the one person who, with her uncanny instincts, would be sure to know.

"Ah, here we are," Brent said, looking out of the window and tapping on the roof for the driver to stop. Emma peered at the narrow grey buildings closely huddled together. It was a poor, mean part of Paris. The streets were filled with rubbish and horse manure, and stray cats and dogs picked among the litter. She held a finger to her nose.

"Aye, it stinks, does it not?" Brent said cheerfully, helping her down. "But a vagabond such as I must lay his head where best he can. Few Jacobites have money to spend on fine houses." Brent took her arm and knocked gently on the door looking to right and left up the street, his hand on his sword. "One must always be prepared," he said. "Newcastle has the Prince followed everywhere; so why not me?"

"Maybe because you are not the Prince," Emma said, and then smiled as the door opened and a timid-looking servant stepped back and bowed the way inside. She spoke rapidly in French to Brent who finally turned with a puzzled frown to Emma.

"There is someone waiting for me upstairs. She did not know whether or not to let her in and then thought she looked such a fine lady that she could not refuse." A sudden light came to Brent's eyes. "A *fine* lady! Maybe it is Analee?" He leapt towards the stairs but Emma restrained him.

"Do not be so hopeful, Brent. Analee is in Carlisle jail. Take care."

187

The smile vanished from Brent's face and he put a hand on his sword. "You had better stay here," he whispered.

"I shall come with you. I doubt a woman would carry a sword."

They went slowly up the stairs and as they did a door at the top opened and a face peeped out. The face looked rather fearful and apprehensive, but still recognizable as the door opened further and the person revealed herself, smiling shyly.

It was the girl Emma had last seen in the convent chapel at her devotions. Emma gave a sigh of relief. " 'Tis an emissary of Mary," she said. "I saw her in the convent chapel."

" 'Tis Anna Cameron," Brent exclaimed, going up to her and taking her hand.

"Do you remember me?" Anna looked past him at Emma.

"Of course I do. Anna, this is my sister, Emma Fitzgerald."

Anna blushed and gave a timid smile. "How do you do. I saw you in the convent."

"And I you." Emma did not smile. "How come you to be here?"

"Sister Mary Gertrude gave me Brent's address. I waited a whole week before she knew it. I have come to bid farewell to him, Mary and John Allonby before I return to America."

"You are returning to America?"

"Yes. I was only here for a visit."

"Come in, come in," Brent said cheerfully. "Do not let us talk in the passage! Ah, good, I see there is a fire lit." He rubbed his hands. " 'Tis cold for spring. Well I am delighted to see you, Miss Cameron, though, I confess, surprised by your news."

"Oh?" Anna paused in the act of divesting herself of her cloak and glanced at him curiously. She was indeed beautiful, Emma thought. She had not met her during

188

her own brief visit to Maryland. She would have been too young to attend the ball where Emma saw Stewart dancing with Elizabeth Cameron. She had hoped she would be plain like her sister, but she was not. No wonder the Falcon was rumored to be enamoured of her. "What news?" Anna continued after a pause, taking the seat Brent held out for her.

"That you are returning to America."

"But why should you be surprised?"

Emma looked at Brent and shook her head in warning; but there was a reckless light in Brent's eyes and he ignored her.

"It is rumored, or so I understand, that Lord Falconer would have you for his second wife."

"Rumors travel quickly, do they not?" Anna said angrily. "It is, I assure you, quite a false and malicious rumor. Lady Falconer is a friend of mine. The fact that she and her husband are at loggerheads has naught to do with me." She shook her head and made to put her cloak round her slim shoulders again. "I see I am not welcome here."

"You are *very* welcome," Brent said placatingly. "Do not misunderstand me, and I apologize if I have believed something false and malicious."

"Nevertheless, I feel I must go," Anna said, standing up. "I do not *feel* welcome. Thank you for receiving me."

"There is no need," Brent tried to bar her way, but Emma spoke quietly from behind.

"Let her go. You know she is lying. Why is she here at all?"

"Because, as I said . . ." Anna was beginning to be afraid. The mission that she had never wanted to embark on was proving a disaster. She did not like the look of implacable hostility in Emma's eyes. Maybe Emma blamed her for the fact that her sister had married the man she once loved.

"I, for one, do not believe your tale," Emma said,

189

gazing at her with dislike. "It is well known that the Falcon has brought this charge against his wife, and Brent, because he is tired of her. The rumor is all over London that you and he are constantly together. I wonder what business you have here when the Falcon is well-known to be desirous of apprehending my brother? You found out where he lived by subterfuge. What is your *true* purpose here, Miss Cameron?"

Anna's face flamed and she wrapped her cloak securely round her, turning her back on Emma, and trod daintily down the stairs. Brent hurried after her.

"Leave her!" Emma commanded, but Brent called back.

"At least I must see her home. The streets are dangerous."

"Then how did she get here? Brent!"

But Anna was by the door downstairs and Brent close behind her.

"Pray forgive my sister, Miss Cameron. I am sure there is an explanation. It is just that we have to be so careful . . ."

Anna glanced back at him scornfully and stepped out onto the road looking to right and left for the escort sent with her by the Falcon. There was no sign of him. Her apprehension returned. She turned to Brent. "Perhaps, if you would. As far as the convent."

"It is no distance. You came with a servant?"

"Yes; but I know not where he is."

Emma stood at the door of the house watching them. It was a quiet street and dark in the late afternoon. No wonder people were frightened to walk abroad.

It was she who saw a tall man detach himself from the shadow of a nearby house and stride quickly after Brent. She started to run up the street and, just as the man closed in on Brent and drew something from his cloak, she screamed.

Brent heard the scream and felt the movement at the

same time. He spun round and saw a dagger coming down at him from a sharp angle. His strong wrist, aided by the quick reflex of one who had been a fugitive for so long, grasped the wrist that held the dagger and with the same movement he took his own short dagger from his belt and drove it into the chest of his attacker. The man gazed at him with an expression of astonishment and then, staggering, fell to the ground without a sound, Brent still clasping his wrist. The dagger that was meant to kill Brent clattered to the ground. A mangy dog with only three legs, which had been inspecting a pile of fetid rubbish, limped up and smelled it. Then, looking disappointed, it limped away again. Brent turned the man on his back and bent to put a hand at the pulse on the side of his neck. "He is dead," he said.

As Anna stared at the face of the attacker a scream rose to her throat, her eyes wide with fear. By this time Emma had reached them.

"Are you all right? Are you all right?" Her hands frantically grasped at Brent's clothing.

"Yes, quite all right. Just. If you had not screamed it would have been a different tale. This rogue was just about to plunge his knife in my back."

Emma looked up. The street remained deserted. Screams were common enough in the streets of Paris without people so much as turning a hair, never mind coming to a door or window to discover what was amiss.

"You must go quickly. Go to the convent and wait there. I will get your things from your lodgings and bring them with me. You must not go back."

"But why not? This was a footpad."

"How do you know? More like an assassin. I saw the way he came from the shadows of the house and strode purposefully after you. He had been awaiting you, Brent. It was you he wanted, not money." She turned and gazed at Anna, whose ashen face was now stained with tears as she stared with helpless fascination at the face of the dead man.

The Falcon, still in his nightshirt, gazed with distress at the stricken woman as she slumped in the chair by the hastily-lit fire. He tried to press some brandy past her lips to stop them chattering.

"I shall call for a doctor," he said anxiously, turning to the servant assisting him. "Go and fet—"

"I need no doctor," Anna Cameron said, looking at him. "I need a priest."

"But, my darling, we cannot be wed until I am divorced."

"I am not talking of marriage, my lord. I am talking of saving my soul. What you have done is to cast me into the depths of perdition."

The Falcon knelt by the side of the chair and put his hands on Anna's cold ones. He nodded briefly to the door and the servant, understanding, bowed. "Leave us now. Now, my darling, tell me what has happened, why you are in this state. Where is Gwyn?"

"Dead." Anna shivered and burst again into uncontrollable sobbing.

"Dead?" The Falcon felt suddenly cold and moved nearer the fire. "You came home alone?"

"All alone, except for my maid. 'Twas a frightful journey."

"Tell me what happened." The Falcon rubbed his cold hands.

"You did not say you wanted to kill Brent Delamain." Anna was stricken by a renewed spasm of sobbing. "You said you had looked for him for years, and I had only to mark the place where he lived. I would not be involved."

" 'Twas true," the Falcon said stoutly, hoping she would believe him.

"Gwyn came after him with a dagger and, were it

192

not for Emma Fitzgerald screaming behind him, Brent would be dead, not Gwyn."

"The fool." The Falcon got up and stared moodily into the fire. "The clumsy, idiotic fool. I thought he knew better."

"Better than what?" Anna's voice grew sharp with renewed terror.

"Than to make a *fracas* in the middle of the street. He was to do it by stealth; certainly not when *you* were there."

"You mean he *was* to kill him?" Anna sat upright in her chair, her body seized by a fresh fit of trembling.

"No, no," the Falcon said hastily, seeing her face. "To bring him here as I said."

"I find it hard to believe you, my lord. I think Gwyn was sent as an assassin and I merely to mark Brent. Like Judas I was to identify him; your henchman to complete the work. Had I known that, my lord, I would never have agreed to assist you in this treachery."

"My little darling," the Falcon said anxiously, putting his arms about her. "I fear for your health. Your mind must be deranged if you think I would do such a thing. I wanted Brent to be tried alongside Analee."

"Then why did Gwyn come after him with a dagger? I saw it myself, a long, ugly thing with a sharp curved blade."

"I should think to frighten him," the Falcon said, inwardly cursing. "He was too inexperienced to have been sent with you. Oh, my darling, please forgive me? *Forgive* me?" He tilted her head and looked into her eyes; but Anna only saw treachery in their dark depths. She longed to believe him; she had already done so much for him. She had betrayed her friends and espoused a cause she despised. What would her father say if he knew?

She shuddered to think. The Falcon enclosed her in

193

his arms; she could feel the heat of his tall, strong body and she leaned her head against it.

She could never go home now. She felt she bore the mark of Judas on her soul.

Lady Yarmouth was very busy indeed; she practically ran the country and at a time of political crisis ministers and potential ministers were forever making their way to the backstairs of St. James's Palace and seeking an interview.

But it was not the Falcon who sought the interview with the most important woman in the country. He was abruptly summoned at short notice and ordered to present himself forthwith.

Even the Falcon dared not disobey.

Lady Yarmouth had always had a soft spot for the Falcon. She admired his combination of manly vigor, cunning, shrewdness and downright aggression. Moreover he had flattered her when she had first come to the country as the King's mistress and many, not realizing the power she was to wield—for the King had had mistresses before—did not pay her sufficient respect. Some were even inclined to laugh at her behind her back. But the Falcon seemed to have perceived that the newly widowed King wanted not so much a mistress as a wife and Amalie Wallmoden seemed very suitable, a queen with the power but without the title. In time she grew very powerful indeed.

The Countess was not yet forty, but she appeared to have aged as the King advanced in years, and she had grown fat. She gazed at him forbiddingly as Lord Falconer was led into her presence, bowing low.

"Pray take a seat, Lord Falconer."

"To what do I owe the honor, Madam?" The Falcon gazed at her, uneasily aware that his chair was lower than hers and that the expression on her face was far from gracious. She was really the only woman of whom he felt just slightly afraid.

The Countess, whose time was at a premium, tapped a document before her. "We have here a petition for clemency, Lord Falconer."

The Falcon noted the royal "we" and bent forward to inspect the document. "Doubtless from my wife, Lady Yarmouth."

"No, *not* your wife, my lord. It is from Mr. Delamain whom you have accused of treason *with* your wife."

"Ah, perfidious rogue!" the Falcon growled. Would that Gwyn's dagger had penetrated his heart as was intended! That bungle had caused no end of trouble, as he knew it would. Anna Cameron was once again making arrangements to return to her native land and the wife of Gwyn Dyffed was making trouble, wanting to know where he was. In truth the Falcon could say he did not know. Probably lying in some pauper's grave in a Parisian burial yard. Bodies unclaimed in Paris streets were not so very uncommon. He didn't have a pang of remorse for the man he had sent to his death; just irritation that the plot had failed.

"He wishes to return to this country, sir. This is a plea to His Majesty for pardon. He renounces the Jacobite cause entirely and begs forgiveness. He says it was for this reason that he met Lady Falconer in Kent."

"Lies, ma'am, all lies," the Falcon blustered, swinging back on his chair and wishing that he were at least on the same level, if not higher than Lady Yarmouth.

"It is supported, sir, by documents I have here." Lady Yarmouth turned to the table at her side. "One is a deposition from Lady Goodacre which confirms this; the other from Sir George Delamain who says that his brother has long importuned him to intercede with the King. It is *this* document, my lord, that has impressed His Majesty most. Sir George has always been devoted to the cause of Hanover, investing time and huge sums

195

of money for arms in support of the King. You do not dispute that, I think."

"Why no, ma'am," the Falcon said sulkily. "Except that the news surprises me. I had thought there was no love lost between the brothers."

"Exactly. That is why it has surprised the King. Sir George has no heir, you know."

"Is he like to die?"

"We pray God that he is not; but it weighs heavily on his mind. The heir to his title is a distant cousin. He has two daughters and we understand Lady Delamain is unlike to conceive again. For this reason Sir George would forgive his brother and entreat the same of the King."

"His Majesty will refuse it, of course," the Falcon said loftily. "Brent Delamain is an unrepentant rogue."

"He seems to be repentant though, sir."

" 'Tis the first I hear of it. He was near hanged just after the Rebellion."

"But *escaped*, sir." The Countess looked strangely at Lord Falconer and he was suddenly visited by an unsettling thought. It was he who, at the behest of his wife, had masterminded the plan for Brent's escape. Supposing this ever came to the ears of the King? Supposing it had come already? Then he, the Falcon, would be tarred with the traitor's brush, too. Maybe he was being warned.

It was a most distressing thought; but, looking into those knowing eyes, that impassive Teutonic face, he did not know the answer. He wriggled uncomfortably in his chair.

"His Majesty, as you know," the Countess sighed, "feels he is coming to the end of his long and illustrious life. He is no longer young. He would leave the throne as strong for his grandson as he can."

"But it *is* very strong, ma'am," the Falcon said indignantly.

"Aye, but can it ever be strong enough? The more

196

who renounce Jacobitism, and are seen to do it, the fewer there will be to plague the new king. This public act of Brent Delamain's, coming when so many others have recently been granted permission to return, will be one more nail in the coffin of that wretched cause."

"So His Majesty is of a mind to grant it?" the Falcon said dejectedly.

"Aye, he is. If not for your sake or that of Mr. Delamain, for that of your wife of whom His Majesty is fond and whom he feels you have sadly abused."

"I, abused?" the Falcon looked at her with surprise.

"Yes, abused, Lord Falconer. His Majesty is very grieved that you should have brought an accusation of treason against her without consulting him . . . or me," her ladyship concluded pointedly. "Lady Falconer is highly thought of at Court. Her virtue and devotion to your lordship—in the face of your lordship's many blatant peccadilloes—are much admired. The Princess of Wales has even made entreaties to us on Lady Falconer's behalf. We have had scores of people approach us to condemn you. In fact, my lord," Lady Yarmouth replaced the papers on the table and folded her hands, looking at him severely, "His Majesty feels that your unpopularity is such that you would be best out of the country."

"Out of the country! Why . . .?" The Falcon half rose from his chair, his face scarlet with rage.

"For your own sake, sir, so that you are not mobbed when Lady Falconer is released."

"I can take care of myself, ma'am." The Falcon bit his lip with chagrin.

"It is *not* to be banishment, my lord," the Countess smiled at him at last with some of her former affection. "His Majesty is very sensible of your many good qualities."

"Gratified, ma'am, I'm sure."

"He values you highly as a diplomat, a soldier, a

197

statesman. He would have you go to the court of King Frederick and consult with him on strategies in the forthcoming war. Since the French signed the Treaty in Versailles with the Russians and Austrians in May, there is no doubt but that there will be a war. Here we are very exercised as to who is to run the country. Newcastle is weak, Fox vacillates too much and the Duke of Devonshire is not sufficiently experienced. We may have to turn to Pitt."

"You could do worse, ma'am."

"I agree with you; but so far the King does *not*. However, Lord Falconer, what say you to this suggestion, which I may say came from the King of Prussia himself?"

The Falcon preened himself and leaned back again in his chair, his legs stretched out before him. "The King was good enough to say he admired my qualities when I was in Potsdam last."

"He thinks *very* highly of them. He would value your counsels and it would be a chance to be out of the way, would it not, for a while? Might not that be a good thing? You have accused your wife of treason on insufficient grounds. You must give her time to recover from the wounds you have caused her. Then maybe when she sees you again she will be in a better frame of mind. I would also advise you to get Miss Cameron out of the way . . . *well* out of the way. After what has happened to Lady Falconer, the King does not approve of *her* at all."

The Falcon looked at her and knew that he was beaten. How could he now say that he wished to divorce Analee and marry Anna? The King would never grant permission, never allow a bill to be laid before Parliament. The Falcon knew he was in a weaker position than he had ever been before. Now he had no wife and the woman he loved would leave him when she heard this news. The King did not even *like* Anna?

198

What chance of her being a duchess now? He groaned inwardly.

Once again the spell of the Enchantress had succeeded.

Chapter Twelve

Brent Delamain, pale and tired from lack of sleep, stood facing his brother. He had not been asked to sit. Sir George leaned heavily on a stick, his frame trembling slightly. Brent was as much shocked by how old and feeble he looked as by what he had to say to him.

"I have done all I can for you, brother, to avoid a scandal . . ."

"I am grateful . . ." Brent began, but George held up a hand.

"I want none of your gratitude. What I did was for the family and not for you. I did not want our name dragged yet again through the mire. Through the goodness of the King you have received a full pardon. He may forgive you, but I never can. I hope not to see your face again before I die."

Sir George staggered and collapsed into a chair. Brent wanted to go over to him, but dared not, besides being frozen into immobility by his brother's words. Sir George breathed heavily and took a sip of water.

"Then what am I to do?" Brent said when his brother had sufficiently recovered to listen to him. "I have no home, no money, no work."

George shrugged. "You have managed before; you must contrive to do so again. I am sure your wits will sustain you; they always have. But pray do not take up with your Jacobite friends again, or the next time it will be the gallows, I myself standing underneath to enjoy your last."

"You sound as though you hate me," Brent said bitterly.

"Well, I have little love for you, I'll confess. I have no reason to feel otherwise. You and our brother Tom, to say nothing of the Allonby cousins, have brought only shame and disgrace on this family. It has been an intolerable burden and has made me a sick man. Oh, do not look so hopeful, I am not like to die yet." Sir George coughed painfully. "Nor for many a long day. I would not have this estate fall into your hands for all the world, not *my* hard-earned money. I hope it will be to your children that it will go and not you. You have done nothing to deserve it. So that is your first duty, Brent—to marry and raise children . . . a son must be sired quickly."

"I have no plans to wed," Brent said quietly.

"Then you'd best make some. If you bring a wife here I may receive her and if you produce an heir I will have him educated at my expense. Henrietta is barren," Sir George paused and looked in front of him as though without seeing. "I had in mind once to divorce her and take another. But I cannot. In my way I love her. I could not do it. I am not such a hard man, am I, Brent?"

"No." Brent looked at his brother and thought how different they were; they looked different and their natures had never been complementary. Theirs had always been a rivalry, a mutual distrust. George always careful, thoughtful, parsimonious—Brent the very opposite, impetuous, careless, generous. "Not as far as others are concerned; but to me, yes."

"Did I not go to the Court and plead for you? Lie for you? Humiliate myself for you? What more did you want me to do? Embrace you?"

"I hoped you might forgive me and take me to your heart."

"Well, I cannot. You are not welcome here. I have thrown you out once before and I do so again. You

200

must pay your respects to our mother, who is aging fast, and then you must go from hence. I daresay Rigg will be able to give you some kind of employment. He is growing very rich. He is a good fellow. Maybe you can lodge with our sister. I hear her house is finished."

"You know I cannot!"

"Because of Hugo? I thought all that was in the past?"

"I detest the fellow!" Brent glowered at his brother who got slowly to his feet and came over to him until he was within an inch or two of his face. Then he grasped the lapel of his coat and shook him.

"It is time you dropped these likes and dislikes, my good man. You are over thirty years of age and have not a penny to your name. It will take you a lifetime to restore yourself with society—to repay your country for the harm you have done."

Sir George let go his lapel and staggered back, his face working with emotion. He raised a trembling hand and shook his finger at his brother. "And take care to keep away from that woman, that witch who has brought so much disaster in her wake. You know who I mean, don't you? You *know*?"

Brent nodded his head and his heart began to beat more quickly. He knew, but he said nothing.

Morella gazed with interest at the uncle she had never seen. She sat with a docility unusual for her, her hands gripping the edge of her chair. She had on her best dress with a long bow hanging down the front and her fair, almost white hair was carefully arranged in neat ringlets which clustered at the base of her neck. Her clear cornflower-blue eyes looked out at him unsmilingly; but she did not trouble to conceal her admiration. This tall, blond, good-looking man was so unlike Uncle George with his choleric temper and his meanmindedness.

Looking at them, comparing them, Brent's mother

201

was sure her suspicions were right. Years ago, before the Rebellion, her son was rumored to have become hopelessly enamored of a gypsy—and Morella was a gypsy's child. Yet what gypsy would acknowledge that white skin, that straw-colored hair, those very deep blue eyes? Besides, there was so much of Brent in Morella—she was impulsive, carefree and warm-hearted. She made friends easily and people loved her; she was a madcap, always courting trouble. How like the young Brent who had grown up in this very castle. How unlike his brother George. She had no proof and she dared not ask; but, putting two and two together, she had long ago reached the opinion that Morella was the daughter of her son and Lady Falconer, erstwhile gypsy; that Morella was her granddaughter, her very own blood.

Susan sighed sadly as she looked at the son she had not seen for over ten years. The weeping was over; just to know that he was safe and at home was enough, though there was still a long way to go . . . a very long way to go, it seemed.

"Then you must live here."

"I cannot, Mother. My only hope really is with Rigg. I am sure he will give me a job on one of his boats. I do not necessarily want my old position. Hugo has that! I am a good sailor, an expert fisherman."

"Oh, Brent, you will not be tempted to . . ." His mother looked at him anxiously, glancing at Morella. "My dear, will you leave us for a moment and go and play? I want to talk privately with Uncle Brent."

"I want to hear," Morella said in her clear voice.

"But you can't."

"But I can!" Morella's eyes sparkled and she banged her fists on her lap.

Mrs. Delamain stood up and gently took hold of the child, propelling her towards the door and giving her a playful slap on her little behind. "Now off you go and do as you are told."

202

Brent watched her, laughing; he leaned against the window with his arms folded. "She is a scamp. She is the gypsy child I sent you?"

"Yes, all those years ago." His mother looked at him solemnly. "You remember it?"

"Aye, very well." Brent scratched the back of his head. "I was riding along after the skirmish at Clifton and all our men were in disarray. Then a gypsy troupe came along, and a woman carrying the sick baby. I told her to seek you out and you would give her refuge. She made me a promise that has sustained me through my life."

"And it is?"

"She said I would endure much suffering but that in the end all would be well. I would have my heart's desire."

"And what is your heart's desire, Brent?" His mother dropped her voice and looked searchingly at him.

"I cannot tell you, Mother; not yet. But when I have it, I shall; and that day will come. It will."

"I hope it will, my son, for you." His mother bowed her head and sat heavily in a chair. "Oh, I hope so; you have endured so much and now you have humiliated yourself by begging the Hanoverian King for pardon."

He looked up at the bitterness in her voice and came over to her, squatting by her side. "You are angry with me, Mother? You think I should not have done?"

"I am not angry with you; I know the circumstances. I am sorry it had to happen, that is all. All my life I have hoped for the return of the Stuarts. Your father and I were exiled for years for the cause and he died a broken man because of it."

"Would you have had *me* die in exile, Mother? Would it have been better?"

"I don't know," Susan said brokenly. "I really don't know. But what I was going to say to you before I sent

Morella out, was to beg you not to jeopardize your life again. Leave the Stuart cause to others. Is there, do you think, any hope?"

He took her hand and brought it to his lips. "Mother, in your day there was still hope. The Hanoverians were newly on the throne. There was King James with his two lusty sons and everyone full of hope. But now there is none, Mother. The Prince is unfit to be a King; *he* has lost the loyalty of all who loved him in a way his old father never has. The King in Rome is still our King; but he is the last of the line. All our people are bitter and in disarray, Mother; there was even an attempt to have me assassinated in Paris."

"By one of *your* people?"

"Who else? I was staying at a Jacobite house. No one else knew I was there. The Prince felt I had failed him in England and tried to throw me out of his house. It is my suspicion that he then sent someone to try and kill me with a dagger. 'Twas Emma saved me."

"Oh! She never told me!" His mother put her hands to her face.

"She would not want to worry you; but that is what made me decide to ask for pardon. I could trust no one, Mother. I knew not where to turn."

"I understand, Brent," his mother said slowly. "Now I do understand why you came home. I did not know things had come to such a pass."

"It was not easy for me to recant, Mother; to sign the paper and swear the oath of loyalty to King George. I shed bitter tears; but I had no option."

"I know you didn't," his mother said, "and thank God you are safe. But where will you go if you will not stay here?"

"I am going to see Rigg. George thinks he will give me work. I will do all I can to make my fortune, Mother, and to bring you happiness. You have suffered so much for all of us."

"But you have suffered, too. George hopes you will

marry and provide . . . an heir." His mother turned away with embarrassment and he saw her lips tremble. "There is a lot I do not know, Brent, about the past; but some of it I have guessed. I hope you will be able to make a new life and do as George bids?"

But Brent's heart was too full to answer. Analee, his precious Analee, was only a few miles away resting at her home in Lakeland after her release from Carlisle Castle with a full apology from the King on the part of her husband, now disgraced and sent abroad.

"I shall be happy one day, Mother," he said at last. "And you will be happy, too."

Lady McKeith had seen better days, both with regard to her face and to her fortune. The passage of time had not been kind to her once-fabled beauty, and her considerable fortune had been gambled and frittered away by her husband Sir Keith McKeith. What little was left had gone to the coffers of the Young Pretender whom Sir Keith followed to France, after the failure of the Rebellion, together with his unwilling lady.

As fond of the bottle as his master the Prince, Sir Keith had succumbed to its effects sooner, not being such a young man, and was laid to rest in the soil of France. Lady McKeith promptly abjured her husband's views and, obtaining a pardon, returned to England, one of the first to do so. She had always been an indifferent supporter of the Jacobites because early on she had seen quite clearly what others had merely sensed: that they would lose.

Isobel McKeith cared too much about fun and fashion to be on the losing side. For a time, when the Prince had appeared to be winning, she had worn the white cockade and even danced with him at a ball in Edinburgh; but after the retreat from Derby she knew quite well which way the wind would blow. She followed her spouse reluctantly into exile, and came joyfully home again after his death. She was still young and a very merry widow indeed. One of the first to help her warm her lonely bed had been the Marquess of Falconer and from time to time he had returned to it until he met the latest object of his desires, a woman with whom he had fallen head over heels in love, for whom he had risked disgrace and finally exile—Anna Cameron.

Shortly after his interview with Lady Yarmouth in the spring, the Falcon had received his orders to proceed to Potsdam or Berlin, wherever King Frederick should be found. He was not to take leave of Lady Falconer who, understandably, was not anxious to receive him, and he was to arrange for the passage of Miss Cameron to her home in America forthwith. He was not even allowed to take leave of the King. It was indeed a kind of exile.

The Falcon did everything he was bid, except for one thing. Under the guise of leaving for America, Anna Cameron left instead for the continent of Europe where, in the company of Lady McKeith, she traveled from one capital to another, doing a kind of grand tour until such time as the Falcon should send for her.

Lady McKeith found it hard to credit that Miss Cameron had so far resisted the considerable charms of the Falcon and that her virtue remained intact. But his lordship assured her it did and that he would be the first, the only man to break it. Until such time, Lady McKeith was paid a comfortable sum to entertain Miss Cameron and keep a very firm eye on her. Lady McKeith did not find this a difficult task: her charge appeared immune to the attention of other men. She neither flirted with them or even smiled very much. Lady McKeith did not know that Anna Cameron still felt the mark of Judas on her soul—that, but for the merest accident, Brent Delamain would be dead and she responsible.

In August 1756 King Frederick invaded Saxony on the advice of the Falcon, who was anxious to see battle. It was put about that the Austrians were preparing to mobilize against him anyway, so he decided to strike first. By October the Saxons had surrendered and their troops had been incorporated into the Prussian army. The victory of Frederick made up for the loss to Britain of Minorca the previous spring and the humiliating disarray of her government.

Under the terms of the Treaty of Versailles, France was obliged to provide Austria with troops if she was attacked, which she did. She also decided to invade Hanover and began assembling an army preparatory to the commencement of operations the following spring.

Lord Falconer threw himself with vigor into the preparations for war; he was the main liaison with the British Ambassador to Berlin, Sir Andrew Mitchell, and it was also through this old friend of his that he managed to send messages to his beloved, hoping for the time when she would be able to join him. Knowing that, by the spring Europe would probably be into a full and bloody war, the Falcon felt he had not much time in which to make her his. But though he was an expert military strategist he could not find a way to unburden himself of his wife; everything he had tried had failed. For a while he thought of having her murdered; but something like that was too risky. The finger of suspicion would immediately be pointed at him, and the way that the attempt on the life of Brent Delamain had been bungled gave him fair warning of what to expect when something delicate was undertaken by one of his underlings. It was a chance he could not take.

Gloomily, the Falcon, when he had time from momentous affairs, pondered the future. The war would be a long and bitter one, of that he was sure. Maybe he could go to India or America and not to return England for years. In that case who would know?

The plan that he finally made was risky; but the Falcon was a man who thrived on risks . . . and, besides, for a few years, months or even days, of delight, was it not worth it?

He sent a message to Lady McKeith, temporarily lodged in Geneva with her charge. One day she came flying into Anna's bedroom waving the paper.

"Oh, it has come, Anna, it has come."

Anna, who was penning a letter to her mother, jumped up from her desk. "What has come, Isobel?"

"The divorce! His lordship has just written. The divorce is made final. He is free to marry. Oh, Anna, I am so happy for you."

She threw her arms round Anna and hugged her. She hugged her tightly and tenderly because she had become fond of her and was sorry for her part in his deception; but how could she disagree with the Falcon? Besides, he kept her alive and in the style to which she was accustomed. She was privy to his plans and he paid her well to keep Anna circulating far away from people who might know more about what was going on in London, who might know that the Marquess and his Marchioness were as wedded as they had ever been, in the eyes of both the law and the church.

"He said he would do it!" Anna gasped, looking at the letter the Falcon had written. The one with the fuller explanation was carefully locked away. "Oh, I did not believe he could do it. Did you?"

"I believe the Falcon can do anything," Lady McKeith said diplomatically, thinking how much had been hidden from the poor girl; she had seldom known such a victim of deception.

"But Lady Falconer *agreeing* to the divorce—and so quickly."

" 'Twas she asked for it, I believe," Lady McKeith said, lies springing as naturally to her lips, due to her many years of political intrigue, as to her paymaster's. "To be accused of treachery was the final straw. Quick now, we must pack. The Falcon awaits us in Berlin."

Anna ran to the wardrobe of the hotel where they

had been staying and flung her clothes on the bed. "Oh, send me my maid quickly, Isobel. I cannot believe I shall soon be a marchioness."

Action suited his lordship. Although there was as yet no English troops engaged in hostilities he had managed a skirmish or two against the Saxons. His only dread was that the Duke of Cumberland would be sent out in command of the Hanoverians and his bigamy would be discovered. There were few English in Berlin. His beloved would be effectively cut off from sources of gossip. Yes, it was worth it. She was lovelier than ever. As his eyes alighted on her he trembled at the thought that he would soon hold her in his arms.

Anna's first glimpse of the Falcon in his magnificent uniform made her feel shy. She had not seen him for over six months, his letters were cursory, few and far between. He was not a man used to pouring out his heart on paper. Lady McKeith discreetly left them alone and for a moment they gazed at each other. Then he went swiftly over to her and folded her in his arms.

"Oh, my beloved." She was trembling. He lifted her chin and looked into her turquoise eyes brimming now with tears. "Why, darling, are you not happy?"

"Terribly, terribly happy," Anna brushed her eyes and tried to smile but her chin still trembled. "I cannot believe it. 'Twas so easy."

"Oh, 'twas not *easy*," the Falcon said, mentally banishing his own misgivings. "But the King was anxious to please me."

"Does he know that we are to be wed?"

The Falcon held her away from him and looked at her gravely. "Oh no, my dear, and nor must anyone for the time being."

"But why if . . ." A shadow had fallen over her face and he quickly kissed her cheek.

"It would not be seemly. You understand, when the

209

divorce is only just granted, it would not help my reputation to marry again in such haste."

"Then we have to wait?"

"Oh no, my dearest . . . What! do I see desire in your chaste eyes, you saucy girl? No, no, we can marry at once, but we must be discreet. You see that, don't you?"

Anna Cameron looked over his shoulder and the expression on her face relaxed. It was not lust he had seen in her eyes—far from it. He had been mistaken for thinking the desire in her eyes was for his embraces. It was simply her longing to be made respectable after all these months of doubt and waiting; to be a marchioness and secure in the strength of his name.

Lady McKeith sobbed all during the short ceremony performed, in a room of the house the Falcon had rented in Berlin, by a Protestant minister who had not been alerted as to the circumstances of the marriage. If he had his suspicions he kept them to himself. He was receiving a most generous fee and a case of brandy to boot. Besides, he neither spoke nor understood a word of English and what papers he was offered were passed by him unread.

The Falcon looked nervous and kept on glancing over his shoulder as though at any moment he expected the door to fly open and his wife to appear on a broomstick. But if Analee divined his intentions she gave no sign. He was well and truly, if bigamously, married. There was now nothing to prevent him claiming his prize.

Anna was the most calm of those present; besides herself there was her groom and the parson, Lady McKeith and two members of her husband's entourage. She felt serene in the knowledge that she had attained her goal—the goal for which she had lied, cheated, betrayed and nearly murdered.

She was now a marchioness. When they were pronounced man and wife she gave the Falcon a brilliant smile of gratitude. He misinterpreted its meaning and his loins burned with renewed desire.

The new Marchioness of Falconer lay nervously in bed. The time had come. She tried to calm her misgivings by thinking that her virginity was no sacrifice; she had kept it long enough, and for good reason. It had not been difficult. She had never experienced the slightest desire to divest herself of it. Lady McKeith, who had helped her change from her wedding clothes into night attire, murmured a few words but received no answer. She was surprised by the state of the young woman's ignorance. However, it was no concern of hers. The Falcon was quite used to this situation, he would know what he was about. She thought rather wistfully of the times he used to take advantage of her favors, and went sadly to her lonely bed.

The door from the adjoining room opened and the Falcon, magnificently attired in a crisp white nightshirt and an embroidered gown, entered. Anna sat up in bed with her hair brushed back; he could see the swell of her breasts beneath her lawn chemise. He took a deep breath and went up to the bed. Anna raised her lovely eyes and looked trustfully at him. He sat on the bed and leaned over towards her, gently brushing her lips. They were cold and did not give easily under his pressure. He tried to insert his tongue between them but they did not yield. He straightened up and looked at her. "Would you like some wine, my darling, to relax you a little?"

"I am quite relaxed, my lord," she said nervously. "I had plenty of wine at supper. It has made me sleepy."

A doubt came into the Falcon's mind but he put it aside. He would have hoped that, after all these months, she would have been a trifle more willing even if her desire was, understandably, not equal to his. He took her in his arms again and crushed his mouth more

211

firmly against hers. She still didn't yield but remained wooden and upright; her mouth tight shut, cold as ice.

He put a hand down her bodice and tried to fondle a breast. She began to struggle and he sat up again. "What is it, my beloved? I have come to love you. You must not resist me. I am your husband."

"Could we not wait until morning?" Anna gave a yawn. "I am so tired. The excitement of the day, the wine . . ."

A red cloud came over the Falcon's eyes, momentarily obscuring his vision of the beloved. His heart throbbed so painfully that he felt short of breath. The sight of her loveliness, her bewitching mouth, her enticing breasts . . . He leaned down and, seizing the sheets, threw them back.

Anna immediately curled up and put one hand protectively across her bosom, the other at her groin even though it was fully covered by her night attire. Her youthful form made him sick with desire; he could just see her trim bare ankle beneath her chemise. Anna looked frightened and a lock of her red hair fell over her face.

The Falcon delicately touched an ankle and let his hand slowly travel up her leg. "My darling, do not tremble. Anna, I am your husband. I want you. I need you so much."

"Could we not wait until morning?"

He slowly eased her chemise up her legs, resisting her attempts to lower it again. He made soothing noises and then leaned over to nuzzle her cheeks, his tongue gently trying to prise open the aperture of her lips. Surely she must at least *begin* to experience some desire now? He grasped her thighs and eased his hand into her groin, trying to part her tightly-closed legs.

Anna gave a little cry and started to struggle once more, resisting him. The Falcon inserted his hand more firmly, the other clasping her behind the back, his lips pressing on hers. But everything remained tight. The legs, the lips; her whole person was barricaded against him. He felt a wetness on her cheeks and reluctantly raised his head.

His bride was weeping. He took his hand away and pulled down her chemise. Then he got off the bed and went and poured himself some wine from the cooler by the side of the bed. If she did not need a drink, he did. When he turned round she had drawn up the sheets over her shoulders and was pretending to sleep. The Falcon gave a deep sigh and went and stood by the fire, warming himself as he slowly sipped the wine, wondering what to do. The cold in the room was causing his desire to ebb. Perhaps he should get into bed and snuggle up against her? He would at least be warmer?

He finished his wine and removed his gown. He then went to his side of the great bed and slipped under the sheets. Anna moved as far away from him as she could, her back towards him. She was curled up in an attitude of self-protection, as though against attack.

Angus lay for a while and stared at the ceiling. This was very different from his last wedding night. He thought of Analee and her wicked wanton ways. He thought of her lovely luscious body and her beguiling black eyes; of how her lips moved and how she arched herself abandonedly in the act of love, imprisoning him with her knees. He tried to put away the image and replace it with that of Anna. It was very difficult.

He put out a hand and touched Anna's back; he felt her recoil. He edged up to her until he could feel the warmth of her body. He put a hand gently on her shoulder. "My beloved, let me lie against you and warm myself?"

"I am *very* sleepy."

"If I let you sleep, will you love me a little in the morning?"

"Yes."

He lay silently beside her, feeling her trembling. He

blew out the candle and moved away from her. The trembling ceased and her breathing became deep and regular. She was certainly exhausted, but he had never had such failure with a virgin. By the time he reached the supreme moment, usually they were eager to yield. His technique was legendary. His stiff and frustrated member gradually subsided and he turned on his side and fell into a fretful sleep.

When he awoke the bed was empty. He sat up and adjusted his eyes to the gloom. He could hear the birds singing and knew it was dawn. With a curse he leapt out of bed and looked for his robe. It was bitterly cold. He found a tinder and lit the candle and went over to stoke the fire. His bride sat huddled in a chair, fast asleep. She looked so pale and pathetic that his heart went out to her. The tears were hardly dry on her cheeks. The Falcon put down the candle and knelt beside her. She opened her eyes and stared at him.

"You look scared half to death."

"I did not know it would be like this."

"But I did *nothing*. My darling, it is the most deli-. cious . . ."

"But I *am* frightened."

He took her hand and kissed it, holding it to his face. "Anna, you have to know some day. 'Tis the lot of women."

"I know; but must it be yet?"

"Well, when can it be then?"

"When I am ready." She started to shiver.

"My darling, you will freeze to death before you lose your maidenhead. Come, let me take you to bed."

"Oh no, please!" She curled herself up in the chair like a very frightened little girl.

The Falcon got up and, bending down, put one hand under her knees, the other firmly round her neck. She gave a little cry and started to kick, but he carried her to the bed and gently laid her down. "There." He covered her with the bedclothes and looked at her. "Now I

214

will get in with you and lie with you, just to keep you warm."

"Only that?"

"Yes."

Angus took off his robe, blew out the candle and climbed into bed beside his beloved. It was almost daylight. Anna was as near the far edge of the bed as she could get, but he moved over towards her, his arm encircling her. She put a hand on it and tried to move it away. He held on to her more firmly and then moved his body up against hers, molding himself to her, his groin pressing into her buttocks. He cupped her breast through her chemise and played with the nipple; it remained soft and flat. She had no desire for him. She seemed to have no desire at all.

He kissed her ear and moved his face over hers. She tried to turn it into the bed. The Falcon felt he would burst. He had never had such a recalcitrant female, never mind one to whom he was supposed to be married. He had a right. How long would she expect him to be patient? It could last for days, weeks.

The Falcon threw back the clothes and got out of bed. He went over to the fire and tried to rekindle it with the tinder with which he had lit the candle. He was not used to this menial work and he was not very good at it; but at last he managed it. Then he went to the washbasin and washed his hands in the freezing cold water. He poured himself more wine, left over from the night before, and drank it at a gulp. Then he went and stood by Anna. She was gazing at him with one eye, the other shut. He suddenly reached for the hem of his nightshirt and, in one movement, pulled it off. Anna shut both eyes and her mouth opened to scream. The Falcon swiftly threw back the bedclothes and jerked her chemise over her hips, exposing the beautiful thighs he had never seen, her delicious mound covered quite thickly with red-gold hair. He stared lustfully at it, his desire knowing no bounds, and as she

215

began to scream he put a large hand over her mouth, and with the other he roughly prised open her legs.

Then he positioned himself on her and thrust himself into her, her legs knocked wide apart by the force and size of his body. She struggled and squirmed, trying to call out, and he knew he hurt her a great deal. Then, as she lay limp, he positioned himself the length of her body and, with a cry of relief, poured his essence straight inside her. He lay on her with his heart pounding, aware of her inert, slim young body beneath his heavy frame.

"I didn't mean to do it this way," he said at last, gazing at her, feeling slightly abashed now that it was over and the desire was spent. She didn't reply and her eyes were closed, her face as white as the sheets. He gently eased himself out of her and the place where he had entered was like a wound, red with blood. He had been very savage and harsh and he felt ashamed. He had never defiled anyone against their will; it had never been necessary.

He would spare her more shame and let Lady McKeith attend her. He drew down her chemise and covered her gently with the bedclothes. Then he pulled on his nightshirt, put on his robe and sat beside her his hand on her shoulder. "It is over now. It will never be like that again. Your maidenhead is pierced. I'm sorry, Anna. I have desired you for so long. I could not contain myself. I'm truly sorry."

He gazed at her face, but her lids remained shut though he could see her eyes moving rapidly beneath them. The color was returning to her face. He leaned down and kissed her cheek, patting her shoulder, once again feeling inadequate.

Then he went slowly and quietly out of the room.

The Falcon had appointments all day. There was a lot to be done in the winter to prepare for the war in the spring. He wished his mind could linger happily on his

216

bride, but it could not. Every time he thought of her he felt deeply ashamed. She was not even his bride, his wife. He had wished to deflower her sweetly, to make it an occasion to remember. She would certainly never forget it.

He bought her a jewel; but he knew he delayed going home and was late. Lady McKeith received him with reserve and glanced at him reproachfully.

"Is she all right?" he whispered in the hall.

"She had a terrible shock."

"I tried to do it gently. She would not let me."

"You should have left her a while to get used to the feel of a man beside her in bed. It is a strange experience for a maid."

"But she is twenty-three!"

"It does not make it any easier being older. You should have been more gentle. You owed it to her to be more patient. I am surprised at you, my lord."

"Is she in bed yet?"

"No, she awaits you in the drawing-room. I have talked to her gently all day, explaining to her the ways of men. I *think* she will be more compliant; but take care to be gentle with her, sir. She is very sore in that particular place your lordship ruptured with such violence."

The Falcon lowered his eyes and fingered the box with the jewel in his pocket.

"If you could not have restrained yourself last night, if your need was so urgent you should have waited until she slept and come to me. I would have accommodated you quite willingly." She glanced at him archly.

The Falcon raised his eyes to the ceiling and then looked at her. "I didn't know you could have a surrogate bride on a wedding night. But it may come to that yet." He patted her arm and went upstairs to the drawing-room.

Anna had taken a lot of care with her appearance and greeted her lord with a brave smile, her lower lip

217

trembling. The Falcon went over to her and pressed the box into her hand. Then he kissed her cheek. "Am I forgiven?"

"I was very ignorant. I did not know what to do."

"I should have had Lady McKeith instruct you in the absence of your mama."

"She tried, but I would not listen. I couldn't believe it when it happened."

"The trouble is you *seem* so grown-up, so assured. 'Twas hard to believe you were not." He kissed her cheek and she trembled. During the meal, which was served à *deux*, he talked about the day he had had and the war that was to come.

"Oh, I *wish* we could go back to England," she said, "that the war could be averted!"

"My dear, we shall not be able to go back to England for a long time. I have much to do here."

"But we can't stay forever on the continent. I wish to be properly presented at Court as your Marchioness."

The Falcon poured some wine into her glass with a hand that shook slightly. "We shall have to be patient, my dear."

Despite her determination to be different, Anna felt herself tremble involuntarily as her spouse got into bed beside her. Lady McKeith had spoken to her with great tact but great frankness for the best part of the day. The more she relaxed in her husband's arms the more pleasant it would be, she was told. She should respond to his advances in order to enjoy herself. But when she felt the Falcon reach for her, inwardly she shrank into herself and put her legs, with that sore place in between, tightly together.

"I will only embrace you and kiss you tonight, my darling," the Falcon murmured, "so that the tear I made can heal. It is quite natural and will soon be better. I promise you, you will love this act like most women do. In time. In time."

Still the bed continued to shake beneath her.

The Falcon tried again. "See, if I caress your breast it will give you pleasure, like this." The Falcon eased his forefinger over her bare nipple but he could feel the gooseflesh of her cold skin. She was as cold as a corpse, as taut as the string of a bow. After some more attempts he gave up and turned his back on her, lying with his eyes open until he heard the long, slow regular breathing of sleep.

Then, when he was sure she would not wake, he crept out of bed and went quietly along the corridor, knocking gently at the door of Lady McKeith.

Her bed was warm and enticing, snug and inviting. Her body pliant and sweet-smelling. She encircled him with her arms and drew his body hungrily against hers. "I knew you would come," she said. "I don't think Miss Cameron is made for love."

"Never?" The Falcon looked at her with anguish, rubbing his suffering loins against her eager, receptive thighs.

"I have the feeling that she does not take kindly to the art and never will."

The Falcon groaned and buried his head in the rounded, ample, willing bosom of Isobel McKeith.

"If you had asked me before I would have told you."

"Why did you not say?"

"Would you have listened? I never saw or heard a man so besotted with love."

"No, I would not have listened. I could not believe it. She is so nubile, so beautiful."

"Alas, beauty of form is not always accompanied by a passionate nature. Beauty is deceptive," Isobel said, accommodating him between her thighs, welcoming the delight of his presence again. How foolish the girl was when she could have him every night! "I knew at a glance she was cold. How could she have refused *you* for all this time; for you attempted before, of course, did you not?"

219

"Of course. She resisted me most virtuously. She wanted marriage. It made her only more desirable to me. I never dreamt of this. Who would?"

"Men are fools," Isobel thought but she did not say it. Unlike Miss Anna Cameron, she could never get enough of the attentions of a man and was grateful for them when she did.

Chapter Thirteen

Analee found that the bruise to her soul caused by the perfidy of her husband took longer to heal than any physical wound. Despite the apology from the King himself, despite the many letters of support and sympathy from friends, despite the knowledge that she was respected and loved on a scale she never dreamed possible, it was still the knowledge that her husband had wanted to destroy her that seemed so hard to bear.

For many weeks after her release from Carlisle she was languid and depressed. She found that even her beautiful Lakeland home in the spring and summer, and the presence of those who loved her, were insufficient to lift it.

But in time Analee grew better, maybe because she realized that this really was the end of her life with the Falcon. Whatever happened now, whatever he did or said, nothing could ever be the same as it was. She came to accept her status as a woman without a husband and her thoughts went to building a new life around her family.

Her first joy was getting Duncan back from Falcon's Keep. With the Falcon abroad no one dared disobey her command. She was even more powerful now than she had been before her imprisonment. So Duncan was returned to her from that gloomy fortress, little worse for his banishment. He was such a bright and attractive boy that he had completely won the heart of his stern tutor who came with him to Furness to continue his education.

So the spring passed into summer and summer into autumn. When the winter came the news from abroad was worse than before, but by the beginning of the new year Mr. Pitt was firmly in command of the government, Admiral Byng was shot on his quarter deck for his failure to hold Minorca and the spirits of the country rose.

Analee thought frequently of Brent and their daughter Morella. He was in Laxey in the Isle of Man operating the bulk of Rigg's extensive fishing fleet. He had begged her to see him but she refused, saying that, their names having been brought together, it would be folly to meet until the business was forgotten. Any word of it back to the King or the Falcon could destroy all that had been done . . . and one must not forget that their release was based on an untruth. She had always felt worried about what Catherine Walkinshaw might say; but, doubtless for reasons of her own, that good woman had decided to keep her knowledge to herself.

One day Analee was working at her embroidery listening to a story read by Clare. Beyrick and Charlotte sat at her feet, their mouths open, their eyes wide with interest as their sister took them through the mysteries of Aladdin's cave. It was a peaceful scene: a large fire in the grate, the smell of burning logs, the dogs asleep on the floor, a cat sitting on the low bench that ran along by the window. Outside the skeletal branches of the tree beat against the mullioned window panes and the haze of winter obscured the distant hills. Except for the crackle of the logs and the piping voice of Clare, no sound disturbed the tranquillity. Analee snipped a piece of wool from her tapestry and prepared to thread a needle with a fresh color. She had been aware of the thud of hooves along the lonely road that led to the Grange in the recesses of her mind, but it was not until they grew louder and entered the courtyard that she raised her head and glanced out of the window. A dust-covered stranger descended from his horse and passed rapidly out of sight into the house. She wondered who it could be. Few people passed this way in winter and most provisions and the post came from Keswick by boat.

There was a flurry outside the door and a servant stood back as the stranger she had observed on the horse entered and bowed low. Analee put down her sewing and bade Clare stop reading.

"My lady," the messenger produced a letter from beneath his cloak, "I bring very sad news."

"The Falcon!" Analee gasped. "There is something wrong with my husband?"

"I am from Delamain Castle, ma'am. Sir George Delamain is dead."

Analee felt a *frisson* run through her body. Nelly, hovering in the background anxiously, having been as disturbed by the presence of the stranger as Analee, hurried forward and dropped a curtsey. "Shall I take the children, my lady?"

"Would you, Nelly? I am so shocked I must have time to recover my wits." She managed to smile at her children and bade the messenger take a seat.

"Thank you, my lady, but I will not sit in your presence. I am but a servant of the late Sir George."

The *late* Sir George. Was it possible?

"Then you must have something to eat and drink in the servants' quarters before you leave. Pray tell me, how did this distressing event occur?"

"Sir George had been ailing all winter, ma'am, prey to one bout of ill health after another; but there was nothing serious or untoward until three days ago when he was suddenly struck with the smallpox. Such was

222

his weakened state that he died within twenty-four hours."

"Oh! I am appalled," Analee put her hands to her spinning head. "Oh, and how is poor Lady Delamain?"

"She has taken it very badly, ma'am."

"I must go to her."

"I think her sister is coming, your ladyship. There is also Sir George's mother and his brother, now Sir Brent, has been summoned. The funeral has already taken place because of the risk of infection."

Infection. Morella! Analee's heart raced and she sat down quickly. The dreaded smallpox could spread like fire.

"I simply came to tell you, ma'am, and I am on my way to inform others who knew Sir George, including Mr. Rigg and Mr. Fitzgerald. I am bound to Whitehaven and Cockermouth now."

"I will write to her ladyship before you go," Analee said, rising from her chair. "Pray go now and take nourishment before you proceed on your journey."

The servant bowed and withdrew and, for a long time, Analee stood by the window gazing onto the lake.

Sir Brent. Sir Brent Delamain. Far, far before anyone could have dreamed it, he had come into his own. He was the sole heir to his brother's great fortune and estates, the owner of Delamain Castle. It was almost as though George had foreseen his untimely death. If this had happened but a year ago Brent would have been an exile, a renegade, a traitor and the title would have passed to a remote cousin who lived in Wiltshire.

Analee put her face in her hands and sobbed— whether through grief for Sir George or relief for Brent she could not tell.

Sir Brent Delamain stood silently by the tomb of his brother. Next to it was that of their grandfather, the last person to have been buried in the family vault.

223

The body of Tom the Jacobite priest had been buried on the battlefield, his brother having refused to have it with the family. Now he, Brent, would alter that; the bones would be lovingly reinterred in their rightful place.

He did not grieve for George; how could he? Yet he mourned his passing even though it had improved his own fortunes beyond his wildest imaginings. In many ways he had been content to spend the rest of his life as a fishing skipper. He had commanded a number of wherries and enjoyed plying between Ireland, the Isle of Man and the English coast. He was careful never to go near France. It would be too easy for people to misconstrue his actions and accuse him of serving the Jacobites.

For a time he had thought of going to America to fight in the war along with his cousin Stewart—this time on the side of the Hanoverian British and against the French. But the life of a vagabond would have begun all over again. In Laxey he had a small house and, nursing dreams of his final reunion with Analee, he had been content to bide his time.

Bitterly as he regretted her command for him not to visit her, he knew it was sensible. The Falcon was too foul a blackguard to trust, and his house would be full of spies ready to bring news of a visit of Brent to his wife.

There was a movement behind him and Emma stood by his side. Mourning did not become her; her frame was too thin and her face too white. She did not look well either and fear suddenly gripped at his heart. It surely was not grief for brother George whom neither had loved.

"Emma, you do not look well."

"I am tired," Emma said, passing her hand over her brow and sitting on the edge of their grandfather's stone. It was cold in the vault which stood in the castle grounds near to the chapel.

"How is Mama today?"

"She is well. The doctor thinks the pox will not infect anyone else."

"Thank God for that. I dread seeing Henrietta. She looks at me with such reproach."

"I think she would rather have you than cousin Edward Henning; but of course she would rather have had George. She loved him."

"And he loved her. The only person he did love. A man I never understood." Brent put on his hat and took Emma's arm. "Come, it is cold in here. When are you returning to Whitehaven?"

"There is no hurry," Emma shook her head. "My husband will not miss me."

Brent's anxiety was renewed. This was the reason Emma was so pale and tired. She was not happy. "I did not expect he would make you a good husband," Brent said bitterly. "He is too full of self-love."

"No, 'tis not that. He does not love me and I do not give him a child. If I could do at least that he might like me better. But I am barren. Two years wed and no child, or sign of one. I think it is because he does not love me that I cannot conceive."

Brent put his arm around his sister's shoulder and said gently, "Love is not necessary to make babies, Emma. How do you think women who are raped on the roadside have them?"

Emma suddenly put her head against Brent's chest and burst into tears. "Then it is as I feared. I will never conceive."

"But, my dear, it is not too late."

"It is, it is," she sobbed. "Most women conceive within a month of two of their wedding. Look at Sarah; she hardly ever stops. It is not fair; it is not fair. I cannot go through life without a child."

"You must go and see Analee," Brent said quietly.

"Analee?"

"Could she not give you a spell?"

"Her spells don't work," Emma said, drying her tears.

"How do you know?"

"I do. That is all."

"I have known them to work, sometimes. Go see her and give her my love, my tenderest respects. Ask her if one day soon I may call."

"Maybe I will go," Emma said, taking his arm. " 'Tis all the hope I have."

Analee shook her head and smiled at Emma sadly. "My dear, my gypsy spells no longer work for me. I am too far gone from nature, from my gypsy ways. Maybe you are too withdrawn from your husband?" She looked sympathetically at Emma, thinking of her own fecundity. It was difficult to share the agony of a woman who could not conceive if, for you, it had always been easy; but with her abundant compassion Analee could imagine how Emma felt.

"Brent said a woman could conceive even if she were raped."

"It is true, alas." Analee gazed at Emma, so worn and thin.

She was not happy, different from when she'd last seen her. Her own meeting with Hugo on that fateful occasion had broken the spell on him. She felt somehow that she owed it to Emma to make up for the misery she had unwittingly caused her, and also to thank her for acting as an intermediary with Brent. "The spells from Reyora are the most powerful ones," she said. "She still practices as the *cohani* of her tribe. Let us send for her again. I love seeing her here."

"But last time her spell did not work."

"It did! He came to see you. He *did* love you."

"But why does he not love me now?"

"I know not," Analee said, turning away. They were walking through the garden by the side of the lake, taking some air although the day was cold. "But then,

226

the Falcon does not love me either. Men's affections are very fickle, Emma; you should know that." She looked gravely at the girl, noting the pink flush that stole up her cheeks.

"Who knows it better than I?" Emma said quietly. "First Stewart and now Hugo. It appears I am not to be loved. At least if I can have children I can love them. Otherwise I do not give much for the chances of happiness in this life."

"Yes, children are a great source of happiness." Analee turned along a path that ran through the wood. "Without my children I would be bereft, having lost the love of the Falcon. You see, my spells did not avail me there."

"You have Brent's love," Emma said. "He told me to send you his tender regards and asks when he may come and see you."

"I will send him word," Analee said. "As long as my lord is alive I cannot see Brent. His lordship would make too much mischief out of it. He has spies everywhere, as we know. There are also people in London who could do me harm. I must be very careful. Now I will send for Reyora. She will examine you and tell you why she thinks you are barren."

"Oh," Emma said, blushing. "Will it be unpleasant?"

"To be barren is not pleasant either, is it?" Analee said lightly. "And Reyora is very skilled; such matters are her specialty."

Reyora came into the drawing-room, a frown on her face. Analee had waited downstairs while Nelly assisted Reyora in her delicate task.

"There is no reason she cannot conceive," she told Analee. "Her inside is perfectly formed. It may be the fault of her husband. It is sometimes the man."

"You can hardly ask to examine him!" Analee said, smiling. "Is there naught you can do?"

"To do what I did for Lady Delamain is useless, because she is perfectly formed. The womb is young and healthy; but yes, I can give her something for her husband. She can mix it with his food and we shall see what that will do. It is not pleasant-tasting."

"Your potions never are," Analee said fondly to her friend. "I wonder they ever work at all."

Hugo spat out the meat and wiped his mouth on his hands. "That meat is foul! Are you trying to poison me?"

"Of course not. Why should I?"

"Let me taste *yours*." Hugo leaned over and speared the beef on his wife's plate, chewing it thoughtfully. Then he took her plate before him, and put his in front of her. "*You* eat it," he said. "Yours tastes perfectly all right." Emma went white and gazed at the plate, her lips trembling.

"Go on!" Hugo said, staring at her, his eyes bright with suspicion. "Let me see you eat it."

Emma put down her knife and gazed at him. "I cannot eat it."

"There you are, 'tis poisoned! Give it to the dog and see it die!"

Hugo bent over and, picking up a piece of the meat, threw it on the floor. Emma flung herself after it and retrieved it just before the bull mastiff opened its enormous jaws to devour it. Hugo got up and seized her wrists, dragging her before him, shaking the hand that held the meat.

"Eat it yourself! Eat it yourself!"

"I cannot. I will not." Emma gazed at him and burst into tears. "It is not poisoned, I swear."

"Then what is it?" He tossed the meat on the table and stood with his back to the fire. "If you do not tell me I will beat you until the truth comes out of you."

"It is for fertility."

"*Fertility?*" Hugo roared, the look on his face one of

incredulity. "Fertility. For me? *I* have naught wrong with me."

"Nor I with me. I want a child. I want to conceive."

"And what did the doctor say?" Hugo lowered his voice.

"It was not the doctor. 'Twas a gypsy."

"A gypsy!"

"Reyora the gypsy, a friend of Lady Falconer. I saw her because I was afraid my barrenness would make me lose you. I want a child, Hugo. I so want a child." Emma flung herself onto a chair, sobbing. Her husband looked at her with scorn.

"*I* have naught wrong with me. I can fulfill my function very well. 'Tis with you the fault lies. Tell the gypsy that."

"Did you ever make a child?"

"Not that I know of, though I have lain with many women," he said boastfully.

"She said it is not me. She felt inside me and found everything in order."

Hugo stared at her, screwing up his nose. "You let her touch your intimate parts! You disgust me."

"She is a midwife, like a doctor. Analee says that she is very skilled."

Vividly Hugo recalled the bite that Analee had administered to his wrist. As he thought of her his eyes narrowed. Maybe Analee had sent him the poison.

"Why should Lady Falconer want to help you?"

"Because she is a kind person."

"I find her not kind. I dislike her intensely."

"She is a good friend to my family . . . and to me. Please, Hugo, eat the meat, although it tastes bad. See, I will eat a little too and you will know 'tis not poisoned."

Emma picked up a small piece from her plate and put it on her tongue. It did indeed taste vile; knowing what was in it she was not surprised. She should have put it in a stew heavily flavored with herbs, not spread

229

it on a piece of meat. She grimaced. "It does taste bad; but it is not poison. Oh please, Hugo, eat it for my sake, for our sake. Do not we *both* want a child?"

"Aye." Hugo looked at her thoughtfully. She had grown so plain, so unattractive. He never really knew why she had captured his attention in the first place. But maybe it was because of him. He knew he neglected her. He could desire her in the marriage bed, but he had felt no love or tenderness for her ever since that day he had seen the Enchantress at Delamain Castle. Every time he made love to Emma, or any woman—those in the brothels in Whitehaven—he imagined it was Analee. Would he could get her into his bed.

Hugo Fitzgerald was not a happy man. He felt he had missed something in life. He had a very good job and prospects; the house he had built was gracious with a fine view of the sea. He had married well, into the gentry. But he knew he was cold; there was something lacking. He yearned for the excitement that had come during his years as a spy—first for one side, then another. He had felt necessary and important. He wished in a way that those days could come again. He studied the piece of meat, now cold on his plate. Picking it up he put it in his mouth. It tasted vile but he swallowed it; then another; then another until his plate was clean.

He leaned back and pushed the plate away from him. Suddenly there was a terrible cramp in his belly; he felt a choking sensation in his throat and he could not get his breath. He stood up and, clutching his belly, staggered across the room. He felt he was on fire and longed for water to quench his terrible thirst. Suddenly he saw a stream before him, its clear crystal waters tumbling over the brown and grey pebbles and rocks beneath. Oh, the welcome of those translucent depths! Crying out he rushed towards the water and dived in.

230

The Enchantress stood by his bedside gazing at him with that look he knew so well, her dark eyes full of meaning, her lips slightly apart showing her even white teeth. She ran her tongue sensuously over her lips and bent nearer to him. She wore a loose robe and from her came an odor of peculiar sweetness. She reached out a hand and he pulled her down towards him, half rising to greet her, to kiss those lips. The gown she wore fell away from her body and her naked form, brown and gleaming like a gypsy, her large aureoles a dusky red, aroused in him inexpressible emotions; such rapture as he had never hoped to experience.

He turned back the sheets and she lay beside him still grasping his hand, still looking at him. He put his head down and began to suck one of her breasts and the elongated nipple was like a teat from which poured milk of such richness and sweetness that it seemed to flow through his veins and fill him with life. Her long, brown, supple body lay on the bed and she raised her legs for him and parted them, inviting him to enter, pointing to the secret place, her eyes alight with desire.

He lay on her and she clasped his back, urging him into her, squeezing him between her thighs, entrapping him. He would forever lie between the loins of the Enchantress as he had always desired, filling her with his seed, drinking her milk for the rest of his life. Sustenance for a king. He kissed her gently and then put his head upon her breast, feeling the strong beating of her heart beneath his. He closed his eyes, weary now, so happy, his essence mingling with her juices to make their child.

Emma had never felt so ecstatic. She lay beneath her husband looking at his dark head on her breast, his eyes closed. She wanted to lie like this forever, knowing the happiness of love, the thrill of being so wanted and desired. It was the first time he had loved her with passion, murmuring endearments and inflaming her with his ardor. The pleasure in her own loins, never

231

experienced before, had been almost intolerable. It had seemed to flame up through her belly to her heart, and all her skin was alive with sensation. He had seized her so unexpectedly as she stood anxiously by his bed expecting him to die. The servants had taken him up from the floor and carried him to bed thinking either he had had a seizure or his wife had poisoned him. For a while he had tossed and turned, calling out in torment, but then abruptly he lay still. Finally he opened his eyes and, greeting her with a smile of rapture, pulled her into the bed and took her in his arms.

She closed her eyes in thanksgiving, knowing the child had been conceived, that the magical, marvelous gypsy spell had worked.

Anna Cameron was very bored. She was bored with embroidery, bored with reading, bored with the sights of Berlin, bored with the company of Lady McKeith who sometimes seemed like a jailer. They couldn't do this and they couldn't do that. They went nowhere in society, neither to the Court of the King or even the British Embassy.

"You must consider it as though the Falcon were in mourning," Lady McKeith had said, trying to temper her impetuosity. "It would never do for him to parade his new wife so soon after getting rid of the last."

"I don't see why. She wanted to divorce him. She *asked* for a divorce."

"Yes, but among the nobility such things are done with delicacy. You do not just put off your old wife and take another."

"I think his lordship is ashamed of me."

"Of course he is not! You know he adores you."

"Does he?" Anna Cameron had looked at her chaperone; but Lady McKeith had lowered her eyes, refusing to meet her gaze.

That was a few months ago. Now the spring had come and the plans that King Frederick had been working on all winter were on their way to maturity. He had prevailed upon the English to return all the Hanoverian and Hessian soldiers who had been hastily summoned to meet the threat of a French invasion. They were also to subsidize Brunswick and Saxe-Gotha to provide troops to swell Frederick's army. The new army was to be called the Army of Observation and King Frederick hoped the British would send a contingent of cavalry. But England was too committed elsewhere to send any troops; and, moreover, she was busy raising more regular regiments to send to India and America.

The Falcon was often away. He went with Sir Andrew Mitchell to arrange for the subsidy to Brunswick and inspected the Brunswick troops. He met Lieutenant General von Schmettau who had been sent as an emissary by Frederick to Hanover and discussed tactics with him there. In February it was rumored that the Hanoverian government was trying to arrange neutrality with Austria. But, also in February, Pitt convinced the nation of the importance of the alliance with Prussia and began to put England on a proper warlike footing.

Then the one thing the Falcon dreaded happened. The Duke of Cumberland was appointed to command the Army of Observation. This meant that the British would start to flock to the Continent and his awful secret would be out. What would the King have to say to a bigamist? The Falcon had tried to get Prince Henry, brother to King Frederick, as commander; but the King wanted the son of the English monarch who was also Elector of Hanover. In April the Duke of Cumberland was due to arrive at Stade on the mouth of the Elbe and the Falcon was to be sent with others to welcome him.

He left his new "wife" behind. He only wished that when he returned she would have gone forever, disappeared from the face of the earth. His bigamous mar-

233

riage had been a terrible failure. In all his considerable experience he had never known a woman so bad in bed as Anna Cameron. He was now able to penetrate her with a fair amount of ease, but without any pleasure. Had he not taken her in the circumstances he had he would have left her long ago. Not only did she afford him little pleasure, she clearly took none herself; she never relaxed or unwound but was always on the verge of fear as though in dread of the act. Her body was always cold and her limbs always stiff.

He could not summon up the courage to tell her about his deception. She would surely go back to England and delight in exposing him, just to extract the maximum revenge.

"May I not come with you to greet His Royal Highness, my lord?" She hardly ever called him Angus as though out of fear or exaggerated respect. It emphasized their lack of intimacy.

"'Tis out of the question," he said briefly, looking up from his papers. It was the night before he was due to depart.

"But *why*?"

"Because it is a military occasion. Europe is no place for a woman to travel through now the French army has moved towards the Rhine. We have evacuated Wesel. Hostilities have begun."

"But shall I be safe in Berlin, sir?"

"As safe as anywhere."

"Could I not go back to England?"

"No."

"But why?"

"Because I say so."

"That is not sufficient reason, my lord."

He looked sharply up at her, aware of the bright flush on her cheeks, the light in her eyes. When she was not being unduly submissive she was bad-tempered. She was like a child, capricious, veering between moods. He would treat her like one.

234

"It is quite sufficient for me," Angus said, returning to his papers.

Anna came over and stood by the table on which he was writing. "I *demand* to go back to England! I shall go when you are gone, whether you wish it or not, and take my rightful place at Falconer House."

"*Your* rightful place!" The Falcon glared at her and put down his quill. He stood up and towered over her menacingly. "*Your* rightful place is where I command it. And I command that you stay in Berlin."

"You are a tyrant, Lord Falconer."

He raised a hand and hit her across the mouth. She stared at him and staggered back as the tears sprang to her eyes. A little blood trickled from the corner of her mouth. Even looking at her disgusted him. He had never fallen out of love so quickly, or with such cause. How had he ever considered her beautiful? Why had he been unable to sleep at nights for thinking of her? Why had he plotted and worked for months—for this? She was superficial, silly and unbedworthy. The Falcon went back to his chair and sat down, taking up his quill again; but the sound of her weeping was too distracting. He gazed at her and tried to summon up some pity. On the other hand he felt she had trapped him. He was saddled with her; he could neither send her to England nor to her mother in America. They could not stay here forever. He wanted to go now neither to India nor America, but to bring his own troops over from England and join in this exciting continental fray. The only feasible thing to do was to have her killed; but Isobel McKeith seemed to be fond of the girl. He knew he could not count on her loyalty.

"I am sorry," he said at last, "that I struck you. I find you excessively vexatious at times. You seem to have no interests, no occupations. I know not what to do with you."

"Send me to England."

The Falcon banged the table. "I have told you I

cannot! 'Tis out of the question. I pray you now desist. Desist, I tell you."

"I am not allowed to go abroad, to mix with the Prussians or visit the British Embassy. I, the Marchioness of Falconer, am treated like a prisoner."

"It is for your own protection. Berlin is full of spies, the country is at war."

"I fear you no longer love me, my lord."

The Falcon looked at her and went over to her. He touched her shoulder and kissed the top of her head. "You are a silly goose. You know I am preoccupied with affairs. It does not mean I do not love you."

She gazed up at him, trying to smile, but her cheeks were stained with tears. "I am glad of that, sir, because I am to have your child. I hoped that it would give you pleasure and, if you still love me, I know it will."

The Falcon shut his eyes and hoped that when he opened them she would have gone; but no, she was still there, gazing at him with an expression of trust, even hope.

"You see why I want so much to go back to England, sir? To give birth in your lordship's home. Would you reconsider now?"

"A child?" the Falcon echoed lifelessly.

"Your lordship is not pleased?" Her face clouded with anxiety.

"Why should I be pleased? I am certainly not delighted."

"But why not, sir?"

"Because this is no time to be having children." Lord Falconer got up and began restlessly to pace the room. "What with war, and . . . uncertainty." He looked at her and wondered if he could have her killed and put away without anyone knowing, and the bastard child with her.

"But did not your lordship think I might bear a child?"

No, he hadn't. He thought children came from

236

pleasure, and he had very little and she none. He had told her to use the sponge but she did not like to have such intimate contact with her body and certainly was against allowing him to. He never kissed or fondled her intimate places because she hated the whole thing, such was her prudery, her shame. Her flesh, and his, seemed to disgust her.

"I thought that, as you had not up to now, you might not. I thought you might be barren."

"Your lordship sounds as though you wished it."

"Of course I do not wish it. I simply feel it is not the right time."

The Falcon strode out of the room, banging the door behind him, and sought out Lady McKeith in her room.

"I told her she should not tell you yet. I knew you would not be pleased." Her ladyship shrugged her shoulders. She too hated Berlin and wished to be back in London. She had tired of the whole game, the indifference of the Falcon and the fear and insecurity of his pathetic, unlawful wife.

"Can she not get rid of it?"

Lady McKeith looked at him in surprise. "But why should she? She thinks she is a marchioness and the child will be a lord or lady. She is proud of it. In her opinion it is the only good thing that has come out of lying with your lordship."

"She says that?"

"No, but I know it. You are in a pretty pickle, Angus Falconer, and I know not what you can do." Lady McKeith looked at him with a smirk, as though pleased at his discomfiture.

"I should never have put away my wife, Analee."

"A lot of people said that at the time, my lord."

"They were right." The Falcon looked wistful. "I think of her a lot, comparing her to . . . that!" He glanced towards the door. "I must have been deranged

237

to prefer her to Analee. I was an old fool, bewitched by young flesh. Well, 'tis no use moaning. Not now.

"Look, I am leaving tomorrów for Stade. I will think of a plan and write to you. Meanwhile if you can endeavor to procure an abortion, pray do. I care not how you bring it about, drug her if you like. Send a surgeon to inspect her and have him insert some appliance. I will pay you well if you succeed."

Lady McKeith shook her head, still with the same mirthless smile. "It is no use, my lord. She is determined to have that child. You know her prudery. She will let none touch her. Even the doctor who confirmed what I already knew, that she was with child, could scarce get near her to take a peep. All he was allowed to examine was her belly, which has begun to swell. Were you not so preoccupied you would have noticed it yourself!"

"Even *I* scarce get to see her belly," the Falcon snorted. " 'Tis a rare privilege indeed to see under her nightdress."

"Well," Lady McKeith continued, "it is the one thing in her dreary life to which she now looks forward. She knows she has lost your love, that she cannot please you in bed or share your interests. She feels you despise her. Going back to England and having your child have become obsessions with her and, believe me, she will bring them both about."

The Falcon hit the wall with his stick, swore savagely and walked out of the room banging the door behind him with such force that two pictures in the hall fell off the wall, and the glass broke into tiny fragments.

Chapter Fourteen

Lord Falconer didn't know with whom his irritation was the most profound; whether it was with the French, who had already crossed the Rhine and were continuing to advance; with the Erbprinz of Hesse Kassel, commanding the Prussian and allied troops, who was perpetually retreating; or with the vacillations of his own master the Duke of Cumberland, who clearly wished the war to stop altogether.

The Duke kept on writing effusive letters to the enemy commander Marshal d'Estrées signed *votre ami affectionné*, and doubtless getting the same back. Yet all the time the French gained ground, pouring troops into their advanced positions. By 12 June d'Estrées had occupied Wiedenbruck and then Rietburg. Cumberland, at last, decided to stand and fight—to turn his Army of Observation into one of action—although he was without any clear information about the strength or intentions of the enemy. He himself had thirty-eight squadrons and fifty-two battalions, almost the whole of his army.

On the morning of 13 June, d'Estrées sent his light troops round both flanks of Cumberland's position. Cumberland immediately decided to retire despite the entreaties of Lord Falconer.

"I would remind your lordship," he said haughtily, "that *I* command this army, not yourself. What is more you are merely here as an *adviser*, Lord Falconer, and have no official position at all."

The Duke swept out of his tent and went to consult with officers who were more keen on ingratiating themselves with him.

Angus looked at McNeath and shook his head.

"This is not the man I remember from Culloden. He has gone soft, McNeath. He is totally uninterested in waging this war. He only desires peace. 'Tis because, he says, the Hanoverians have no arguments with the King of France or the Empress of Austria. He fears Hanover will be too easily overcome. I know not where it will end."

But during the night, to the Falcon's fury, the command came to withdraw. Immediately there was chaos as the order did not reach all the troops, and some began to retire through others who thought they should stay where they were. The result was that they fired on each other.

In the dawn the Falcon tried to take command, riding among the disaffected troops and doing what he could to restore order. As the troops slunk back to Bielefeld the French were at their heels and fighting recommenced. The Duke of Cumberland was nowhere to be seen, having moved off at first light to be sure of safety.

"It is useless, my lord. You must retreat," McNeath urged, gazing anxiously into the gloom. "See, there are the flags of the French."

The Falcon put his telescope to his eye. Sure enough they were advancing in disciplined and orderly ranks whereas all around him the Prussian rear guard was in a state of chaos. He suddenly felt ashamed of himself and the men. He was only here as an observer, it was true. Officially he had no part in the war at all; but to see such craven behavior was a sight so distasteful to him that he could not stomach it.

"Come, McNeath," he said peremptorily. "Gather a body of troops and let us charge them."

"My lord," McNeath looked around in consternation, "all the troops have their backs to us."

"Then we alone will face the French."

"I beg you, my lord . . ."

It was too late. The Falcon drew his sword and

charged towards the oncoming French ranks. It was such an astonishing sight that those in the front row of the advancing troops paused, and those behind almost fell on top of them. Then, quickly recovering his composure, a solitary infantryman from the French ranks raised his arm, put his musket to his shoulder and fired. The Falcon fell immediately, his horse charging on without him until it too was brought to the ground.

For a moment there was an eerie silence in the dawn as McNeath flung himself off his horse and knelt beside his master. He was not dead; but a great mass of blood belched from a huge wound in his side. His eyes were closed and his face pale as death. Two French officers came up and gazed with astonishment at the stricken Falcon.

"He rode like a madman."

"To his death. He was bent on self-slaughter."

McNeath looked at them with resignation, expecting any moment the bullet that would finish off his master and then another for him, too. That was how they had dispatched the Jacobites at Culloden, without mercy. He was resigned. He would not plead. But the French were standing around in a state of great consternation, as though it was something they had not seen before and could not understand. Suddenly there was a small commotion at the rear and the body of troops sprang hastily to attention. The two officers bowed and gestured helplessly at the fallen soldier.

Marshal d'Estrées peered to the ground and then looked incredulously at McNeath. "It *looks* like Lord Falconer."

"It is, sir."

"It is impossible. What is his lordship doing here?"

"He was adviser to the Duke of Cumberland on behalf of the King of Prussia, sir."

"Of course." The Marshal straightened up and shook his head sadly. "The retreat of the Prussians and their allies will have sickened a man of such valor.

Take him up gently and carry him to my tent. He will be treated not as a prisoner but as an honored guest—and send immediately for the doctors. Come!" He gestured to McNeath whose eyes filled with tears of gratitude. "Lord Falconer may be mortally wounded, but he will die as the hero he is. How *Le Faucon* must hate this sort of timidity!"

By nightfall Angus had recovered consciousness, but the wound in his side was a terrible one and the French doctors had had to operate on it to remove pieces of shot. McNeath had stood with him administering brandy during the agonizing process, during which the Falcon fainted anew several times. Now the wound was dressed and bandaged and the Falcon seemed peaceful. As he lay in his tent the flap was drawn back and Marshal d'Estrées entered quietly and looked at his prisoner.

"Well, my lord, do you recognize me?" he said in French.

The Falcon stared at him, tried to raise his head and then smiled replying in the same language. "Louis. Louis—César. We meet again on the battlefield. How are you, my old friend?"

The Marshal put a hand out and smiled. "Better than you, my dear Angus. Never did I think to see such a sorry sight."

"Those Prussians have no stomachs," the Falcon growled. "I urged them to advance and they all fled."

"I have not seen you since you were in Paris to discuss the peace in '48, Angus."

"Oh come, have we not met since then? No? Maybe you were too busy plotting with those Jacobites. They . . ." The Falcon paused and gasped with pain. McNeath bent forward and put a glass of brandy to his lips. "Ah, I think I am done for, Louis-César. At least I died with my face to the enemy and not my rump."

"You will not die. We have the best surgeons here

with us. I have told them that if you go to the grave they follow you. No, Angus, your wound is grave but not fatal. We will get you to your own lines, unless you prefer to go to Paris?"

Angus managed a weak smile. "There I think I *will* be despatched to my Maker—by the Jacobite renegades if not by King Louis. No, send me to Cumberland. Thank you, my old friend. I hope you lose!"

The Marshal bent over and kissed both his cheeks. "I hope your force loses, but not you, Angus. I hope to see you in Paris as an honored guest at the Court when we are at peace again."

The Falcon shook his head. "Not for a long time, Louis-César. This will be a very bitter war. But thank you, my old friend. You have saved my life."

"Do not forget to give my regards to Lady Falconer." The Marshal raised his right hand to the sky and kissed the tips of his fingers. "Ah, the Enchantress. Is she here with you?"

"No."

"Then have them send for her. She will restore you to health in no time."

"Sir Brent Delamain, ma'am."

Nelly looked anxiously at Analee and then glanced behind her shoulder.

"Sir Brent . . ." Analee rose to her feet and put a hand to her breast in a futile attempt to quell the rapid beating of her heart. "He is *here*, Nell?"

Nelly nodded excitedly and then stood back, stifling a gasp as Brent gently edged her to one side and came slowly into the room.

"You cannot throw me out," he said with pretended solemnity and then he smiled and held out his arms.

With a cry Analee rushed into them, flinging her head against his chest. He didn't attempt to kiss her, but put his arms around her protectively, hugging her to him.

243

"I knew if I asked you would not let me; but this agony has gone on for long enough. I have come to claim you, Analee."

Analee leaned her head against his chest, aware of his strength and power, his gentleness. She seemed to hear his words from a long way off and the echo reverberated through the room.

"*Claim* me?"

"Aye. I am determined on't. How long is it since you saw that ruffian of a husband of yours?"

Analee didn't reply and a hand lingered on his chest before she left him with reluctance. "I have not seen my lord for eighteen months; but he is still my lord, my husband, Brent. Now he is with the Duke of Cumberland in Germany."

"Aye, and badly the war is going, too, from all I hear."

"It makes no difference, Brent."

He strode over to her and seized her shoulders, drawing her close to him once more. With unaccustomed delicacy Nelly quietly withdrew and closed the door, staying outside in case anyone should try to venture in. Analee heard the door click and smiled to herself. She put her face up to Brent and he gazed at her lips. Then he gently kissed her. For a moment the desire she felt for him was overpowering. To feel the impress of his lips, the warmth and strength of his body was almost too much for a passionate woman like herself who had been for so long without a man. He felt her trembling and his hands tightened round her.

"Take me here, Brent, if you want."

She felt him quiver, but he gently eased his mouth away, keeping his arms about her. "I want, but I will not. I want to wed you, Analee. I have thought long about it; debated within myself, sought advice from those I trusted."

"But how can we be wed when I am wed to another?"

"There is such a thing as divorce. It is not easy, but I am sure the King will grant it, having in mind the way the Falcon has treated you."

"I am sure His Majesty will do no such thing. There are many husbands who abuse or ignore their wives. If they were all allowed divorce where would it end? A woman is meant to be resigned—and chaste. I find both a burden, being tempestuous and hot-blooded by nature. Maybe if in ten years I neither saw or heard from my lord he might be prepared to consider the matter. But what is eighteen months in a lifetime?"

"It is not only eighteen months separation, Analee! You know that full well. It is what he has done; having you put in jail, humiliating you."

Analee kissed his cheek and moved away. His proximity was too much for her; she felt too weak. "Brent, although to you the time seems unendurable—and it is, aye, for me as well as you—it is not such a very long time for others. Do not you think the King would immediately be suspicious if I petitioned for divorce? He would ask why and I would have to say to marry you. He would recall that we were accused together of treason and all my friends would disperse, like the waves receding from the shore. People, alas, are all too fickle and there are many who know I was born of a gypsy—not that I am ashamed of it, as well you know; but they would soon start to talk and mock, pointing a finger and saying I had the morals of a whore. I have my children, Brent; they come first. I would never bring shame to my children."

Analee felt more in possession of herself and turned to Brent, her color high, her bosom quickly rising and falling. "My children are very precious to me, Brent; more important to me than my own happiness. As long as their father lives—and God grant that will be for many years—I would do nothing to make them ashamed of me; even if I have to live in this way, like a nun, for the rest of my life."

Brent squeezed his hands together and his whole frame shook with anguish. "I wish I had taken you when you asked."

"You thought it was nobler to ask me to marry you than to lie with me? You did not used to be like that, Brent. I think inheriting a title has made you more aware of your responsibilities. Or is it that, now you are a baronet, making love on the floor is undignified?" She smiled at him mockingly. The old Analee coming to life.

"Oh, Analee, do not talk like that! I only wanted you to know I had not just come for that one thing—that precious thing, your body. Of *course* I want to lie with you and love you. Every occasion has been exquisite to me and lingers forever in my memory. Have we not lain on a forest floor as well as in a soft bed? But you have told me not to come and see you. You forbade it. I obeyed your command because I saw the sense of it; but I think of you every day, not once but many, many times. Without you my life will never be complete, never be happy. I am a lost man without you, Analee. Without you I cannot function."

"I am only half a woman, too," Analee murmured, her hand stealing into his. "And that half is broken. I have given such love to the Falcon, to have him smash it in my face. For months someone tasted my food in case he tried to send poison to me. If there were noises in the night I feared that an assassin had been sent to kill me. I felt such waves of evil from that man. I cannot tell you."

Analee put her face in her hands, her eyes shut as though with horror at the memory. "Oh, do not think that I would have risked the life of my servants by getting them to taste poisoned food! 'Twas *they* who did it without my knowledge. Nelly told me. They all feared the Falcon, even those who had once loved him, as I did. Oh, not as I did. No one could have loved him, as I did."

"Do not talk to me of your passion for him!" Brent wrenched his hand away and went to stand by the window. How elegant he looked in his suit of brown alpaca, Analee thought, a full white cravat at his throat and lace at his wrists. He wore his own hair unpowdered, tied back with a brown velvet ribbon. He looked like the elegant *gadjo* she had known all those years ago, as he stood at the back of the tavern outside Penrith watching her dance. Now, twelve years on, the lines on his face had deepened, his hair was darker; but age had given him an air of distinction that he had lacked as an impetuous youth. His frame was still powerful and muscular, no surplus fat anywhere, and there was an ascetic quality about his eyes and lips that told her he was not a profligate like her husband. The Falcon had grown sensual and a dissolute look had replaced the once disciplined fervor in his eyes. She knew that Brent saved himself only for her.

"It is no longer a passion, Brent," Analee said quietly. "I fear him. When he comes back from the war I know not what he will do; for I think he hates me and would do all he could to endanger me."

"Let him try!" Brent said, shaking a fist at the ceiling.

"What could you do? We are both powerless. Maybe he will stop in London, contenting himself with his amours, the younger women he likes increasingly to disport himself with, trying doubtless to recapture his own youth. But, Brent, I live only for today. I never know what tomorrow will bring, or the day after. I have all my children in good health and vigor, for which I thank God. My servants protect me and love me and I grow increasingly enchanted with this lovely country, this Lakeland. I have the pleasure of watching the seasons day by day as they change the character of the woods and meadows, the hills and pasturelands, even the water itself. I am become resigned, nay, content."

"I want you more than ever," Brent whispered, closing his eyes. "Merely to hear your voice is a torture to me."

"Then you should not have come to torture yourself," she said gently and she leaned her head on his shoulder and placed an arm lightly around his waist. He bent to kiss her when they were disturbed by a hammering at the door and sprang apart.

"Madam, it is I, Nelly. Oh, may I enter?"

"Of course, Nell." Analee went quickly to the door and opened it. By Nelly's side was a stranger, covered with mud, his face caked with dust and dirt. He breathed quickly as one who had ridden for a long time without stopping.

"Who is this, Nell?" she said in alarm, drawing back and looking at Brent.

"I am come from the Duke of Cumberland, Madam. He bade me ride as I have never ridden before, and I obeyed his Grace's command, one horse even dying beneath me."

"Yes, yes?" Analee said, trying to stifle the panic in her breast.

"It is your lord, Madam. Lord Falconer is gravely ill."

As she swayed, Nelly put an arm round her to support her. Brent didn't move from where he stood, transfixed, by the window. Nelly took Analee to a chair and helped her sit down. Analee stared in front of her, strangely unaware of anything or anyone. Then she said slowly, "The Falcon, gravely ill?" Her eyes focussed on the stranger, and she struggled to rise, but Nelly held her back. "Where? I must go to him."

"He is on his way home, ma'am, slowly by coach. He was wounded near Minden and appeared to make a good recovery as he was well taken care of by the French. But his condition deteriorated once he was brought to Hanover and his Grace wished to send for you, as his lordship cried for you continuously. His Grace then thought that he could not possibly reach you in time and the Falcon said he wished to go home. But the journey is slow and painful and I do not know if he will die on the way."

"But where, where, *where* is he now?"

"Last time he was on the Dutch coast, ma'am, ready to cross the sea. For all I know he may now be in England. They will send fresh word to you as soon as he is."

The man staggered and Analee looked at him with concern. "Nelly, you must see this good man has food and rest. Go now and then return to me when I have recovered my wits."

Nelly led the messenger to the door and Analee stared after him as though she had seen a ghost. Brent went to the door and closed it then came over to her and knelt by her side.

"I know not what to say."

"Why did I not know something was wrong?" Analee said. "In the old days my powers would have alerted me. Yet I have slept like a baby, my dreams were sweet and happy. How did I not *know*?"

"Because you no longer love him." Brent gently took her hand and brought it to his lips.

"No, it is because my powers are no longer with me. I cannot see things as I did. I am mortal, after all, Brent." She tried to smile. "No longer an enchantress."

"For me you are *always* an enchantress. Oh, Analee, what will happen now? If he dies . . ."

She quickly put a finger on his lips and pressed them firmly. "Shhh, do not say it. I would never wish that Lord Falcon should die if I could do aught to prevent it. And did you hear? He asked continually after me. If he is well enough to travel there is hope. Go now, Brent. I know you are a Christian, so pray for me. Pray for us both, Angus and myself—for if he dies what will become of us all, his children orphaned and me, a widow?"

"If he lives it will be worse," Brent began but Analee put her hand across his mouth and stared at him, fear and distress obliterating the customary light in her eyes.

As the boat came over the water Analee stood on the jetty shielding her eyes. Although the sun was behind and above her it cast a glare upon the water, and the harsh reflections of the surrounding mountains made it more difficult to see the slim outline of the skiff that bore the Falcon home.

No sooner had the messenger left than Analee received fresh word that her husband was stronger and would make the rest of the journey to Lakeland. Every day brought news of him, where he was, the state of his health and how much he longed to see her.

The Falcon, she thought ruefully, was like a child. Whenever he was ill he needed her. This time she would harden her heart to his need; she would be a good and dutiful wife and nurse but nothing more. She would never allow him to tear her heart again. But as soon as she saw his battered body being carried out of the boat she experienced such waves of shock, tenderness and compassion that her stern resolutions fled from her as she ran to his side and gazed at his stricken face.

He did not speak, but from the deep recesses of his sunken sockets his eyes blazed out at her, full of love and the desperation that had forced him to make a journey many would have given up long ago. For every tilt of the carriage, every lurch of the boat had been agony; but his spirit was borne aloft by one thing: to see Analee again.

As she looked upon him and smiled, stroking his brow, the expression of desperation was replaced by contentment, and he closed his eyes as they bore him into the house and up the stairs to the bedroom that overlooked the lake and, in the far distance, the jaws of Borrowdale looming like sentinels.

250

He had shrunken to half his size; his frame was like that of an old man. His hair was almost white and his growth of beard grizzled and grey. She helped to strip his body and then she washed it down, dressing and bandaging the terrible wound herself and noticing how it still bled and festered; a huge suppurating sore. The Falcon opened his eyes, following her as she moved quietly around him assisted only by a weary McNeath and Nelly. He seemed either too exhausted to speak or incapable of speech. She did not know. The bowl of water to bathe him was refreshed time and time again and finally she put a clean nightshirt on him and, between them, she and McNeath gently pulled the bedclothes over him and tucked them tenderly around him as though he were a baby. He then closed his eyes and, sighing deeply, fell into a deep sleep, a slight smile hovering on his mouth.

Analee, pale and distressed, stared at McNeath. "He did not utter a word. Can he still talk?"

"He is worn out, ma'am. He has scarce spoken since Derby. Only every now and then he called your ladyship's name, repeating it to himself, 'Analee, Analee,' but every time we wanted him to rest he forced us to go forward. I have hardly stood the journey and I don't know how his lordship has. Some demon drove him on." McNeath looked sadly at the Falcon and swayed slightly, passing his hand over his brow. Nelly took his arm, supporting him as Analee said:

"McNeath, you too must go straight to bed and Nelly will bring you refreshment. First you must tell me how my lord came by this terrible wound; but before you do that I must send for Reyora. She is the only one who can help him now."

After McNeath had told his story and two messengers had been sent for Reyora, Analee went slowly up to the bedroom and sat by the bed where the Falcon still slept peacefully, breathing gently, never turning once, the expression on his face serene. Analee took

251

his hand and at her touch he trembled and his eyelids flickered. The late afternoon sun stole through the window and the gentle lapping of water, the sighing of the wind in the trees were the only sounds, apart from his deep regular breathing, that could be heard.

Maybe he would recover . . . Surely he should be dead by now from that wound? Already the color of his face had improved. In her care his wound would heal and he would put on weight, recover his strength. Maybe once again . . .

"Analee . . ."

"Yes, my lord, Angus?"

" 'Tis you, then, and not a vision?"

"I think you have a vision, sir, for your eyes are still closed."

"I am dreaming of you then. I am still in Hanover in the palace of Herrenhausen and a little bird taps at the window."

"No, no Angus, that was many years ago. Then you were also healed and came back to me. You will be again. I have sent for Reyora and I am here. It *is* real."

His eyelids flickered but still they did not open. Once again he smiled and slept, Analee continuing to hold his hand. How could she *not* love him, this man she had married in the midst of war, who had given her his powerful name and three beautiful children? How could she *not* love him when, although he was not true to her, she was the one he needed when in pain and distress, when only the thought of seeing her kept him alive? All her old love for him returned, flooding her, suffusing her being as though he had never caused her such heartbreak and pain. McNeath said that many were the times he thought the Falcon was on the verge of death, but he had only to say her name to gain the strength to continue.

Perhaps she still had her magical powers. She closed her eyes as she pressed his hand, willing all the

252

strength into the Falcon to restore him to life. She had done it once before, after Culloden. She would save him yet again.

The sun sank below the hills and a mist rose on the lake. The sighing through the trees became a soft breeze and night slowly fell. Nelly entered with candles and stood by Analee's side gazing at her master.

"How does he, Analee?"

"He sleeps very peacefully. He has spoken to me, but I think in his sleep. He thought he was in Hanover. But I do not like his weakness, Nelly. I wish Reyora would come."

"Are you sure Reyora *will* come?" Nelly said gently, a hand on Analee's shoulder.

Analee looked at her, startled. "Of course I am sure Reyora will come! Why should she not come? She has never failed me yet."

The expression in Nelly's eyes was enigmatic and Analee grasped her hand and shook her. "Why do you look at me like that, Nelly?"

Nelly avoided Analee's eyes. "I have no reason; I merely wondered, 'tis all."

"Then if you have doubts we must send another messenger. He must command her to come. If she does not come I will go and get her myself and drag her here!" Analee bit her lip savagely, looking at the sleeping Falcon; but her heart now was troubled. Supposing Reyora would not come. What then?

"Calm yourself, ma'am," Nelly said. "I am sure she will come if you think so. I will get you some food. The children are anxious to see their papa."

"Not yet. Not until he is better. Tell them they will see him in good time."

That night Analee got into bed beside her husband and pressed her naked form against him, willing him life. His breathing was shallower and a feverish sweat had broken out on his forehead. As she molded herself to him she raised his nightshirt so that his bare skin

253

could feel the touch of hers, the impress of her full breasts, but he didn't move or stir and she gently stroked his body trying to infuse him with life, the life that had given life and brought life. Then she put her arm about him and the tears started to flow as she thought back on the happy times they had shared. Her memory kindly obliterated the many bad moments that had intervened, the times when he had neglected her, cast her into prison, undoubtedly wished her dead. She remembered only the great love they bore each other for so long.

During the night his fever rose and at dawn she got out of bed and went to summon Nelly, who clung to McNeath as though she never wanted to be parted from him again.

"Nelly, the Falcon is worse! You must get up. Reyora should be here by now."

McNeath stirred as Nelly left his side, but she kissed his cheek and bade him stay where he was.

"I will go send another messenger," she said, dressing quickly. "Do you wish me to send McNeath?"

"No, let him sleep. We will now have sent three messengers. *Why* is Reyora not here?"

Nelly ran down to despatch yet another servant on horseback and Analee returned to her bedroom, clasping her gown around her in the cold morning. The Falcon now tossed in his bed and the moaning he made filled Analee with fear. When Nelly came back they bathed him again, but saw that the yellow pus round the wound was turning green and an evil, sickly-looking slime was oozing from it together with fresh blood. The smell was vile.

"Oh, I *would* I had the potions and herbs I used to have. I *would* I remember the spells." Analee clasped her head, her face stricken with anguish. Just then they heard the sound of hoofbeats and Analee ran to the window, flinging it open and looking out.

254

A solitary rider climbed wearily off his horse and ran into the house.

" 'Tis Gilbert. The one we sent first. Quick, bring him up there."

Gilbert, sodden with the dew and pale with weariness, was brought into Analee's room and sank to his knees in front of her. "She is gone, ma'am."

"Gone? Reyora?"

"She has gone from the tribe."

"I do not believe it!"

"They were all very *silent*, ma'am, and acted peculiar. I had the feeling she was somewhere in the camp but would not come out."

"But did you look? Did you look?"

"I looked everywhere and besought them to find her for your sake. Tom has stayed on to scour the neighborhood."

Analee reached out and gently drew him up. "Do not distress yourself, Gilbert. You have done well. If Reyora does not come I myself will go and fetch her. She is there, I know. Is she not, Nelly?" She motioned Gilbert out of the room and then turned to Nelly. "Is she not? You *knew* she would not come?"

"Did you not say, Analee, that she would not help him again? Did she say it because of the way he treated you?"

Analee nodded, her eyes haunted. "Aye, she did, and she has no right! I want him well. I *love* him. I will have him better. I will go and fetch Reyora myself."

Nelly took Analee's hand and pressed it. "Do not go, Analee. If the Falcon should die while you were away you would not forgive yourself. Perhaps it is his time," she looked over towards him, gravely shaking her head, "and Reyora knows it."

"But Reyora could stop it. You know she could . . ."

"Did she not say he was on borrowed time? Once you saved him, once she saved him and now . . ."

The Falcon cried out and Analee ran to him. His body was burning, his face flushed. He gazed at her in agony. "Oh, Analee, I hurt so much. My body is burning. Pray give me water . . ."

Nelly filled a glass and gave it to Analee who held it to the Falcon's lips, supporting his head with her arm. He sipped greedily and then leaned against her breathing harshly. "I am going Analee. I have seen death in the night beckoning to me. Oh God, I would not leave you now! How I repent of all the follies of my life . . ." He lay against her, too weak to continue and his harsh stertorous breathing frightened her. She bathed his body again, covering him lightly with the sheet, and his pulse grew less rapid, his breathing easier. He took her hand and smiled at her.

"I repent all the follies of my life, my injustice to you . . ."

"Do not speak of it, Angus." Analee sat by his pillow and took his head on her breast. He snuggled up to her and clutched her as a small child does when it is frightened.

"But I have always loved you, Analee. Always. You might not believe me, might not think it possible, but 'tis true."

"I know it is true, Angus, and when you are well we shall enjoy life together as we did before."

"Oh, would that we could." Tears ran down the Falcon's face and Analee gently stroked his cheek with her hand, brushing away the wetness. "But I think God will not give me another chance. I am a cruel man, bent on having my way and prone to do injustice. I loved you so passionately and yet I abused you most vilely; but all the time, Analee, even in Berlin, my thoughts turned to you."

He looked up at her and Analee saw shame stealing over his face; he averted his eyes.

"Berlin . . ."

"Yes, even in Berlin. Oh, how I do repent . . . oh."

The Falcon gave a convulsive shudder and his head fell from Analee's bosom. His eyes stared in front of him and he seemed in the grip of some seizure.

Nelly, who had been standing in the shadows by the window, rushed up and together they straightened his body, terribly twisted and tormented by spasms, while froth ran out of the corner of his mouth and his eyeballs swiveled in his sockets.

" 'Tis a fit," Nelly said. " 'Tis the fever. Oh, pray God . . ."

McNeath came into the room and went quickly to his master's side, his face contorted with grief. He seized him and held him down and after a while the spasms ceased and the Falcon's eyes closed, and once more he went into a deep, weary sleep.

"McNeath, *you* must go for Reyora. Tell her I command her; that if she does not come I will never speak to her again; that I will have no love for her and wish her only harm."

"The second messenger has come back, my lady. He cannot find her."

"Then you must go. She is there. Speak to the head of the tribe."

"Aye, ma'am, I will."

"Take another servant with you to show the way. Only *you* can bring her back, McNeath."

McNeath turned and, kneeling by the side of the bed, brought his master's hand to his lips. As he kissed it the tears poured down his face and he leaned his head against the bed, sobbing. "Oh, I cannot go. I cannot leave him. I have loved him and served him all these years, my lady. How can I leave him now?"

"It is the only way to save him, McNeath. The only way."

Analee gently helped him to rise and turned her head away, her own eyes filled with tears, as McNeath bent once more and kissed the Falcon's face. Then he turned abruptly and left the room, Nelly following him.

Analee could hear the preparations for departure downstairs, but it only seemed to enhance the silence in the room. She sat on the bed and put her hand on the Falcon's heart. The beat, at first unnaturally fast, was now very feeble and his breathing was light and jerky. She thought for a moment that he had overcome his crisis and would recover, but the pallor of his face told her otherwise and there was a strange rasping in his throat like the prelude to the death rattle. She threw herself across his body and clasped it, willing her life to flow through him, willing him to live, but she felt no force go from herself to him. She kissed his cheek and his lips, tenderly stroking his brow, and all the time that urgent summons was going from her body to his until she felt almost weak with exhaustion. But she knew there was no response. Her powers had failed.

"Analee," His voice surprised her by its calm and strength. Her heart leapt and she sat upright and gazed at him.

"Angus. You are better?"

"I feel better. Suddenly I feel better," he said and gazed at her lovingly. "You enchantress, you are at work again, are you not? Healing me? Making me strong?"

"Yes. Oh yes." She leaned her cheek against his breast but still the heartbeat was very faint, almost a flicker. With difficulty he drew his arm from beneath the bedclothes and put it around her, his fingers on her bosom.

"I still desire you, enfeebled though I am."

"But soon we will lie together, Angus, as we used to. I know it."

"I do not think so, Analee." The Falcon shook his head.

"But I am making you strong. You said."

"It is pretense, is it not?" the Falcon whispered, his eyes clouded with grief and pain. "You and I are deceiving each other. It is too late. I feel my life ebbing away. Oh, would I could stay here with you; but it was

258

here I wish to die, Analee, if God wills that I die. Once here with you, in our beloved home, among our children. I felt I could die in peace. Now will you bring the children to me?"

"Oh, Angus, no, no!" Analee put her arms around him but Nelly, always hovering in the background, came forward and leaned over her.

"The children are outside, my lady. I told them to expect a call to see their papa. You must be strong for them."

She opened the door and, preceded by Duncan, the children trooped in, Clare taking Beyrick and Charlotte by their hands. Timidly they approached their father's bed, the youngest scarcely able to peep over the top. Between them Analee and Nelly propped him up on his pillows and he gazed at his children from his sunken pain-wracked eyes. Then he put out a hand and drew Duncan to him.

"You will be the head of a great house, Duncan."

"Yes, sir." Duncan looked at him solemnly.

"But your first duty is to your mother. You must always look after her and protect her. I charge you with that. Is it clear?"

"Yes, sir." Duncan gazed impassively at his father, showing no emotion.

"Good. The rest is taken care of." For a while the Falcon gazed at him and then sighed and patted him on the cheek. "Give me a kiss, then."

Woodenly Duncan bent down, pecked his father's cheek and turned away. His eyes were quite dry. But Clare, as she approached, was already weeping. As her hands left those of the younger ones they tried to scramble on the bed but Nelly stopped them.

"Now then. You must not disturb your papa. He cannot romp with you until he is better."

"But will Papa get better?" Beyrick said, looking at him with interest.

The Falcon smiled. "Of *course* I will, you rogue. My

Beyrick." He ruffled his tousled head fondly and put a finger playfully on his nose. "My favorite son," he murmured.

"But why must Duncan look after Mama?"

"Because I may not see her for some time. I am going away."

"To the war?"

"A sort of war." The Falcon's voice sunk to a whisper and he kissed Beyrick and Charlotte holding them both briefly, seeming to grow feeble with the effort. As Clare bent to kiss him she threw herself across her father in a torrent of weeping.

"Oh, Papa, Papa, do not go. I beg you."

"There, my little Clare." The Falcon held her tenderly. "You will be like your mama, I know, a beauty. You could do worse than try and emulate her for the rest of your life. She is not only beautiful, but wise and faithful, virtuous—a good and loving wife and mother, a woman to admire. Hold her always before you as an example." He kissed the top of Clare's head and, as his eyes closed with exhaustion, Nelly shepherded the children away, the younger ones running before her, Clare still weeping, trying to cling to her father. Only Duncan remained unaffected, solemn and detached. He was the last to leave the room and, as he stood on the threshold, he turned and stared thoughtfully at his father before closing the door behind him.

The Falcon gazed at the door for a long time. "Yes, I think he is my son. I still do not like him, but he has all my ways. He will be a very ruthless man, Analee. You will have to bring him up strictly. And now you, my sweet wife." He beckoned to her, and she came over to him dragging her feet, her heart so heavy she thought that it, too, would stop. Watching the children make their farewells had been a terrible trial to her. She sat by him and he stroked her hair, caressing the tresses which fell onto her swelling bosom.

"See, even the sight of your breasts makes a strange stirring in my loins and I am dying."

Analee undid her bodice so that her breasts, full and rounded, were exposed to his gaze. She leaned over and he fondled them, grasping each nipple momentarily between his lips, as though trying to suck sustenance from her. In the dark recesses of his mind he could recall her shimmering beauty as she lay with him in the act of love, giving herself to him, receiving from him the life that quickened into their progeny. And how they had loved! What blind stupidity, nay, madness, had driven him from her side? It was too late now for regrets.

Gently once more he caressed each breast and then reluctantly let them go. "I wish they could give me life," he said, his eyes shining. "When you suckled our children your milk was like nectar. You were always the most beautiful woman I ever lay with, Analee. The only one of any importance, the very best. You do know that, don't you?"

"I do, Angus." She fastened her bodice again and as she hid her breasts she could see the light fade from his eyes.

"But, Analee, there is something I would tell you now that I am dying; for the thought fills me with grief and remorse."

"What is it, Angus?"

"It may cause you pain."

"Even then, tell it me."

"You remember Anna Cameron?"

Analee felt her heart give a little leap. "Yes."

"Of course you remember her. Well, you know I was an old fool, having my last fling, but I mistakenly became attached to her."

"I thought as much, Angus."

"In fact," the Falcon paused and seemed to be fighting for breath, "she was with me in Berlin. I want you to look after her, Analee. I did not treat her well. Look

261

after her for me. Go and fetch her when I am gone. Will you do that?"

Analee swallowed and nodded; but the tears rushed to her eyes, making her choke. That, on his deathbed, he could think of another woman!

He pressed her hand. "Be brave, Analee, be generous. Compared to you Anna Cameron was nothing to me, but I regret the incident. She has to be looked after. Do not reproach me. Retain in your heart only love for me; because that was all I ever had for you. Analee . . ."

He gazed at her as though wanting to continue and he opened his mouth, but no words came. He clutched at her arm and half drew himself up, his face illumined by a brilliant smile. But suddenly his grasp on her arm slackened and he fell back on the pillows, his eyes still open, the smile remaining on his face.

For a long while she looked at him, her hand on his silent heart. She leaned forward and, drawing his lids over his eyes, imprinted on each of them a silent lingering kiss. She continued to sit by his side until darkness came, holding his hand as it grew cold, its lifeless fingers in hers.

When Nelly gently tiptoed in Analee did not know how long he had been dead, or how much time had passed. For a long time Nelly gazed at him, then she turned and kissed Analee.

"Reyora is here. She came with McNeath."

Analee turned and behind Nelly stood her old friend, with her wrinkled face and wise eyes, her bag of potions and unguents in her hand. Analee stared at Reyora who returned her gaze unblinkingly.

"You are too late," she said.

"I know."

"Why did you not come before?"

"It was his time."

"But, oh, Reyora, you could have . . ." Analee burst into tears and threw herself against Reyora who put

262

down her bag and enfolded her in her arms, hugging her.

"No, my dear. I could not. There was nothing I could do. He was on borrowed time as it was. And look how he misused it. Have you forgotten that?"

"Oh, but he would have changed. I know. We should have been as we used to. Happy, this time, forever."

Reyora shook her head slowly, her face resigned and sad. "He would never have changed, Analee. I knew that."

"And *that* was why you did not come?" Analee still shook with sobs and Reyora stroked her shoulders tenderly.

"I knew that it was his time. There was no point. No point at all."

She continued to hold Analee until her wild sobbing ceased and a feeling of calm pervaded her. Analee took a handkerchief and, wiping her eyes, straightened up, looking at Reyora whose calm enigmatic face gazed back at her.

She would never know the truth.

Chapter Fifteen

The journey had done much to assuage her grief in those awful days after the death of the Falcon, his burial in the family tomb at Falcon's Keep and the legal and civil complexities connected with the death of a great nobleman and the accession to his title and estates of his eldest son, the eight-year-old Duncan. Many people journeyed up from London for the funeral, including Mr. Pitt and the Duke of Newcastle. The King sent a personal representative, his mistress the Countess Yarmouth. No higher honor could have been given, but perhaps her ladyship had her own, more personal reasons for wishing to bid farewell to the remains of the mighty warrior. For a hero he was. The King was increasingly displeased with his son's reverses abroad and the brave, though futile, act of the Falcon had restored him to the nation's favor.

Analee bore it all with calm, good humor and dignity. She was supported by her father, who had hurried over from Spain on hearing of the Falcon's illness and now accompained her to Berlin where they had arranged, in advance, for a house to be rented for the short time they were thcre.

Berlin was a frenzied place in which to be, with troops passing through it and much of the civilian population packing up ready to leave in case of a French invasion. Apart from being with his beloved daughter, the Earl of St. March had not enjoyed journeying through embattled Europe.

"I shall be pleased to be home," he said, looking out into the deserted streets—a curfew of sorts had been imposed. "You should have sent for this woman, Analee."

"He asked me to go myself; it was his last wish."

"But *why*?" The Earl of St. March gazed at Analee, noting with concern her weariness and dejection.

"I felt I owed it to him."

"You owe him *nothing*. To fetch his mistress! 'Tis a monstrous thing to ask."

"Then perhaps I wanted to get away. I must say I do not relish the thought of seeing my husband's last mistress—the last of many. Maybe he felt an especial affection for the girl."

"But he came back to you."

"Yes, and I know he loved me. He had such flights of fancy and I suppose he would have continued to have them." Analee got restlessly up from her chair and began to pace up and down. "I know not. However what is done is done and he is gone." She got out

264

her handkerchief and removed a tear from her eye. "And I miss him. I always will. I would always have forgiven him and loved him again. I know that now, Father. The Falcon was something so special to me that I cannot replace him. Ever. I will never try."

The Earl bowed his head and took his daughter's hands between his. "Aye. There was a chemistry between you and only you knew it. Only you and he, and he can feel it no more. Now, my dear, if you will see this woman, let us get it over. I detest this place. Will you take her back to London?"

"Yes, and see that she is shipped off to her home in America. I must say I thought she had gone there long since. I did not know he had taken her with him. Maybe I would not have welcomed him back so kindly it I had."

"You have a generous heart, my dearest Analee. What other woman would have done this—gone and fetched her late husband's paramour?"

"The Falcon was no ordinary man and I am no ordinary woman. That is why," Analee said, riffling through a notebook that she had taken from her bag. "Now let me see, McNeath gave me the address. Yes, here it is . . ."

"I will call the coach. Let us . . ."

"I must go alone, Papa."

"But, my dear . . ."

Analee held up a hand and shook her head. "No. I must go alone. It will not be pleasant for me; but 'twill not be pleasant for her either. The last legacy of the Falcon was typical of him—guaranteed to cause a lot of distress all round. I will greet Miss Cameron, talk to her and then arrange for the lease of the house to be surrendered. Of course, I also wish to see if my husband left any effects, jewels, notes and such like. That is another reason I came. I have to leave his affairs in order, Papa, you know that."

"And then what will *you* do, my Analee, have you thought of *that*?"

"It is early days, Papa. The children are still grieving their father—all except Duncan, who mourns his passing not at all. It is very strange."

"But his father was so stern with him."

"Yes, but nevertheless you would have thought some spasm of grief would have touched him, for he is a sensitive, gentle boy. No, they disliked each other. My lord even showed that on his deathbed. Ah well, Duncan now as the Marquess of Falconer has his own important way to make in the world. And I must be by his side to help him. That is my duty now."

"And Morella?" The grandchild he had never seen. There was a question in the Earl's eyes as he looked at Analee.

"Ah, Morella," Analee sighed. "I would like very much to set that situation to rights; but I do not know what to do."

"But Sir Brent Delamain is her father, living in the same place as she and not knowing of the relationship."

"I know," Analee agreed, passing her hand wearily across her forehead. "There are some things that one does in life, Father, that are a permanent source of sorrow and regret. Yet, at the time, one did not know what to do for the best. That is how it was with me. Two things have happened that I could never have predicted. Brent Delamain has succeeded his brother and Lord Falconer is dead. You are right, once I have sorted out these various affairs to do with the Falcon's death, I must turn my attentions to the problem of Morella. Now would you kindly call the coach for me, Father, and direct the coachman as to the route he must take."

The house near to the Royal Palace in Berlin was larger than the kind of establishment Analee expected the Falcon would have taken for such a short sojourn.

Maybe he had wanted to impress his mistress! The door was opened by a doorman and yet two others greeted her in the large paved reception hall. She did not give her name but said she wished to see the mistress of the house. She kept her cloak on and her face hidden by a hat with a large low brim.

Analee felt apprehensive as she awaited Anna Cameron. Did she, for instance, know of the Falcon's death? What would she say? What would they both do? Now it *did* seem unfair of her husband to have given her this task. Only now did she regret she had not ignored his last wishes. What had made her come? Curiosity? Duty? Or maybe a mixture of the two, combined with a desire to get away from England, to travel abroad in the company of her father who would leave her after this and return to his home in Spain.

The ornate clock on the marble mantelpiece struck three. She was being kept waiting, perhaps deliberately. Had Anna Cameron spied her arrival from some hidden vantage point? She began to tap a foot impatiently when the door opened and a servant, stepping back to hold the door open, bowed at Analee announcing: "The Marchioness of Falconer, madam."

Analee rose to her feet with a smile, only realizing a moment later that the woman who had been announced as the Marchioness of Falconer was not her! She stared as Anna Cameron came slowly and haughtily into the room preceded by a second servant and followed by a third. Behind her was a gentlewoman some years older, probably a companion. The surprise at the style of announcement was nothing to the shock Analee got when that lady advanced, her large belly thrust out before her, obviously in a fairly advanced state of pregnancy. Analee closed her eyes momentarily, her senses reeling. *This* was why the Falcon had wanted her to look after Anna! She was carrying his child.

Analee, rapidly trying to recover her wits, held out a

267

hand as Anna stopped her stately progress and gazed imperiously at her.

"Why, 'tis Lady Falconer."

"Indeed, Miss Cameron."

"*Lady Falconer*, too, if you do not mind. Although it is confusing I understand that both past and present wives bear the same title."

"Past and *present* wives," Analee said with amazement, the light at last beginning to dawn. "Am I to understand that you consider yourself *married*, Miss Cameron?"

Anna Cameron flushed and the woman beside her came forward. "May I introduce myself, Lady Falconer? Lady McKeith. I think we met briefly in Paris in 1748."

"How do you do, Lady McKeith," Analee took her hand with her usual friendly smile, though she had not the fainest recollection of ever seeing her before. "Of course we did."

"I am afraid something very untoward has occurred, your ladyship," Lady McKeith said, glacing nervously at her companion whose air of haughtiness was gradually yielding to one of bewilderment. "Lady Falconer . . . er, Miss Cameron, that is to say, has undergone a ceremony of marriage with Lord Falconer. As you see, she is shortly to bear his child."

"I see that quite clearly," Analee said, unfastening her cloak with a grimace. "Getting her with child was one thing and, I regret to say, not such an uncommon one; but his lordship was in no position to marry Miss Cameron being, at the time, married to myself."

"There was no divorce?" Anna cried shrilly.

"None of which I am aware and, even with one so unpredictable as his lordship, I think that even *I* would have heard of that."

"You never petitioned for a divorce?"

"Never. His lordship was married to me until the day he died."

268

At this Anna, who had been growing visibly paler, fell to the ground. Lady McKeith rushed up to her, kneeling by her side and taking her pulse. She too had gone white and gazed at Analee.

"Until he *died*, Lady Falconer?"

"Alas, his lordship died over a month ago from wounds sustained during a fracas in June against the French. How far gone is Miss Cameron?"

"Seven months, your ladyship."

"I see. And no word of him reached you?"

"No word at all. Berlin is in absolute chaos with a French invasion expected any moment. The Court is in a turmoil, preparing to move to Magdeburg. In any event I was under instructions from his lordship not to allow Miss Cameron to go to the British Embassy."

"You knew why?"

Analee gazed at her severely from under the brim of her wide hat, a large ostrich feather concealing her eyes.

Lady McKeith was very busy fanning Anna's face, and avoided her gaze. "Yes."

"Then you were a party to the deception? How cruel of you, Lady McKeith."

"Believe me, Lady Falconer, I had no alternative. You know how determined his lordship can be . . . I'm sorry—could be."

"Indeed I do know. You had best see that Miss Cameron gets up to bed and rests. Poor child, she has had a double shock. She is not married, and her paramour is dead. Then come down and attend me, Lady McKeith, and we shall decide what is best to be done. Why he could not bed her without pretending to marry her I do not know."

"She would not do it, my lady. She was adamant."

Analee raised her eyebrows and permitted herself a wry smile. "Undoubtedly a challenge to his lordship."

"I am afraid so. He was obsessed with her and then

when he had got her there, it was not the paradise he thought it would be."

Analee held up a hand and glanced at Anna. "Pray spare me the details, Lady McKeith. It is, I assure you, of not the *slightest* interest to me. Now do as I say."

A week later Analee said goodbye to her father and, accompanied by Lady McKeith, set off for home traveling through a continent ravaged by battle, and arriving in London after a long and wearisome journey undertaken by stealth and at great speed. Analee installed Miss Cameron at Falconer House, dismissed Lady McKeith to whom she had taken a dislike for her obvious duplicity, and set about deciding what to do with the woman who would shortly bear her late husband's child.

After two days, when she thought Anna would be rested, Analee went into her room to find her sitting comfortably in a chair, looking out of the window. Her color was better but she still looked pale. The shock about Angus's deception and subsequent death had been so profound that she had scarcely spoken at all during the journey home. She looked at Analee as she came in, but did not smile.

"May I sit down, Anna?"

"Of course, it is your home."

Analee drew a chair up as close to her guest as she dared. "Anna, his lordship's final charge to me was that I should befriend and look after you. This I want to do."

"How can you be friends with me? We are rivals."

Analee sadly shook her head. "Not for a man who is dead. We are his widows."

"He cared nothing for you. He adored me." Anna shut her eyes, the tears rolling down her cheeks.

Analee swallowed hard, summoning to her aid the best of her nature, banishing jealousy and bitterness. "I am sure he adored you, Anna; after all what he did was no light thing. A bigamous marriage is a very grave offense; but I feel that I must point out to you the fact that, when mortally wounded he came all the way back to me. He wanted to die with me at our home in Lakeland. That is the final test of fidelity, is it not? In marriage and out of it."

"He knew not what he was doing. They brought him home."

"No. He *asked* to be taken home. The pain of the journey undoubtedly hastened his death. I was his wife, Anna, in spirit and in body, and it was with me he wished to die." Analee got up and slowly began to pace the room. "Now, having said that, I do not desire rivalry or jealousy between us. What is done is done. On his deathbed his lordship asked me to look after you. He did not tell me you were with child, although I should have guessed it. He certainly did not tell me he had bigamously wed you, and that must remain a secret. I hope I have paid Lady McKeith enough to keep her mouth shut. No one but you and I knows about all this, and I am going to take you to Lakeland to have your baby. If we summon a doctor or midwife in London all the world will know about it."

"I am not ashamed," Anna said, raising her chin and gazing at Analee with dislike.

"Good. You should indeed be proud to bear his lordship's child, a lasting memento of him. Then what will you do, Anna?"

"*Do?*" Anna gazed at Analee. "I have never thought what I should *do*. I thought I was his wife, a marchioness, well provided-for, secure for the rest of my life, whatever happened to Lord Falconer. Now I know that I have no title, no wealth and my child will be a bastard. What do you *expect* me to do?"

Anna's voice rose almost to a scream and Analee knelt by her, taking her hand. "Hush, my dear. There, you have got it out and it is over."

Anna put her head in her hands and sobbed. "I

271

thought my child would be a lord or a lady. It will be nothing. A bastard."

"It will be a child, boy or girl," Analee said with calm practicality, continuing to stroke Anna's hand. "I myself was born, as they say, on the wrong side of the sheets. I find it no disadvantage to have parents who were not wed. Indeed, sometimes it is an advantage. My father loves me dearly and I only have beautiful memories of my mother. Your child will have had a distinguished man for a father, and a beautiful, brave-spirited girl for a mother. I think that a fine inheritance."

"*Fine?*" Anna stared at her, her lips curling. "But what shall I tell my family?"

"Tell them that your husband died. We shall invent one for you; maybe a soldier you married in Berlin. Maybe . . ."

"Oh, I cannot, I cannot return to my house unwed and with a child."

"But no one will know."

"I told my mother that I had married the Marquess of Falconer, that we were blissfully happy and expecting a child."

"Oh." This was a complication Analee had not thought of. Of course the girl would tell her mother.

"I told my mother that I would bring his lordship to America and . . ."

"Oh dear, oh dear," Analee said. "Well, I will assist in any lie except that of deceiving people into thinking my husband had divorced me. That I will not do. It would be a slur on myself and my children; also to his name because I know he did not *wish* to divorce me. Now, Anna, let us be practical. Even though you are not ashamed of your condition—an attitude I fully applaud—it would be wiser, would it not, to move out of London?"

Anna hung her head and gnawed at one of her fingernails. "Maybe."

"Good, that is what I think," Analee got up and shook her skirt.

"But after that, after the child is born?"

"Well, we have to go one step at a time," Analee said. "I will always protect you because that was what his lordship asked of me. You and your child will always enjoy the protection of the Falconer family. That I promise you. If you wish to return home there will be money for the journey. If you wish to stay here we will devise some plan. I will protect you. Never fear. Your child will always be provided for. It is what the Falcon would have wished." Analee smiled and turned to the door, not seeing the look of hatred that Anna Cameron cast at her back.

"I can't think why you did not warn me," Analee said to McNeath, who hung his head and shuffled his feet. Behind him stood his wife, her arms akimbo, face flushed. She looked as though, as soon as she had her husband to herself, she would give him a good hiding.

"I did not *dare* say anything, my lady."

"You did not even tell Nell!"

"No, ma'am." McNeath stole a guilty look at his wife. "I thought it best your ladyship should find out yourself. I couldn't find the words, ma'am."

"You could have found them for *me*, you nincompoop!" Nelly screamed. "I would have spared her ladyship such an encounter."

"Perhaps 'twas as well," Analee said, shrugging her shoulders and gazing thoughtfully at the lake. "I might have lacked the courage to go at all."

"But what will you do with her, my lady?" Nelly said in a hoarse whisper, looking over her shoulder although Anna Cameron was safely in her room resting from the journey.

" 'Tis a bitter legacy from the Falcon. She is not a pleasant person, such as I remember her, but has become brittle and hard. She is greatly embittered and resents anything I do for her. I do not know what will become of her. I cannot bear to think about it. But she will be the mother of a child by his lordship. I cannot reject her, and she does not wish to go home, having told her family that she is married to him. When they learn of his death they will think she is a widow, but eventually they must learn the truth.

"My father thought she would be best off abroad, posing as some widowed, respectable lady with a child. Of course, I would provide the money for her to live in a suitable state. But she rejects the idea. I think she prefers to be a thorn in the side of his wife, seeing that she cannot have my husband. Anyway, Europe is no fit place in which to reside at the moment though my father says Spain is quite safe. However, he does not want her there! We shall see, Nelly. Maybe she will be of a more pleasant disposition when her child is born."

Anna Cameron resented Analee, disliked her children and made herselef generally unpleasant about the house. She also gave herself the airs of a marchioness even if she had no right to the title. Sometimes Analee thought that Anna was indeed the owner of the house and not her; her little bell rang imperiously all day long to summon servants to fetch this and bring that. Gradually Analee felt that she had a rival in her own home and her resentment of Anna grew as her attempts at friendship were continually firmly rejected.

"I do not see how we can live together if you persist in this attitude," Analee said, confronting Anna one day after a bout of unpleasantness involving Nelly. "Nelly McNeath is a very old friend of mine, not a mere servant."

"But I will not have her children near me!" Anna said, wrinkling her nose with disgust. "They ran alongside me as I walked by the lake, as though I were not a person of quality."

"But they run alongside *me*! They play with my children all the time. They are all like brothers and sisters together."

Anna looked down her nose and pursed her mouth in an expression of comtempt.

"It seems to point to your own humble origins, Lady Falconer, does it not? It must have been *very* difficult for you to slough off your gypsy past and play the marchioness. I, of course, was born to parents who were legally married and in possession of a considerable fortune. The children of our servants are never allowed anywhere *near* us!"

"I am surprised to hear you talk like that, Anna," Analee said, her voice rising. "Take care you do not go too far with me! I am obeying my lord's wishes with regard to you, but not my own inclinations. Yes, out of compassion I was at first prepared to welcome you and treat you as a sister, despite my distress at learning of your close relationship to my husband. I was prepared to overlook all this in honor of his memory; but you are making it *very* hard for me. I cannot endure endless abuse."

"His lordship was married in spirit to me," Anna said contemptuously. "I regard myself in fact as his lawful wife, his widow. He loved me passionately, desired me . . ."

"Oh, pray do not bore me with the details of your intimacy," Analee said, putting down the embroidery she had been unsuccessfully trying to work. "I am glad you gave him pleasure in his last days; but when he wanted comfort in his extremity and dire need, he knew to whom to come. *Me*, not you!" Analee thrust an imperious finger at her own breast and, gathering up her work, marched out of the door, cannoning into Nelly as she did.

"That girl' she is intolerable! she will make my life a misery. What did I do to deserve this?"

"Analee, Reyora is here."

"Reyora?"

275

"She knows not if you will receive her."

"Of course I will . . ." Analee paused and gazed at Nelly. "Because of the Falcon?"

Nelly nodded. "She is very upset about it. McNeath found her skulking in a tent that day and dragged her here. He has told me I should send her packing; but, as she is such as old friend of yours, of course I could not."

"Of course." Analee took a deep breath and squared her shoulders. "How many things have been sent to try me in these days. Will there be no end to it?" She smiled at Nelly and opened the door of the small parlor where Reyora was sitting hunched over her special bag. As Analee came in she got to her feet and looked at her humbly.

"Oh, Reyora!" Analee felt a surge of emotion and clasped her friend to her bosom.

"I am forgiven, Analee?"

Analee stood back and looked at her. "You did what you thought was right."

"I was right. My powers are not limitless, you know. I could not have saved him."

"But why did you hide?"

"Because I knew I could not help and you would blame me. The forces that wanted to take him into the other world were too strong. They had been pulling at him for some time, summoning him . . ."

Analee shuddered and clasped her hands about her arms in an attempt to warm herself. "Oh, do not speak thus. It is as though a ghost is walking on my grave. So why have you come now, dear Reyora?"

"Because you need me."

"I need you?"

"Yes. You are still surrounded by evil forces, Analee. Someone in this house hates you."

"Oh no!"

"They would do you harm."

"Harm *me?*"

276

"Push you out of the window or into the lake. Drug you at night. Someone who would benefit by your death."

Analee sat down, too shocked to speak. "But who would benefit . . . Oh no!" She clasped her head in her hands and rocked back and forwards.

"You know who it is?"

"My husband had a mistress. She is to bear his child. They entered a bigamous form of marriage."

"And she is *here*?"

"Yes."

"Then she must be got away. She is too dangerous. I cannot control her from afar."

"But what can she do? She is large with child."

"I know not how she will do it, but she will. She wishes you dead. Maybe then she can say she is legally married to his lordship. Is that a possibility?"

"I do not know; but she does hate me. I wanted to be friendly towards her and put myself out; but it is of no use."

"You must send her away."

"I cannot! She is very near her time. Any day."

"You must be protected night and day . . ."

Reyora looked up as Nelly came in carrying a parcel, holding it out before her, looking at the card with it. "Analee! Someone has sent you a present. See, a parcel came all the way from London. It just arrived on the boat with the mail."

"Who would send me a parcel?" Analee gazed at the card. " 'From a well-wisher.' I seem to recognize the writing. Do you not, Nelly?" She handed it to Nelly, who laughed and gave it back to her.

"Analee, you know I have not your accomplishments. I can neither read nor write."

Analee smiled and began to open the parcel. "I must have you taught, Nell; so that you can be a fine lady like me. Oh look! Chocolates and bonbons—all beautiful wrapped. I wonder who could be the well-wisher?"

Analee raised a large nut to her lips, offering the box to Nelly and Reyora; but Reyora suddenly was seized by a spasm, stared at the ceiling and dashed the chocolate from Analee's fingers.

"Do not eat it. It is poisoned!"

Analee jumped and the box fell from her hand, the chocolates and bonbons scattering on the floor.

"Really, Reyora . . ."

"This is the danger I spoke to you about." Reyora surveyed the scattered confectionery. "You said you recognized the writing? Try again."

Analee picked up the card and scrutinized the writing. " 'From a well-wisher,' " she murmured slowly. "I know. I think it is Lady McKeith. She wrote me a letter of thanks before she left. I am sure it is her writing, a fine, bold hand. Why should she send me poisoned chocolates?"

"Who is Lady McKeith?" demanded Reyora gravely.

"She was the companion to . . . Oh!" Analee paused and stared at her friend. "The companion to Anna Cameron, the mistress of my husband."

"Then that explains it, does it not? It is a plot to get rid of you and say she is the legitimate widow of the Falcon."

"But it is an *absurd* notion."

"No matter. Two stupid, greedy ambitious women are hardly likely to think of anything very profound. Maybe they thought there was a chance."

"But how can we prove it?"

"Offer her the chocolates." Reyora began picking them up from the floor with a smile. "See what she does."

Anna Cameron was resting in her room when Analee walked in bearing the box of chocolates, an anticipatory smile on her face. "See! Someone has sent me a delicious present of bonbons from London! I must have a secret admirer." Analee selected a luscious

278

chocolate and held it to her mouth, holding the box to Anna. "Try one, Anna, please."

Anna Cameron changed color and clutched her stomach. "Oh, no thank you, Lady Falconer! I am not well enough."

Analee paused in the act of pretending to put the chocolate to her rounded mouth and stared at her guest in feigned surprise. "Oh? Are you unwell?"

"It may not be good for my stomach."

"But you ate such a huge dinner."

"That is why. Maybe I ate too much." Anna heaved her cumbersome form from the bed and propped herself on her arms. Her face was quite ashen and her lower lip trembled. She stared at Analee as though transfixed by a shocking sight.

"Anna, you look most *unwell*," Analee said with concern, putting the box by her bedside. "Maybe it is your time?"

Anna clutched her stomach and wriggled uncomfortably. "Yes, I have had cramps all afternoon in the belly."

"Well, I will just eat my chocolate and then go and fetch some help."

Analee very deliberately selected a fresh chocolate, slowly took the wrapper from it and then made as if to pop it into her mouth, glancing at Anna from the corner of her eyes as she did so. She saw Anna close her eyes, clutch once more at her distended stomach and then, lurching up, she grasped Analee's hand and the chocolate fell to the ground.

"Do not eat that!"

Analee raised her eyebrows in mock surprise and gazed at the chocolate on the floor. "Why, Anna, whatever made you do that?"

"There may be something wrong with it."

"But why should there be?"

"You never know."

Anna burst into tears and Analee picked up the dis-

279

carded chocolate and placed it with the others, putting the box safely out of the way. Then she sat on the bed and placed her hand on the shoulders of the weeping girl.

"*Is* there something wrong with them, Anna?"

Anna nodded her head, weeping violently.

"Are they poisoned?" Analee said sadly. "Did you want to kill me so badly then?"

Anna first shook her head and then nodded, as though unable to make up her mind. "I hate you!" she sobbed. "But I do not want to see you die. I couldn't lie there and watch."

"I should have done it quietly, out of the way, was that it? Indeed I would have, had not a friend warned me in a most uncanny way."

"They say you are a witch," Anna blubbered. "I should have known it would not succeed."

"But how could it? You would have been accused of poisoning me. 'Twas Lady McKeith sent them, was it not?"

"She said I would then be Lady Falconer because I had married his lordship."

"But your bogus marriage to him was while I was alive, Anna! You could never have been Lady Falconer, even with me dead."

"I did not know. She said it, not I. She said, anyway, that with you dead I would have a claim on the Falcon's vast fortune on behalf of the child I would bear him."

"I see," Analee sat back. She felt very sad and dejected. "I am sad that you hated me so much, rejected my friendship."

"How could I *like* you? I hated you! You were so condescending, so grand. I had nothing in the world and you . . . everything!" Anna made a gesture and then her face crunpled with pain.

"I did not mean to be condescending or grand," Analee went on. "It was a difficult position for me, but I wanted to do my best. I see I failed."

"What will become of me now?" Anna cried again, her face grimaced in a spasm. "I think my time has come, Lady Falconer. The agony in the belly grows greater."

Anna labored all that day and part of the next. Forgetting that she had wanted to kill her, Analee waited on her tirelessly, holding her hand, bathing her face, changing her chemises soaked with prespiration, talking to her with soft words of encouragement. Reyora sat by the bed massaging her belly, deftly probing in the birth passage with her skilled hands, but by late morning on the following day she shook her head.

"The child is lodged in the womb, Analee. You can only take it out by cutting open the stomach and I cannot do that."

"But you helped me when Morella was born. You cast a spell."

"This is different. The passage has not opened as much as it should. You must call the doctor immediately and tell him to bring his instruments with him. It is the only way the child and the mother can be saved."

A messenger was sent swiftly to Keswick and within the hour the doctor and midwife were on their way by boat. All the time Analee talked to Anna bringing her words of comfort.

"I will die, I will die, I will die," Anna screamed. "I can stand the pain no longer."

"No, you will not die. The doctor is on his way. Because the Falcon has given you such a fine, lusty child he will need instruments to deliver you. But do not be afraid, he is skilled in *accouchments*."

"I will die," Anna said, looking distractedly at the ceiling. "I will die for my crimes against you and God."

281

"No," Analee smiled, stroking the hair back from her feverish brow. "I forgive you and I am sure God will, too. When you are well, Anna, and rested, you will go with your baby maybe to Spain or Italy where there is no war, to rest and ponder on the future."

"I will die," Anna repeated tearfully. "I will never live to see another day."

"No, you are young and strong; but tired. The baby will be delivered before dark."

Analee went to the window and for the tenth time looked out into the lake. She was worried about Anna, who was showing signs of weakening. Reyora squatted beside her massaging her belly and murmuring soft incantations; but her eyes looked troubled as she gazed at Analee and from time to time she shook her head.

"Look, there is the doctor!" Analee cried. "Nat is rowing him in the boat. Soon your troubles will be over."

Anna began to cry and Analee went and sat with her again, telling Nelly to go down and welcome the doctor. She took her hand and squeezed it. Anna's eyes were tired and her face pinched and drawn. She beckoned to Analee, who put her head close to that of the suffering woman.

"He *did* love you. He murmured your name in his sleep. I was no use to him as a woman. I was fearful of the marital act. I hated him to touch me. I wanted to be a marchioness for the happiness it would give my family. I was too vain, too ambitious. Now I am paying for it all. I am cursed."

Analee's eyes filled with tears and she found it hard to swallow. She grasped Anna's hand and turned away, trying to compose herself before the doctor came.

An hour later the baby was delivered, cut expertly from its mother's belly; a fine healthy girl who cried lustily as the doctor drew her out of the womb. But despite the undoubted skill of the surgeon, Anna Cameron, exhausted and frightened after her protract-

282

ed labor, too frail to stand the pain of the operation, only lived long enough to see the child she had endured so much to bear. She seemed to make a supreme effort to gather up her strength and smile at the child as if in farewell before she sank back, her eyes closed. A few minutes later she died, her head resting in the arms of Analee who, throughout the terrible ordeal, had nursed her with such tender care, never leaving the side of the woman who had done so much to wrong her.

Chapter Sixteen

Catherine Walkinshaw tapped her snuff box and looked shrewdly at Isobel McKeith before opening the lid and delicately putting a pinch in her right nostril.

"Do you take snuff?" she said, holding out the box.

Isobel shook her head. She thought women taking snuff was a revolting habit but, unfortunately, a common one. Catherine Walkinshaw managed it very deftly, there was only a tiny trace of the brown powder at the base of her nostril. She repeated the process with the left nostril and then shut the box and stowed it away in the pockets of her capacious skirt.

"So," she said. "What you have to say is a very grave matter."

"I have had it on my conscience, Catherine. I did not dare approach her Royal Highness with it; but thought first to discuss it with you." Isobel shifted uneasily in her chair, her bright, artificially colored golden curls bobbing about beneath her lace cap. She was really raddled now, rouged, powdered and patched but with an artifice that managed to bestow on her a semblance of past beauty.

283

"But what you are saying is that Lady Falconer murdered first her husband and then his mistress."

Isobel lowered her eyes. "I can see no other explanation. They both died within weeks of each other. Lord Falconer was considered fit enough to make the long journey from Hanover, only to die shortly after reaching home. As for Miss Cameron, I know how well she withstood the journey because did I not travel with her? She was a fine healthy girl, fit to bear many babies. But what happens? When we got to London I was curtly dismissed by Lady Falconer, without so much a a 'thank you' or 'call again,' and Miss Cameron is whisked up to the cold north of England, away from the best obstetric surgeons, where she dies in childbirth—supposedly." Lady McKeith lingered heavily on the word "supposedly."

"But what was Lady Falconer's *motive*?" Miss Walkinshaw murmured. "What had she to gain?"

"To rid herself of a rival. I know the Falcon was bent on divorcing her and marrying Miss Cameron. 'Twas but a matter of time."

" 'Tis a very serious charge." Miss Walkinshaw looked thoughtfully at Lady McKeith, whom she had known since a girl. She did not really trust her but then she trusted no one, living in the same twilight world of truths and half-truths, loyalties and divided loyalties as others whose sympathies were or had been part Jacobite, part Hanoverian. For many years she had just tried to do her work as a lady in the service of the Princess of Wales; latterly endeavoring to forget the shame of the liaison of her youngest sister with Prince Charles Stuart, but people kept dragging her in. "How would you propose to go about making it public, if that is what you wish?"

"I thought if you had a word with the Princess, expressing your own doubts."

"You expect *me* to stand in a court of law and accuse Lady Falconer of murder?"

"Oh no, Catherine, nothing like that; but I do not think she should go unpunished. I feel very strongly about it."

"Lady Falconer has but recently emerged from Carlisle jail on suspicion of high treason. She was so clearly vindicated—do you think the King would listen to fresh rumors?"

"He might, if there were more substance. Lady Falconer had a very strong motive for getting rid of her husband. Very strong indeed. And was he not a hero? Do you think the King would condone *that*?"

"I will see what I can do," Catherine Walkinshaw said reluctantly after a while. "I do not like to see wrong go unpunished, but neither do I like to interfere where matters of such gravity are concerned. Now tell me, Isobel, what are you doing with yourself these days?"

She picked up her embroidery and leaned forward, indicating that the subject was at an end.

Princess Augusta's plain pockmarked face remained impassive as she listened to the story told by her friend of many years' standing, one of the few members of her household whom she felt she could completely trust. Since the death of her husband and the knowledge that she would never wear the crown of England as its queen, she had become more settled in her ways. She was, for instance, on better terms with the King because she was anxious that her son George should get on well with his grandfather. She had been very careful to divest herself of Jacobite sympathies; but even then the factions in the two courts continued—some politicians, such as Pitt, favored by Leiscester House, others by St. James's Palace. Her special friend and confidant was Lord Bute who had enhanced his power by supporting Pitt and Newcastle to form a ministry in the summer, shortly after the death of Lord Falconer.

When Catherine Walkinshaw had finished speaking,

the Princess did not at first say anything, but smoothed the tapestry that she was working on, regarding it from a distance with a critical eye. "Do you think the color of that rose is too loud, Catherine?"

Miss Walkinshaw bent forward, inspected the work and shook her head. "It will tone down, Your Royal Highness. Maybe a paler shade for the flower on the right?"

"I think you are correct." Princess Augusta nodded and, removing her spectacles, placed them on top of her work which she put on a table at her elbow.

"Catherine, why are you telling me all this?"

"Because I feel an injustice may have been done, Your Royal Highness."

"To whom?"

"To Lord Falconer and his unfortunate mistress."

"Yes, a pretty girl." The Princess looked wistful. "He used to parade her in a very unsubtle manner at Court. The King was quite taken by her, but of course his loyalty was for Lady Falconer, as it will be again. If I were you I would forget all this tittle-tattle, Catherine. I would put it out of your mind."

"But I have known Isobel McKeith since we were girls in Scotland, ma'am."

"But she is flighty, is she not? As soon as Prince Charles Edward fled to France she tried to get her husband to petition for clemency to the King of England on the grounds that he had never taken up arms against him."

Catherine shrugged. "Ma'am, were there not many people with a duality of purpose? Even Lady Falconer herself . . . Why, it was not so long ago, I hesitate to say this, ma'am, that her ladyship came with a message from the Prince wanting to know the dispersion of those with Jacobite sympathies in the English Court."

The Princess's face puckered with horror. "Lady Falconer! An emissary of the Prince?"

Catherine spread her thick fingers on her skirt and regarded them gravely. "I told her ladyship that I had no dealings at all with Jacobites, and disapproved of my unfortunate sister's connection with the Prince. She apologized for having misunderstood the situation."

"I am dumbfounded," the Princess said. "I am horror-struck, for it would be after that that the Falcon accused her of treachery. He knew the truth."

"Yes, ma'am."

"And she *was* a traitor?"

"It would appear so, ma'am, a *kind of* treachery."

"I am amazed to hear it had gone so far. And her own husband a trusted counselor of the King! Maybe she did have cause to murder him. Oh dear, I wish I had not this information, Catherine."

"I too, ma'am. Believe me, I spent a very troubled night, tossing and turning, wondering whether or not to approach Your Royal Highness. You see, I feel that if I do nothing Isobel McKeith might noise it abroad until she had some vindication. There is no doubt that she nurses a bitter vindictiveness towards the Marchioness of Falconer. Very bitter indeed."

The Earl of Bute, when consulted, was equally appalled. Like the Princess and, before her, Miss Walkinshaw, his immediate instinct was to do nothing; but the Earl knew that the King's memory of the Falcon was tainted by the knowledge that he had falsely accused his wife of treachery. That he might have been done to death by this same wife was a monstrous state of affairs.

"She was but a mere gypsy after all," he said, gazing at the Princess. "She has no real breeding as a lady."

"She is very much loved by many people," the Princess said defensively. "I have always been very fond of Lady Falconer and there is no doubt her husband treated her shamefully . . ."

"All the more reason to kill him."

287

"But he was very badly wounded."

"Yet well enough to travel such a distance."

Lord Bute put his hands under the tails of his coat and walked to the windows that overlooked the formal gardens of Leicester House. "I will talk to Mr. Pitt," he said. "He may be more objective, although he had high regard for the ability of Lord Falconer and was dismayed when the King sent him abroad. He will know what is best to do."

Hector Cameron stared at Isobel McKeith, his eyes puckering with tears. She drew him to a chair and bade him sit down. She then went to the sideboard and poured from a decanter of brandy into two glasses. She needed to give herself courage as well as him. "There, sir. Pray drink it at a gulp. It will steady your nerves."

With a trembling hand Hector raised the glass to his lips and did as Lady McKeith had bid him. But his hand was still shaking as he replaced the glass on the table. "My daughter, *murdered* by Lady Falconer?"

"What else can I deduce, Mr. Cameron?" Isobel McKeith shook her head. "She was a strong girl, the pregnancy uncomplicated."

"But have you any *proof*, Lady McKeith?"

"Who can get proof, sir, from the wilds of Lakeland? It is as though Lady Falconer rules over her own domain there. Who would bear witness against her ladyship? No one, I am sure."

"But there is a child, my granddaughter. Lady Falconer wrote to me of her when she told me about the whole sad business. My wife, who has been made ill by the whole affair, bade me travel here at once. That our daughter should bigamously marry a man, thinking herself a marchioness, give birth to his daughter and then die . . . 'Twas too much for the poor lady, who has never enjoyed good health. The last we had heard from her was of her marriage in Berlin and that she was expecting this child and ecstatically happy. The next that she was dead, and the marriage had been illegal."

"I can image the shock," Lady McKeith sighed sympathetically. "And how did Lady Falconer speak of your granddaughter?"

"That she is a beautiful girl; that she is taking good care of her."

"Well, that's a wonder," Lady McKeith sniggered. "I suppose even *she* balked at the thought of three murders. Though 'tis a wonder she did not bury her alongside her mother, and consider the task well done."

. . Hector Cameron held up a hand, his lips trembling. "I cannot bear to entertain such a suspicion, Lady McKeith. Lady Falconer seemed a much abused woman, by her husband, by my daughter. She seemed to have shown nothing but goodness and consideration in return."

"Ha!" Isobel McKeith threw up her head in a gesture of scorn. "Do you really suppose *that*? Her ladyship is a gypsy, and gypsy ways are evil—everyone knows that. It was not for nothing that she was known as the Enchantress. She is a witch. She should be burnt at the stake for witchcraft; I hear it is still done in some parts of Lancashire."

"Oh I hope not, Lady McKeith! It was common practice in my country in the early settler days, but is now stamped out. I would not like to see such a thing happen to Lady Falconer. If she is a murderess the law should take its due course; but burnt at the stake . . . no!"

"And *do* you think the law will take its due course?" Lady McKeith said mockingly. "Or do you not suppose her ladyship to be above it? I do. There is only one way to touch her."

"And that is?" Hector Cameron got out a handkerchief and rubbed his watery eyes hard.

"She must be accused in public. *You*, sir, must vindicate the foul murder of your daughter and point the finger of suspicion directly at the Marchioness of Falconer, so that all may know the truth."

Analee looked from the Princess of Wales to Lord Bute, the amazement on her face more telling than any expression of indignation. "I know not whether to laugh or cry," she said at last. "That *I* should murder first my husband, then his mistress? Is is possible anyone would believe it? Do you not know, does not everyone know, that the Falcon should have died of his terrible wound in Hanover, and was only supported by his longing to die in my arms?"

"That *is* what I heard," the Princess said, looking at Lord Bute doubtfully.

"His lordship's wound was green and riddled with maggots. He was a corpse when he came home, as any number of witnesses will tell you. It was only his love for me that sustained him."

"But his mistress . . ."

"I knew naught of Miss Cameron's position until *after* his death. I only discovered that she was his mistress, and with child *and* thinking herself Marchioness of Falconer, when I went to Berlin on his lordship's instructions. You think that I then plotted to bring her back and *murder* her? Oh, 'tis monstrous!"

Lord Bute gazed at her with admiration. She was a beautiful woman, a forceful character, there was no doubt of that; but was she telling the truth? He swiveled his eyes round to look at the Princess who appeared to be having her confidence in Lady Falconer vindicated. She smiled with relief.

"I agree it is monstrous," Princess Augusta said at last. "And I for one am satisfied. Are you not, Lord Bute?"

"I never doubted for a moment that the story was without foundation," the Earl said ingratiatingly. "But I knew it would spread further if we did not stop it."

"By whom, may I ask?" Analee gazed fearlessly at

them. "May I not know the name of my accuser, or accusers?"

"I am afraid not," Lord Bute said diplomatically. "We gave our word . . ."

"Then how can I be satisfied unless I confront him, or them, or is it *her*, myself?"

The Earl shrugged and glanced at the Princess. "We will see that it gets no further."

"I am *not* satisfied," Analee said, her eyes smoldering with anger. "I demand justice!"

"Oh please, Lady Falconer," the Princess gazed at her pleadingly. "Leave it here; let it drop. Catherine Walkinshaw . . ."

"Ah, Analee said, looking at Lord Bute. "It *was* Mistress Walkinshaw. I thought her a good friend of mine. Why should she spread such a lie?"

" 'Twas not Catherine Walkinshaw in the *first* place," Princess Augusta said cautiously, fanning herself despite the cold of the room. "But she told me of the rumor. I told Lord Bute. That is as far as it has gone."

Except for Mr. Pitt, Lord Bute thought, who undoubtedly had told half the Cabinet by now. He shuddered at the idea of what they had put in motion.

"But why should Miss Walkinshaw believe such a scandal?"

As Lord Bute gazed at his feet, Analee knew. The one weakness; the misguided deed she had done out of pity for the Prince. Such a little thing, a stupid error that might ruin her whole life.

" 'Twas because I went to her," she said without waiting for an answer, "and told her of the Prince's request. She thought I was a traitor?"

"No, she didn't think you were a traitor," Princess Augusta said earnestly. "She was disquieted enough to speak to me about what she had heard. It was thought there might be ample reason for you to kill your husband—because he had caused you insupportable pain."

"I am, I was no traitor," Analee said quietly, her white hand on the medal of Falcon gold she wore round her neck. "But I admit I *was* unwise. I was merely an emissary between the Prince and Miss Walkinshaw, the sister of his mistress. His Royal Highness mistakenly thought . . ."

"But how could he *think* such a thing? He must know that her family abhors the action of Clementina Walkinshaw?"

Analee shrugged her shoulders. "That is what I do not understand. Believe me, Your Royal Highness, it was never my intention to help plot the restoration of the Stuarts; but I was torn between two allegiances— between loyalty to my husband and pity for my many friends who were in exile. I thought it innocent enough a request and I obeyed it. I was very foolish and repent of doing it. I can see now that it was open to misinterpretation. I deserve to be chastised, maybe; but not to be accused of murder."

The Princess rose and Analee rose with her. Her chin was tilted proudly, but her eyes were downcast. Her lustrous black hair was set in modest ringlets which gleamed against the exposed skin of her shoulders. Her bodice and skirt were of a dark blue that enhanced her coloring, and her stomacher was of delicate lace, matching the lace flounces at her elbows. The Princess thought that if ever Lady Falconer were in the dock, the court would have to be composed of women if its judgment was not to be influenced by her beauty— and maybe even her own sex would be susceptible to her charm.

"I think many of us have mixed loyalties which we have subsequently had reason to repent of," the Princess said lightly. "Even my husband was accused of Jacobite dealings and nothing could have been further from the truth. Happily those times are in the past and our nation is no longer divided. I am sure your ladyship will be very discreet in future. As for this matter," the Princess gestured towards Lord Bute, "I think we should all let it drop. It will soon be forgotten . . ."

"But my accuser . . ." Analee stammered.

"Your acciser will be dealt with, will be spoken to. Have no fear. Put the matter out of your mind and go back to your Lakeland home; but before you do, promise to take tea with me and tell me about your family, the new Marquess who I hear is such a handsome child, and so on."

Analee dropped a deep curtsey. She did not feel satisfied, but she did not know what she could do. She intimated that she would be honored to take tea with her Royal Highness and then accepted Lord Bute's arm as the doors were opened and he led her into the small antechamber of the Princess's apartments. A way was being cleared for them by many who were curious to gaze upon the widowed Marchioness who was said to mourn her husband so much that she shunned the pleasures of the Court, despite his blatant infidelities.

"I assure you, Lady Falconer," Lord Bute patted her hand, "the Princess only brought this matter up with the greatest reluctance, in your own interests . . ."

"I appreciate that fully," Analee murmured quietly so that those around should not hear. "But it has been an ordeal for me, my lord, and I have had so many sorrows in past years. Sometimes I wonder what I have done to deserve them."

Suddenly she looked up as a small commotion started by the door towards which they were walking. A figure unfamiliar to Analee advanced slowly towards her; his arm outstretched, his finger pointing accusingly; but next to him was someone Analee knew very well indeed. She grasped Lord Bute's arm and he too stopped talking and gazed at the stranger who, obviously in the grip of strong emotion, shouted:

"She is a murderess! There! She murdered her husband and my daughter. She is a traitor to her country and murderess! There, behold her: Lady Falconer!"

293

Even Lady McKeith, who had instigated the scene, looked momentarily dismayed by its effects; for no sooner had Mr. Cameron stopped speaking than he was seized by liveried servants and pushed to the floor while shocked and amazed courtiers buzzed and hummed a ceaseless undercurrent of comment and conversation.

While Mr. Cameron struggled on the floor with the servants who were reinforced by others, Lady McKeith held her hands to her mouth as if in horror. She looked up and her eyes met Analee's.

"I see who has caused all this," Analee said slowly. "It is all clear to me now, my lord. Lady McKeith is the fount of this malicious gossip that threatens to destroy an innocent woman. I might have known."

She gazed witheringly at Isobel McKeith, who lowered her eyes while the already high color on her cheeks grew hectic. Mr. Cameron, however, would not be silent and kept on shouting, "Murderess!" whenever he had the chance, until the large hand of one of the servants was firmly clamped around his mouth and he was dragged into an adjoining room.

Lord Bute raised his eyes to heaven, wishing he were in the safe confines of his club drinking porter with his cronies.

"Come, Lady Falconer," he said, taking her arm. "I will have you escorted home."

But Analee shook her arm free and smiled at him. "I am afraid we cannot ignore this, Lord Bute. Now that I know the source of the mischief it is important to extinguish it, for I know it comes from the mouth of one who is indeed a genuine would-be murderess: Lady McKeith herself!"

Analee raised her voice for everyone to hear it and Isobel, who had begun to have doubts about the affair when they set out, now bitterly regretted it. She swayed and clutched the arm of a nearby courtier who moved quickly out of the way, not wishing to be tainted by one who had been instrumental in causing such an unseemly and unprecedented commotion in the apartments of the Princess of Wales. Lord Bute, looking increasingly agitated, demanded the room should be cleared as the door to the Princess's chamber opened and she came out to see what had caused the uproar.

"Why, Lady Falconer!"

"I know who my accuser is, ma'am." Analee pointed a finger at Isobel McKeith, by now cowering in shame. "And glad I am of the chance to rebut her charge in public."

By this time the room had been cleared of all but a handful of spectators, those who were close to the Princess or Court functionaries. It was, however, sufficient as far as Analee was concerned to constitute a small court. She curtsied to the Princess and pointed to the room where Mr. Cameron had been taken.

"I hazard a guess that the poor man yonder is the father of Anna Cameron. He has doubtless been told wicked lies about his daughter. If your Royal Highness will permit it, may he be brought back here?"

Princess Augusta looked helplessly at the hapless Lord Bute as though to say that this business was all his fault.

"I think the matter had best be cleared up, ma'am," he said.

"If you say so, Lord Bute, though I never did think that even my exalted position constituted a court of law."

"I hope it does not come to that, ma'am," Analee said firmly. "But if it does, I am prepared to face trial, and we shall then see who ends on the gallows."

Mr. Cameron, still shaking, but a little recovered from his ordeal, was led into the chamber and a chair placed for him opposite that of the Princess to whom he bowed very deeply before taking his seat, mopping his brow. Analee, Lord Bute and Lady McKeith re-

295

mained standing. Everyone stopped chattering and the air grew tense with expectation.

"Now," Lord Bute said, bowing to the Princess. "What is it you wish to say, Mr. Cameron, against Lady Falconer?"

Mr. Cameron again took out his handkerchief and nervously wiped the sweat off his face, after glancing at Isobel McKeith, who stood agitatedly fiddling with the large yellow bows on her petticoat. "I was informed that Lady Falconer killed my daughter, sir, after murdering her own husband."

A gasp ran round those assembled who edged away from the chief participants as though fearful of contagion.

"We *have* heard this rumor," Lord Bute said pompously, "and have decided it was completely without foundation. *If* you thought this, sir, why did you not take it to the proper authorities? The Court of the Princess of Wales is not a place in which to make accusations of this nature, as you should know, even if you are from the colonies."

"Lady McKeith told me that, because of the eminence of Lady Falconer, no one would listen to me, so I should make it in public."

"I see." The Earl turned to Isobel McKeith: "And do you stick by these accusations, Lady McKeith?"

"I do." Trembling inwardly, Isobel McKeith drew herself up and stared defiantly at Analee.

"Do you have proof?"

"*Proof?*" Isobel McKeith looked at him with concern.

"Proof of the very grave charges you are making. Proof that Lord Falconer and Miss Cameron were murdered."

"The proof, sir, is that they were both well before they set foot in Lady Falconer's house."

"That does not constitute proof of murder, ma'am."

"Besides, it is not true," Analee intervened. "The

296

Falcon was near death and Miss Cameron was delivered by caesarian section of a baby after a long and painful labor. The shock of the operation coming after such an ordeal killed her. You have only to ask the doctor who performed it."

"But Lady McKeith has said that all those who live near you are in your pay." Mr. Cameron objected.

"*Has* she?" Analee looked scathingly at Isobel McKeith. "Does she doubt the probity of Dr. Scarsdale, who performed the operation, his midwife or the many servants loyal to the memory of my husband who were in the house at the time? Has she questioned *them*, for instance? I doubt it. Has she inspected the scar across the abdomen of poor Miss Cameron to see that the birth was not a natural one? I think not. And, as for his lordship, did she see the maggots crawling in the gangrenous wound from which he died? Did she question the many who attended him on his arduous journey? Did she?"

"Did you, Lady McKeith?" Lord Bute stared at her censoriously.

"How could I, my lord?" she complained queruously. "I'm only saying what I *suspected*."

"*Suspected*, Lady McKeith!" Lord Bute thundered. "Did you say *suspected*? When you make charges of such gravity against a person of such eminence as the Marchioness of Falconer, do you not think you should do more than *suspect*? You should have proof; and when the Princess and I heard the facts we dismissed the story immediately, as I am sure all those who are here will, too."

Many heads were nodded vigorously in agreement.

"I think such suspicions spring naturally to the mind of one who herself has entertained thoughts of murder," Analee said quietly. "And for the charges I make I *do* have proof and *can* call witnesses. Lady McKeith was instrumental in sending me a box of poisoned chocolates from which I should surely have died but

297

for the timely intervention of a friend staying in the house who, with uncanny prescience, suspected them."

"Poisoned chocolates, poisoned chocolates," the scandalous words ran round the room.

"*Poisoned chocolates?*" Lord Bute boomed. "And you have evidence, Lady Falconer?"

"I have the chocolates, sir. They were kept in my cellar to preserve them in good condition should it ever be necessary to produce them in evidence against Lady McKeith."

"This . . . this is monstrous," Isobel McKeith spluttered. "Something I heartily deny . . ."

"Do you deny the evidence of your own handwriting?" Analee demanded. " 'From an admirer' or some such words were written on the card. I have it still. I recognized your writing instantly; but more important than that, and said in front of witnesses who I daresay would swear to it on the Bible, Miss Cameron confirmed it before her labor commenced. From her own mouth I have the evidence of Lady McKeith's foul deed."

"But what could Lady McKeith gain by this?" Lord Bute looked across at Princess Augusta, who was clearly transfixed by the whole proceedings.

"Believe it or not, my lord, she suggested to this innocent but troubled girl that if I were dead her bigamous marriage to the Falcon would be validated. That she would become Lady Falconer . . ."

"Lord Falconer entered into a bigamous marriage with this girl?" Princess Augusta understandably found it impossible to maintain the regal silence expected of one in her station.

"I'm afraid so, ma'am," Analee said quietly. "With the connivance of Lady McKeith who, one would think, should have known better. She assisted at this deception, concurred in his lordship's behavior and then, when all failed, tried to kill me—all, I may say, for gain. The Falcon paid her well, and doubtless she expected Anna Cameron to reward her, had her evil plan come to fruition."

"I am appalled," Princess Augusta murmured faintly. "I can scarcely believe such monstrous conduct."

"Lady Falconer will doubtless wish to press charges," Lord Bute began, but Analee held up her hand.

"I do not care to press charges or persecute a misguided woman who can live only on her wits. I merely make the proviso that she should withdraw her accusations against me in writing, to be lodged with Lord Bute, and then I hope she will never trouble me again."

"But, Lady Falconer, if she tried to murder you . . ."

"I am prepared to destroy the evidence once I have the withdrawal from Lady McKeith. Only those here will know the real truth of the matter, and God alone will judge her."

"Treachery, Lady Falconer," the King said sadly, "is something it is impossible to overlook. Whereas you have denied murder, and everyone believes you, you have admitted treachery."

"Foolish conduct, Your Majesty."

The King nodded his head and tried to stretch his foot. He was very old and tired and his sights were already fastened on the next world. The scandal that had rocked London concerning Lady Falconer and Lady McKeith had eventually come to his ears, but he had been urged to take action by his mistress who sat beside him now, as though she shared his throne.

"Very foolish, Lady Falconer, very, very foolish. Your husband may have done a lot of stupid, maybe wicked things in his time, but he was never a traitor."

"Neither was *I*, Your Majesty." Analee, nearly at the end of her tether, felt close to tears. She had

299

known the scandal regarding Lady McKeith would not die down and it had not. Too much was known and those who had been privileged to witness the unique spectacle at Leicester House soon told everyone who had not. Before the week was out Lady McKeith, her withdrawal of her accusations safely lodged with Lord Bute, had fled the country, vowing never to return. Some said she was lucky to escape so easily; some said she only left because she would have been arrested and tried, whatever Lady Falconer wished, and Lord Bute had urged her to go.

But the matter of the treasonable activities remained. Lady Falconer had conveyed a message from Prince Charles Edward to Leicester House and the King could not ignore it. The government urged him to take action in case anyone else should be tempted.

The King leaned forward and looked at her kindly. "I believe you, my dear. You are a headstrong, impulsive woman and your warm generous nature would have ruled the wisdon of your head. I know that. We have known Catherine Walkinshaw for so many years as a good and loyal servant that there was no question of her ever being involved in a plot—but, if she were not loyal, and you did not know that . . ."

"I knew Your Majesty was never in danger, that your throne was secure. I did it as a favor . . . for an old friend. I knew the cause was hopeless, or I would not have acted as I did."

"I hope it is your last favor for that particular friend," the Countess of Yarmouth said, looking anxiously at the tired King. "That friend is finished with, you must know that."

"I do, Lady Yarmouth." Analee bowed her head, her eyes stinging with tears.

"Lady Falconer," the King said, "I am not long for this world and my grandson George, a Briton born in Britain, will be your King. Until such time as he comes to the throne I propose to impose on you a sentence of banishment. You will return to your country estates and remain there until my death is announced and my grandson is King. In saying this I am depriving myself and my daughter-in-law of your delightful company. We shall miss you in London and at Court, Lady Falconer. But justice must be seen to be done by the people; treasonable behavior must not be condoned, however misguided and well-meant. I know you are no traitor, that you loved your husband who, although a great man, was not a particularly good one. I know that you have many, many virtues that outweigh your faults and I know, my dear Lady Falconer," the old King bent down and touched her shoulder as she knelt before him, "that this sentence I am imposing on you will not be too onerous for you to keep, neither is it like to last very long."

The King gave her his hand to kiss and Analee, seizing it, held it to her face and bathed it with her tears.

Analee looked around at the furniture covered with sheets, the carpets rolled on the floor and stacked against the walls. The white outlines of the individual pieces of furniture reminded her of the silent shrouded form of the Falcon, of her vigil beside it in the chapel of Falcon's Keep the night before his funeral. She shuddered and felt the tears spring to her eyes; but they were for the Falcon, not for her banishment or because she was leaving Falconer House for the duration of this monarch's life. She had no regrets about that; none at all.

After one last look round she adjusted her hat in the mirror and began fastening her cloak when one of the servants entered and bowed.

"I will be ready in a moment, Robert. I . . ."

"There is a gentleman to see you, ma'am. A Mr. Cameron."

"Mr. Cameron?" Analee glanced at herself in the

301

mirror, set her hat and finished fastening her cloak. "Pray tell him we are about to leave for the north; but he is welcome to a few minutes of my time."

"I told him, ma'am. He is most anxious to have a word with your ladyship."

A fire still burned in the grate; it was a bitterly cold December, and Analee stood warming her hands, glancing round as Mr. Cameron was admitted. She felt she should be polite to him, but not gracious, and did not offer him her hand to kiss. After all, had he not falsely denounced her in public, in front of one of the premier earls in the country and the Princess of Wales herself?

"Pray come and warm yourself, Mr. Cameron. Two of our servants remain to clear up before the house is closed, so we still have a fire."

Mr. Cameron stood timidly by her side and nervously extended his hands to the blaze.

"I only came with great trepidation, Lady Falconer. I am about to embark for America, but I felt I had to see you before I left. I penned several drafts of a letter but cast them all onto the fire. I wanted to see you myself and . . . apologize."

Analee straightened up and looked at him kindly. Her sympathetic heart always went out to a troubled soul however much she herself had been wronged, and poor Hector Cameron clearly was suffering. He had a film of sweat on his forehead and his upper lip, and kept anxiously tugging at a forelock of unpowdered red hair that had fallen over his brow. Anna had inherited her coloring from him, Analee thought, a good-looking man who had kept his figure, with a ruddy face and red hair, and bushy brows above clear blue eyes with the slight hint of turquoise that had been so strong in Anna.

"Would you had come to me first, sir, rather than listen to that tittle-tattle from Isobel McKeith. You might thus have spared us all."

302

"Would that I had, ma'am. I meant to see you but, as Lady McKeith had spent so much time in the company of my . . . late daughter, I wanted to hear news at first hand from her, never dreaming of the accusations she would make. The woman was clearly deranged."

"No, she was not deranged, Mr. Cameron," Analee said, enunciating very carefully. "She was evil. The two states are quite separate. The person afflicted can do nothing about the one, but plenty about the other. They could pray to God for help to turn them from their wicked ways, but they are too close to their master, Satan. To have hatched such a plot which involved instilling thoughts of murder into your own daughter was infamous. Your daughter actually *wished* me dead; she told me."

Hector Cameron bowed his head dejectedly and folded his hands to stop them trembling. " 'Twas so unlike my Anna. She had the gentlest, kindest nature."

"When I first knew her indeed she had. She was delightful and charmed everyone; unfortunately she charmed my susceptible husband too much and this mutual infatuation turned her head. She wanted to displace me as his wife, to assume my title and finally when all had failed, deprive me of my life." Analee straightened herself and regarded the rings on her fingers, twisting them around. "However, having said that, Mr. Cameron, I have the greatest regard for the memory of your daughter. In affliction and pain she was magnificent and she died nobly and well. I did all I could to save her. I never left her side. What happened to her could have happened to anyone, and those who say the medical care would have been better in London are wrong. Our doctor in Keswick has a very fine reputation for obstetric practice and has performed many difficult deliveries. The amazing thing was that your granddaughter survived the trauma of her birth, for it had proved too much for the mother. We have buried her in Keswick churchyard, Mr. Cameron, and it is my intention to raise a fine stone and keep her grave well-tended. I will honor your daughter's memory and it will live in that of your grandchild."

Hector Cameron was now openly shedding tears and dabbed at his eyes with a large handkerchief.

"Which brings us to your granddaughter," Analee said, setting aside the covers of two chairs and sitting down in one, while indicating to Hector Cameron that he should take the other. "She is now nearly six months old. She is a lovely child with your family coloring, fierce red hair and her mother's beautiful turquoise-colored eyes. I already love her as my own, so gentle and sweet is her disposition. She is also the daughter of my late husband, whose memory I will always cherish and respect. I am quite willing to bring her up as my own, though of course she will never bear a title; this cannot be. It could never be thought she was my daughter because everyone knows the Falcon and I were separated for eighteen months before his death, and that when he did come home he was ready to die and in no condition to beget children; but I will bring her up as my child. I will adopt her unless it is your wish that she should be brought up by you and your wife in her mother's home. If you wish that, then I will willingly, though sadly, give her into your care."

"Oh no, Lady Falconer!" Hector Cameron held up his hand and shook it from side to side. "My daughter's shame must never become common knowledge. That I should bring up her bastard . . ."

Analee's lips curled. "In that case, sir, I think you do well to leave her with me. I have no prejudice against children conceived out of wedlock. Indeed, I am one myself."

"Oh nor I, ma'am, I assure you," Hector Cameron protested cravenly. "But in our society . . . it is so small and *narrow*, ma'am. I'm sure you understand."

"But was it not thought your daughter was *married* to Lord Falconer?"

Mr. Cameron grimaced. "Well, yes it was; but too many people return to the old country for the truth to be concealed forever. It will come out one day and when it does it will be better—for her, you understand—that my daughter's child were not living with us. Her prospects for marriage would be negligible. But, of course, if your ladyship would be so kind, I would be glad enough of news from time to time of . . . what is her name?"

"I have called her after Stewart's wife, Elizabeth. I felt there should be some family connection. If you agree, she will be known as Miss Elizabeth Falconer."

"Oh, that is capital, Lady Falconer! I am sure my daughter Elizabeth—she would be the least influenced by considerations of impropriety—will be highly gratified. She loved Anna. My eldest daughter, Perdita, would . . ." Hector Cameron made the same uneasy motion with his hands, "not be so pleased."

"I never thought to call her Perdita, sir. It would never have come to mind for I did not know how your eldest daughter was named. Now, sir, it is time to go. My servant will escort you to the door."

Analee got up and pulled on her gloves. She was already tired and had a long journey before her. She had many things to think of and much to tell her children.

But more than anything else she had to write to Brent Delamain and tell him of her banishment and the unwisdom of their meeting for as long as it should last. She had saved him from implication in the supposed treachery; his name had never been mentioned as it was thought she had had direct contact with the Prince. As it was, he never came to London because it was understood that as long as this King lived he would never be received at Court.

But in her heart she did not really wish to see Brent.

She had buried the Falcon, but not her love for him and, for the foreseeable future, she was content to embrace the long years of exile and widowhood.

Chapter Seventeen

Sir Bret Delamain put down his quill and gazed at the three girls playing in the garden—his nieces Mildred and Jessica, and his mother's ward Morella, who was the eldest by three years. They were playing with a ball and a wooden mallet, knocking the ball through hoops and every now and then the play was interrupted by gales of feminine laughter and one or other of the girls would be chased round the lawn by the others wielding their mallets like clubs.

"They get on so well," Brent said, turning to his sister-in-law who sat sewing by the fire.

"Who, the girls?"

"Yes, they are like sisters."

"Would my two had Morella's beauty."

"They have nice dispositions. *That* is important, too."

"But so has Morella. She is altogether a most exceptional child."

Henrietta put down her sewing and came and stood by Brent.

"She is the light of Mother's life," Brent said. "Sometimes, I think, of mine, too."

"Yes, you are very close."

"I am inordinately fond of the child," Brent sighed. "Occasionally I feel that I have missed being a father."

Henrietta put a hand on his shoulder. "But it will not be too late for that, Brent! With men it is never too late! You could sire a child in your fifties or sixties and you are but thirty-seven years of age, is it not so? You were ten years younger than poor George."

"Yes, poor George. I hope he would have approved of the way I have looked after his estate."

"Oh, I am sure he would! You have been a model landowner and businessman. To tell you the truth, Brent, I never thought it was in you."

Brent smiled and toyed with his pen again. He was writing a report on the potential for breeding pigs on one of the home farms where the soil was poor. "You thought I was a scatterbrain. Well, I was. I never thought I would settle down to gentlemanly pursuits and the joys of cattle-rearing and pig-breeding!"

"All you need is a family of your own, Brent. A wife and . . ."

"Do not say it, Henrietta." Brent's smile vanished and his face assumed that severity she was used to whenever she introduced this topic.

"But, Brent, you cannot remain forever in love with Lady Falconer! She will not even see you."

"She has her reasons. It is not that she does not love me."

"Are you sure?" Henrietta clasped his shoulder and looked into his eyes. He roughly brushed her hand away and got to his feet.

"Of course I am sure! She feels her banishment keenly. What she did was to protect me, so that my name should not be associated with hers in this disgrace. *That* shows she loves me."

"But, Brent, that was two years ago, nearly three! The King could live forever."

"I can wait. He cannot live forever and he is a great deal older than I am. Analee and I will be happy one day. I know it. Ask Reyora. She promised it."

"Does she still?"

"I have not asked her, but I am sure she would say 'yes.' "

But he was afraid that she would say "no." That was

307

why he avoided Reyora whenever she came to see his mother or Henrietta. It was a long time since her prophecy—nearly fourteen years. Besides, he had not told his sister-in-law everything. It was true that Analee had written about the banishment and her desire not to implicate him, but she also told him that, when her husband lay dying, she had discovered a renewal of her love for him. That to honor his memory she did not wish to see Brent.

How long could a memory last? And was it true that she loved him after the way he had treated her, leaving her with a natural child by his mistress to bring up? How much love could a woman have for someone like that? Or was it merely that, conscious of her dignity as Lady Falconer, she felt she owed it to the memory of a great lord to remain chaste?

They gazed for a while at the children playing, each wrapped in their thoughts. Henrietta was envious of Morella's beauty, the Delamain beauty—blond hair and deep blue eyes. But Morella was not a Delamain! She often thought that she was because in so many ways she seemed to resemble Brent and Emma, whereas her two children took very much after her side, the Dacre family, who tended to be dark and short, a rather cruel gift of nature—when it came to women, anyway. They were amiable, sweet-natured girls; but they would have to fight hard for husbands when they grew up, whereas Morella . . .

Morella, breathless with laughter, stopped playing and suddenly looked at the long window where the people whom she knew as aunt and uncle now stood. She waved at them and then she beckoned to them to come down.

"What does she want?" Henrietta asked Brent.

"She wants us to go down."

"She wants *you* to go down. She adores you, Brent. You had best take care, with those devilish eyes . . ."

Brent again stopped smiling and looked at his sister-in-law severely. "Henrietta, I am old enough to be her father! Indeed she regards me as the father she never had. I assure you there is nothing else in her simple affection for me."

"Are you sure? She is uncommonly well-developed for fifteen, and with the mind of a woman, too. I declare the way she behaves with you is sometimes close to being flirtatious."

"Oh come!" Brent protested. "I would feel highly flattered if such a young girl should find me attractive; but it is not the case. I can assure you of that. However, let us go down and see what she wants."

"You go," Henrietta said, turning towards the fire. "It is too chilly down there for me today."

Whenever Morella beckoned, Brent went. It was true he was half in love with the girl though he could not, dared not, call it an adult passion. He liked to think of himself as a fond uncle; but he knew that he was attracted to her, that he felt a little better when he saw her, better still when he was with her, and altogether bereft when she was not there.

"I shall be glad of some air," he said and walked swiftly along the huge stone corridors, down the central staircase and across the wide hall to the great front doors where Morella waited for him.

"I knew you would come," she said, holding out her hand.

"You know I can't resist you," he said laughing, "you little minx!"

"I am no minx, Uncle Brent!"

"You are! You can twist me round your little finger. I was writing a report on pigs."

"*PIGS*!" Morella exploded with laughter and put her fingers to her nose, "Ooo, *PIGS*!"

"They are very useful animals. They are easy to feed and rear and their yield is prodigious. I am going to become one of the biggest pig-breeders in the north of England."

Morella put her arm through his and drew him away from the lawn. He fell into stride alongside her in a companionable way and knew that she felt as he did: they wanted to be alone together. They enjoyed each other's company. They could talk so easily, whether it was about pigs or the progress of the war, or books, or Brent's adventures with the Prince, whom Morella fervently admired. She could never hear enough of Prince Charles. But today she wanted to talk about something else, something she hardly ever touched upon and when she did she was always met by a wall of silence, whether she asked Brent or Henrietta or the woman she called Aunt Susan.

"Uncle Brent." She stopped and looked into his eyes. Anyone seeing them then would have been astonished at the likeness, but as each only saw the other—and neither was given to gazing in the mirror—they were unaware of it. "Uncle Brent, do you *really* not know who my mother was?"

He gazed back at her gravely. He knew it was something that disturbed her, as, in a way, it disturbed him; he wasn't quite sure why.

"No, I do not, my dear."

"But it is said she was a gypsy. Do you think it is Reyora?"

"No, I don't. Why should Reyora not claim you if you were her child?"

"She is like a mother to me, so fond when she comes; but she will never speak to my mother. It is a subject she forbids me to mention. Maybe she thought I would be better reared in a castle than a gypsy camp. Uncle Brent, I wondered if, when she comes again, you would ask her for me. Would you Uncle Brent? *Please.*"

Brent avoided Reyora, but for his own reasons. What a lot that unfathomable woman could tell if she wished. It was even rumored that she had refused to

310

save the Falcon; had hidden when Analee sent messenger after messenger begging her to come.

"All right, I will speak to her," he said, recommencing their walk. "But I fear she does not tell you because the truth is quite simple."

Morella gasped and again they stopped walking. "And what is that?"

"I think she does not know. They were very painful days. It is difficult to imagine them now as you survey our peaceful land; but fifteen years ago much of the countryside was pillaged and plundered by bands of marauding soldiers crazed with hunger. Families were split up and separated; many went into exile and never saw one another again. I often think that you are the child of such a house, maybe a noble house such as ours, and that Reyora found you and took care of you—perhaps feeling later that she had done wrong. Maybe she wished to return you and could not. That is all I suppose."

"So my mother might not have been a gyspy?"

"I don't think she was. I never have."

"I do," Morella said gravely.

"Why?"

"I have a feeling she was. It is a very strange feeling. That is all I can say. I sometimes feel I can see into the future and that my mother is there, waiting for me."

Brent squeezed her hand and said gently, "I hope you are right, my dear. I know it meant a lot to you, to find your mother. I . . ."

"Sir Brent, Sir Brent! Miss Morella!"

They both turned at the shouting that came from the direction of the dower house and a servant began to run towards them waving his arms in agitation. They were just about to descend the slope of the bank to the river and stopped abruptly. Brent started to climb up the way they had come.

"Oh, Sir Brent . . ."

311

"What is it? What is it?" Brent clasped the arm of the breathless man.

"Oh, it is your mother, sir. She has fallen and will not get up. Oh, Sir Brent, I think she is dead. Oh, Sir Brent . . ."

The man blubbered pathetically and Brent turned to Morella who was already clambering up the bank. He took her hand and they ran towards the house. Already a small crowd of servants awaited them at the door, anxiously huddled together. They stepped back as Brent and Morella ran inside and made their way to the small parlor where Susan liked to sit by the window and sew. She now lay on the floor as though she had simply fallen from her chair, the tapestry that she had been working on still clasped in her hand. Her eyes were open but she lay perfectly still.

Brent knelt by her side. "Mother?"

She did not look at him or move. He felt her neck, and her pulse beat feebly. "She is not dead. She has had a seizure. Morella, get two of the men to help me take her to her room."

Although she was very slight and weighed hardly anything, it took a long time for the men, carrying her gently, to negotiate the winding corridors and staircases of the old house, some parts of it older than Delamain Castle. For some said it had once been a hunting lodge in the days of the Conqueror, and the castle had been built by one of the Marcher barons left by the Conqueror who used to hunt in the great wood which had stretched south from Penrith.

Susan Delamain lay on her bed, her eyes still staring in front of her, and Brent and Morella covered her with a blanket while one of the maids tried to light a fire. It was very cold in the room.

"What happened?" Morella asked.

"No one knows. She was apparently sitting on her own and they heard a bump."

312

"I left her on her own, embroidering. She seemed perfectly well but tired."

"She has been tired for a long time," Brent said, the tears coming to his eyes. "Someone must go for Emma."

"Is she . . ."

"Shh, I do not know how much she can hear. The doctor will tell us more. He is on his way."

Susan Delamain had had a paralytic seizure and the doctor could not tell how long she would live. Maybe for a few hours, maybe for years. All her senses were affected and she could not speak or move. The first twenty-four hours would be critical. So that they could all look after her, she was moved into the Castle and a member of the family sat by her bedside all the time. Emma arrived first with Hugo and then Sarah came, leaving her large family behind. The sister of her father, Jonathan Allonby, she had always been a favorite aunt—Susan Allonby, who had married Guy Delamain.

Sarah took charge because Henrietta did not react well in a crisis; she immediately felt ill herself and was glad to take to her bed for hours at a time. Emma never left her mother's side, so Sarah took over. To her surprise she found her best helper was Morella, the orphan whom her aunt had so oddly decided to adopt. She was a wonderful help—calm and good humored. She knew where everything was to be found. She never flapped in a crisis or relaxed too much when things were smooth. She was alert and seemed to anticipate everything; her blonde head bobbed up all over the place accompanied by a willing smile.

"Let me do that, Aunt Sarah."

Sarah smiled at the strange, beautiful girl. She didn't really know her well. Her duties kept her at home and Morella had only occasionally visited Cockermouth with Susan.

"You're a great help, Morella."

313

"I like to be useful." Morella smiled back and took the tray that Sarah was carrying to the large kitchen table before a footman took it upstairs. Sarah made all Susan's food herself, preparing the thin gruel and creamy custards which were all she could take. "Do you think Aunt Susan will get well?"

Sarah looked at the glowing girl and shook her head sadly. "I do not think so, Morella. I don't see how she can live on the little she is able to eat. She must surely fade away."

"But Uncle Brent thought she was a little better. He says she can even recover completely."

Morella arranged the things on the tray with a little bouquet of twigs and late flowers she had found in the garden.

"How long can you stay, Aunt Sarah?"

"Only a few more days. My own family will miss me."

"Oh I wish I could see more of them!" Morella clasped her hands, her eyes shining.

Sarah looked surprised. "Then you must come over more often. You must come and stay whenever you like."

"It is because I do not have relations of my own. I feel that when Aunt Susan dies . . ." Morella faltered and gazed at the ground.

Sarah carefully placed the pot she was stirring on the hob and put her arm round Morella. "You must not think you will be on your own, Morella. You *are* part of our family. We regard you as one of us, and we love you. All my children are your cousins and you must come over and stay whenever you wish. Why, Elia is only a year older than you and Henry is quite a young man! He will adore you. You must not think you will be alone. Besides, you have Brent."

"Oh yes, Uncle Brent." Morella brightened. "Maybe I can move into the castle and live here with him?" Her eyes shone again and she went about her tasks with a spring in her step. Sarah gazed at her thoughtfully, a little apprehensive, before turning back to the stove.

Hugo Fitzgerald and Brent Delamain were uneasy in each other's company. They met from time to time because of their mutual business interests; but their memories were too long and they had little liking for each other. Hugo was chafing to get back to work.

"I think I shall leave Emma here," he said, accepting the glass of whisky that Brent offered him. "There is no saying how long your mother . . ."

Brent shook his head. "None at all. The doctor said that if she didn't die soon she would probably live for a long time. Yes, leave Emma here, she is very welcome. But will not your children miss her?"

"Oh they are well taken care of, and the baby has a wet nurse."

"I long to see the baby," Brent said.

"You must come over." Hugo's voice was indifferent. "Thank God your mother saw him before this happened. Ah, here is Emma. I was saying I should get back to Whitehaven, my dear. Is there any news of your mother?"

Emma shook her head. She was pale and there were dark shadows under her eyes. "There is neither good news nor bad news. She lies there quite calmly; sometimes I fancy I see a faint smile. And she *is* definitely trying to talk; she plucks at the sheets with the effort."

Hugo stood up holding his glass, his right hand in the pocket of his waistcoat. His general air was one of impatience. It made everyone uneasy. "I feel I must be getting home."

"Of course; but I must stay here."

"Shall I send the children to you? It might give your mother pleasure to see them."

"Yes, I think she would be happy to see them. And so should I. I have never been parted from them since they were born."

315

As she knew they would be, Emma's children—two boys, Connor and James, born within a year of each other—had been her main joy in her marriage. Her husband was, on the whole, a cold man and their relationship a loveless one except for the rare occasions when he unexpectedly showed the passion which had resulted in the conception of their first-born. She felt then that he was making love to some ideal woman of his imagination because he seemed not to be aware of her at all, and to be disappointed when he discovered that the object of his ardor was his own wife. However, he was a good father, and a careful and meticulous husband and provider. Their house was one of the finest in the district and they entertained all the local gentry, people of quality and those who had made their fortunes in business. Emma felt she had very little to complain about, except for the lack of that one, longed-for ingredient that had so far tragically eluded her in life—love.

"Then I shall be off after dinner," Hugo said. "I shall be home by nightfall if I ride over Honister."

"Honister?" Brent said, looking up. "Would you care to pass by Furness Grange and give to Lady Falconer the news of my mother's illness? She is so fond of her."

"Lady Falconer?" Hugo hoped they didn't notice the tremor in his voice. "Why, certainly."

"I'll pen a letter for you."

"Pray don't," Hugo said. "I am perfectly capable of explaining the matter." He looked at his timepiece. "Well, if I am to stop at Furness I had best be gone. I shan't even wait for dinner."

Now that he was going he was in a fever of impatience. Emma noticed and was puzzled by it. But somehow she did not link it with the visit to the Enchantress.

316

So her banishment was over. Analee let the letter fall on to her lap, the stiff parchment that had arrived from London by special messenger telling her of the death of King George II. His young grandson was on the throne—a Briton born in Britain. Now she could go where she liked, do what she wished. But where did she wish to go? Nowhere. What did she wish to do? Nothing. Sometimes she felt half dead, that her life was over and what remained she lived only in her children.

Four months of the year, the winter months, she spent at Falcon's Keep so that her children would be aware of their ancestral home. The spring, summer and part of the autumn were at Furness. In October they returned to Falcon's Keep and it was just as she was packing up, preparing to move the household, that the letter from Lord Bute, a favorite of the new King, arrived.

Hugo Fitzgerald stood at the door looking at her, even before she knew he was there. He had left his horse in the wood by the house and walked round, thinking she might refuse to see him. The last time he had left her house in disgrace nursing a wound in his arm and shame in his breast. He had not seen Analee since that night he had tried to rape her at Delamain Castle—well, "make love" was the term he preferred; but Analee would have thought differently.

As he coughed she turned and looked at him with instant disapproval showing. Hesitantly he advanced into the room.

"I wonder you have the nerve to show yourself, Mr. Fitzgerald," Analee said haughtily. "The last two occasions on which we met were not propitious ones."

"Is that why you do not call on us in Whitehaven? I know Emma asks you to."

"It could be the reason," Analee said, standing up, the letter falling to the floor. She neither asked him to sit down nor gave him her hand to kiss. "Could you state your business now?"

317

"Is there no forgiveness, Lady Falconer?" Hugo looked as her wistfully. If only she knew that he could only make love passionately to his wife when he thought of her, when he thought it was her body he lay upon.

"I think you have put yourself beyond the pale, sir. No doubt your attachment to me had dissolved with the years, but . . ."

"It has not." Hugo came up to her and she backed away, alarmed by the light in his eyes.

"Then you had best depart at once." She went to the bellrope and made as if to pull it; but he got there before her.

"You haunt me, Analee. I am not a good husband because of you. When I make love to my wife I think it is you . . ."

"Oh, la!" Analee turned her head aside to hide her amusement. "I am grateful that I do not suffer its effects."

"It is true. That is why I work so hard, to put you out of my mind. You are the Enchantress and you have enchanted me. I feel I will never be free of your spell until I hold you in my arms, lie with you . . ."

"I assure you, Mr. Fitzgerald, that is unlikely to occur." Analee spoke sharply because he was a big man and he could easily overpower her. "I must warn you that if you come an inch nearer I shall scream. My servants are never far away."

"That will not be necessary," Hugo said sulkily, stepping back. "I came to bring you a message from Delamain Castle where I have recently been staying with my wife."

"Oh?" Analee's hand flew to her heart in alarm.

"Mrs. Delamain is near death. Sir Brent asked me to give you these tidings because he knows you are attached to the old woman."

"I am indeed. What has happened?"

318

"She had a seizure a week ago. They do not know how long she can live."

"I am very sad to hear it. We are leaving tomorrow for Falcon's Keep and I shall stop at the castle on my way to pay my respects." Analee tugged sharply at the bellrope. "Thank you for calling, Mr. Fitzgerald, and conveying this message. I hope we do not meet again too soon."

Analee stood with her two eldest children and kissed first Emma and then Henrietta. Behind them stood Brent. She gave him a sisterly embrace and realized it was the first time she had ever been so near him without an instant feeling of passion. She looked briefly into his eyes and then greeted the girls who stood shyly at the back of the room—two rather dumpy and plain and one extremely beautiful. Analee's heart skipped and Morella met her gaze.

"Do you remember me, Morella?"

"A little, Lady Falconer."

"You are a very big girl now, so tall. I suppose I should say, a young woman."

She glanced at Brent, who was staring at Morella with undisguised admiration. At Morella, not her. Analee felt a pang of disquiet as she followed his gaze and then bent to greet the two younger Delamain girls.

"I hope you did not mind us calling, Brent." Analee ushered forward her two eldest children. "I have sent the carriages with the staff and the younger members of my family on to Falcon's Keep; but I had to stop and enquire after your mother. May I introduce Lord Falconer—Duncan, my eldest boy?"

Duncan stepped forward and gravely took Brent's hand, shook it, and then politely kissed those of the ladies. He bowed to the girls and Analee saw his eyes linger on Morella.

"And this is my first-born, Clare."

Clare was as dark as Morella was fair; but the two were of a similar height as they were close in age, separated only by two years. They also both possessed an unusual degree of beauty. Already, at thirteen, Clare was developing a womanly form but her breasts were tiny compared to those of Morella, who had the figure of a full-grown woman with a firm bustline that showed to advantage even above the high décolletage of her simple girlish dress. Clare had black lashes. She had the regal, imperious gaze of the Falcon, whom she closely resembled. She was undeniably his daughter.

When the introductions were completed, Analee asked to be taken to Mrs. Delamain. Emma came forward eagerly to escort her, whereas Analee perceived how Brent held back. Was their passion dead, then? Finally interred after all these years? She remembered the way he had looked at Morella. It was not a fatherly expression he bore in his eyes.

"I hear you have two lovely babies, Emma," Analee said as she was escorted along the stone corridors of the castle.

"Two boys, Analee! I am so overjoyed to have them. It is thanks to Reyora, I am sure."

"The spell worked?"

"In the most extraordinary way. I thought I had killed my husband. He fell insensible to the ground after eating the potion that I had spread on some meat and was then violently ill; but when he recovered," Emma blushed at the memory, "all was well."

"And is all *still* well?"

They turned to mount the final flight of stairs.

"He is a good husband. He is not passionate, except on occasions; but I cannot complain, seeing that he never really loved me. He has done well for himself and is someone people respect. He is a magistrate and commands the local militia. I wish he loved me, that is all." Emma sighed as they stood outside her mother's door.

"Love often grows in marriage," Analee said. "I know that. In the end I came to love my husband in a different way from when we were first wed. That is why I still honor his memory. I hope it will come for you, too, but before it is too late."

She entered the room quietly and Sarah, who had been sitting by her aunt's bed, stood up. Analee greeted her with a kiss and then bent low over Susan Delamain, looking into her eyes. She took her hand and pressed it.

"I have come to wish you better."

There was no answering squeeze from the paralyzed hand, but the eyes seemed to smile.

"They tell me you are not suffering and that you will slowly recover."

The expression in the eyes looked sad and Susan seemed to be trying to speak. Her lips actually began to move and both Emma and Sarah exclaimed in astonishment.

"She is trying to talk. Her lips moved!"

Analee continued to gaze at the stricken woman and there was suddenly a noise in her throat.

"She is speaking. Oh, Mama!" Emma threw herself beside the bed and grasped her mother's hand. "I *knew* Analee would make you well. Oh, Mama, you *are* going to get better."

"Lady F—F—" Susan said slowly. "Lady F—Fa—"

"Lady Falconer. She is speaking to you, Analee."

"Yes, I know." Analee bent nearer to her and continued to gaze into her eyes. "Do you think if I were alone with her the struggle might be less agonizing?"

Sarah and Emma looked doubtfully at each other. Then Sarah nodded. "We shall be within call," she said and tucked her arm through Emma's. "Come and show me the new Lord Falconer. I hear he is very handsome."

"And Lady Clare is extremely pretty. Analee is indeed fortunate in her children."

Analee listened to them as the door closed and their footsteps grew fainter. Then she sat by Susan Delamain's side and took her hand. "You wish to say something to me, don't you?"

Susan nodded, her eyes pleading.

"It is about Morella?"

The rasp in the throat came again and, with difficulty, she mouthed the word "yes."

"You have known for a long time that she was my daughter?"

"Yes," again the faltering word. Analee squeezed her hand.

"You know that I could not claim her; but I have always had her and her welfare close to my heart. I knew that with you, her grandmother, she was in good hands."

Susan's eyes grew wide and Analee felt a faint return of pressure on her hand.

"Yes, her grandmother. I was the gypsy Brent lay with before we were separated by circumstances and the war. He never knew he was Morella's father, for shortly afterwards I was forcibly captured, taken to a gyspy camp and made to wed. When Morella was born Reyora assisted at her birth. It was at once clear, from her fair complexion, that she was not the daughter of two dark-skinned gypsies, such as my husband and I were. So I was urged to escape from the camp and Reyora promised to look after Morella until we could be reunited. Alas, we never were. I despaired of finding my daughter alive again because I knew what had happened to the Buckland gypsy camp and I was then loved and wooed by Lord Falconer. The rest you know."

"And n—n—ow. A—f—ter my d—death?" Susan Delamain whispered.

"She will be well taken care of. Brent, after all, is her father."

"T—e—ll him," Susan said hoarsely. There was an

322

agonizing look in her eyes. "Very f—f—ond of Morella."

Analee looked sharply at the stricken woman. "He is *very* fond of her? Yes, I have already perceived that; but how could a man of his age have anything but paternal affection for such a young girl?"

But as she spoke Analee knew in her heart that it was perfectly possible, especially as Morella looked so much older than she was, like a young woman. Analee too had been well-developed at that age, and she herself was born when her own mother was only seventeen.

Analee laughed as lightly as she could and her grip on Susan's hand tightened. "Why do we talk so gloomily? They tell me you are better every day. I pray to God that you will be with Morella for many years to come and that what we have spoken about will not be necessary."

"Pr—o—mise me." Susan Delamain's eyes were pleading.

Analee gazed at her solemnly. "If you die I promise you I will see that Morella is well taken care of."

The pressure of Susan's hand on her increased and a distraught expression came into her tired eyes.

"P—ro—mise to t—e—ll Br—ent."

Analee squeezed her hand reassuringly but said nothing. She knew that telling Brent of Morella's paternity would be the most agonizing thing she would ever have to do after all these years . . . especially if his passion for her had cooled and he no longer loved her. And why should he? She had kept him waiting for so long, with no promise of future reward; why should he wait for her when she spurned him, telling him that she was in love with the memory of her husband? For how long could fidelity be expected of a man?

But as she walked slowly along the corridor towards the drawing room, Analee felt an emptiness in her heart, and she knew that, for many years, the knowledge that she was loved single-mindedly by one man had sustained her.

Susan Delamain did not die and indeed she did slowly begin to recover. Her speech was halting but understandable if attended to with patience, and she managed to take a few steps from her bed and sit in a chair by the fire or the window.

Sarah and Emma went back to their prospective homes and the castle household returned to normal. Everyone said that Susan's recovery dated from the arrival of Analee. The spell of the Enchantress had worked once more.

Brent found that he went about his tasks much as he had always done but with a new awareness of Morella who, the following June, had her sixteenth birthday. England had done well in the war, in India, in America and on the Continent, and although Pitt had left the government, feelers were being put out for peace. England was now an increasingly prosperous, well-ruled country, Brent thought as he rode around his estates looking with satisfaction at the acres of rich land he owned, as far as the eye could see.

He had a sense of exhilaration and expectation. This was the night of Morella's sixteenth birthday. He intended to talk to his mother about her as soon as he could. Maybe she would tell him to wait a couple of years, for the sake of decency. After all he was twenty-two years older than she was. But he would. He had waited so long for one love; to wait a little while longer for another was, to one so accustomed to patience, no hardship.

But would she have him? Or was she only flirting? She had been over to Sarah for part of the summer and had returned full of talk about Henry Rigg who, at nineteen, was a tall solemn-looking young man, erudite and with impeccable manners. Brent was relieved to discern that the spirited Morella had really found him rather dull. She was only trying to tease him, and he had stifled his jealousy. But there was no doubt—from Sarah's letter—that young Rigg had fallen in love for the first time with his mysterious cousin. It was partly the reason why Sarah had sent her home earlier than had been expected. "She is a little temptress," Sarah had written, "mature for so young a girl and too aware of her charm and her power."

Power? It was a curious term to use; But Brent knew what she meant. Morella had power. She exercised a fascination over most people with whom she came in contact. They seemed immediately to admire her. The only woman he had ever known with this sort of attraction had been Analee. Yes, in a curious but unmistakable way, Analee and Morella were alike; not in looks—no two women could be more different—but in temperament. Morella too was a little enchantress.

He looked at the sun and turned his horse towards the castle. He had come a long way, partly for the pleasure of riding and partly to think on this warm day with the countryside at its rich, verdant best. He had not eaten since breakfast and he felt hungry. He turned by the side of the river and chose the path that ran up through dense woods to the castle. Suddenly, in a ray of sunlight that splashed through the trees he caught sight of a bright dress, of a head of flaxen hair. He reined his horse and called out.

"Morella! Is it you? Morella!"

He set off to weave his way among the trees, taking care not to let his horse trip in the tangled undergrowth. Suddenly he saw the skirt again and then it disappeared. He heard a trill of laughter. She was playing with him! He got off his horse and tethered it to a branch then stole silently through the wood, a smile on his face.

"Here! Here!" A voice called and he turned to the left.

"Here!" It came again from another direction.

"Morella, I'll spank you when I find you! You have no right . . . you are too far from home."

Unless she had followed him? His heart began to beat quickly with excited speculation. Suddenly he saw her head bob round the tree trunk in his path and his arms reached out and caught her. "There, you monkey!"

Her face was very close, he felt her pliable, young body immediately yield to his. He grasped it, closing his eyes as his arm encircled her tiny waist. Thoughts of the most deliciously lewd nature rose up to torment him. He had not lain with a woman for so many years, he, Brent Delamain, who had once had such a reputation for women . . . before the Enchantress enslaved him. She had bewitched him, unmanned him. Now he felt his loins on fire. He opened his eyes and her own blue ones, almost the color of his, were very close. She parted her mouth slightly and he bent his head.

She was sixteen. A maid! What was he doing? Abruptly he wrenched himself from her, and he saw the disappointment in her face. His heart hammered in his breast and his jaw worked furiously.

"Uncle Brent?" she said differently. "Do you not like me?"

"Of course I like you, dammit! But, my dear, I am your guardian. I am old eonugh to be your father."

"So what does that matter?"

She tilted her pert chin at him, her eyes sparkling with merriment. "In *what* way, pray?"

"You know, you minx!" he groaned.

He caught her again and this time he pressed his mouth down on her cool, chaste lips. Oh, the delicious thrill of the encounter! His hands roamed over her taut virginal breasts and he was overcome with such powerful desire that he felt he would be unable to restrain himself.

"I want it, too," she whispered and looked at him. "I am a woman, you know."

326

"I know, I know," he groaned again, "Oh, how I know. You shall tempt me, my darling Morella; but not yet . . . not yet."

"Now," she said and moulded her young body to his again, "I want you to do it. You."

Once more he crushed her to him, an arm encircling her waist, a hand kneading those tender breasts. Yes, he would take her here as she wished, and then they would announce their betrothal at her birthday dinner party. They could be wed immediately, tomorrow. There would be no shame. What if he was a lot older? It was not uncommon. He was not yet forty and he had so much to give her. He could make Delamain Castle her own. Lady Delamain. At last all his years of suffering and loneliness would be over. They would have the children he so longed for; many. Oh, how he yearned to breed from her, peopling the great castle with the fruit of their loins. A lifetime of happiness with the beautiful Morella suddenly seemed a possibility. And *she* wanted it! *She* wanted him, as urgently, it seemed, as he desired her.

And somehow now it seemed so right that the baby he had saved so long ago should become his wife. She would no longer be a foundling, but a lady of status with her own home and servants.

He put a hand under her skirt and began to caress her thighs, gently lowering her to the ground so that they could rest comfortably on a green sward. Shortly he would see her beautiful nubile body that he had so often imagined in his dreams. She was panting and moaning now and held up her arms for him as he lay down beside her, beginning to unfasten his breeches. The excitement was such that he fumbled clumsily at his clothes like a first-time lover. If he was not careful he would spill all his seed before it got to her and she would despise him for his clumsiness. He drew a deep breath and tried to control himself as, held tightly in her encircling arms, he began to ease her skirt over her

327

thighs, gently so as not to frighten her, murmuring tender endearments. Even the boldest maid usually felt some trepidation at her first encounter and indeed Morella had begun to tremble, the passionate expression in her eyes slightly tempered with fear.

"Do not worry, my darling. I will be so gentle with you. Oh, my love." Just as he bent to kiss her, his hands about to explore further, a movement—he thought a tree bending in the wind—made him look up and there was Analee standing before him, her eyes severe, her full red mouth twisted in scorn. Suddenly he held not Morella in his arms but Analee, and they were again in that moonlit glade making love on the forest floor as he was about to do here.

"Do not do it," Analee said, speaking clearly. "Do not touch her." He gazed up at Analee, who wore a long blue cloak, her face partly obscured by a wide-brimmed hat.

"If you touch her you will regret it all your life," she said, and held up a hand to him in admonition.

Brent sat up and, rubbing his eyes, looked at her again; but where she had stood was only the blackened half-trunk of a blasted tree. Analee had gone.

Brent stood up, shaking, and hastily fastened his breeches. Then he looked at Morella and quickly drew her skirt down to her ankles. He felt unclean and all the excitement had gone from his limbs. Morella sat up, her eyes blazing with wrath, her slender form shaking.

"And *why* was that, pray?"

Brent put out a hand and helped her to her feet. "I was too ashamed of what I was doing."

"But I *wanted* it."

She tried to come close to him again, but he backed away, standing against the tree where he had seen Analee so clearly. "You are too young. It was a wretched thing for me to do, to deflower a maid who is my own ward. I cannot do it, Morella. Forgive me."

328

"You have made a fool of *me*," Morella said furiously "For I have shown you that I want you."

"There is no shame in that, my dear," Brent said tenderly, but the feeling of passion he had for her had evaporated. "I am an older man, used to the world; you are well-developed for a maid. But I cannot take you here, or introduce you to the delights of love. I would never forgive myself."

"But *why* . . . Brent?" It was the first time she had used his name alone.

Brent put a hand to his head. "I cannot tell you. I was about to take you and then someone told me it was terribly wrong. That is all I can say."

"*Someone?*" Morella said crossly, dusting down her pink dress put on with special thought to its effect on Uncle Brent, for she had come into the woods intent on seducing him.

"I mean some*thing*, of course," Brent said desperately. "Something inside me told me it was wrong. Now come, let us go home and prepare for your dinner party tonight."

Brent went to his horse and untied it. He had meant to get her to ride behind him, but now he did not dare. What he had wanted was evil and unclean, and he did not know why. Many much older men married women half their ages. Why could he not? Why had Analee come to him at that time? Because he knew in his heart that she had. It was not a vision; it was her actual presence, the Enchantress once again at work.

The dinner party was a sober affair with Morella unusually quiet and Brent very formal and reserved. Mrs. Delamain, of course, did not attend and, beside Henrietta and her daughters, there was a sprinkling of worthies from the locality. Everyone noticed Morella's unaccustomedly low spirits.

"It is because she is getting old," Brent said with an attempt at levity, and he felt his face redden when

329

Morella gave him a glance of scorn. The conversation at the table was dull and the evening seemed interminable. He would be glad when it was over and he could go to his room.

Morella avoided his eyes for the rest of the evening and he avoided hers. He knew that, whatever else happened, nothing could ever be between them as it was. She had thought he did not desire her and her pride was hurt. She would never understand.

He suddenly thought of his beautiful young bride Mary and how he had been unable to prove his manhood with her, so besotted was he by the memory of Analee. Was he, for all his life, to have her come between him and his desires?

Wrapped in his thoughts he hardly noticed the guests going and when he looked round only the family was still there and one or two stragglers who were reluctant to leave the good smuggled French brandy that Ambrose Rigg kept Brent supplied with.

"Brent, you are out of sorts tonight?" Henrietta said smilingly.

"I have a headache. I think I will go and say good night to Mother. It is time these young girls went to bed anyway."

He went over to Morella, who was simmering in a chair near the fire toying with a golden curl which hung over her eyes. She scowled at him as he bent down and kissed her chastely on the forehead. "Good night, my dear ward. Do not stay up too late."

Then he kissed Mildred and Jessica likewise, bowed to Henrietta, clapped the two remaining guests on their shoulders and went along the corridor and up the stairs to his mother's room.

A candle still burnt beside her bed, and a maid sat with bowed head by the embers of the fire. She was asleep. Brent tiptoed to his mother's side and knelt to kiss her. To his surprise her eyes were wide open and the hands that had scarcely been able to move

330

clutched at him. He felt their strength and was astonished.

"Mother, you are recovered!"

"I am dying, my son, and God had given me this p—ower to sp—eak to you before I go."

Her voice was so clear and strong; she hardly faltered at all. He sat by her side and grasped her hands.

"Mother, you are well! You *are* recovered."

"Do not spe—ak and listen to wh—at I have to sa—ay."

"Yes, Mother, I will."

"B—end your h—ead in case that st—upid girl hears."

"She is asleep."

"D—do as I sa—ay."

Brent smiled. His mother was not only better, but had recovered all her old powers of authority. He bent his head obediently. "Yes, Mother."

"It is about M—Morella."

"Yes, Mother?" Brent's heart sank.

"I kn—ow you are f—ond of her."

"Yes, Mother."

"But not as a f—ather."

So she had noticed too.

"It is wrong, Brent, because—" Susan was suddenly seized by a spasm and the hands that had grasped his so strongly seemed lifeless once more. She shut her eyes and her teeth bared grotesquely in the rictus of death. He grasped her shoulders.

"Mother! Mother!"

Susan Delamain half opened her eyes, and once more her breath came raspingly, painfully. There was a rattle in her throat. "As—k A— An—alee," she said and, before she could say more, her spirit left her and she remained as she was, her form inert, her half-opened eyes gazing unseeingly before her.

Chapter Eighteen

Analee received Brent in her private sitting-room where none were admitted, not even her children, except with prior permission. She knew that here they would be able to converse quietly. The room overlooked part of the great fortress that was Falcon's Keep, but from a second window there was an aspect of the grounds of the castle and, in the distance, the Cheviot Hills that formed the border with Scotland.

Analee wore a comfortable morning dress of patterned silk without hoop or bodice. With her hair loose and hanging over her shoulders she almost looked the young woman Brent had first met sixteen years before. He bowed gravely and kissed her hand.

"It is good of you to receive me so soon, Analee."

"Your message sounded urgent, Brent. Pray sit down."

It was very formal for two people who, for so many years, had enjoyed reciprocal feelings of passion, for a man who had sworn that he would never marry another but her as long as he lived. But sixteen years was a long time and now a blonde, blue-eyed girl, very junior to Analee but with some of her qualities, had intervened.

"My mother is dead, Analee."

Analee felt a catch in her throat and impulsively took his hand. "Oh, Brent, I am so sorry."

"She lived much longer than was expected and I think was not in pain. She was serene. She enjoyed her grandchildren, Henrietta's girls and Emma's boys—Emma is breeding yet again—and the company of . . . Morella." Brent paused before saying the name and looked at Analee.

332

"Morella must be grief-stricken. She was so fond of your mother."

Brent took the seat she had offered and crossed his legs. "It is about Morella I have specifically come to see you. Hers was the last name my mother mentioned before she died. Hers, and yours."

"Mine?" Analee felt her heart quicken uneasily. This was the moment she had tried to avoid for so long. Indeed at times she had thought it might be avoided altogether; that the truth of Morella's parentage need never be revealed; that the secret, so long hidden, might remain buried forever.

"My mother tried to tell me something about Morella. For an instant she gained an extraordinary strength, such was the urgency of the message she wished to impart. She seized my hand and spoke almost normally. But she never finished her message. She said I should ask you. Analee, what is the secret about Morella?"

Analee rose from her chair and began agitatedly to pace the room. Brent admired her as she swept past him, the faint trace of perfume, the delicious subtle body odors of one he knew so intimately, though the number of times he had lain in her arms could be counted on the fingers of one hand. A wave of longing, of nostalgia swept over him, momentarily obliterating from his mind the constant image of Morella.

"Brent, have you formed an attachment with this young girl?"

Brent nervously cleared his throat. "I am very fond of her."

"But is it, shall we say, the *normal* affection of an older man for a much younger girl?"

"Normal? I know not what you mean."

"Is it *paternal*, Brent?" Analee's voice sank to a whisper.

"No." Brent uttered the brief word and was silent.

"That is why your mother wished to tell you something. You should have been told long ago. I know it now, and I reproach myself bitterly."

Brent sprang up and grasped her arms, pulling her towards him. "What is it about Morella I must know?" he shouted. "Why is it so important that *I* know it?"

Analee shook herself free and rubbed her wrists, red from his painful grasp. He was still towering over her breathing heavily, angrily, and for a moment she feared him. She took a few paces back so as to put some distance between them and then she lifted her chin and gazed at him.

"Morella is our daughter, Brent, yours and mine. She was conceived the night you first took me on the forest floor and born nine months later when I was the wife of Randal Buckland."

"Then how do you know she is *my* daughter?" Brent spat. "She is more like the daughter of the *husband* you so perfidiously took. You have lied to me all your life, Analee, and you lie yet again."

"I do not lie, Brent. My husband Randal Buckland was dark-skinned and black-haired, as I am, with eyes the color of mine. A child of ours could not have had fair skin, blue eyes and blonde hair. Never. It was because Reyora saw this that she kept Morella while I fled so as to save me from the wrath of the tribe. As she was the *cohani* they would never dare to touch her or the baby; but they would have stoned me to death. That was when I ran away and found the Allonbys. For a long time I did not know what had happened to Morella because, as you know, I found the gypsy camp burnt and Randal dead. That was when I met Lord Falconer. I think you know the rest."

"Then the baby I met with Reyora on the road was my own daughter?" Brent said incredulously. "Why did she not say?"

"She did not know; maybe she guessed. Your mother guessed. She saw how greatly Morella

334

resembled you, as a child, and bit by bit pieced the story together."

"But why did *you* not tell the truth, tell me when you found out about Morella? How did you find out?"

"Nelly saw Morella and Reyora at the castle. She then told me that Morella was safe and in good hands. She advised me to leave her there."

"Because you wanted to marry a marquess, of course!" Brent hurled at her contemptuously. "You would let your daughter be brought up by strangers so long as you . . ."

Analee put out a hand and wearily sat down. "*Please*, Brent. You must know that is false. I did not think this would ever be pleasant, which is why I unwisely delayed telling you. I wanted to leave well alone. I had suffered so much. What could I offer Morella? When Nelly told me where she was it was my intention to stay on the road as a gypsy. I had run away from the Falcon to look for her. I did not intend to go back to him until I was sent for because he was dying. I knew that Morella was with her own grandmother who loved her, the best possible place for her to be.

"You know how the Falcon hated you. What would he have done to us all if he knew Morella was our child?"

"Our child." Brent repeated the words as if he could not believe them. Then he put his face in his hands. "If you knew how I longed to have children by you in those days when I still hoped . . ." He gazed at her.

"And you no longer hope?" Analee said quietly, her voice close to breaking. "It is past?" Brent didn't reply and Analee continued: "I asked too much of you, to wait. I realize now that I put myself first, myself and Lord Falconer. I thought you would wait forever. How stupid we are to take too much for granted."

"Beautiful women usually do," Brent said bitterly. "Aye, you put me second always. Who, after all, was I? Not *Sir* Brent Delamain, owner of vast estates and a

335

considerable fortune, but plain Brent Delamain, a homeless, penniless vagabond. Did I not even command a fishing wherry and pull in the haul with the men? Certainly not someone for *Lady Falconer* to consider . . ."

"Brent, you know that is not true. Wealth and position never mattered to me and still do not. Remember it was you who were first unfaithful to me. You fell in love with Mary Allonby . . ."

"Until I saw you again!"

"I did not know that. You had proved fickle once, why should you not again?"

"But from then on I was constant, my marriage shattered because of you. I wanted to take you away from him, to give you a life—but no. You pretended to love that ogre!"

"I did love him," Analee said solemnly. "His mettle matched mine. I said I would venerate his memory and I do. I have been faithful to my marriage vows."

"In a way *he* never was!"

"He was certainly not faithful. But he had a different understanding of the roles of men and women."

"He thought of women as chattels!"

Analee bowed her head in agreement. "In a way he did; yet he was so dependent on them! But he was the most remarkable man and I shall remember and honor him until I die."

"You were not exactly *true* to your marriage vows either," Brent said slyly. "There was a time you took me in your arms . . ."

"I do not deny it. Can you not love two men, Brent? Is it not possible? You know my affection for you went beyond mere friendship. I loved you and I love you still; but circumstances have always intervened. I felt I had to live a number of years as a widow out of respect to my late husband and in deference to his children; but after that . . ."

"You expected me to come running."

"No. I hoped that . . . we might come together eventually, if it suited everyone concerned."

"Oh, who is concerned beyond you and me?"

"The children," Analee said simply. "My son Duncan is the Marquess of Falconer. He is now twelve years of age, my daughter Clare fourteen. And then . . . there is Morella."

"Morella," Brent said bitterly. "How she has longed to know her mother. It has tormented her. She even said to me once, 'I feel my mother is there somewhere waiting for me.' "

"Oh, she said that!" The tears ran down Analee's cheeks. "Oh, I feel I have done such a wrong. The worst of it being that you imagined yourself in love with your own daughter."

" 'Tis a monstrous crime!" Brent said savagely. "But how did I know? How *was* I to know? My mother knew. Why did she not tell me?"

"She did not know for sure until last winter when she was like to die. I told her then to comfort her; why she did not tell you when she got better I cannot say. Maybe, like me, she was content to leave well alone."

"But all was not well! My affection for Morella was deepening, couldn't she see that? Everyone else could. My sister Emma even said she thought Morella was a little young for me. I nearly made love to her, my own daughter! Imagine that! I lay on the ground with her, in a clearing as we once did, she urging me to take her and . . ." Brent, ashen-faced, stared at Analee. "You appeared to me. It was physical. I could have touched you. It was no ghost. You bade me to have nothing to do with her or I should regret it for the rest of my life. My desire ebbed immediately and before any harm was done, thank God. To have ravished my own daughter!" Brent kept his hands over his face for a long time, his shoulders jerking with sobs.

Analee went over to him and touched him. "Brent, you can never blame yourself, never. Yes, I know I ap-

337

peared to you. I sometimes in the past have had the sensation that I am leaving my own body. I had it quite often in the war or when the Falcon was ill. He once saw me when he lay wounded after Culloden, emphasizing, as you did now, that it was not a dream. A few days ago I was very disturbed in my mind and anxious about you. I kept on seeing you and Morella . . ."

"You wore a blue cloak and hat . . ."

"Yes, I was walking in the grounds here. You know at this time of the year we are usually at Furness, but Duncan had some studies to complete and Clare had been in London, so I waited here for them, It was a beautiful day and I was walking in my own rose garden when I had that sensation that I was elsewhere . . ."

"Well, you were watching me attempt to make love to my daughter!"

"Oh no. I could not see anything. I never can. It is just an odd sensation in my body. I do not feel normal. I cannot really explain it to you; but, yes, I know the day. I remember it. I was thinking of her, and you. I wore my blue cloak, and a large hat to shield my eyes against the sun. Morella's sixteenth birthday."

"Yes," Brent whispered.

"You would have taken her virginity then, would you? Fie on you!"

"She *begged* me to."

Analee gave a bitter smile. "I am glad she does not lack passion. In that, at least, she resembles her mother."

"She resembles her mother in many ways," Brent said. "I know it now. She has your spirit, your temperament. Oh, Analee, what have we done?"

He gazed at her pitifully and her heart went out to him in love. Yes—love—not passion, but gentle, understanding love. She felt as a couple does when they have lived together for many years and raised children.

"It is more what I have done than what you have done," she said gently. "I should have spoken years ago. Your emotions would never have got the better of you then, and she would have known who her mother and father were. I was a coward. I confess it now." She sighed and turned to the window. "I have made many mistakes in this life, but this I feel is one of the greatest, one of the most important, with consequences that went far beyond my control. Morella is now in love with you. What will her reactions be when she finds out that the man she had desired, idolized maybe, is her own father? Who will she blame for denying her this knowledge?" Analee paused and once more the tears came into her eyes. "She will blame me, her mother, for you were as ignorant in this matter as she was. Will she hate me now?"

"We must find out," Brent said, rising to his feet. "We must go immediately and tell her."

Henrietta Delamain paced anxiously backwards and forwards, gazing out of the window. The reason for Brent's sudden visit to Lady Falconer so shortly after the burial of his mother was unknown to her; but the messenger she had sent to bring him back had been told to ride without stopping and now it was twelve hours since he had left. Yet, even as she looked she saw the carriage drive through the gates in the far distance, the messenger she had sent riding alongside, and she fled down the stairs to await them on the porch, twisting her handkerchief in her hands, so great was her feeling of guilt and responsibility.

Brent was out of the carriage door almost before it had stopped and he ran round to the other side to open the door for Analee before her own postillion could get to it. They had met the messenger outside Penrith as they were on their way and, apart from the urgent summons from Lady Delamain, knew no futher details.

When Henrietta saw Analee she ran down the steps, tripping over herself in her anxiety to welcome her distinguished guest. "Oh, Lady Falconer! Pray what

339

brings you here? Welcome, Analee." She kissed her cheek but Analee noted the pallor of her face and clasped her hand as she said anxiously:

"You do not look well, Henrietta. What has happened?"

Henrietta looked from one to the other, her handkerchief by now a twisted rag. "I know not how to tell Brent," she said, "Oh, I blame myself."

"But what is it? What has happened?" The look Brent gave her was so menacing that she felt frightened. She lowered her eyes.

"Morella has gone. She has run away."

"Morella? Gone?"

"Yes, without a note, without her maid or packing any clothes. She went in the night like some spirit and her bed was empty when her maid went to wake her the next morning. She has taken nothing with her. Oh, I only fear that out of grief for Susan, or for some other reason I know not, she might have killed herself."

"But why should she kill herself?" Analee intervened. "Was she not a happy girl?"

"She has been so depressed since Mrs. Delamain died. She has scarce smiled or spoke a word. Then, the morning after Brent left, she had gone. I dread her body being dragged out of the river."

Morella knew the gypsy camp was near, but not where. She made several false starts and sometimes came back to the point from which she had started. She knew she had to go south, not north.

As night fell she grew afraid and she kept to the woods to be out of sight of wandering beggars or thieves. Once she saw some charcoal-burners in a clearing; but she did not dare approach them, despite the tempting smell of roasting meat.

At dawn she rose, thankful that it was the summer and she could sleep outside without freezing with cold.

When she woke she looked around for berries and drank water from the stream. She found that such activities came naturally to her and that the life suited her.

The food in her belly and warmth on her back renewed her courage, and during the day she was not afraid to approach strangers on the road and ask them where the Buckland gypsies were. Everyone commented on her fine clothes and the way she spoke; but no one molested her. Finally, in the late afternoon, she came to the spot she sought, the gypsy tents around the fields, their horses tethered in the shade. In front of the tents were many fires and the men squatted around while the women prepared the evening meal. Groups of children played with sticks and hoops or balls made of rags and wrapped round twigs and leaves.

They all had the black hair and brown faces of their race; they looked at her with curiosity as she timidly made her way past the tents, not quite knowing whom to ask or what to say.

"Can I help thee, lass?" A fine young man sprang up in front of her, his chest bare, his eyes gleaming in admiration.

"I'm looking for Reyora," Morella said. "Can you tell me where to find her?"

"Reyora is the *cohani*. She will be in yonder tent." The young man pointed and Morella glanced at him with approval, noting the fine hairs on his brown torso, the red gleam of his nipples. He looked virile and vibrant with life. "I'll take you to her," the young man said. "How are you called?"

"Morella."

Reyora squatted by her fire, looking into the flames as one of her daughters prepared the meal. Although she was not old in years she sometimes felt old because of all the hardships she had been through, especially during the Rebellion when her tribe had been almost annihilated. But the Buckland tribe, with true gypsy

341

vigor, had revived itself. It had intermarried and married into neighboring tribes. It was now large and as vigorous as it was when Randal Buckland had captured a bride and brought her there and Rebecca, old Rebecca, had been the *phuri-dai*, the wisest and cleverest woman in the tribe. Now Reyora had held that position unchallenged for many years.

Reyora felt she was seeing a vision as she glanced up and saw Morella, carefree and laughing, walking alongside the tall frame of Timothy Buckland—one of her many nephews. She got up and drew her shawl closer against the chill evening, but Morella trailed her cloak behind her and seemed quite happy in a thin muslin dress, the hem of which was very dirty and torn from her long walk.

Reyora went slowly towards her and when Morella saw her she paused in her chattering and ran to her. "Oh, Reyora! I have found you." She threw her arms around the older woman and kissed her.

"But, Morella, where have you been? Your clothes are dirty, Your face . . . Your hair."

"I have been wandering, Reyora, like you told me the Buckland gypsies used to do. I left home yesterday and took the wrong road. I then had to sleep the night in the wood; but I covered myself with dry leaves and ate berries and drank the clear water from the stream. I've enjoyed it, Reyora. I feel at home in this life!"

"And do Sir Brent or Lady Henrietta know where you are?"

"No, I have run away for good. I have left home. I want to be a gypsy and live as you do. I like the life. I knew I would."

Morella looked archly at the handsome Timothy Buckland, who hung on her every word.

"Be off with you now, Timothy," Reyora said. "I must talk to Miss Morella."

"Oh, not 'Miss Morella'! Morella." The blonde girl burst out laughing and Timothy felt dazzled by her beauty. He had never seen such a lovely creature in his life.

"Dance with me afterwards," he whispered. "When it has grown dark we sing and dance round the fire."

"Be off with you. Shoo!" Reyora made a gesture with her hand, but to herself she was smiling, remembering all those years ago when Morella's mother, Analee, had bewitched the Buckland tribe by her skill as a dancer, had made all the women jealous with her striking looks, "Now Morella, come to my tent and tell me why you are here. I will have food sent in."

Reyora drew Morella past the curious glances of her family into her large tent. She lit a candle and bade Morella sit on the pile of soft cushions on the floor where she used to squat to weave her spells or simply to meditate.

"Oh, I like it here!" Morella said mischievously. "I feel at home. May I stay here."

"First," Reyora said, squatting opposite her, "you must tell me why you are here."

Morella faltered a little at first; but then the story came out. How she admired her Uncle Brent, how about a year ago she began to dream of him and weave fantasies around him. How she was convinced now that she was in love with him and he with her. How she had tried to tempt him in the wood but he had changed his mind at the last minute.

"He said 'someone' stopped him. I then challenged him. 'Someone?' I said. 'Some*thing*,' he corrected; but I think he meant *someone*. That night my Aunt Susan died and from then to the funeral Uncle Brent hardly ever looked at me. He never smiled and he ignored me. As soon as Aunt Susan was buried he left to visit Lady Falconer. I know not why. I decided to run away and become a gypsy like my mother." Morella reached out and grasped the hand of her old friend. "Reyora, my mother was a gypsy, was she not? Tell me the truth. Tell it now. In the past, whenever I have asked you,

you have evaded it. Uncle Brent said he thought it was because you did not know; but I think you do. I want to know *now* about my mother, and I want to know why Uncle Brent has changed towards me and does not love me. Am I not attractive?"

"You are very attractive." Reyora nodded and scratched on the floor of the tent with a twig she was holding. She wrote some magical gypsy letters, a kind of charm, to bring her luck in the difficult task ahead of her. "That is part of the trouble. It was the trouble with your mother, too. Her beauty was of little advantage to her. It brought her so much sorrow."

"You are going to tell me about my mother?" Morella clasped her hands together. "Oh, Reyora, pray go on!"

"I am going to tell you about how it was long ago," Reyora answered, "When this land was very troubled. A beautiful dark gypsy girl of undoubtedly noble bearing, but a gypsy for all that, fell in love with a nobleman. He had to go the war before he knew that this woman he loved was to bear his child. He was on the side of the Stuarts and you know what happened to those who supported the cause?"

Morella nodded gravely. "They were defeated."

"Defeated and stripped of their lands and rights. The man was sentenced to death but escaped and the beautiful gypsy, who also underwent many vicissitudes and had been forced into a loveless marriage, eventually gave birth to a blonde baby with fair skin and blue eyes who, it was known, could not possibly be the issue of herself and her dark-skinned gypsy husband."

"That was me?" Morella gasped.

"Yes; I was present at your birth and helped to bring you into this world. Already I loved your mother, and I urged her to flee because otherwise she would be killed by her tribe for lying with a *gadjo*, a non-gypsy. I would look after you and restore you to her in time. Well, that was not to be. Our camp was invaded by the

Jacobites and you know how I took you on the road and, on the way, I met a man who took pity on us and directed us to his mother."

"*Uncle Brent?*"

"Yes, and your Aunt Susan."

"And what happened to the gypsy?"

"Well, for a while she did not prosper. She had no home and no money and lived on the road, eating berries as you did last night, and sleeping under hedges or in caves. It was a bitter winter the year of the Rebellion, the year you were born, 1745. She had heard by chance that you were safe, in a good home with people who loved you. She wished to reclaim you, but was advised not to in your own interests, not hers. She did what she did for the best. She knew where you were and that you were happy. You must always believe this, Morella; what your mother did was what she thought was in your best interests. She never thought of herself. That I know."

"You *know*? My mother is still alive? Oh, where is she? Can I see her? Is she here among the gypsy people? Pray take me to her, Reyora."

"It is not all that easy, Morella."

"But why not? Does she think I will be ashamed of her because she is poor? Of course I will not! I forgive her anything, just to see her."

Reyora got up and looked out of the tent towards the camp. It was now dark and the fires blazed, lighting up the faces of those around.

"I will have to think what to do," she said at last. "Let us eat now."

She had not imagined it would be easy, but it was proving more difficult than even she had thought.

The girl was dancing, her lithe body weaving intricately in and out of the assembled gypsies. To see her dance you would have thought she had done it all her life, that, from being a small girl, she had learned the steps

345

and how to click her fingers above her head and sway her hips.

But Morella had learned it in two nights, ever since Timothy Buckland had taken her onto the grass after her talk with Reyora. For two hours they had spun and twirled until the whole camp had gathered to watch them and called to those who were inside to come out and see the blonde *gadja* who must surely have gypsy blood to dance with such skill.

That night Morella had slept in Reyora's tent and the next day, dressed in a gypsy skirt and blouse, she had lived the way the gypsy women did, cooking and cleaning and chatting as they chewed their nuts, sitting apart from the men. Then in the afternoon she had ridden with Timothy bareback and once even standing on the horse fearlessly, her fair hair streaming in the wind, while Reyora had gone on a mysterious mission, promising to be back at night.

Now the assembled concourse clapped and one or two played gay cheerful gypsy tunes on their tin whistles, while the fiddler did his best to keep up with them.

The tears came into Analee's eyes as she watched her daughter and, but for the coloring, she could see herself as the girl she had been, dancing for her living in taverns, in the houses of the great, just as the Buckland gypsies still did.

"You can see she is your daughter," Reyora murmured. "She has your talent. It came to her naturally as one born to it. See, Analee, if you now went into the crowd you could dance as well as Morella. You still have your figure and your skill."

Analee pulled her cloak about her feeling herself trembling in the chill breeze. She had ridden over, through the forest with Reyora, and she wore a riding skirt and high polished boots. Her feet tapped to the music, but she smiled ruefully at Reyora's words.

"I have borne five children since I danced, Reyora.

Even my greatest admirers would not say the girth of my waist is what it was." But she found it difficult to joke. She was too full of trepidation as to what Morella would say. She wished Reyora had spared her the task.

"Who is the boy she dances with?"

"He is my nephew, Timothy Buckland. The son of my sister Rose."

"He is a fine-looking boy."

"He *is* a fine boy. He is nineteen."

"He never stops looking at her."

"Or she him. He is more her own age. Morella had to meet boys of her own age. If she had, she would not have fallen in love with her father."

"He knows that now. In time they will both forget it ever happened."

"And is he in love with you again?" Reyora looked at her slyly.

"No, not yet." Analee glanced knowingly at Reyora. "But I am using the last of my failing powers to try and ensure it will not be for long. I will never tease him again for, now that he does not want me, I find I passionately desire him."

"Hush, they are stopping." Reyora looked anxiously at Analee. "Now you must tell her."

But Morella had disappeared, and it was a long time before they found her at the back of the camp with Timothy Buckland listening to his stories of horse-trading and dancing in the fairs.

"Oh, I would love to come with you!" Morella's eyes shone. "I would like to stay here forever. My mother was . . ." Morella looked up and saw Reyora and with her a lady in a long cloak with the hood pulled well down over her face. Something about her was familiar. Morella stopped talking and ran over to Reyora. "Did you see me dancing? Where were you today? Why . . . ?"

The lady dropped her hood and smiled timidly at Morella who gasped with amazement. "Lady Falconer! Whatever brings you here?"

"I have come to see you, Morella."

"Me?" Morella looked at Reyora. "Oh, you have come to take me home. Uncle Brent is too angry to come himself. He has sent *you*."

"Yes, but I have also come to talk to you." Analee took her arm and led her away from the crowd. The only light came from the flickering fires, some being dowsed down for the night.

"What did Uncle Brent wish you to say?" Morella enquired petulantly, "That he did not dare come himself? Well, tell him I like it here. I want to stay. I hate the castle and the boring, stilted life."

"It is true Sir Brent did not wish to come himself, but not because he did not dare. I wanted to talk to you and explain why it was that the gypsy let her baby go, the blonde baby who was found on the road sixteen years ago."

"But why should you know that?" Morella said, her eyes already showing a glimmering of understanding.

"Because, my dear child, *I* was the gypsy and you are my daughter, Morella."

Morella gazed at her mother, her mouth wide open with shock. She moved away from her and, for a moment, turned her back to hide emotion. Analee braced herself, resigned to whatever would come. When Morella slowly turned to her again, tears were streaming down her face.

"But why did you not tell me before? I have seen you throughout the years. Were you so ashamed of me?"

"Oh, Morella," Analee was weeping now, and she drew her daughter to her. "I was proud, *proud* of you! It is of myself I am ashamed; but, you see, I felt you had made a new life and that if I came into it, it would only upset and disrupt you. Besides, there was Lord Falconer. Not at first, but later. I loved him, but he was a harsh man. I had other children and I thought that if he knew about you he might send me away. Part

348

me from them too. He never liked your father. He hated him. I admit I was afraid and I have always repented of this cowardice and always shall."

"You preferred your other children to me?" Morella's lip was trembling.

"Of course I did not! I always loved you best, my first-born. I thought of you constantly. Did we not like to play together when I came to see you? Were you not attracted to me?"

"I thought you were beautiful. I wished my mother was like you. Now that I know . . . I am not so sure."

"But why, Morella?" Analee's arm tightened around her.

"Because I think it is too late. I have grown up without the love of a mother, with my mother pretending to be someone else, a stranger. You see it is very hard for me."

"It is hard for me too. Morella, to show you how much I love you and always have. Even if you reject me now I will always love you. Besides I gave a promise to your father."

"My father? He is alive too?"

"This is the hardest part," Analee said her voice choking. "For the man I loved and lay with all those years ago, the man who met Reyora on the road and out of compassion, directed you to his mother—although he did not know who you were—was Brent Delamain, my lover and your father."

Morella gave a scream and ran off into the dark. Reyora, who had been watching nearby, ran after her and Timothy, who had been standing with her, ran faster. As Morella tore across the field and into the forest Timothy reached her and grasped her, holding her tight as she struggled against him, beating his hard young body.

"Let me go! Let me go!"

She tried to bite his hand, but he held her until Reyora came and, at the sight of those wise eyes, Morella's struggles grew less frantic and she calmed down.

"Come with me," Reyora said. "I will give you something nice to drink. It will blot out all the unhappiness and when you wake you will feel better."

"Tell *her* to go! I never want to see her again," Morella muttered, her eyes blazing with rage and humiliation, pointing to where Analee stood in the shadows. "I never want to see either of them again. Her or *him*, as long as I live."

Chapter Nineteen

"Thus," the Marquess of Falconer said, as though explaining something to a simpleton, "the earth goes *round* the sun. 'Tis not the other way about."

"I see," Brent replied, "that you would make a fine sailor."

"Oh no, sir, I wish to be a scholar."

"Not a soldier like your father?"

"No indeed!" Young Lord Falconer's aristocratic features wrinkled in horror at the very idea. "That is the ambition of my brother Beyrick. He plays with toy soldiers all the time. My mother has to send for them to London. I don't enjoy warlike things. I wish this war was over."

"They say it soon will be," Brent observed, looking out of the window for a sight of Analee. "But England has made splendid gains. Was there ever a year like 1759? Hardly ever in our history. We shall drive the French into the sea and capture the whole American continent. And India, too. Are you not proud of our country?"

"Of course I am proud," Duncan said. "But I do not

350

wish to be in the military. I would like to serve her by peaceful means—in the cause of science if possible."

Brent smiled and leaned against the window sill of Duncan's large room filled with apparatus and instruments. Analee complained that he studied too much, whereas Beyrick, completely different, gave vent to his aggressive nature by drilling his toy soldiers and ordering the servants about all day long. Brent felt rested and at home at Furness where the Falconer family had gone for their usual summer retreat. The nagging irritation about Morella seemed less intense here, the reason he ostensibly came to see Analee.

"Ah, there is your mother now," he said, eagerly glancing for the fiftieth time out of the window.

"Are the girls with her?"

"Yes. Your sister Clare is a beauty. I hear she loves London."

"She is too giddy." Duncan said derisively. "She can't wait until she is presented at Court! She has no love of the country as Mama has."

"Let us go down and greet them."

"I would like to finish this experiment, Sir Brent. I will join you soon."

Duncan bent his head to his piece of apparatus and Brent left the room and ran downstairs with a feeling of excitement he could not altogether explain in his heart.

Analee had stayed on the terrace where the servants brought out chairs and refreshment because of the warmth of the day. Little Elizabeth Falconer sat near her; she hardly ever left her side if she could help it, while Charlotte and Beyrick went to the water's edge and started playing with the boat that was at anchor there. Charlotte was a tomboy and copied everything her brother did.

Clare was a languid girl, not given to overexerting herself unless it was at a dance or riding in Richmond or Marylebone fields or occasionally here on Manesty

351

Moor. She had already the air of a grand lady and lay stretched out in her chair, one arm trailing to the ground, her eyes closed, panting slightly.

"Oh, I am puffed! The heat is too enervating."

"You do not take enough exercise, Clare," Analee said. "You will get fat and . . ."

"Oh, Mama, do not say such a thing!" Clare looked at her in horror. "You know I am so careful about what I eat. I *never* let a chocolate past my lips or . . ."

"No, darling, I was only teasing." Analee leaned over to her and took her hand. "You are lazy by nature, but you will always have too much care about the opinions of others to let yourself get fat. But, Clare, I do not wish you to grow up *too* soon. You are but fourteen. Enjoy your youth. Your head is full of dances and parties and . . . men." Her mother leaned heavily on the last word.

"Mama, Lady Agnes Dulcimer is already wed and she is just fifteen!"

"She is too young," Analee said primly. "I do not want thoughts of marriage to enter your head until you are at *least* seventeen, and I would perfer it a good deal later. Ah, thank you, Nell." Analee looked up as Nelly put a cushion behind her back. "Now Nelly makes me feel like an old lady, always fussing about me. Nelly, did I see Sir Brent at the window of Duncan's room as we walked past?"

"Yes, ma'am. He rode over to see you."

"He is always here, isn't he?" Clare said, glancing at her beautiful mother meaningfully. Though the two were deeply attached there was a slight air of rivalry between them. Analee ignored her remark, looking towards the door.

"And here I am," Brent said, walking onto the terrace and extending his arms. "What a beautiful day! I could not resist saddling my horse and coming to see you all." He gave Clare a friendly smile, deliberately

352

offhand. He knew Analee thought him too susceptible to young females.

"Is everything all right?" Analee glanced at him anxiously, Morella being a constant source of worry to them both.

"I would like to talk to you later alone, but there is nothing really wrong," Brent said while Clare gazed at them both beneath the long black lashes that tantalized all the beaux in London.

"We do see a *lot* of you, Sir Brent," she said haughtily.

"I am a *very* old friend of your mother's," Brent replied, "and having no family of my own to speak of I am very fond of you all."

"What do you mean 'to speak of'? I thought you had no family of your own?"

"Well, I have my sister-in-law Henrietta and her daughters, my sister Emma and her sons and my ward Morella."

"Ah, Morella," Clare said with a laugh. "Mama said she is living with gypsies! How outrageous!"

"Not 'Living' with them, Clare," Analee said reprovingly. "She is staying with our old and valued friend Reyora."

Clare managed a grimance of distaste and shuddered. "Oh, I should hate it! Imagine in a tent, and all those common people . . ."

Analee's eyes glinted dangerously. She found Clare the most unlike her and the most difficult of all her children to cope with on account of her fine airs and graces, her exaggerated manners. But still, she was the daughter of a marquess, and Analee supposed that daughters of a marquess felt entitled to give themselves airs. Not having grown up as one of them she didn't know. She was perpetually correcting her daughter, which was why Clare spent such a lot of time under the chaperonage of a sister of the Falcon, Lady Amelia Duguid, in London.

"Take care, Clare, what you say. Remember I am one of those 'common people' by birth."

"Oh, Mama!" Clare scoffed, "and your father an earl! Common person indeed."

"Yes, Clare, but as you know, he did not bring me up. I grew up among the gypsies and Morella is like . . . that," Analee finished just in time, having been on the verge of saying "me." None of her children had yet been let in on the secret of Morella's parentage.

"Well, how long will Morella stay with those 'dear' people?" Clare looked at Brent, who shrugged, the expression in his eyes unfathomable.

"Forever, as far as I can see. She shows no desire to come home."

"Oh you cannot allow it, Brent!" Analee expostulated. "She cannot stay there forever! I shall have to go and talk to her."

"But why you, Mama?" Clare enquired curiously.

"Because she listens to me, that is all. Or rather she listens to Reyora, who listens to me. I must say I can make very little headway myself with that willful young lady." She glanced at Brent in despair. Their worry over Morella had brought them close, and he got on so well with her children. Duncan loved him and valued his comments on his work. Beyrick liked him because he had fought in the war and played soldier with him. though always on the enemy side, Beyrick being a staunch Hanoverian. Charlotte was obviously fond of him; but his favorite was Elizabeth, beautiful fragile little Elizabeth, who had never known her father. Brent was especially tender with her and he was gazing at her now playing tranquilly by the side of the woman she called Mother.

"Do you think we could have a word inside, Analee?"

"But you are not going back too soon, are you? Why not stay a few days with us?" She gazed at him and he felt a sudden excitement, a quickening of the pulse as

354

when he used to look at Analee in days of old. He thought she was looking at him in the same way, too. How well he recalled that expression; amorous without being too blatant, seductive with a pleasing hint of diffidence.

"I cannot do that just at the moment, but I would like to take it up in a week or two," he replied slowly. "The thing is that with Morella it is beginning to be a little serious."

Analee got out of her chair and took his hand as he helped her up.

"Serious? You must tell me at once. Clare, keep an eye on the children." She put an arm through his and together they walked slowly into the house, Clare's eyes on them, not on her small charges.

"Now what is it about Morella?" Analee turned to Brent as soon as they were inside.

"Reyora came to see me yesterday. She feels she must stay no longer in the camp."

"But why? Is she not happy there? I hoped she would grow out of it naturally and wish to come home!"

"Oh, not a bit of it," Brent laughed and, taking off his coat, put it over a chair. "I hope you do not mind, Analee, but I am very hot."

"Of course not." How handsome he looked in his shirt and breeches Analee thought, his unpowdered hair still thick and fair, his jawline firm, his figure that of a much younger man. She closed her eyes and thought sadly of what might have been; but now they were like two elderly parents anxious about their errant daughter, clucking rather than billing and cooing. "Tell me about Morella."

"Reyora fears she is in love."

"In *love*?"

"With that scamp of a gypsy, her nephew Timothy."

"Oh my goodness! I am afraid that Morella will always be in love from now on. She is rather like Clare in her attraction of the opposite sex."

"All they have in common, I fear. Clare is much too elegant for Morella. Reyora says that Morella has become the complete gypsy—wears gypsy clothes, her hair in a band, never washing. She is always slinking off with Timothy and Reyora has to keep a very close eye on her and is growing tired of it. She wishes that you would come and speak to her. Ask her to go home. Clearly, as she is in love with Timothy, she is no longer a danger to me."

"And you? Are you a danger to her?" Analee gazed at him, her voice scarcely above a whisper.

"Of course not! That is long since gone. I . . ." he looked at Analee and then lowered his eyes.

"Yes, Brent?"

"Well I . . . I come over here a lot, do I not?"

"Yes, you do," she replied lightly. "As Clare has noticed."

"It is not just to see the children, fond as I am of them."

"And they of you."

"Duncan is a very fine boy. I feel he will enrich the scholarship of this land."

"His tutor hopes so, too. He feels he can teach him no more and Duncan will shortly go to Oxford to study with new tutors there."

"Oh, Analee, I am so glad!" Brent looked at her, his eyes shinning. "What a credit to his father."

"A real credit to his father," Analee said, gazing at Brent. "Or should I say a credit to his real father?"

"But what do you mean?"

"I cannot tell you now, Brent, but I may some day."

"You mean the Falcon was not Duncan's father?"

"It cannot be proved, but that is my suspicion. They are neither alike to look at or in temperament."

"Yes, I noticed that. Duncan is very different from the rest, who all have the Falcon's imperious expression, even little Elizabeth. Duncan is gentle . . . Analee," he gazed at her, the feeling of excitement returning. "Do you mean to tell me . . ."

"I can tell you nothing, Brent, not yet anyway."

He came close to her and took her hand, drawing her to him. "You tease, you Enchantress, you! So you did not keep your marital vows too well after all? That is *two* men, at least you lay with while you were wed, for I don't suppose *I* am Duncan's father?"

"Most certainly not."

"How many more?"

"Children or men?" Analee said provocatively.

"Oh, you . . ." He crushed his mouth down upon hers, feeling her yield to him as she had in days gone by. His head swam with desire for her; she was so familiar, yet always strange, new. She put her arms round his neck and drew him to her.

"I would imprison you forever in my arms," she murmured.

"Forever?" Brent's voice was hoarse. "You *mean* forever?" She let him go and he stepped back panting, his eyes alight. "Oh, Analee, if we . . ."

"I was afraid the magic had gone; but it has not."

"It never did! I only saw you in Morella, I know that now."

"And you are definitely *over* Morella?" she said slyly.

Brent threw up his hands and gazed at the ceiling, the veins on his forehead bulging. "Oh, never bring that up again, that folly! It has ruined my relationship with my daughter, but it is not too late to repair it with her mother. Analee . . . will you?"

He knelt down and took her hand, bringing it to his lips.

"Really, Sir Brent, is this a formal proposal?"

"You know it is, my darling. A passionate proposal for you to become my wife—at last!"

357

"And I accept you, Brent, with great joy. Oh, how I feared I would never awaken desire in you again . . ."

"You need never fear that, my Enchantress . . ."

Analee put a hand on his head. "No, Brent, the Enchantress is gone. It is Analee, the mother and wife I have become."

"But when you appeared to me? What was that if not magic?"

"That was because I was a mother. I could not let you have carnal knowledge of your daughter. I was being a mother then, not an Enchantress." She bent and kissed his head and, drawing him up, led him to a seat by the window. "Now, my darling, we have to think what to do about Morella. My only interview since I told her I was her mother was unpleasant; she was rude and sullen. You have not seen her at all. She presents a real problem to us, but do you know what I think will suit our wayward young daughter?"

"No?" Brent looked at her, still not believing his good fortune.

"A spell in a convent."

Brent threw back his head and roared with laughter. "A convent! Morella in a convent?"

"Only for a short time. I did not suppose she would wish to take the veil; but yes, why not? I thought of Mary, who would gladly look after her, supervise her studies and maybe teach her a prayer or two."

"But Morella does not like to study."

"It will do her no harm, before she is ready to be presented."

"You *are* serious about this, are you not?"

"Very."

"And what do you suppose Morella will say?"

"Once she is confronted with the wishes of her *united* parents she will have very little say in the matter."

"United? You mean we are to be wed, that soon?"

"As soon as I have the permission of my eldest

son." Analee kissed him once more and then she led him through the house and up the stairs.

Duncan was still in his room when they went to find him. A candle was alight under a jar in which liquid slowly bubbled and his head was bent over a book. When he saw his mother he stood up and took her hand and kissed it. Instinctively his manners were as exquisite as those of Prince Charles.

"Mama, how good of you to visit me!"

"Sir Brent told me of your conversation. He is most impressed with your knowledge, Duncan."

"I am honored, Mama." He bent his head and smiled. He was an extraordinarily handsome boy with the dark hair of his mother, but with fair skin and the distinctive regal air of the Stuarts. Fortunately he had not inherited his father's rather weak chin; but bore closer resemblance to his great-uncle Charles II as a boy. He was very tall for his age and moved with unusual feline grace. When his mind was made up nothing could bend him, but he was thoughtful and tolerant. The only thing he could never stand was any mention of the Falcon. He would close his lips tight and his eyes remained fixed while the virtues of his supposed sire were extolled.

"Will you not come into the sun, Duncan? We have had so many miserable days this year. Much as I love my Lakeland, the climate . . ." Analee shuddered. "I think when you go to Oxford I shall come to London for a while and then, when the war is over, I am going to visit my father in Spain."

"Alone, Mama?"

She looked at him with surprise. "Alone? Well, if you mean my servants and maybe Clare . . ."

Duncan folded his hands gravely in front of him, a slight color to his cheeks. "Mama, if I am speaking out of turn pray forgive me, and you, sir." He bowed solemnly at Brent. "But I have noticed how often Sir Brent is over here of late. I welcome his company, but

359

I have reason to think he does not come to see me or my brother and sisters. It is you, Mama, he comes to see."

Analee glanced at Brent, her expression half-hopeful, half-fearful. Brent was looking at Duncan, something of the same emotion showing on his own face. It seemed for a moment as though their future happiness was in the hands of this twelve-year-old, but very mature boy.

"It is true I am excessively attached to your mama ..." Brent began nervously.

"Then why do you not *marry* her, sir?"

For a moment there was silence accentuated by the sounds of laughter from the terrace below, the splash of water as the children played with the boat.

"You would *like* us to marry, Duncan?" Analee looked at her son through tears.

"I would like nothing better, Mama. You have been a widow too long, and I know you are lonely even though the best of mothers to us. Sir Brent seems like an excellent choice to you."

"Oh, my darling, we are all of one mind," she said, throwing her arms round his neck. "It was your permission to do this very thing that we came to seek."

"Then you have it, Mama, and my blessing," he said and drew Brent also into his arms.

The only one who objected to her mother marrying again was Clare. She thought she was much too old to contemplate such a step, and Brent likewise she considered in his dotage. However, when they said that they would still like the opportunity to support each other in their senility, she grudgingly agreed.

The wedding, which was not long delayed, was a very quiet one in Keswick Church with only members of Analee's family and staff attending. Brent did not want any word of this to get to Delamain Castle before they had seen Morella.

* * *

360

He lay alongside her and she looked at him with wonder, his long lissom body with its fine hairs, the big tuft at his groin out of which that interesting appendage was slowly growing to an enormous size. Morella gazed at it with astonishment.

Although she was in no doubt about wishing to shed her virginity, she had undressed completely with some show of reluctance despite Timothy's eager help, especially when it came to exposing her breasts to those excited male eyes. He cupped them in his hands and placed the nipples between his lips, first one and then the other and a delicious commotion began in her loins as she felt the rising member stiffen beside her.

"Is *that* it?" she said with wonder. "What do you do with it?"

"Aye, it is my cock and I put it inside thee."

"Then do it quickly," Morella demanded urgently. "Because I need you." And, with unmaidenly enthusiasm as well as a natural instinct, she lay back and opened her legs as he positioned himself upon her.

Suddenly there was a violent slap on his back and Timothy's senses reeled. A further cuff came to his head and he felt dizzy and sick. The fierce beating of his heart from desire turned into panic, and he rolled off Morella and lay gasping on the ground, his erect member waving helplessly in the air, while she curled up her legs in shame and tried to disguise her naked breasts.

Reyora stood over them with a large stick in her hand and behind her, peeping eagerly through the opening to the tent, was a giggling group of onlookers. The stick thudded on Timothy again and he tried to roll away from her.

"Reyora, please!" Morella cried. "You will kill him!"

"Death is *too* good for him, that is what," Reyora snarled, turning to the tent flap and brandishing her stick. "Get away, all of you. Get away!" The crowd

361

reluctantly retired from the interesting spectacle and Reyora turned threateningly to Timothy again, throwing him his breeches which lay on the floor by Morella's crumpled, hastily shed clothes.

"Well, did you penetrate her?"

"No, Reyora."

"Do you swear it?"

"I swear," Timothy gasped and Reyora looked closely at Morella's crotch for signs of tell-tale blood.

"Well, it seems that you were lucky," she said, straightening up. "Thank God I was in time, for if you had I would have called such a curse down upon you that your overeager member would have withered and fallen off." She shook a finger at him "And *that's* what will happen if you ever touch her again. I am here to look after her in place of her mother and father. What would they think of me if she was deflowered within my own tent!"

"We thought you were in Penrith, Reyora."

"Well, I changed my mind! Thank goodness I did or I would never have looked her parents in the eyes again, especially her mother whom I love so much. Now get up and get dressed, you shameless pair. And wait until I see your mother, Timothy. You'll get such a hiding, I'll guarantee that. Morella, you are sent for to go to Delamain Castle and I am to take you there whether you like it or not."

"I won't go," Morella said.

"Oh, yes, you will. You have been here too long. I wrote a month ago and told your father so; but he had other things on his mind it seems. Besides, it is nearly winter and you will find it very different from the hot summer we have had."

"Oh, Reyora." Morella threw herself into the older woman's arms. "*Please* do not send me back!"

"I have to, my dear," Reyora said, her expression softening. "After what I have seen I know your blood is too hot for you to remain here. There is too much

362

temptation for Timothy—and for you! I have been anxious about you too often, and something made me turn back as I started on my way. After what I nearly saw . . ." Reyora put her hand over her eyes as though to banish the awful sight. "How near you came. Oh, my God. Yes, I think your parents have in mind to send you somewhere to cool your blood, and high time, too."

"Well, they *won't!*" Morella said, but she did as she was bid all the same and finished dressing while Timothy was given a fresh smack on the backside with Reyora's stick and sent on his way.

Brent chastely pecked his daughter on the cheek, his arms lightly on her shoulders. The cheek was very cold and she was pale beneath the tan she had acquired in the camp. She had not smiled at all as Reyora had ushered her into their presence, but had stared rebelliously at Brent and Analee who were discomforted enough themselves.

After Brent had kissed her he stepped back, and Analee went over to her, embracing her more warmly. "You look well, Morella."

"I *am* well. I did not want to come back!" She stamped her foot and Reyora looked at her severely, a warning gleam in her eyes. She had promised Morella that if she was rude to her mother and father she would tell them about the incident in the tent.

"But you cannot stay there forever, my dear," Analee said nervously.

"Why not?"

"Because we do not wish it. We have something to tell you, Morella. I hope it will please you." Morella looked at her sulkily and Analee met her eyes. "Your father and I are married, Morella. Last week in Keswick. He has thus legitimized you and made an honest woman of me, at last. You are now legally Morella Delamain and I Lady Delamain . . . still a

363

lady," Analee said with smile, "but no longer, alas, a marchioness."

"But, my dear, you said it did not matter," Brent protested.

"Of *course* it does not. I was joking, trying to introduce a little levity into this solemn proceeding." Analee took his arm fondly. "Well, Morella, I hope it pleases you. We would have liked you to come to our wedding, but we did not know what to do for the best. It is not easy to understand you."

Morella sat down and stared at her parents openmouthed. "Married?" she said.

"Aye, wed. Legally before a parson and witnesses. Just a quiet ceremony. Not only for you, but for ourselves, too. It is something we have long wanted. My other children are happy, they love Brent and you will now have a whole family of brothers and sisters."

Morella burst into tears. Brent and Analee looked anxiously at each other, then at Reyora. Analee went to her daughter and knelt by her, her rich silken gown rustling as she did.

"My dear, we do want you to be happy. We love you so much. You will have what you have always wanted, a large family, your own parents united. Is it too late to begin again, Morella, to undo the misunderstandings of the past?"

Morella leaned against Analee and sobbed more loudly. Analee held her head against her breast and stroked her hair, thinking this was the first time she had held her like this, mother and daughter knowing each other. She put her chin on Morella's head and murmured, "Would you like us to be alone?"

Morella shook her head. "No . . . no. I don't know why I am crying. I don't know whether I am happy or sad. You see . . . Mama," she looked at Analee into whose eyes tears sprang at the word "mama" used for the first time, "I am in love, too! I want to marry Timothy Buckland. Oh. Mama, do say 'yes' and then I will be very nice to you and . . . Papa." She looked at Brent, bestowing on him a calculating smile of great charm.

"Marry?" Analee said, staring hard at Reyora.

"We are so in love, Mama, and you who know all about love, you will understand. He says we can have a gypsy wedding in the camp and there will be music and dancing and oh, Mama, we are going to earn our living as you did, dancing in the taverns. We thought you might ask us to dance here at the Castle and perhaps at Falcon's Keep?" She looked hopefully at her parents one after the other while Brent, who had tried hard to control himself, burst out laughing.

"But, Morella, you are an heiress! You are my lawful eldest child. You will inherit great wealth one day."

"But it does not matter. Papa." Morella stared at him thinking as she did how *old* he looked. The memory of the agile young body of Timothy Buckland haunted her, his rippling skin, his flat pink nipples. How could she ever have imagined this *old* man before her . . . inwardly she shuddered.

"It does not matter at all. I want to live as Mama did."

"Well, you can't," Brent said, aware of the expression in her eyes, and relieved to see it. He could now exercise his full parental authority. "And that is all there is to be said."

"But, Papa, I am in *love*."

"You are also sixteen," Brent said sternly, "and a minor. I hope you will never want to marry a gypsy, but if you do you cannot until you are twenty-one, and that is final."

Morella stuck her chin out at him, but Analee put a hand round her waist, still kneeling beside her. "I see you two are too alike. Stubborn. Morella, seeing that this is intended to be a happy family occasion *I* have a plan. Now listen to me." She held up a hand gleaming with the sapphires and diamonds that Brent had given

365

her as a wedding present. She smelt warm and fragrant, Morella thought, and memories of old suddenly came back to her . . . the beautiful lady who had come to call, looked at her so tenderly and held her in her arms. Yes, she has always been her mother, she had always wanted her—the woman she had dreamed about, whom she had instinctively known was waiting for her. She leaned a little nearer to her and Analee felt the gesture and her heart leapt with joy. Morella needed her; she was going to trust her.

"Listen to me, my darling. I am not saying you *cannot* ever marry Timothy, I am sure he is fine young man; but not just *yet*. Your father and I would like you to spend a little time in Paris."

"Paris?" Morella's expression froze. "So far from Timothy?"

"In a convent."

"A convent!" Morella leapt up and stared at her mother, her eyes blazing. "A *convent*?"

"Not as a *nun*, my dear, but as a young lady learning good manners and how to embroider and such—an education for a lady that I missed myself. It is very common for daughters of the aristocracy to be finished on the Continent, and now that things are more peaceful we would like you to spend a year or two with your Aunt Mary, your father's first wife, who is related to you, as she was his first cousin."

"I never knew I had an aunt who was a nun," Morella grumbled, clearly not enchanted with the idea.

"Well you have. There are all sort of relatives you don't know about and what a joy it will be discovering them. Now Paris will be such fun, Morella, after the war! I had a wonderful time there in 1748 with my late husband. We went to balls and met the King and Madame de Pompadour who was greatly taken with the Falcon and most kind to me. Although I understand her health is not good, I am sure she would be delighted to receive you, and she still has the favor of

366

the King. Please, Morella, it is a good idea. It will give you time to make up your mind and learn a little about the world. You have been painfully cut off here. If, when you come back, you feel about Timothy as you do now, well, I am sure your father can have no objection . . ."

Analee glanced at Brent who clearly would object very much, if his face was anything to go by. She quickly looked away again. She felt she was going to have a hard time in cementing relations between father and daughter who, now that their mutual infatuation had become a matter of repugnance to both of them, clearly did not see eye to eye. She could see that Brent would be a strict parent, and Morella . . . well, she was her mother's daughter after all.

"Well," Morella said with a grimace, "if that is what you want I will do it. I would *quite* like to see Paris, but I tell you I am quite determined to marry Timothy and lead the life of a gypsy just as soon as I can. I will wait for him all my life if need be." She flung back her golden head and gazed defiantly at everyone in the room.

Mother Mary Gertrude could see at once that she was a spirited girl and doubtless she would have trouble with her, but she liked her. She was the image of Brent. She smiled at her and took her hand.

"I think we shall get on," she said.

"I think so too," Morella said, quite surprised by this nice aunt who must have been pretty and still had a beautiful smile.

"It is not as quiet as you think. We have some very nice girls here from the best families all over the Continent."

"I intend to marry a gypsy when I go home," Morella said. "I am going to live in a gypsy camp and wear gypsy clothes, and have gypsy babies . . . eventually."

"Well, doubtless the girls will be very intrigued to hear that, and perhaps a little envious." Mary looked over her head and smiled at Morella's parents sitting nervously behind her. "I am sure you will have a lot of them visiting you in your new home."

Morella gazed suspiciously at her aunt. She was not quite sure whether she was mocking her or not.

Analee stood up. "I can see you two will get on. I knew you would. We are to stop for a few weeks in Paris, Mary, to see old friends. Brent has taken a house for us near the Bois. So we shall see that Morella settles down. Mr. Pitt, having learned of our intended visit, has even asked Brent to engage in a little diplomacy while we are here. He is very anxious for the war to be over."

"Are not we all?" Mary said piously. "We have petitioned Heaven for so long. God must be deaf. But I should not say that. Now, my dear Morella, I am going to get one of the girls to show you to your room and unpack while I have a word with your dear mama and papa."

Mary rang a little bell and a lay sister entered. "Sister, would you take Miss Delamain to the Comtesse de Beauséjour? She is waiting for her in her room."

"Yes, Mother." The sister smiled, bobbed at Morella and took her arm. Morella glanced anxiously at her parents who smiled encouragingly.

"Do not worry," Brent said. "I shan't make you take the veil."

Morella grimaced and stuck her tongue out at him before turning her back and following the nun out of the room.

"She is a lovely girl," Mary said. "I knew about her from Emma."

"But not that she was our daughter?"

"I knew there was *something* special about her. I have often prayed for her. I know not why. But, Analee and Brent, I am so happy that at last what you have always wanted has come to pass. Believe me I am overjoyed."

"I do believe you, Mary." Analee smiled gratefully. "I think you are really happy in your vocation and am I wrong in thinking that you are advanced in the hierarchy of your order? *Mother* Mary Gertrude?"

"I am professed now," Mary said. "We have to serve many years as a novice. When we take our final vows we are given the title 'mother.' We are choir nuns and sing the Divine Office in the choir. I am also to be in charge of the novices, to instruct them in the duties of our faith and our holy Rule. But what is this about Morella and a *gypsy*?"

"Oh, Morella is always in love," Analee said airily. "Her father and I are hoping it will pass in two years. I, naturally, have nothing against gypsies myself, but Brent hopes for a more—er—suitable marriage . . . though he who takes Morella will need a strong head, firm hands and a warm heart. We hope she will meet a number of suitable young men in Paris to take her mind off Timothy. But have her carefully chaperoned, Mary. She is very . . . hot blooded." Analee glanced at Brent, who averted his eyes.

"Oh, I will take the greatest care of her, never fear. Most of our girls here are young puppies. Alas, very few of them feel called to serve God and take the veil. They are never allowed to see young men without the closest supervision." Mary smiled and moved her chair close. "Now, my dears, I have some very particular news for you. We have here under our roof a very important personage. I know you will want to see him "

"Oh?" Brent and Analee looked at each other.

"His Royal Highness Prince Charles is sheltering here. You know that his common-law wife Mistress Clementina Walkinshaw left him last year with their six-year-old daughter Charlotte? He has since then scoured the country for her and seeks her in every convent."

"But do you know where she is?"

"No, I do not and I do not want to. It is some convent in Paris, but I know not which. She has very powerful patrons. Some say King James in Rome himself supports her. But His Royal Highness is *here*! We could not deny him refuge, poor man. Besides, our Reverend Mother is a member of a distinguished English family impoverished and exiled by long support of the Stuarts. A family like the Allonbys."

"But how long will he remain?" Analee said incredulously.

"Until a safe way can be found for him to leave Paris. He has never ceased his intrigues, of course. He has grown rather fat and drinks copiously, which is why she left him. He treated her vilely—but I still have some love for him. Do you not?"

"Yes," Analee whispered.

"No," Brent declared, standing up. "I do not; most decidedly I do not. I have no wish to see him. I too heard of the foul way he treated this woman of good family who bore him a child, who gave everything up for him. I stayed in their house in Switzerland and saw myself how he abused her. I have finished with the Prince. I have no desire to see him. I have made a new life."

"But, Brent, for the sake of the past?" Analee's eyes were pleading.

"The past is finished, Analee. I have made my peace with the English King, who has been gracious enough to indicate he will receive us together at Court when we return. Mr. Pitt has charged me with very delicate diplomatic negotiations. Do you think I want it put about that I have consorted with the young Pretender in Paris? No I do not, and forbid you likewise."

Brent looked at her severely and Analee bowed her head, acknowledging once more the absolute rights of a husband over her very existence.

* * *

370

Mary greeted her at the side door and drew her in.

"Where is your carriage?"

"I came by cab."

"It is *very* dangerous."

"I am used to danger, Mary. My servant will wait outside and call another cab when I am ready."

Mary held up her candle and gazed at Analee. "Does he know?"

"Brent? Of course not. He is dining with the Duc de Choiseul. Do you know, Mary, he has developed a taste for politics? I believe he will forsake the life of a country gentleman as soon as he can. Every day, unfortunately, he gets more and more like the Falcon in some ways."

"Oh?" Mary looked at her in surprise.

"I only mean in his liking for this kind of life," Analee said quickly. "In other ways no, I am glad to say. I believe him to be very faithful, as I am. His eyes never stray and I don't think they will. He gives me a security in love I never enjoyed before."

"He always loved you," Mary said with resignation, the scorned woman momentarily showing through the sombre habit of Mother Mary Gertrude.

"He is also a devoted family man," Analee went on quickly. "My children love him—well, Clare is a *little* jealous perhaps. I think she considers me in my dotage and too old to marry again."

"But you are still a young woman in your thirties!"

"Thirty-six, Mary. It seems a great age to a girl of fourteen."

"I hope you and Brent will have children of your own, more children."

"I think he would like it," Analee agreed. "It is not impossible, though doubtless my eldest daughters would be shocked by the idea. He *would* like an heir. It is understandable because there is still that distant cousin who stands to inherit Delamain Castle and all its wealth if Brent has no son."

371

The thought of motherhood all over again was slightly daunting to Analee, whose youngest child, Beyrick, was now a sturdy eleven-year-old. But Brent *did* want a son and she wanted to give him one if only as as expression of their deep and profound love. Brent had proved to be right. Their passion was not spent and it renewed itself over and over again in endless manifestations of mutual love and regard.

She put a hand lightly on her belly, wondering if she had already detected signs of quickening life and gazed at Mary, who smiled.

"And you, you want a symbol of your love. It is understandable. I hope your womb will prove fruitful, Analee. I will pray for you. Now come. The Princes is eager to see you."

"And I felt I *had* to see him."

"He is not the man he was." With a warning look Mary led her swiftly, silently along the corridors of the convent, dimly lit and smelling of beeswax and candle grease. The statues with their lamps in front of them loomed out of the dark like ghostly emanations, and several times Analee was surprised and rather frightened.

"It makes me quite nervous," she said.

"It is not always as dark as this. It is on account of the hour. We go to bed very early because we get up before dawn. Now here is the Prince's room. I will wait for you outside." Mary stopped and, shielding her candle, knocked quietly on the door before standing aside to allow Analee to go in.

The Prince was sitting by the fire. Analee hardly recognized him. He had grown very fat and his face had a debauched expression that had replaced the nobility she always associated with him.

She knelt before him and took his hand. "Your Royal Highness."

The Prince started up as though he had not heard her enter and gazed at her for a long while. "Ah, it is

Lady Falconer! Now, let me see . . . Paris, oh, about ten years ago, was it not?"

"1748, Your Royal Highness."

"Ah yes, I remember it." A lecherous look came into the Prince's rheumy eyes and he lowered his gaze fixedly to her bosom. "Still as beautiful as ever, Lady Falconer. They called you the Enchantress. Indeed you were."

"It is Lady Delamain now, sir. I married Sir Brent after he succeeded his brother."

The Prince's expression grew petulant. "Oh, yes. Brent Delamain, once a loyal supporter, now a traitor like the rest."

"He is no traitor, sir."

"They are *all* traitors who left me. I am alone, Lady Falconer, alone in the world. Did you know that?"

"I had heard that good times still do not attend your Royal Highness. I am very sorry."

"My mistress left me, Lady Falconer . . ."

"Delamain, sir, Analee Delamain."

"Well I liked not *him* either, the Falcon, I mean. I was delighted to hear of his death. Good riddance."

Analee lowered her eyes, blushing with anger. She was sorry she had come. This gross, inebriate man bore no resemblance to the hero of her memory—Duncan's father.

"You may get off your knees, Lady Delamain, and pour me some more whisky." The Prince held out his glass. "I am uncommonly fond of this stuff. It is all I have. It makes the world barely tolerable. Yes, she left me, craven whore. You know she gave herself to me without the marriage bond? What *lady* would do a thing like that? I ask you? She was forever bragging that she came from the Scottish nobility. She was always begging me to marry her; but no, I have my sights on a Princess of France. It will happen, you will see. Those old hags, the unmarried daughters of the King, will have anybody, and I am not *anybody*," the

373

Prince added hastily, swallowing his drink as if to blot out the memory of the King's unmarriagable daughters. "You can be sure Lady . . . Analee, I will yet sit upon the throne of England; then see Sir Brent Delamain and others like him come running. I will put them all in the Tower, I can tell you. Aye, all of them. Never forget, my father was the *son* of the last Stuart King of England, James II. These Hanoverian Georges are mere upstarts."

The Prince lifted the bottle by his side and poured a glassful of whisky. "Ah yes, she took my daughter. I had a daughter, you know, Charlotte. I loved her. She took my daughter. I will never forgive her for that. Never!" He leaned back and closed his eyes, a tired man only just forty but prematurely aged. "If only I had had a son." He opened his eyes and stared at her. "Do you know I think if I had married properly and had a son it would have made all the difference to me, all the difference in the world."

The tears came into Analee's eyes as she thought of beautiful young Duncan with all the world before him, and this pathetic hopeless man, his father. Yet he had once been a great man, a brave Prince. His only misfortune had been the times into which he had been born, the circumstances of his sad life. He carried the blood of the Stuart's in him and this blood flowed on in her son. How could she not be proud?

"God grant that you will wed as you wish, sir, maybe a Princess of France, and have sons."

"Yes, King Louis wished it, I know," the Prince said, closing his eyes. "By God, I am very tired, Lady Delamain. Your husband is not with you?"

"No, sir."

"He did not wish to see me, I suppose. No one does. I have few friends. Will *you* be loyal, Lady Delamain?"

"Always, sir." She knelt again and took his hands. "I will always honor your memory and that of your Royal House."

374

"God bless you, Lady Delamain." The prince yawned drunkenly and began to unbutton his coat. "Thank you for coming. It is good to know I have some friends left."

"Thank you, sir," she whispered. "Thank you for everything."

But the Prince did not seem to hear her. He waved her away and began to shake off his boots, pressing the toe of one against the heel of the other. "As you go out tell my valet to come in and put me to bed," he said.

She rose and went slowly to the door. There were two empty bottles of whisky on the table together with some remnants of food. The nuns were good to him. He could only rely now on people's charity. But he still had his pride. She knew he had no valet, that he was here on his own. She stood by the door and looked at him before knocking on it to bid Mary unlock it.

Suddenly there arose before her eyes a picture of Brent, her husband and lover, his blue eyes alight as he made love to her. She had a mental image of his vigorous, youthful body and the comparison between him and this sad dissolute man in front of her was almost grotesque. She yearned to get back to Brent's arms, to enfold him to her breast, to smother his face with her kisses. The Prince was the past and Brent was the present and the future. The future for as long as she could see. What was more it was a happy, secure future. Of that she had no doubt, something that she could never say of her relationship with the man she had also once loved—the Falcon.

Yes, the Prince was the past; the Falcon was the past, even though in herself and her children she retained something of him and always would. She caught her breath, anxious to be with Brent, to reassure herself and him that the past was indeed gone and the future only beautiful.

"Goodbye, Your Royal Highness," she whispered urgently.

He suddenly looked at her sharply and sat up. "I remember it now," he said. "I recall it well. Aye, Analee. I asked you to be my mistress. Well, you would have done a better job than the other one. I am sure you would have given me sons. I might have married *you*." He leaned back again and waved his hand. "Farewell, Analee. Farewell, Enchantress." He kissed the tips of his shaking fingers and gave her a bleary smile as his hand flopped by his side.

Analee tapped on the door and asked to be let out. As it opened she glanced again at the Prince. But the last hope of the Royal House of Stuart was fast asleep.